COTTON'S WAR

Spring, 1941. Britain's fortunes in the war had reached their lowest point and the German Swastika fluttered confidently over the capitals of Europe. It was then that the Mediterranean suddenly blazed into action, as the Nazis began to make up for the deficiencies of their Italian allies by storming their way through Greece. Beyond lay the Greek Islands, notably Crete with its incalculable value as a naval base. The British were ill-prepared for its defence, but they proved to have one formidable asset in the person of a particularly reticent, particularly single-minded corporal of the Royal Marines: Mihale Andoni Cotonou. Better known as Michael Anthony Cotton.

COTTON'S WAR

A novel of the Aegean campaign 1941

John Harris

THE SHERIDAN
BOOK COMPANY

This edition published in 1994 by
The Sheridan Book Company

First published by Hutchinson 1979
Arrow edition 1980
Random House, Vauxhall Bridge Road, London SW1V 2SA

Printed and bound in Great Britain by
Cox & Wyman Ltd, Reading, Berkshire

ISBN 1–85501–650–8

Author's Note

For the benefit of those who don't know, perhaps it would be an advantage to explain what was happening in Europe in the spring of 1941, when this book begins. At that period of World War II, when Britain's fortunes had reached their nadir and the German swastika fluttered confidently over the capitals of Europe, the Mediterranean suddenly blazed into action.

In late 1940, eager to emulate the German successes in France, Norway, Denmark and Holland and half-expecting it to fall into his lap like a ripe plum, Mussolini had attacked Greece from Albania, which he had occupied before the war. Immediately, the Greeks asked the British government to stand by a promise made in 1939 that Britain would go to her help in the event of invasion. Unfortunately, while this idea had been fine in 1939, in 1940, with the British in North Africa already conducting half a dozen campaigns at once, there were too many commitments elsewhere and, apart from a few dozen aircraft, a British mission and a token force of troops, there was precious little assistance Britain could afford to give.

Nevertheless, there was one big strategic prize to be snatched from under the noses of the Italian invaders. Crete, with its fine natural harbour of Suda Bay, afforded a valuable advanced fuelling base for naval operations in the central Mediterranean, and at the invitation of the Greek government it was occupied by British forces just three days after the Italian attack. As a result, Admiral Cunningham, C-in-C, Mediterranean, was able to establish a much wider sphere of control, and almost immediately took advantage of his new base by attacking with carrier-borne aircraft the Italian fleet at Taranto.

7

It also happened that the Greeks ran rings round the Italian invaders and tossed them smartly back into Albania. But then, in the spring of 1941, a new threat appeared. Concerned with the Italian navy's failures and the Italian army's lack of success in North Africa, which seemed likely to impede the German war effort, Hitler despatched to their assistance units of the Luftwaffe – a very different proposition from the Italian Regia Aeronautica – and, immediately, Stuka dive bombers closed the Mediterranean to through convoys. With seaborne supplies threatened, there was a great need for land bases for aircraft and, with the threat of a German invasion of Greece through the Balkans, a British army was put ashore in that country.

One month later the long-expected German attack came via Yugoslavia, Bulgaria and Rumania. Outnumbered on the ground and in the air and deprived of supplies by the needs of North Africa, the British and the Greeks were immediately in trouble, and almost from the outset were fighting for their very survival.

Prologue

Crete lay like a basking lizard in the spring sunshine. The warm waters of the Aegean lapped at the brown rugged inlets that scarred the sides of the rocky outcrop which ran like the lizard's scaly backbone the whole length of the island.

The slopes of the coastal plain were covered with scrub and brown grass, with here and there small areas of cultivated terraces among the olives and cypresses and the acres of flowers that softened the arid harshness of the land. Masses of small white irises and big daisies grew among the oleander, tamarisk, poppies and flowering thistles, and the valleys hid bright birds and gorgeous butterflies. It was easy to see why the land had been so beloved of Byron and Rupert Brooke.

Staring from the window of a hut beneath a tamarisk tree near Retimo, Lieutenant-Commander Henry Kennard studied the light-grey shapes of naval vessels across the harbour and the groups of men marching through the dusty sunshine, passed and repassed by lorries towing guns or carrying ammunition along the gritty tracks. Kennard was a man in his forties, greying and with a face wrinkled like a walnut, a reservist who had served throughout the other war and had found himself recalled to fill a vital job ashore so that a younger man could go to sea. As he stared through the dusty glass, he heard the cheep-cheep of the wireless operator's set behind him and turned.

'Sir! Signal! It's *Loukia*!'

A short square pipe sticking from his sun-reddened face like the muzzle of a gun, Kennard stood behind the operator as he wrote.

'*Loukia to Scylla. ETA 1315.*'

Kennard read the signal as the operator set it down. Then, picking it up and slanting it down on to his desk, turned to the civilian sitting in a deckchair alongside.

'Estimated time of arrival just after lunch,' he said. 'They're almost there, Ponsonby.'

He glanced through the window. A destroyer group was just entering the harbour and he could see the signal flags moving up to the yard-arm in bright splashes of colour. The sun caught the glass below the bridge and picked out the smooth barrels of the guns, and he could make out white-clad men forming up on the foredeck. The ships looked sleek and deadly, but Kennard knew how vulnerable they were to German dive-bombers.

'I think those bastards back in England have landed us properly in the dog's dinner this time,' he said. 'They can't have had the slightest idea what they're expecting us to do, chucking the pongos into Greece like that. All that bloody talk about keeping faith. Was your office behind it?'

Ponsonby gave him a cold stare and was just about to reply when the radio cheeped again.

'Sir! *Loukia* again!'

'She's not arrived, surely?'

Kennard reached for the message, read it and passed it to Ponsonby. '*Blenheim bomber landed in sea to east. Investigating survivors.*'

Ponsonby frowned. 'They haven't time to investigate crashing bombers,' he said. 'We want them in Antipalia.'

Kennard glanced quickly at him but Ponsonby was quite serious and Kennard reflected that he looked like the sort of man who took great care that his own survival was never likely to need investigation, the sort of man who would never be in a ditching Blenheim or swimming for his life to a rubber dinghy.

'We'll just have to wait and see,' he said coldly.

It was a quarter of an hour before the next message came.

'*Observer and air-gunner picked up,*' Kennard read. '*Names: PO Travers, Sergeant Kitcat. Pilot missing.*'

'Now get on your way.' Ponsonby, who had read the message over Kennard's shoulder, spoke quietly, urgently, as though trying by the force of his own will to drive the unseen men back to their task.

The day grew hotter as the sun moved further west, baking the dry earth on the sides of the Cretan cliffs and among the undergrowth in the inland ravines. The sky grew brassy with its heat, and, bored, Kennard went for a cup of tea to a small square white house down the road where a movement office had been set up. It boasted a kettle and an electric cooker, and had kept him in tea and gossip ever since he'd arrived. When he returned the radio was cheeping again, and the radio operator put the message into his outstretched hand without a word. '*PO Travers died,*' he read. '*ETA 1500.*'

'They've lost two hours,' Ponsonby said.

'They're sailors,' Kennard snapped angrily. 'No sailor likes to see another man drown. It might be his turn next. Because that's what happens, you know. They go down into the darkness, gurgling and blowing bubbles and trying to shout to their God, to their mother, to their friends, and unable to, because the salt sea water's choking them. "Lost at sea" or "Lost with the ship" doesn't really sum it up, you know. That's newspaper stuff – something dreamed up by the hurrah departments – all a bit remote, even a bit romantic. Drowning's what happens and *that's* slow and agonizing.'

Ponsonby stared at him coldly and Kennard knew he had no idea what he was trying to say. How could he? Probably the most dangerous thing Ponsonby had ever done was climb up the gangway of the destroyer that had brought him to Crete.

The radio cheeped again, unexpectedly, and the operator's voice cracked. 'Sir!'

'*Loukia?*'

'Yes, sir. Trouble.'

'Now what, for God's sake?' Ponsonby's voice was fretful and

11

angry, as though he resented the minor incidents of the war interfering with his carefully laid plans, and they leaned over the operator's shoulder to watch as he wrote.

'*Am being attacked by MAS boats,*' the message read and the two men behind the operator stared at each other.

'There's another coming, sir. '*Casualties. Damage. Am attempting to reach nearest land!*'

Ponsonby turned away, his eyes angry. 'It's not the nearest land we want,' he said. 'It's Antipalia.'

Kennard didn't reply. This corner of the Mediterranean had become damned dangerous lately, he thought. A backwater from the mainstream of the war, it had just lately become a place where it was wiser not to linger long on a clear day. The time when the Royal Navy had lorded it over the place after the battles of Matapan and Taranto had gone.

'Damn,' he said quietly, his voice grieving and full of a serviceman's bitterness against those who hazarded lives for politics, and ships for victories that would count in the press at home.

'Damn,' he said again. 'Damn, damn, damn!'

PART ONE
Defeat

1

If it hadn't been for the shopkeeper in Heraklion on the north side of Crete, Cotton might never have been involved.

The Cretan was obviously a student of the three-card trick and switched Cotton's coins so fast it deceived the eyes of most of the people looking on. But Cotton had seen it done before in the Portobello Road in London and, grabbing the Cretan's hand in his big fist, he wrenched the missing coins free and jammed them into his pocket. Then, lifting the slices of melon he'd bought, he glared into the Greek's glittering charcoal eyes, his face red and angry.

'*A'fu 'den to xri'azome*,' he snorted. '*Oa tu to xa'riso*.' And shoved the ripe slices of melon in the Cretan's face.

His features dripping with juice and dark with fury, the Greek reached for a knife. Cotton snatched it from him and flung it away and the two of them spat at each other in Greek until more Greeks arrived and things started to look nasty. That was when Patullo appeared.

'You'd better hop it, Corporal,' he said casually. 'I'll sort this out.'

Cotton didn't argue. Lieutenant Leonidas John Patullo was well known aboard the six-inch cruiser *Caernarvon*, in which Corporal Cotton was an insignificant member of the Royal Marine detachment. Patullo was Wavy Navy, a languid ugly-handsome smiling man of enormous wealth who, despite his manner, had made his presence felt in no uncertain way, even among the stiff-necked regular denizens of the wardroom. Patullo was a nutter, an oddity. With umpteen degrees in Balkan languages, he'd been in the Piraeus, the seaport of Athens, when war had broken out in 1939, and had slipped out to Alexandria in the yacht of a wealthy Greek friend to enlist as an ordinary seaman in the navy.

He did sort out the matter of the melon and the Cretan's face. As Cotton had expected. After all, supported by his wealth, Patullo had wandered intimately in peacetime Rumania before finding his way to Greece long before Mussolini had decided it might look better as an Italian colony. He knew Bulgaria, Yugo-slavia and Greece like the back of his hand and had sailed his own boat among the Dodecanese and Cyclades Islands. But his hope of being a simple sailor had been dashed at once when someone in Alexandria had recognized him. Since everybody even then expected Mussolini to march into Greece at the first oppor-tunity, and since nobody else spoke Greek, and – despite what they always said at home – none of the Greeks spoke English, he had been commissioned at once, posted to *Caernarvon* and put in charge of Intelligence.

The matter of the melon was settled within ten minutes and he caught Cotton up as he was trying to explain to his friends what had happened to the fruit he'd promised to produce.

'Really should be more careful whom you pick on, Cotton,' he smiled. 'That chap had a knife.'

Cotton straightened up, every inch of him a Royal Marine, stiff in starched khaki drill. 'Yes, sir,' he said. 'I took it off him.'

'Might have been nasty, though,' Patullo said. 'Cretans aren't noted for having the sweetest of dispositions and they actually enjoy being warlike. They sometimes even wear empty ammuni-tion belts stuffed with pellets of paper just for the look of the thing, and whole families conduct vendettas for generations.'

Cotton began to see he'd probably been lucky and he stiffened again. 'I expect I could have handled it, sir.'

Patullo looked up at Cotton's square bulk and the blue emery paper of beard on his big chin. 'Yes,' he said. 'You probably could, shouldn't wonder.' He paused. 'You were pretty articulate back there, Corporal,' he went on. 'In Greek, too. Did you know what you were saying to that chap?'

Cotton's face reddened. 'Yes, sir, I did,' he said. 'I told him I didn't really want his bloody melon any more so I'd make him a present of it. I did.'

'You did indeed.' Patullo smiled again, then he paused and stared hard at Cotton. 'Where did you learn to speak Greek like that?'

Cotton frowned. 'When I was a kid, sir,' he said. 'I lived with a Greek family. There's a lot of Greeks round London.' He didn't explain that the family in question was his own and consisted of his mother, father and three adoring older sisters, Elene, Rhoda and Maria, and that if everybody had his own, his name was not Michael Anthony Cotton, under which label he'd enlisted in the Royal Marines, but the Mihale Andoni Cotonou he'd been given at birth.

Patullo smiled again. 'I thought you didn't sound as though you'd learned it at night-school,' he observed.

'No, sir.'

'Well, it takes all sorts.' Patullo seemed happy to have found a fellow Greek scholar. He had never kept himself aloof from the lower deck like some of the officers and had employed his inherited self-confidence, wealth and creative power to splash on the canvas of the everyday life of *Caernarvon* some of the colour of his own past. 'Lafcadio Pringle was an Irishman of Welsh descent, and *he* spoke Old Norse, Flemish, Tibetan, Czech and diplomatic Latin, and he ended up as a corporal of Uhlans in the Polish army. You that sort of chap?'

'No, sir,' Cotton said, wondering why he hadn't kept his big mouth shut and who the hell Lafcadio Pringle was when he was at home.

It was a small incident and it had taken place in late 1940 when the Italians had first gone into Greece. Now, five months later, since he was well aware that he was blessed with nothing else beyond the Greek language in the nature of unusual gifts,

17

Cotton suspected that it was responsible for his being present in this hut near Retimo, standing in front of a scrubbed army table covered with maps, being stared at by Patullo and two other men.

There was a pile of signal flimsies in front of them and Patullo was tapping one of them.

'*Loukia to Scylla* . . .' he read out. '. . . *ETA 1315*. . . .'

Cotton shifted his position slightly. 'Who's Loukia, sir?' he asked. 'A young lady? It's a young lady's name.'

Patullo glanced at the other two men behind the table then at Cotton, his face bland and smiling. 'Yes, it is, Cotton,' he said. 'A *Greek* young lady's name. But, as a matter of fact, in this case, *Loukia*'s a motor launch. That's why she's sending her estimated time of arrival – at Antipalia on the mainland. *Scylla*'s the code name for the base here. These two gentlemen to be precise. Lieutenant-Commander Kennard and Mr Ponsonby, of the Foreign Office.'

Kennard nodded his acknowledgement of Cotton. Ponsonby's expression seemed to indicate that Cotton probably smelled.

Patullo paused, moving a few papers about on the table in front of him. Since the incident with the shopkeeper in Heraklion, he had taken a great delight in getting Cotton to one side so he could toss phrases at him, testing him, teasing him, quoting a lot of ancient Greek poets Cotton had never heard of and saying he reminded him of Homer or Aeschylus. If Patullo hadn't been so obviously normal – his escapades with the ladies of Alexandria had become notorious even with the lower deck – Cotton might have thought he was making advances to him. As it was, he had long since realized it was nothing but Patullo's weird sense of humour at work.

He stood now, stiff and motionless, well aware that there was something in the wind. There'd been something in the wind ever since *Caernarvon* had arrived in Suda Bay, and he was just waiting to see how it concerned him.

'*Loukia*.' Patullo sorted out his papers and raised his eyes again. 'A motor launch, Corporal,' he explained. 'Indeed, a damned fast motor launch. What you'd really call a high-speed motor boat.'

'I see, sir,' Cotton said.

He was giving nothing away. In *Caernarvon* there were a lot of people who considered that Cotton was not particularly bright. In fact, he was brighter than he seemed and he was a sound Royal Marine because the discipline and tradition of the corps had been well instilled into him and he believed in good order and had no objection to being told what to do. He was also an old soldier, and had an old soldier's sharp awareness of 'buzzes', of things that went bump in the night, and duties that might be unpleasant and were best avoided, at one with all those sly, wily men who knew exactly which side their bread was buttered, ancient in the service and all-wise when it came to dodging church parades. Whatever it was that was in the wind, it smelled to Cotton as though it was going to concern him very deeply.

It was Ponsonby who spoke next, taking over from Patullo.

'There were three of these boats originally,' he said in a voice that sounded like a file rasping on the edge of an anvil. '*Claudia, Loukia* and *Irene*. They were a class of boat developed for rich people to enjoy themselves in, and they belonged to the Greek millionaire, Spiro Panyioti, who used them for fishing and that sort of thing. He gave them to us after using them for evacuating his family and personal fortune from the mainland.'

Cotton waited. They seemed, he thought, to be going halfway round the bloody world to reach the point.

'We mounted 303s on them,' Kennard joined in. 'Only Lewis guns, unfortunately, which aren't so hot, but we did get some captured Italian 20 mm cannons from the Greeks, and we put one on the stern of each against aircraft. Unfortunately we lost *Irene* a few days ago. She disputed the right of way with the destroyer *Wryneck*, and not unnaturally came off worst. Now, in what seems to have been the last flicker of life in the Italian navy, *Loukia* seems to have been caught by *motoscafi anti-sommergibili* – fast motor launches to you, Cotton – and has been wrecked, leaving us only *Claudia*.'

Patullo pushed a sheaf of flimsies across the table. 'Better read

19

the messages, Cotton,' he said helpfully. 'They can tell you as much as we can.'

It wasn't difficult because there weren't many. *'Blenheim bomber landed in sea . . .'* Cotton saw. *'Investigating survivors.'* They told a tragic little story in as few words as possible but Cotton, who'd been involved in picking up a few survivors since the war in the Mediterranean had come to life, could well imagine the drama that had gone on in the cramped forecastle of the little vessel, with anxious seamen knowing only a little of medicine and surgery crouched over a soaked and wounded airman gasping out his life.

There was a second or two of silence; then Ponsonby went on. 'They were taken off course by the ditching,' he said, 'and the Italians got them. It seemed that was the end of it, but then a Blenheim of 113 Squadron from Nyamata, in Greece, reported seeing a boat ashore on the island of Aeos and it seemed as if it might be *Loukia*. We got them to fly another recce over the place, and, sure enough, it is *Loukia*. She's beached there and seems to be wrecked. But there were several men standing by her on the sand, waving, so it seems some of the crew survived. We have to find them.'

'Why, sir?' Cotton had never before known the services to be so bloody keen to pick up odds and sods who got left behind.

Ponsonby looked at Kennard, who shrugged; then he lit a cigarette, slowly, carefully, as though he were wondering how much to say. 'You know the situation on the mainland, Corporal?'

Cotton knew it only too well. The British army, which had been put smartly on shore in March, looked very much now, in April, as though it would have to be taken smartly off again.

Kennard picked up a piece of paper. 'On March 4th,' he said, 'at the Greek government's request, we began to land an army. On April 6th, the Germans launched their attack in the Balkans. They have now reached Yugoslavian Macedonia and are approaching the Salonika plain, and the Greeks west of there on the Albanian front are expected eventually to surrender. That would make our position untenable, and a withdrawal to a position round Mount

Olympus has already been planned. It seems that when it starts it will continue to the coast.'

Cotton didn't really need telling. He was no strategist, but the road outside was already dusty from the troops marching from the landing stages where the transports were dumping them from the mainland. That spring of 1941, the Germans could count the divisions they had available in dozens, the British on one hand, and Corporal Cotton had never expected the soldiers to stay long in Greece. Every man in the fleet could have told them what the result would be, even as they'd disembarked them at the Piraeus.

'See you later,' they'd said. 'At the evacuation.'

Ponsonby tapped the ash off his cigarette and spoke again. 'That's old news now, of course. What you probably don't know is that months before the decision to send British troops to Greece was finally taken, Admiral Cunningham set up a plan to bring them all out again.'

'An eminently sensible precaution in view of our track record up to now,' Kennard said.

There was a clear atmosphere of tension and worry, and Ponsonby sniffed. He looked like a man who believed in last stands – so long as he personally didn't have to make them.

'As a result of all this' – he was looking out of one eye at Kennard – 'arrangements were made to hedge our bets in case of defeat. *Loukia* was carrying a consignment of weapons for the Greeks.'

'Quite simply,' Kennard said bluntly, 'we were intending to stir up trouble for the Germans after we'd left. *Loukia* was sent off under the command of Lieutenant-Commander Richard Samways, an experienced small-boat officer, and her bilges were full of rifles, grenades and other assorted weapons. It was hoped they'd be instrumental in starting a resistance movement.'

Ponsonby took off his spectacles and started to polish them. 'We think, from the reports we've received, that this bay she's in' – he glanced at the map – 'Xiloparissia Bay – is a lost sort of place, well covered with trees at one side, and steep and almost inaccessible at the other. It may be that those rifles are still there. We have to make some attempt to recover them.'

By this time Cotton had begun to suspect the route the discussion was taking and he didn't particularly like it. He noticed that Patullo and Ponsonby were both watching him carefully.

Kennard continued. 'Since the navy's hard-pressed and its launches have to be used for coastal escort work, when we decided to send the guns to Antipalia it was decided that *Loukia* was the only boat we could spare. At least she had a speed of thirty-five to forty knots.' He pushed several photographs across. They showed a boat, apparently intact apart from a fallen mast, lying on the edge of a beach half-hidden by trees.

'That's *Loukia*,' he said.

Cotton studied the men beyond the table. Patullo stared at the papers in front of him. He seemed faintly embarrassed. Kennard looked at Ponsonby.

'I think he should know,' he said.

Ponsonby stubbed out his cigarette and looked up. '*Loukia*, Corporal,' he said, 'was also carrying twenty thousand pounds in coinage. Maria theresas and napoleons and silver American dollars. Though those coins are no longer legal tender, for your information they *are* still valuable and most governments manage to have a few under the counter for operations when paper money ceases to have much value. They were also to be used for Greek resistance.'

Cotton's face didn't change. 'Very nice, sir,' he said again.

'We don't want that money to fall into the hands of the Germans,' Ponsonby pointed out. 'We also want the rifles.'

'*And Loukia*,' Kennard added.

Cotton frowned. They didn't want so bloody much, he decided. 'I thought that's how it was, sir,' he said.

Ponsonby gave him a sharp, suspicious look as if Cotton were trying to be clever. 'We expect the Germans to try something here before long,' he went on. 'They're not likely to be happy with an aircraft carrier the size of Crete off their south-eastern flank.'

No, by Christ, Cotton thought, they weren't. Crete had made

a vast difference to the Royal Navy but it had proved a mixed blessing in the end, because the Stukas had already knocked the living daylight out of two cruisers and an aircraft carrier, and Cotton was under no delusions that worse was to come.

Ponsonby looked up again and Cotton decided he didn't like him very much.

'You're Greek, Corporal,' Ponsonby said.

Cotton jumped, and decided abruptly that he didn't like Ponsonby at all.

'Not me, sir,' he said indignantly. To Cotton, Greece was as foreign as Tibet. He knew his mother received postcards occasionally at Christmas from Athens and that he had an Aunt Chrysoula and two cousins, Despina and Eleftheria, who, judging by the photographs, were a bit of all right in the manner of Maltese girls, but he'd never been to Athens to meet them and didn't expect to go.

Ponsonby was staring at him suspiciously. 'You speak Greek,' he accused.

This was something Cotton couldn't deny, though under the circumstances he'd have liked to.

'A bit, sir,' he admitted cautiously.

'Your mother was Greek.'

'Until she married my Old Man, sir. After that, she considered herself an Englishwoman.'

'But your father was Greek, too, wasn't he?'

'My Old Man was English,' Cotton said sharply. 'His family went to London fifty-odd years ago.'

'His name's Cotonou.'

Cotton wondered where the hell Ponsonby had found out because he'd deliberately changed his name when he'd enlisted; he'd been called 'dago' and 'wop' too often in civvy street for him to want it to follow him into the service. He realized Patullo was the culprit and gave him an aggrieved look.

Ponsonby was staring at a sheet of paper in front of him and he lifted his head to peer accusingly at Cotton. 'You know Greece?' he asked.

23

'No, sir, though I've got relatives there, I believe. I reckon they're still there. They weren't millionaires, sir.'

Kennard looked up. He was smiling as if he were trying to take the heat out of the interview. 'One thing you are, without any doubt,' he said. 'And that's a Royal Marine.'

'Yes, sir.' That, at least, was undeniable. In fact, Cotton had always thought it stuck out all over him in large lumps. Joeys were Joeys and couldn't be anything else.

The commander smiled as if he were reading Cotton's thoughts. ' " *'E sleeps in an 'ammick instead of a cot*," ' he quoted, ' " *'an' 'e drills with the deck on a slew. An' 'e sweats like a Jolly – 'Er Majesty's Jolly – soldier an' sailor, too!*" Kipling,' he ended. 'You know Kipling's Marine, Corporal?'

'Yes, sir,' Cotton said stolidly, giving nothing away in the matter of encouragement.

There was a moment's silence, then Ponsonby drew a deep breath and looked up at Cotton. 'It's absolutely essential that what *Loukia* was carrying is brought away, Corporal,' he said.

Cotton was beginning to fight a rearguard action now. 'Suppose it can't, sir?'

'From the reports we have, it can. In addition, we'd rather like to know what the Germans' next move is to be and it's just possible *Loukia*'s money might be used to help. Aeos is a large island not so far from the mainland.'

There was another silence then Kennard spoke again. 'We shall be sending *Loukia*'s sister ship *Claudia*,' he said. 'She'll carry a carpenter–boat builder – from the Merchant Navy, because he's the only one spare – in case we can patch *Loukia* up. There'll be an ERA to take a look at her engines, and a crew of eight under Lieutenant Shaw, of ML137. We have several volunteers already : Two RASC men from military lighters, some sailors, and one airman who speaks German. They're a mixed bag but we couldn't just help ourselves where we fancied. They'll be issued with Greek money and their orders will be to pick up *Loukia*'s survivors and the arms and money. If it's possible, they will also effect repairs on *Loukia*, tow her off and bring her back, too, because we're badly in need of boats. Since they may have to inspect her hull, there will be a diving suit on board. Do you know anything about diving, Corporal?'

'No, sir.'

'Well, it's a shallow-water closed-circuit re-breather type and there'll be a man aboard who can use it.'

Cotton knew what was coming next. 'Who's in charge of the show, sir?' he asked.

Patullo gave a small embarrassed smile. 'Me, Cotton. I was conscripted into offering my name.'

Cotton knew exactly what he meant: 'Three volunteers. You you and you!'

'Now we need one more,' Patullo went on. 'Greek-speaking.'

'Me, sir?'

Patullo smiled. 'I thought of you at once, Cotton.'

Cotton decided he was about to volunteer for something without even opening his mouth. And volunteering was something an old Joey – or an old anything else, for that matter – just didn't do. It could get you into trouble. A friend of his in the Royal Scots had volunteered for a driving course and had ended up as a cook in Singapore. All that seemed to be missing was a bed of nails and a couple of hair shirts.

'We have a lot to do,' Patullo explained, 'and not much time to do it in. It was decided under the circumstances that more than one Greek speaker would be an advantage. That's where you come in.'

With an effort, Cotton managed a slightly bitter smile.

'I thought it might be, sir,' he said.

2

Unfortunately for Corporal Cotton, Lieutenant Patullo, Commander Kennard, and Mr George Ponsonby, of the Foreign Office they were not the only people who had an eye on Aeos.

From Belgrade in Yugoslavia, Wehrmacht Field Marshal Wilhelm List, who was in command of the over-all operation for the subduing of the Balkans, had sent out instructions to General Johann-Helmuth Ritsicz, of the German 12th Army, who had set up his headquarters in Sofia, Bulgaria, a mere hundred-odd miles from the great Macedonian plain. Well placed for communications with the valleys of the Danube and the Struma, Sofia was a curious mixture of Thracian, Roman and Turkish civilizations and at that very moment, in a room near the Buzuk Džamija Mosque, a certain Major Renatus von Boenigk Baldamus – until wounded in the invasion of France the previous year, part of the 346th Panzer Grenadiers – was just being informed of the part he was to play.

Ritsicz's headquarters were in the Bălgarija Hotel near the Narodno Săbranie and, with the city already subdued, General Ritsicz was walking confidently up and down as he talked. His thick legs breeched with the red stripe of the General Staff, he stumped heavily backwards and forwards between the window and the door. Major Baldamus listened in silence; a smooth-faced man, young for his rank but intelligent, clear-headed and – despite the air of insouciance he affected as part of his stock-in-trade – decisive when necessary. From where he sat, he could see the Russian Church of St Nicholas and, beyond the Narodno

Săbranie, the towers of the Alexandar Nevski Cathedral. After his light-hearted fashion, he had come to the conclusion that they provided a much more impressive vista than General Ritsicz who had the heavy jowls of a man who liked his food. Son of a wealthy Ruhr manufacturer, Major Baldamus was never inclined to drop on one knee before his superiors, and, while he was shrewd enough to see the advantages Hitler had gained for Germany, he was not even a Nazi.

For the tenth time General Ritsicz turned by the window and faced him. 'Your orders,' he said, 'which have come direct from Field Marshal List, are to land on Aeos and take possession of it. There must be no mistake, and nothing half-hearted about it. You will *be* in possession.'

You will advance to the right in threes, Major Baldamus thought cynically. You will keep your barrack room tidy. You will engage in a football match. You will capture London, shoot Churchill and take the King of England prisoner. All part of the scheme. The army never suggested that you might not. You will, it said, and that didn't mean, you will have a go. It meant, quite simply what it said : You will.

But though Major Baldamus was under no illusions, he also had no personal doubts. 'What opposition can we expect, sir?' he asked politely.

Ritsicz stopped and turned to face him again. 'None,' he said. 'There will be none. Intelligence states quite categorically that there is no organization for opposition. There are no troops on the island, except perhaps a few in the capital in the north, attached for Customs duties and things like that. There may also be a few sailors attached for harbour service, but there are no naval ships in the harbour, and there are no aeroplanes.'

'There's an airstrip, sir.'

'Civil.' Ritsicz gestured airily. 'Chiefly used by wealthy Greeks from the Piraeus flying in to their island homes. Spiro Panyioti for example. He built it and he was the major user. He has a home at Xinthos nearby, where he went when the cares of business became too pressing.'

27

'Poor chap!'

The general's expression didn't slip. 'It's supposed to be a country house,' he explained. 'But, in fact, it's more like a palace. You will keep an eye on it.'

'Perhaps I can billet myself there,' Baldamus smiled.

'You can *not* billet yourself there,' the general said sharply, beginning to wonder if Baldamus' light-heartedness was an indication of a flippant nature. He had heard that Baldamus had done well in France, but so far he hadn't given much indication of any ability. 'There will be no troops in Panyioti's place,' he went on. 'For the simple reason that it may well be needed later for something else. I had not failed to notice its existence or its value. But it's been earmarked for a special purpose and you will do no more than look it over and keep an eye on it. You will be informed by signal when to use it, and when you are informed you will immediately realize why.'

'I see, sir.' Baldamus rose. 'I think that covers everything.'

'You have your men?'

'I have, sir. Engineers, pioneers and lines-of-supply troops. I think there will be more than enough.'

The general eyed him shrewdly. For the first time Baldamus was beginning to behave like a commander.

'I have also a good second-in-command,' Baldamus continued. 'He was with me through France and I can trust him implicitly.'

'Can he keep his mouth shut?'

'Like an oyster, sir.' Baldamus paused near the door. 'When do we leave, sir?'

'At once.'

'Embarking where, sir?'

The general indicated the envelope Baldamus held. 'It's all in there,' he said shortly. 'It will be made clear as soon as you read your orders.'

'Of course, sir. I was merely thinking of earmarking the ship.'

The general smiled. 'You will not be going by ship,' he said.

Baldamus' eyebrows rose in surprise and Ritsicz smiled at his expression. There was something engaging, he saw now, about this young man when he allowed it to emerge, and he began to feel reassured. 'You will be going by air. Everything has been laid on at the Italian airfield of Lushnje in the plain west of Tirana in Albania. Aircraft of *Fliegerkorps IX* are awaiting you and your men there at this very moment.'

'Let's hope the Italians haven't been driven out of it before we arrive,' Baldamus said mildly. 'After all, it's only about a hundred and fifty kilometres from the Greek frontier and the way the Greeks behave to them they might well.'

Ritsicz's smile widened. 'I think the Greeks are a spent force,' he said, 'and this time the Italians will not give way. Indeed, they had better not or the Führer will want to know why. The Junkers 53s you will use have a range of 900 kilometres – though I believe wise pilots prefer to regard it as considerably less – which gives you plenty spare to reach Aeos. Our friends on the island have provided fuel for the return journey.'

'It should be interesting,' Baldamus observed mildly.

'It should certainly be quicker,' Ritsicz said.

Quite unaware of Major Baldamus and what he had been instructed to do, Corporal Cotton stood staring at *Claudia* lying alongside a sleeper-built jetty in Suda Bay. The water round her was dark, oil-slicked and drab, and on the slipway nearby scum and rubbish had collected in the form of sticks, bits of paper and orange peel. The smell was one of brine, oil and rotting wood.

Across the water, the harbour was almost empty, with only a few odd destroyers and oilers and one charred wreck nearly out of sight. It was a mellow evening and Crete looked superb. The mountains inland shone with a soft lustre as the setting sun caught each succeeding ridge. On the slopes were scrub bushes and grass, and a few flowers. In the rifts, there were cypress and olive trees and little cultivated patches, and occasionally an almond tree in full blossom.

Claudia was a handsome-looking boat. Freshly painted in the pale blue-grey of the Mediterranean fleet, she had sweet, clean lines running from a yacht-like bow down to a blunt square stern.

'Seventy-three feet long, nineteen-foot beam, fifty tons displacement, double diagonal ma'ogany planing hull, with hard chine.' Duff, the chief engine-room artificer who'd been sent from the motor launch flotilla to accompany them, was a long lean, gloomy individual with a laconic manner. 'They're adapting 'em as MTBs for the navy at home, with three Packard V12 supercharged 1250-horse engines. We've only got two – millionaire's bloody meanness, I suppose. That's how they get to be millionaires. It gives us less power, but as we don't carry as much all-up weight as a fully-armed torpedo boat, the maximum speed ends up roughly the same – thirty-five to forty knots.'

Cotton nodded and continued his inspection. The foredeck, complete with a small hand winch, was broad and swept back to a large varnished wheelhouse, with doors on either side opening like hatches. Inside the wheelhouse was the bridge, the commanding officer's cabin once occupied by Panyioti himself lush with civilian blankets and even curtains; and opposite another cabin once occupied by the boat's skipper but now filled with radio equipment. Beyond that, still under the wheelhouse deckhead, was the engine room containing the two huge Packard engines. From this a door opened on to a large well-deck, part of which had been built over just forward of the after hatch and mounted with the captured 20 mm Italian cannon. On either side of the wheelhouse, almost jamming up the gangway, was a Lewis gun on a stand, and at the rear end of the well there was a canister containing chloro-sulphonic acid for making smoke, below it the tanks containing the 100-octane petrol that gave the boat a range of around one hundred and forty miles at a speed of twenty-five knots.

Cotton fingered the wheel. The boat had originally been fitted with hydraulic steering for fingertip control so that her millionaire owner would not have to exert himself too much when he wished to turn to port or starboard, but this had been replaced by the navy with a direct wire system. The deck seemed to be unbelievably cluttered up with drums of petrol and oil, ropes, water casks, guns, fenders, Carley float and crash nets. Lashed along the starboard side, where a small rubber-covered hand line was threaded through low lightweight stanchions, were planks. Heavier timbers were stuffed underneath the cannon platform and below deck were two rifles, a tommy-gun, and a large wooden box with two handles containing a closed-circuit re-breather diving equipment consisting of a flexible breathing bag, tube and canister of CO_2 absorbent, a helmet vaguely like a gas-mask with goggles and mouthpiece, gas cylinders, weights and boots to which lead had been attached. It looked remarkably old-fashioned and well worn and Cotton wondered where in God's name it had been dug up.

There was a thump of feet on the black wooden piles of the jetty as Patullo appeared with Lieutenant Shaw, a thin-faced dedicated-looking officer who didn't seem to be relishing the job he'd been given. Like Cotton, like everybody else, he wore a white submarine sweater.

Patullo introduced Cotton with a smile. 'This is our Ulysses,' he said. 'Corporal Cotton, Michael Anthony, Royal Marines. He speaks Greek as well as I do. Perhaps better. He ought to prove useful.'

Shaw's eyes were bleak. 'Let's hope so,' he said. 'I gather the Germans have already reached Rhodes, which'll make this place rotten uncomfortable if they use it for their Stukas. And I gather this bloody boat's already had her share of bad luck. Old Panyioti's brother-in-law was shot dead aboard her by his wife a couple of years back when she found him in bed with her maid. Panyioti's money fixed the law, of course, but there was another bit of shooting, too, before they left the mainland. Several members of the family, who thought *they* ought to have a chance to leave as well, put their point a bit forcibly, and a man was killed and another wounded.'

He sounded disgusted and disillusioned by the whole business, and Cotton frowned. Like all seafaring men he was intensely superstitious. Women on boats, like death and sailing on a Friday, were bad, and this boat had seen more than its fair share of women and death, it seemed.

As the two officers disappeared into the wheelhouse, Cotton began to loosen the bow rope. One of the RASC men waited quietly by the stern.

There was a dull explosion as the engines leapt to life one after the other and *Claudia* began to surge forward for a second at the creep of the propellers. Lieutenant Shaw reappeared, his head through the starboard hatch, his cap on the back of his head. He glanced round him and nodded.

'Okay,' he said. 'Let go springs.'

As the springs were taken in, he spoke to Patullo inside the cabin, then turned to the soldier on the stern.

'Let go aft !'

'All gone aft, sir !'

'Let go forrard !'

'All gone forrard.'

Standing alongside the winch, Cotton thrust gently at the wharf with his foot and *Claudia* edged away and began to glide slowly across the basin towards the sea. From inside the radio cabin, the cheeps of the wireless set began abruptly.

The sun was already disappearing behind the mountains and the dark water looked like black silk. The crews of tugs, oilers, transports and naval vessels watched them in silence as they slipped past, the white ensign trailing limply from the mast. There was no cheering, no interest even. They were just a very small launch moving out on to the dark sea.

'We should be well on our way before nightfall,' Cotton heard Patullo say as *Claudia* headed towards the entrance to the harbour. 'We should be able to do most of the trip in darkness, and, one thing, there are plenty of islands and they're not far apart. We ought to be able to slip from one to the other without being seen too much.'

He called to Cotton. 'Get the crew's names, Corporal,' he said.

Cotton set about the job carefully. He regarded it as his right. He was senior man on board after the officers and Duff. He had a record sheet unstained by black marks and a good, if unimaginative character. He made out the list on canteen notepaper in his neat hand.

Lieutenant Shaw, in command.
Lieutenant Patullo, i/c operation.
Chief ERA Duff, engine room.
Corporal Cotton, Royal Marines.
Stoker Docherty.
Pte Howard, RASC.
Pte Coward, RASC.
LAC/WOp Bisset, RAF.
Mr Gully, carpenter–boat builder, civilian

Gully was a pink-faced, foul-mouthed man in his late thirties, fat and unhealthy from too much boozing, with greying hair that looked as though it had been cut by placing a basin on his head and snipping round it. He wore false teeth that looked as though they'd been rifled from a corpse, all dingy grey-green molars and bright-red vulcanite gums, and his jacket and trousers were of a standard of cleanliness that Cotton wouldn't have been seen dead in. He carried a boxful of tools, a concertina and a brown-paper parcel containing his belongings. 'One of these days,' he had said as he climbed aboard, 'I'll make meself a kitbag.' Over one ear he wore a cap with a broken peak, so that Cotton – his own cap top-dead-centre, like Cotton himself, straightforward, squared away and no nonsense – considered him the scruffiest thing he'd ever seen and felt he ought to identify him firmly on his list so that nobody could blame the navy.

He'd been carpenter on one of the Glen Line vessels which were being used as assault ships by the army and, at least, he didn't appear to be put off by the nature of what he'd undertaken.

'I hope you know what you're in for,' Cotton said.

'Sure I do.' Gully's dreadful teeth flashed in a grin. 'I've lived off burgoo and bloody Ticklers all me life.'

'In case of emergency, naval discipline. Okay?'

'Oh, Christ, hark at him.' Gully grinned again. 'I was too young to be in the last war, me old flower. I'm going to enjoy this one. I'm a bloody good chippy – best there is – and I ain't got nothing to worry about.'

Only the Germans, Cotton thought.

Howard and Coward, the RASC men, were both young and – except for the position of the spots from which they both suffered – surprisingly alike even to their names. Anonymously blond, blue-eyed and with cheeks that looked bare of beard, they were like cherubs and were already known as the Heavenly Twins. Leading Aircraftman Bisset, of the RAF, was a Jerseyman, tall, thin-faced and intelligent-looking. Because of his accent, Cotton assumed he was a Hostilities Only and was startled to find he was a Regular like himself; a sort of gentleman-ranker out on the spree, he decided, and immediately jumped to the conclusion that he had a shady history and wouldn't be much cop in a tight corner. He'd been working naval frequencies for a long time, however, and knew what to do, though his ability was largely hidden from view by a sleepy-eyed manner and a smile of enormous charm that only served to make Cotton, on the look-out for dodgers, all the more wary.

'Jimmy Bisset,' he'd introduced himself. 'LAC/WOp, RAF. Sounds like a chemical formula, doesn't it?'

Apart from the officers, Cotton had found them all living in an aeroplane packing case on the wooden wharf where *Claudia* lay. They'd made themselves comfortable with a stolen stove to which they'd attached as a chimney an old cast-iron drain-pipe from God alone knew where, and Cotton didn't expect any problems with any of them save Stoker Docherty.

In all ships, merchant service or Royal Navy, the black gang were considered to be tough guys and troublemakers, and it seemed Docherty's ambition was to be the toughest and most troublesome of them all. Cotton suspected he'd been chivvied into the job because the ML flotilla he'd come from had had enough of him, but that he wasn't half as tough as he liked to pretend, and was more than a little mad, with his slicked-down, greasy hair, crazy eyes, permanent grin and twisted sense of humour. His head was full of thoughts of women, singing and dancing, in that order, and he was irresponsible, uproarious, rebellious and noisy. His arms tattooed with a tombstone bearing the legend 'Mother', clasped hands, and 'Home Sweet Home' on a length of ribbon, his reputation had arrived ahead of him through Chief ERA Duff, who knew him well.

'Nickname's "Rammer",' he said. 'For obvious reasons. Only one bloody thought in his mind. He can't keep it in his trousers. He's supposed to have taken a diving course for inspecting underwater gear.' He didn't seem very impressed by Docherty.

The stoker had spent his first day aboard *Claudia* pinning up the most salacious set of pin-up pictures Cotton had seen – and in the navy Cotton had seen a few – all button-hard nipples and thrust-out rumps.

'You sex-mad?' Cotton asked.

'Yeh.' Docherty's grin was unabashed. 'It's dead smashing. I'm a connoisseur of tits, legs and bums.'

He stacked up a row of what he called his 'dirt books', white-jacketed paperbacks each bearing a picture of an undressed girl in the last stages of torture or rape. Cooped up with him in a small boat seventy-three feet long, with a forecastle no more than fifteen feet across at its widest point, smelling of dust and old fag-ends, and shared with everybody else on board, Cotton wasn't sure how they'd cope.

They had taken on the extra drums of petrol that afternoon so they could fill up before entering Xiloparissia Bay and be able to leave – in a hurry if they had to – with full tanks. Other odds and ends – including a couple of unhappy-looking pigeons – had also been loaded on board, together with extra ammunition for the 303s and the 20 mm.

'Which,' Docherty said gaily, 'will probably tear itself out of the fucking mounting when we fire it.'

Altogether, Cotton decided, Operation Long John Silver, which was the fancy code-name Ponsonby had thought up for the affair, looked like being a pretty dicey do. Although the navy was watching out towards the north, the Germans already seemed to hold almost everything in that direction and there was the possibility that the Italian fleet, despite the pounding it had suffered at Taranto, might also rouse itself sufficiently to join in.

Cotton climbed on to the gangway alongside the wheelhouse to remove the covers from the Lewises. Since he was supposed to be an expert on weaponry, it was his job to maintain them in sufficiently good order that the two pongos – who, being RASC, couldn't be expected to know anything about guns – would only have to press the trigger and point them in the right direction if they were attacked. In action, it would be Cotton's job to fire the 20 mm, with Stoker Docherty standing by with the full drums of ammunition.

As they edged along the coast of Crete and began to turn north past Canea, Cotton could see small vineyards, olive groves, paddocks and half-acre plots for oats, barley, lentils and broad beans. They could smell the land, the dry breath of rock, dust and rotting driftwood. There were two white caiques anchored just in front of them, which, but for the Italians and the Germans, would have been sponge-fishing deep inside the Adriatic. Otherwise, there seemed to be nothing else in sight, not a mast or a sail, just the spill of the wine-dark sea the wind was freshening into little waves, a brown-blue island on the horizon and a windmill just visible over the top of a small hill.

Cotton stared round him stolidly. He wasn't afraid. In the past when people had dropped bombs on him he hadn't panicked – not even when *Caernarvon* had been hit and temporarily put out of action. He'd always assumed this was because he wasn't very well endowed with brains, but at least he was immovable and didn't flap, and was sufficiently well trained to know what to do in emergencies. Besides, he was a dedicated serving soldier. He'd joined the Marines before the war because he'd watched his father return home every night, grey-faced and exhausted from his job as a waiter, to shout at his mother, who, short, fat and dark-eyed, had never ever answered back. 'Yes, Cotonou,' she'd said. 'No, Cotonou. Three bags full, Cotonou.' Unknowing in his youth the fears, the needs and the worries that held together two middle-aged people no longer attractive to look at when they seemed unable to be civil to each other, to Cotton she'd seemed to be everlastingly pliable and far from being the wife Cotton wanted when he finally got around to getting hitched himself.

Watching them, he'd sworn that *his* home wasn't going to be like that; and that, although most of the London Greeks he knew ended up in restaurants, *he* wasn't going to – certainly not like his father, short of money and married to another wop with wop relatives and blessed with a brood of kids all yelling in a foreign language. He'd been halfway out of the cage even before he'd joined, in fact, because he'd become a Catholic, which was near enough to Greek Orthodox and seemed safer and better, and everybody at the bus depot where he'd worked as a clerk had called him 'Mick' and thought him an Ulsterman.

Briskly, efficiently, his mind devoid of doubts, he finished checking the guns, then went in search of the RASC men. He found Howard in the galley between the wheelhouse and the forecastle brewing tea.

'I've fixed the guns,' Cotton said stolidly. 'It's your job to make sure yours is kept all right.'

Howard looked round. 'You an expert on guns, Corp?' he asked.

'A bit.'

Howard grinned. 'I'm glad you're on our side,' he said. 'I like to have the experts on my side. Giz a kiss, Royal.'

Cotton sniffed. Coward and Howard, he'd found already, were a bit too big for their boots for RASC wallahs. After all, the bloody RASC hadn't got its knees brown yet, while the Marines had been founded in 1664 by Charles the Second when it was the Duke of York and Albany's Maritime Regiment of Foot. Cotton had had the corps history drilled into him so much he didn't even have to think. He knew every campaign through Belle Isle, Egypt, the Sudan, the Boxer Rising, Gallipoli, Jutland and Zeebrugge. The RASC existed only to keep better men supplied with beer and fags when they hadn't time while holding off the king's enemies to go and get them themselves. Besides, Coward and Howard didn't look old enough to have been in more than a month or two, anyway, and were only there, he suspected, because better men were busy on the mainland repelling aggression with not much more than their teeth and bare hands.

'When do we get there?' Howard asked.

'We reach Iros tomorrow,' Cotton said. 'We lay up during the day and leave for Aeos tomorrow evening.'

'I suppose the captain told you, did he?'

'No,' Cotton said. 'Patullo did.'

Howard pulled a face to indicate that he thought Cotton was an arsehole creeper, toffee-nosed, slow on the uptake, and a bit regimental. It didn't worry Cotton. Even in a jersey, his cap badge was polished and his trousers were pressed, while Coward looked as if he'd been dragged through a hedge backwards. He moved aft to check the 20 mm. An idle Marine was an inefficient Marine. It had been drummed into him so many times, he believed it himself. Keep them occupied. Keep their thoughts away from home and women and comfort. They had to be moulded. The lower deck always said that Marines came in batches of a dozen while sailors were always different, and he supposed that was true enough. But sailors' jobs were more varied than Marines', and being a Marine demanded stolidity rather than the flashy independence of the navy. Although he was barely aware of it, Cotton had an enormous pride in his corps and, for that matter, in himself, too.

'Cup of tea?' Howard said when he returned to the forecastle.

'Thanks.' Cotton accepted the tea and sipped at it. 'Very nice,' he said and he saw Howard grin.

When he went on deck again, it was already dark. Not far away he could see a rocky shore with low cliffs and a low hillside, and he assumed it was one of the smaller islets to the north of Crete. The sky was clear and filled with stars, and the night hung about them like cool velvet because the wind had died away so that only the breeze that came from their own speed blew into his face.

He did his spell on the wheel, watching the RAF-type compass with which the boat had been fitted, listening to Shaw talking quietly to Patullo at the back of the wheelhouse as he filled in the log.

'We should arrive at Iros at daylight,' he was saying. 'Refuel and hide ourselves among the caiques and wait there all day. There'll probably be aircraft over.'

'Got your watches sorted out?'

Shaw grunted. 'Fat lot of watches there'll be with only three deck crew,' he said. 'I've arranged for one man to be on the wheel, one on look-out and one below, the man below to be responsible for cooking and brewing up.'

'What about those two RASC chaps?'

'They know their stuff.' Cotton was surprised to hear it. 'They crewed a lighter over from Alex.'

'And the chippy?'

'I can hardly fit *him* into the pattern, can I? He's a civvy. He'll probably go on strike. We'll just have to see.'

When Cotton was relieved at the wheel by Howard, he went below to find Gully at the galley stove. He grinned at Cotton and spooned a mixture of rice and bully-beef on to a plate for him and slammed a mug of tea down on the table.

'Thanks – er – ' Cotton said. 'What do we call you, anyway?'

The ghastly false teeth flashed. 'Same as all carpenters: Chippy'll do. They christened me Frederick 'Oratio but nobody never called me nowt but Chippy.'

It was after midnight when Cotton got his head down on one of the bunks. Gully, curled up in a ball, lay on the other. When Coward shook Cotton's shoulder it was light enough to see the sea through the scuttle. Howard was asleep on the other bunk.

'Who's on the wheel?'

Coward handed him a mug of tea. 'Chippy.'

'Can he handle a boat?'

'Says he can. Seems to be doing all right. At least, it makes one more to work and no passengers. You relieve him.'

As it happened, however, Cotton didn't. When he went on deck, it was raining in a thin, drizzling grey mist that wavered down from an unexpectedly dark sky. Through it, he could see an island just ahead and a bay with greyish cube-like fishermen's houses round it. Faded gardens lay on the slopes behind, where misty mulberry trees grew in profusion, bamboo hedging them against the wind. Beyond them, the bony soil on the gentle rise of the hill lifted up darkly, ending in a violet early-morning sky.

The harbour was crowded with caiques and rowing boats, and large dinghies with lateen sails for the inspection of shellfish baskets and inshore fishing; on the wharves donkeys and mules were waiting to carry away their loads.

'Iros,' Shaw was saying.

The place looked gloomy and forbidding, but the rain stopped as they entered the harbour and the sun came out strongly. As the clouds parted, the wet concrete of the mole began to steam at once and the place was transformed immediately, the greyish houses becoming dazzling white, the dulled colours of the flowers beginning to glow once more.

'There's nothing here but bloody rock,' Docherty observed from the gangway near the bridge.

Patullo heard him and smiled. 'I suspect this part of the world was some of God's early work,' he said. 'We'll just have to do the best we can with it.'

3

As *Claudia* entered Iros Harbour, a thin ragged figure on the jetty began to wave its arms at them, indicating they should moor where it was standing. There were other figures on the jetty – fishermen, women in black and a few children – but none of them moved, and they knew very well why.

Bisset had tuned the radio in to the BBC that morning, and it had made no bones about the extent of the disaster on the mainland. The German mechanized divisions were heading for the Rupel Pass and the Monastir Gap from Yugoslavian Macedonia and everyone knew that if they succeeded in getting through, the British forces, outnumbered and faced with fierce air attacks, would have to fall back because an outflanking German thrust towards Salonika would compel a further withdrawal; while the Greek army, weakened by their five months' struggle against the Italians, would be unable to withstand the tempo of the German bombing. It was already on its last legs, and the evacuation of the British looked inevitable, so that the islanders, viewing the possibility of the Germans' arrival in the Cyclades with alarm, were waiting in a nervous, hostile crowd, afraid that any sign of their having helped the British would be dangerous.

'They look as if the cook's spat in the soup and thrown the ladle at the mess cat,' Gully said.

'Don't look exactly welcoming,' Patullo agreed. 'Cotton and I'll have to entertain 'em with verses from Sophocles.'

'Who's Sophocles, sir?' Goaded, Cotton decided to find out once and for all, but it was Duff who answered.

41

'Played full back for Fulham,' he said in an unexpected burst of humour. 'Took the penalty that knocked Arsenal out of the Cup.'

Shaw placed them neatly alongside the stone mole. The sky was a piercing blue by this time and against it the white houses stood out with the bareness of old bones. As the engines were cut, Patullo climbed with Cotton on to the jetty. Behind him, Shaw was detailing Howard, who was now carrying a tommy-gun, to act as sentry. Patullo was already arguing in swift incisive Greek with the crowd, trying to make himself heard over the excited shouting.

'Discussion among Greeks can't ever be conducted quietly,' he observed over his shoulder to Shaw. 'They're intensely patriotic, of course, and think we're being too flippant about losing the war here. I suppose you'd say we consider *they*'re taking it too dismally.'

As he plunged once more into the argument, Shaw pushed Cotton forward and indicated the ragged figure who had waved to them. 'Okay, Corporal,' he said. 'Get on with it. Let's see what you can do. The mayor's supposed to have drums of 100-octane fuel waiting here for us. Ask him where he lives. He looks as though he might know.'

Cotton couldn't see why they couldn't wait until Patullo was finished but he didn't argue.

'Good morning,' he tried in Greek and the scarecrow figure on the jetty smiled at him and said 'Good morning' back.

'You from the mayor?'

'Yes.' Their guide was only a boy. 'I am to take you to him. I have everything – petrol, donkey, a stick to hit it with. Would you like to follow me? I know the way exactly.'

He reminded Cotton of the urchin who used to stand outside the Marine barracks in Alex calling, 'Chocolates, cigarettes, French letters. Would you like my sister? She is very clean and white inside, like Queen Victoria.'

He passed on the message to Shaw who nodded. 'Right,' he said. 'Off you go, Corporal. Lieutenant Patullo's better here.'

Cotton wondered how much Shaw was influenced by the freemasonry that existed among officers and the thought that if anybody was going to disappear down a dark alley and have his throat cut, it might as well be Cotton and not Patullo who would then remain available to help Shaw to get away to safety.

Cotton didn't think much of the situation but he hitched at his trousers and prepared to do his best. Gully climbed after him with Private Coward and Chief ERA Duff. Gully had lit a cigarette but Shaw barked at him about fire and he stubbed it out and stuck it behind his ear.

'No peace for the wicked,' he said in his thick north-country accent. 'Off we go, boys, sixpence round the bleedin' lighthouse.'

The boy who had met them was curly-haired and dressed in ragged trousers and shirt with rope sandals on his feet. Cotton regarded him with disdain. The boy looked as though he hadn't had a decent meal for a week, and this, Cotton realized, was the very thing he'd fought against all his life – this image of the Greeks everybody had in England. It was this which had persuaded him to change his name when he'd joined the Royal Marines so there'd be no questions asked – something that still made him feel a little guilty.

The boy's donkey was moored to one of the ring-bolts in the quay. It looked hardly bigger than a rat and not in the best state of health into the bargain. Gully gazed at it with contempt.

'What's he expect to do with that?' he demanded.

Patullo, occupied with the shouting men, heard him and turned. 'Greeks regard their donkeys as Americans regard their cars,' he said helpfully. 'And there's no limit to what they're expected to carry. If it collapses it'll get no sympathy. It'll just get dragged to its feet and beaten for being difficult. I'm sure it's aware of the conditions. It'll make it, don't worry.'

They followed the boy between two lines of tiny houses, each one joined to the next; but with its door, patio, balcony with flowers and outside stair leading to the square flat roof, all differently spaced and placed from its neighbour's, as though in an effort to preserve individuality even in poverty. There were a few flowering trees behind them which threw bars of brilliant colour

43

across the road, and at every turn they could see the dark water of the harbour sparkling between the white walls.

They climbed a set of wide, shallow steps and found themselves in a narrow alley with high, almost Moorish walls running up to dark windows, and foliage spilling over from an array of flower pots. The boy stopped at a door carved with arabesques, that clearly belonged to someone of greater importance than those who inhabited the smaller houses they'd just passed. The courtyard was leafy and shadowed by climbing roses, geraniums, wisteria and the magenta of a Judas tree. After the rain there was a smell of thyme in the air.

The boy banged on the door with his fist and after a while it was opened by a small plump woman dressed in black, with a grey shawl on her head. She looked like Cotton's mother. Behind her was an old man, equally plump and with a large black moustache. He was tall, however, with square, strong shoulders and still looked powerful. He seemed nervous.

'Ask him if he's the mayor, Cotton,' Duff said.

Cotton did as he was told and the big man nodded, so that Cotton decided he'd been elected chiefly because his size enabled him to quell any disagreement among the islanders under his authority.

'Komis, Konstantine,' he announced. 'At your service.'

'Tell him we've come for our petrol,' Duff said.

Cotton translated and the mayor's eyes flickered from one side to the other.

'I have it hidden,' he said. 'It's best that way. There are a few on this island who don't like me and they might well tell the Germans that I have helped you, when they come. Enter, please.'

They pushed into the house, which, despite its more imposing exterior, was sparsely furnished. The hall was empty except for a single cane chair, a small table bearing a wine glass with a solitary flower in it and, above it on the wall, an ikon. Beyond, the back of the house was very different. They could see a dirt yard and chickens wandering in and out, and even as they watched, a goat relieved itself on the doorstep.

44

Komis showed them into a room with bare plaster walls and a wooden floor, which was clearly his office. It contained a woven rug, a desk, a dowry chest, an assortment of plants and calendars, a wooden filing cabinet and four chairs in a line with embroidered antimacassars over their high wooden backs, clearly there for those seeking Komis' favours. The men stood in a group, five of them with the boy, filling the small room with their bulk, all a little awkward and ill-at-ease. The shutters were closed and the room was dark and smelled of the damp which had peeled the tinfoil decoration from the frame of a gaudy religious painting of an agonized Christ facing a paternal-looking God through a circle of heavenly clouds. Komis sat down and gestured at the chairs, but they all remained standing. The woman brought a tray and offered them loukoumi, tsipero and Turkish coffee.

'I shall not come with you,' Komis said.

'Why not?' Cotton asked.

'Because it's not safe to do so. There will be fighting in these islands when the British have gone. There are a few Fascists, and a lot of ELAS who are willing to kill Germans but are also anxious that their own unlovely Communist creed should be brought here.'

Cotton guessed that the mayor was a Fascist and might even welcome the Germans, but that he was afraid of the Communists and was hedging his bets by offering help.

'They shot up the square of Mandalani on Siphos,' he went on. 'They came over and machine-gunned the people. There were seven dead.'

Whether the mayor was a Fascist or a Communist, he seemed concerned, at least, that no Nazi frightfulness should be visited on Iros, and he was not unhelpful.

'Nico will show you where the petrol is,' he went on, indicating the boy. 'It's in a shed behind the town. There are six drums.'

'I was told eight,' Duff said. 'I'll bet the corrupt bastard's hidden two for himself.'

They followed the boy up the narrow street and down white steps between more flat-roofed buildings. Against one of them was

45

a wooden lean-to, timbers and old tyres piled against it. The boy gestured and began to move the tyres until eventually, they saw a padlocked door. The boy took a key and unlocked it. Inside the shed, there were seven drums and several new tyres. The boy banged the drums; one of them sounded empty.

'How do we get them to the boat?' Duff demanded. 'The bloody moke can't carry 'em.'

Cotton asked the boy, who vanished, leaving them awkward and uneasy because they were aware of the hostility on the island towards them and didn't know where the Germans were. After a while the boy returned pushing a small cart. It looked little bigger than a child's barrow but he began to hitch it to the donkey.

'Let's have a ramp of some sort rigged up,' Duff said and they managed, with the timbers that had been leaning against the shed, to build a sloping platform against which the boy backed the cart. Manhandling the drums up, they loaded three of them into the cart and the boy locked the door again and began to pile the timbers up against it.

'We will come back,' he said.

The weight of the drums in the cart seemed almost to have lifted the donkey off the ground and Gully eyed it speculatively.

'It's never going to be able to pull those things,' he said.

But, with the wheels wobbling and screeching on the axles, the minute beast tottered off, its hoofs click-clacking on the cobbles.

'The bloody thing'll have a heart attack,' Gully said.

Duff took the rifle from Coward and handed it to Cotton. 'Stay here, Cotton,' he said. 'You, too, Gully. Keep an eye on this place. I'll go back with Coward and turn the stuff over and then come back.'

Cotton and Gully watched them disappear behind the houses towards the bay. Gully took his cigarette end from behind his ear and lit it. After a couple of puffs, he passed it to Cotton, who also took a couple of puffs and handed it back to Gully to finish.

'What you make of this bleedin' lot?' Gully asked.

'Which bleeding lot?'

'Us. You and me. Where we're goin'. It's a right carry-on, innit?'

Cotton shrugged. It hadn't occurred to him to wonder. Having been recruited into the enterprise, he had accepted it with his usual unflappable logic. A Marine didn't ask questions. He got on with it.

Gully studied Cotton for a while, puzzled by his silence. Gully was a man who liked noise and believed in making plenty. He'd grown up in a house full of people and was uncomfortable when everything was quiet.

He spat. 'How long you been in?' he asked.

Cotton's head turned. 'Nearly four,' he said.

'Poor bugger!' Gully grinned. 'I could never 'ave joined the navy. I like to be free to 'op it when I feel like it. "Just let me shake the dust of this old cow off me feet," I always used to say when I was at sea. But then I'd come ashore and get into the first bar I saw and, afore I knew what had happened, I was spent up – even me railway fare 'ome – and I was back aboard the bleeder again, flat broke.' He gave a boozy cackle. 'I was never one for discipline though. I mean – ' he ran a hand over his greying, grubby-looking thatch and looked hard at Cotton's neat haircut ' – they ought to give you gas for a haircut like you've got. After all, a feller's got to have enough left to brush and comb, ain't 'e? Give me a haircut like you got and I'd have broke down and cried like a child. I pride myself on a nice eddervair.'

Cotton thought it might have been an even nicer 'eddervair' if he'd bothered to wash it occasionally but he said nothing and Gully went on cheerfully.

'You look like the sort of chap who'd capture a battleship with a jack-knife,' he said.

'I might.' Cotton didn't smile. He wasn't given to smiling much. He was a slow-speaking, slow-moving man not willing to quarrel. 'The Marines have been around a bit.'

'Why'd you join?'

Cotton considered. For a long time as a youth he'd wondered what he was going to do with his life because he'd never intended

47

to spend the rest of his life writing down in ledgers the petrol consumption of London Transport buses.

'Fancied it,' he said.

'But why the Marines?'

Cotton shrugged. In fact, he'd seen a poster of a Marine corporal, smart in his best blues and white helmet, talking to a blonde in a bathing costume with palms and a foreign blue sea behind him, and his mind had been made up at once. It hadn't turned out quite as the poster showed, of course. He hadn't noticed, for instance, such a fat lot of blondes – they seemed to be reserved for the officers; the other ranks got the brunettes with a touch of the tarbrush who didn't make the wardroom dances – but he'd been to Bermuda and Jamaica when *Caernarvon* had shown the flag in the Caribbean before the war, and he supposed he had to take what came. After all, *Per Mare, Per Terram*. That was the Royal Marines' motto. *By horse, by tram*. You didn't argue about it.

'Bit of excitement,' he said.

'Get any?'

'Here and there.'

'What did you do before you joined?'

'I dunno.' Cotton was not one to encourage discussion of his private affairs. 'I've been in so long, I've forgot.'

The donkey reappeared, apparently none the worse for dragging the three heavy drums through the village. As they loaded the last drum on to the cart, Gully looked round the shed to see if there were anything he could scrounge.

'Come on,' Duff said. 'Let's be having you.'

Gully spat and emerged with a tyre.

'What the hell do you think you're goin' to do with that?' Duff demanded.

'Be worth a bit in Alex,' Gully said. 'Them Gyppos'll give a lot for this.'

'Shove it back,' Duff said. 'We depend on these bloody people for their good will. And they'd be delighted, wouldn't they, if they found we'd been pinching things?'

Gully replaced the tyre unwillingly and they set off back towards *Claudia*. Docherty and the two RASC privates had manhandled the first three drums on board when they arrived.

'We'll top up at Aeos,' Shaw said. 'That'll give us full tanks for the return trip.'

The sun was high now in a sky that had become startlingly blue. More men and boys had appeared on the jetty to watch them and, at the landward end, the women stood like black vultures, obviously discussing them.

'We'll move among the caiques,' Shaw said, 'and wait until dark before leaving.'

But the fishermen resented the movement of the boat among their vessels. They were well aware that the Germans weren't far away and had obviously decided that if a prowling German plane spotted her and returned to drop a bomb, their own boats would suffer.

A large man in a jersey and wearing ear-rings acted as spokesman. He was obviously enjoying his position and the fact that the women were giving him admiring glances.

'*Philótimo*,' Patullo explained. 'The Greek male's sense of honour and pride in his own worth. A self-image that keeps him in conceit of himself and demands revenge for insult. It gets a bit swollen by a loud voice and great physical strength.'

It took a great deal of concentrated arguing to make it clear that it was best for everybody if they managed to hide *Claudia* rather than moor her separately across the harbour, and it was Cotton who pulled the trick in the end.

'If we moor over there,' he said, pointing, 'and a German plane comes, they'll spot her at once. And if bombs are dropped they're as likely to hit your boats as ours. If we hide her among the caiques, they'll probably never see her and then there'll be no bombs at all.'

'You should take an interpreter's course, Cotton,' Patullo said as the fishermen unwillingly withdrew their objections. 'It would be worth a bit extra, and we might be glad of a few Greek speakers in the Med before the war's over.'

The idea struck a spark. If nothing else, Cotton thought, it would mean he'd be relieved of sentry duties and might even get three stripes on his arm. To Cotton that was the very pinnacle of military glory and he decided to make enquiries when he got back.

Then he paused. *If* he got back, he thought.

4

The plain of Kalani on the north side of the island of Aeos was like a plate, with the Phythion Hills running along the south coast and dropping steeply to the sea over narrow bays overhung by trees. The north coast, less rugged, less open to the sea because of the shelter of the mainland of Greece, was fringed by more hills, but these were gentle slopes rising to the port and capital of the island : Kalani, a sprawling town of white houses round the Bay of Xinthos.

The plain was fertile but low-lying and intersected by marshes, so that across its whole length it was studded with windmills with small triangular-shaped sails, oddly like the celluloid toys children placed on their sandcastles on English beaches in summer. It was said that here Odysseus set up camp after landing on his journey to Ithaca. In addition to lemon, orange and olive trees, it contained cherry, almond, fig and quince as well as bougain-villaea and oleander. In one part of the plain, however, near Yanitsa, to the south of Kalani, there was a stretch of land which was surrounded by cotton and tobacco, and its burning noonday heat was softened by the prevailing north wind. Here, occasion-ally, light aeroplanes from nearby Athens had been in the habit of landing wealthy passengers heading for their summer houses away from the bustle and heat of the metropolis. A small, narrow landing strip had been built with one hangar and a set of huts to serve as workshops, stores and offices.

It was here, on 7 April 1941, that the two or three clerks, mechanics and labourers who were employed there, stood staring at the sky as a heavy three-engined aeroplane came in to land. It was made of ribbed metal, its centre engine placed in the nose of the machine. The Greeks watched it, open-mouthed, and it was only as it drew nearer that they realized that on the wings and fuselage it carried the black crosses of the Luftwaffe and on its tail the crooked cross of Nazi Germany. Knowing already what was happening on the mainland, they watched, petrified.

The radio had been full of an appalling bombing raid the day before on the Piraeus, the port for Athens and the only shipping centre of any consequence in Greece.

It had been congested to the point of chaos and three ammunition ships had been alongside, one of them with her cargo of explosives only partly removed when the first wave of bombers had arrived. The blast had showered debris everywhere, igniting small craft, while the violence of the explosion had reduced sheds to rubble. In all, eleven ships had been lost and the Piraeus had ceased to function as a port.

As a result, the people on the landing strip at Yanitsa were worried to see the Junkers coming in to land. Aeos was so far south of the fighting on the mainland they couldn't imagine what the aeroplane was doing there. It was only as it touched down that they realized a second and a third and a fourth aircraft were coming in behind it.

The first machine had landed and was taxiing towards the hangar and the hut that was used as an office. As it slowed, the pilot jammed on his brakes and swung it round in a tight circle. The blast from the propellers raised a cloud of dust which it blew through the open doors and windows of the office, scattering papers and filling the place with blinding grit. Immediately, a door in the side of the machine opened and men in packs and helmets began to pour out. Behind them was an officer, in full uniform and wearing only a revolver.

He jerked a hand towards the row of cars standing outside the office. 'Seize those vehicles,' he said. 'If anyone argues, shoot them.'

The men ran towards the line of cars as the second, third and fourth Junkers touched down. Somebody obviously did argue, because there was a short burst of firing; then, as the aeroplanes cut their engines, a shocked silence and a woman's wail of terror. Driven by the German soldiers, the cars edged out of line and, heading towards the officer, drew up in front of him. By this time, the second, third and fourth aircraft were empty of men and the officer was pointing to the north.

'Off you go,' he said. 'We want all the chief officials, port authorities, military and naval men and the Mayor of Kalani. Lock them up. If they argue, shoot them. We haven't time to discuss things. Let it be known that if there's any resistance, I'll have the Luftwaffe obliterate the place.'

'Jawohl, Herr Major!'

'We have one hour to get control. Once we've got Kalani, it's done. See to it.'

'Jawohl, Herr Major!'

'Commandeer any vehicle you want on the way.'

Packed with armed men, the cars swung round and began to head towards the north, roaring over the grass in the direction of the port, while the German major deployed the rest of his men about the airstrip, setting up heavy machine-guns and establishing them in and around the office and the hangar.

They had barely finished when the telephone rang. The man sitting by the radio that had been set up answered it and handed the earpiece to the major.

'Captain Ehrhardt, Herr Major,' he said.

The major took the telephone, sat down in the chair behind the desk and put it to his ear. As he listened, he looked like a business-man attending to the first call of the day.

'Well done, Ehrhardt,' he said.

Replacing the telephone he clicked his fingers and, as the radio-man handed him a signal pad, he began to write, addressing the message to General Ritsicz, 12th Army, Sofia.

'Objective captured. No casualties. Await orders. Baldamus.'

He signed it and handed it to the signaller with a smile. 'I think this will startle the British,' he said. 'At least, it should discourage them from putting men ashore here.'

This time it was Major Baldamus who was wrong, because *Claudia* was only waiting for dusk before pushing on with the next stage of her voyage.

A sort of dread seemed to have settled over Iros. As the day advanced they began to hear the soft thud-thud of guns to the north and the distant hum of aircraft which never came close enough to be seen. Otherwise all was extraordinarily quiet, the islanders moving about in small silent groups as if in need of constant company. There were no voices, not even the voices of sea birds, and the women in the low fields by the shore seemed to speak in whispers, because it was impossible, even in the still air, to hear them.

Occasionally, groups of prune-eyed children or old men came down the jetty to look at *Claudia*, moored among the caiques and disguised with blankets over her guns; but no one asked about her, or the purpose of her voyage. It was obvious the islanders suspected that no good could come of her visit and they were all holding their breath, wondering when nemesis was going to arrive in the shape of a prowling German aeroplane.

Even the harbour wall was silent and deserted except for a man using a six-inch nail to splice an eye in a heavy wire hawser.

'He'd do better with a spike,' Shaw observed and Patullo smiled.

'He'll manage,' he said. 'It's a habit of the Greeks to use things for multiple purposes. I once saw the fire brigade turn out in a suburb of Larisa, complete with engines and brass helmets, to water the flowers in the public gardens.'

Gully pulled his concertina from under the dreadful heap of rubbish in the brown-paper parcel that he called his gear and tried a few notes. 'I'm a flying fish, sailor, just 'ome from 'Ong Kong,' he began.

Docherty stopped him. 'Gi'e us something proper,' he said.

'What sort of proper?'

'Know "Ramona"?'

''Oo's she?' Gully asked. 'That bit that used to wait outside the docks at South Shields?'

But he started to play the tune and Docherty sang in a breathy tenor, doing dance steps round the forecastle. 'These bloody navy jobs,' he complained. 'They get me chocker. No room to move. If I'd built this scow for meself I'd have had a bar and a big double bed for the bints.'

'Your mind runs on rails,' Bisset said.

Docherty grinned his mad grin. 'It's a short life, so you might as well make it a merry one. I was in Singapore before I come to the Med. The bints there were all right – one of coffee, two of milk, and red hot in bed.'

At midday Bisset managed to pick up the BBC news again, and they listened with hearts that seemed to be clutched by cold fingers. The Axis troops were active again in North Africa and Tobruk was still besieged, while to the north in Greece the British army was as hard pressed as it seemed to have been everywhere since the war had wakened up the previous year.

'The situation is grave,' the announcer said in the smooth, cool tones of someone sitting out of the way in London. 'The Greek government has left Athens and the whereabouts of the king are at present unknown. Australian and New Zealand troops are taking up positions –'

'On Crete,' Bisset put in.

' – and a British fleet is in the Adriatic –'

'Assembling for evacuation, I bet.'

' – Naval units, assault ships and A-lighters are being gathered.'

'That *makes* it evacuation,' Cotton said bluntly. 'The assault ships are the Glen Line vessels and the A-lighters are tank landing craft. They carry a lot of blokes.'

'And they're bloody unhandy jobs into the bargain,' Docherty observed, rolling a cigarette with his oil-stained fingers. 'As far as I'm concerned, you can stuff 'em where the monkey stuffed its nuts.'

They'd all known that evacuation was inevitable but the news that it was now clearly a fact depressed them all a little, even Docherty.

Later Bisset picked up Berlin and crouched over the set, listening with his head cocked, his eyes thoughtful.

'Where did you learn German?' Cotton asked.

'At school.'

'Can you understand it?'

Bisset smiled. 'It was rather a good school,' he said. 'I even spent a year in Heidelberg – officially studying the German language, unofficially chasing the German girls – all at my father's expense.'

Cotton's family had never had enough to send him even for a week to Brighton, and he frowned. There was something about Bisset that puzzled him. With the world falling about their ears, he seemed quite unperturbed.

'I never know when you're pulling my leg,' he growled.

Bisset beamed at him. 'As a matter of fact, neither do I. And now I think you'd better fetch Patullo. They're having a bit of a gloat about what they're going to do and he might like to know.'

Patullo and Shaw arrived in a hurry and listened with grave faces. 'They're hoping to get Junkers 87s on the Salonika airfields,' Bisset said. 'Supported by transports. They're beginning already to move through the Monastir Gap and the Rupel Pass. They say they intend to seize the Corinth Canal.'

He was about to say more when the harsh German voice started again. As it stopped, Bisset sat back. 'They're flying out to the offshore islands,' he said. 'They mentioned Aeos.'

Patullo frowned. 'Probably won't affect us,' he decided, but he didn't sound too sure. 'Aeos is a big island and the airstrip's up in the north near Kalani. They'll probably not get around to Xiloparissia Bay for a couple of weeks. With luck, we ought to be able to pick up what we want and get out before they notice us.'

As the officers disappeared and Bisset switched off the receiver, Cotton studied him again. He'd met men like Bisset before –

56

strange types from happy homes who'd decided on uniform and were content enough not to want to throw it off, indifferent to commissions or promotion.

'Patullo's a nut,' he said. In front of a member of the idle rich like Bisset, Cotton was vaguely pleased to be associated with such a character and such wealth. 'It was him got me into this. He once told me he took part in a Greek cavalry charge in some rebellion in the thirties and was allowed to keep his horse, saddle and sword as a reward. And I once heard the commander telling the captain that he'd interrupted a dinner at Shepheard's by standing up at his table and reciting a Horatian ode in honour of a Cantacuzene princess who was one of his girl friends.' Cotton paused. 'What's a Horatian ode?'

'An ode by Horace, I expect. He was an ancient Roman poet.'

'And a thingy princess?'

'A descendant of Cantacuzenus, I suppose.'

'Who's he when he's at home?'

'He became Emperor of Byzantium.'

Cotton frowned. 'You seem to know a bit too,' he said.

'It's been noticed,' Bisset smiled.

'Are you married?'

Bisset gazed at Cotton. The Marine was big and clumsy but there was something about him that impressed – if it were only his size.

'Not much fun courting, getting engaged and all fixed up on Naafi notepaper,' he said. 'No, I'm not.'

Cotton was still feeling his way. Bisset's speech was precise and devoid of service slang and was one more reason why Cotton needed to know more about him. He tried him with the eternal introductory question of all regulars.

'Why'd you join?'

Bisset's smile came again. 'I got taken in by that poster of the blonde. My family said it was a waste of a good education, and I suppose it was. But, you know, a training in classics is no more use to a career in business than it is to the service.'

Cotton gestured. 'Why didn't you try for a pilot?'

'It did occur to me.' Bisset gave his wide smile again. 'But it turned out there was a bit of a problem in telling brown from green. I'm colour blind.'

Cotton frowned. 'It was the blonde that got me,' he admitted. 'I'd read all the stuff, of course. It was the Marines that captured Gibraltar. Gibraltar's the only battle honour worn on *our* colours. No flag's big enough to hold 'em all.'

Bisset was watching him with mild, amused eyes. He came from a family which took everything for granted – even its own worth – and it was a change to meet a man who was naïvely proud to belong to something simply because of its record.

'When they invaded Holland last year,' Cotton went on, 'they fell in two hundred of our lot at Chatham – cooks, clerks, barrack stanchions, the whole shebang. Within twelve hours they were defending the Hook of Holland. When they came out they brought Queen Wilhelmina with 'em. Didn't lose a man either. In fact they had an extra anti-tank rifle.'

'Why didn't you join the commandos?'

Cotton sniffed. 'What's the point?' he said. 'We *are* commandos. We always have been.'

A wrinkled crone, covered in black against the heat like an Arab, came down the jetty, making the sign of the cross over them as she passed. She was riding on a mule that was decorated with a string of blue beads on its forehead, and they all leaned on the wheelhouse roof to watch her.

'What's them bead things for?' Gully asked, addressing the question to no one in particular. 'They've all got 'em. 'Ouses, babies, mules, carts, boats.'

'To guard against the evil eye,' Bisset said.

'Whose evil eye?'

'Nobody's.' Bisset smiled. 'Just the evil eye. It's responsible for all maladies in humans, the malfunctions of boat engines and the dropping dead of overloaded donkeys.'

In the heat of the early afternoon, Shaw allowed them ashore for a drink, leaving only Chief ERA Duff on board in command of the boat and Howard to do sentry-go with the tommy-gun.

Docherty was at his most intractable, staring at the signs outside the shops with a disgusted look, as if all Greeks were mad.

'Bloody funny language,' he said at the top of his voice. 'Looks like a fly fell in the paint-pot and crawled all over it. It's worse than that gyppo writing you see in Alexandria.'

The café was vine-covered and inside people were eating red mullet with retsina and white demestica wine. In the lee of the wall, sponge fishermen were slapping the sand out of their sponges, clipping away the dirt and stones, then soaking them and stuffing them into sacks. A flock of lambs came past, driven to the jetty for transport to the mainland which would probably now never want them, and the air was full of their bleating.

The sponge fishermen, a boy mending a net, and an old man making a new one from thread, hooking and knotting with dexterity, looked up as they arrived. There was a buzz of chatter going on in the shade inside over the sound of the radio batting out a Greek Orthodox liturgy from the mainland, and their arrival stopped the conversation so that the radio said, 'Kyrie eleison! Kyrie eleison!' so loudly everybody looked round.

Docherty tasted the thin, pale, watery beer cautiously.

'Tastes like horse-piss,' he complained.

'Shut up,' Cotton said. 'They might understand English.'

'Who?' Gully asked. 'Wops?'

'They might,' Cotton said, faintly shamefaced but also slightly indignant that Docherty should regard Greeks as something less than human.

As they drank, the village priest went past, in his black robes and flat-topped hat, pushing back the sleeve of his robe, then an old man appeared from the café, holding a glass of raki, and stopped in front of them. He wore a beard, a fringed turban, elaborately embroidered waistcoat, cummerbund, tall black leather boots and a pair of voluminous knickerbockers with a baggy seat.

'Known as crap-catchers,' Patullo said to Shaw at the next table.

The old man grinned and waved his hand. 'Welcome,' he said

59

in English. 'Rooly Britannia. Goss-savey King.' He gestured at the radio and lapsed into Greek. 'That is the true liturgy,' he said, and Cotton translated for the others. 'We have the words of the Fathers. The true confession. We have the ikons and the blessed Eucharist to cleanse and unite us.' He stopped and looked hard at Cotton. 'You are Greek, my son?' he asked. 'You look Greek.'

'No,' Cotton said quickly. 'I'm English.'

'You have the Greek language. You speak it well.'

'I learned it,' Cotton said. 'I learned it at school.'

'You speak it like a Greek too. You have a good accent.' The old man paused as Cotton grew more uncomfortable. 'Where are the Germans now?' he asked.

'I don't know. North somewhere.'

'They will come soon. We shall be prisoners. God grant that they will be haunted by the spirits of their victims. They no longer rest quiet in their graves.' The old man sniffed. 'The Italians – *pò-pò* – ' he gestured contemptuously with his fingers ' – they are mere jackals. The Germans are vampires from hell. But a Greek is a man with a long memory.' He looked hard at Cotton. 'That boat of yours,' he went on. 'Panyioti, the millionaire, had one like that.'

'It used to be Panyioti's boat,' Cotton explained.

The old man spat. '*Aie!* That was no Greek. He only visited Aeos once a year, and he spent all the time throwing ten-drachma pieces to the poor from his shiny car. True Greeks believe in things. Every day the newspapers report how somebody has been chopped to the navel with a meat cleaver because somebody else didn't agree with him.'

They went inside to have a meal because they suspected they'd be living on bully beef and biscuit before long. Patullo paid and it consisted largely of lamb, which Gully suspected and Cotton knew was goat. But with it there was fresh bread and young wine, light, sparkling and cool. Gully inevitably preferred the beer.

The food was brought by a dark-eyed, dark-haired girl with moist lips, big sticky eyes and a large bust. Gully eyed her gleefully, nudging Coward energetically. Docherty watched her with a hot, longing look in his eyes, as if he'd have liked to wrench the clothes from her back and fling her down across one of the tables.

'Bit of all right,' Gully said. 'Look smashing with a feather in 'er 'at and no drawers.'

Cotton said nothing. He'd lost his virginity soon after joining the Marines but he'd never gone for lush dark-eyed women. Because of his rejection of his background, he'd always chosen blonde, blue-eyed English-looking girls, but they'd always seemed to lack the steam and passion to match his own. 'Steady on, ducks,' one of them had once told him during a bout of intense love-making on the settee with her mother asleep upstairs. 'You don't have to go at it as if you're starving.'

They had cheese that was strong enough to remove the roofs of their mouths and washed it down with cherry brandy at a penny a glass, so that they returned on board feeling mellow and ready for anything. Later in the afternoon, they lay the boat alongside the mole and took on water. Then they slept in the heat, with only Cotton on deck, watching the sky. He didn't feel like sleeping and had offered to do aircraft look-out. Uneasily he felt that something was stirring in him that was spiritually connected with this island, as if the place was calling to him; and he realized that when the old man had been talking about Greek courage and bravery, he had even felt a certain amount of pride. It was disturbing, because all his life he'd tried to believe he was entirely British.

As the sun sank, people filled the café, drinking cocoa and wine, and music from a couple of fiddles and a bouzouki started. The sun was setting and the evening was one of beaten gold when the lone Heinkel came over. As it flew off towards the west, they smiled with relief.

'He's missed us,' Patullo said.

But the aircraft returned a few minutes later, grey-green and sleekly streamlined, and circled the harbour about two thousand feet up. Everybody on the wall stared upwards, watching it, men, women and children, holding their donkeys and their fish baskets and their shopping. Then, as the aircraft came overhead again, Cotton noticed that the bomb doors were open.

'He's going to bomb!' he yelled, and they all ducked behind the wheelhouse.

The black crow-like shapes of the women started to run and the wail that went up could be heard over the noise of the engines. Then the yelling was drowned in an iron howling as the aeroplane swept overhead and they saw the bombs drop away. At first they thought they were intended for *Claudia* but they passed in a descending curve over the boats and landed in the town. Lifting their heads, they saw the explosions puff up in four mushrooms of brown smoke that contained twisting tiles and pieces of wood. Then the aeroplane swept over the town and out to sea towards the north.

'Come on!' Patullo said, and they started to run down the harbour wall.

The bombs had fallen among the huddled white houses. Two had gone wide and done no more than dig holes of fresh, pulverized smoking earth in a plot of gardens, but the other two had flung down two of the houses and the Greeks were just dragging out a woman and a child. A donkey lay dead nearby, its blood soaking the earth in a huge sticky pool, and the priest, his face agonized, his hands red, was standing among the rubble muttering a prayer.

As they lifted the child clear, ominously still, the woman wrenched herself free, her face, her clothes, her hair, white with plaster dust. As she flung herself on the child, wailing, the aircraft passed over the harbour again and released a cloud of pamphlets which showered down to litter the streets.

Patullo caught one as it fluttered past. ' "To the Greek islanders," ' he read aloud so they could all hear. ' "Be warned! The Greek government on the mainland, having directed hostile actions against the Greater German Reich and her allies, the Führer, Adolf Hitler, has decided the time has come when the Greek people must be taught a lesson. They have the choice of being ruled by their own decadent and corrupt government, or accepting the German army of occupation – " '

'Same bloody stuff they dropped on France,' Shaw said sourly.

The anger of the islanders seemed to have knotted into a bitterness that was directed not against the aeroplane but against the British, and they saw a crowd gather near the end of the mole. The corpse of the child was lying on a slab, the mother still wailing over it. The rest of the village, led by the priest, drew together and began to march towards them.

'I think we'd better go,' Shaw said. 'Start her up, Chief.'

As the engines crashed to life, the crowd stopped dead and only the old man who had talked to Cotton was on the mole to see them off. He seemed to know where they were going and seemed to feel no resentment towards them because there were tears in his eyes as he made the sign of the Cross over them.

'May God go with you,' he said. 'May God in his openhandedness bless you with a fine night.'

Cotton replied automatically as he'd heard his mother call after departing guests. 'Thank you. Perhaps God will assist us.'

Staring back, he frowned, uncertain and worried. He'll need to, he decided.

5

In the headquarters he had set up in the Hotel Potomakis in Kalani, Major Baldamus sat back and considered his position.

He had done well in France and his promotion had been rapid, but he was also clever enough to have kept his nose clean without claiming that he was part of a master race. He hadn't particularly wanted a war but, having got one, he was determined to get the best out of it; especially here on Aeos, where he felt he was ideally suited for the job he'd been given. He spoke excellent Greek, had spent a lot of time as an archaeological student in the islands during the thirties, and had used his money to make sure he did it with a certain amount of aplomb. He was, in fact, a German version of Lieutenant Patullo, whom, oddly enough, he had even once met in the Parthenon Hotel in Athens before the war.

A flight of Messerschmitts had just reached the island to support him and, to maintain them, two more transports loaded with fuel, spares, fitters and riggers. Every public office was already controlled by his men, under the efficient Captain Ehrhardt, and the mayor and the island officials were still under lock and key until he could decide what to do with them. Everything seemed highly satisfactory and he was happy that he had not been obliged to call on the bombers to break the islanders' will.

He shifted in his chair and lit a cigar. Contemplating the blue smoke with a certain amount of satisfaction, he felt he had a right to be pleased with himself. It had been a bold stroke to take over Aeos so far in advance of the Wehrmacht. It had been captured entirely by airborne troops and, as General Ritsicz had said, could well be a pattern for the future. Because of the speed, with every hour that passed Baldamus' position grew stronger, and there was no doubt in his mind that eventually the Germans would control the whole of the mainland and the Greek archipelago as well. From the outset of the Balkan campaign, the British and Greek troops had been falling back in the face of strong and determined attacks.

Belgrade and Skoplje were secure now, he'd heard, and the panzers were already pouring into Greece. The British would inevitably have to form a new line near Mount Olympus and the River Aliakman – and then only until the growing German flanking movement in the west compelled a further withdrawal. They hadn't a chance. They were suffering intensely from bombing, because when Field Marshal List's 12th Army with twelve first-class divisions and over 800 aircraft had started their advance, the RAF in Greece had possessed only eighty usable machines out of a strength of 150; the rest were already unserviceable on airfields all over the country. Once the panzers were completely through the passes and had seized the Salonika plain to establish fighter bases supported and maintained like his own by transports, there would not be a single British unit that could not come under intense and constant air attack, while in the rear every sector of military organization, ports and aerodromes could suffer incessant bombing.

Major Baldamus decided he didn't have a lot to worry about. He had the island nicely wrapped up. The population chiefly lived in the north round Kalani and, since he controlled that and the airstrip at Yanitsa, it seemed his worries were over. Surely there could be only a few more days to hang on. The transports and Messerschmitts were merely the first of the supporting units to arrive and, with the build-up going well, he no longer had any fear of a rising against him because the rest of the island consisted of mere hamlets and groups of farms. Though he could hardly patrol them all, he preferred in any case to keep his people close together. It was one of the first principles of soldiering and, since

65

Major Baldamus was rather out on a limb on Aeos, he considered it wiser to avoid trouble.

It was while he was in this euphoric state that Captain Ehrhardt appeared. Ehrhardt was a small man, with a brown wrinkled face. His uniform was dusty and his sleeves were rolled up to the elbows. Strapped and buckled like a carthorse in his equipment, he presented a perfect picture of a tough German fighting man. As he laid the signal he was carrying on Baldamus' desk, he gave a slow grin at the reaction he knew it would produce.

Baldamus looked at the sheet of paper with a lazy eye, still full of thoughts on his own future. Then, as he read the words, he sat bolt upright and stared at his second-in-command with startled blue eyes, his handsome face full of consternation.

'*Another* British launch?' he said.

'Yes, Herr Major.'

'Like the one the Italians drove ashore near Cape Annoyia?'

'Yes, Herr Major. It's just reached Iros on its way north. It seems we have sympathizers there who have passed on the information.'

Baldamus stared again at the signal. 'But heading north?' He gazed at Captain Ehrhardt, frowning. 'What are they after?'

'Perhaps,' Ehrhardt said, 'they're on their way to look for survivors from the other one. Though we've seen no sign of them. I gather the boat's a total wreck – holed forward, engines wrecked, underwater gear buckled. The islanders seem to have been poking around it already because the dead have been buried and everything movable's been pinched. Still – ' he shrugged ' – perhaps the British *think* somebody escaped.'

Baldamus stared at the signal again then he grinned. 'If another of those boats *is* on its way,' he said, 'then we might as well collect that one too. We could have our own fleet. I'd like to be an admiral. Inform the Luftwaffe to look out for it.'

He smiled, sat back and drew on his cigar again. 'As a matter of fact,' he went on, 'I understand there were originally *three* of these boats – all belonging to Spiro Panyioti. What a feather in our caps it would be if we had them *all*. We could use them for evening drinks, Ehrhardt, and trips round the island. One for me, one for you, and one for the Luftwaffe. Since the war's going our way, we might as well enjoy it.'

It was raining again as *Claudia* turned north and Docherty stuck his head out of the engine room. 'Roll on my twelve,' he said. 'I thought it was always bloody fine in the Med.'

They headed north all night, all of them quiet and depressed by the bombing of Iros. They still had a long way to go and Shaw wanted to cover it slowly to conserve fuel. There were so many islands, he had to pick his way between them in the dark, busy at the chart table all the way.

As daylight came the next morning, the islands multiplied, each bare hill and blue-grey cliff appearing from behind the last boulder-strewn headland. Beyond them were more leagues of ruffled sea the colour of delphiniums, and in the distance more green headlands, each hazier than the one in front. Despite the islands, however, the sea appeared blank and empty and vast. With the Germans on the march, the islanders were staying ashore for safety and there wasn't a boat to be seen.

After Iros, Cotton was keenly aware of a sense of danger surrounding them. With every beat of the engines, every turn of the screws, they were getting closer to the Germans, and he took to studying himself to see if he was afraid. He was pleased to find he wasn't.

The sky was free of clouds as the boat knifed across a sea that looked like a dark silk sheet. They had rounded Xiros and Kafoulos and were heading directly towards Aeos. To the north they could still occasionally hear the distant thud-thud of guns, even above the beat of the engines.

'Army's having itself its usual happy time,' Patullo said.

'Poor buggers,' Shaw growled.

There was also the constant sound of aircraft, a low distant throbbing hum in the sky that they knew meant danger to the unprotected army, and disaster to themselves if it appeared overhead.

'Aeroplanes,' Shaw said.

'They won't be British,' Patullo commented.

'No.'

'Better get the Flit gun ready.'

Then Patullo pointed towards a shadowy shape between two other islands.

'That's it,' he said.

'We'll increase the revs,' Shaw said. 'Turn the wick up a bit, Howard. And let's have a message off, operator, to say we've arrived.'

He turned to bend over the chart with Patullo. 'Here we are,' Patullo said, jabbing with his finger. 'Approaching Cape Annoyia. Kharasso Bay's on one side of it and Xiloparissia Bay's on the other.' He gestured ahead. 'That's Cape Asigonia, the easternmost tip of the island, and that – ' his arm moved again ' – that's Cape Kastamanitsa, the southernmost tip.'

'What about towns?'

'Fishing village here, the other side of Xiloparissia Bay – Ay Yithion's the name. There are two more – here and here – Skoinia and Kaessos. The capital's in the north across this plain. The air strip at Yanitsa's just to the south of it.'

There was a pause then Patullo went on, sounding faintly depressed. 'Let's hope the islanders' views are the same as ours,' he said. 'Greeks enjoy arguing, whether it's about God, that part of Macedonia which used to be Greek, or their own eternal cunning, and they're very sensitive about politics. Bodies are left about stabbed like colanders every time the prime minister makes a speech. Thank God nobody but us and Iros knows much about the bombing there.'

An hour later they were edging in to their landfall. To port, just beyond Cape Annoyia, they could see a small bay surrounded by houses and a curving stone wall lined with masts.

'Is that it?' Gully asked.

'Yes,' Cotton said.

They could see Shaw studying the island through his glasses. Then he bent and called down to Howard on the wheel.

'Starboard,' he said. 'Let's take a look at Xiloparissia Bay. If we can get straight in there, we might just as well.'

As they approached, the water shelved so that they could peer into water, only a few fathoms deep, that was teeming with fish in the blue-green light. The sea clattered against the rocks and the breeze came through a gap in the hills towards them.

'Keep your eyes skinned,' Patullo warned.

They edged in closer, their eyes on the sky, Patullo studying the bay with his glasses. It was narrow, the shore overhung by trees; from the narrow beach fringed with rocks, the coast rose steeply in a slab-sided hill covered with boulders and foliage to a high ridge.

Then Shaw spoke. 'By God, there she is!' he said.

He cut the engines while they were still a long way out, but it was just possible to see the shape of a boat lying bow-on to a beach under the cliffs at the eastern side of the bay. She looked as if she'd been badly hurt, and was blackened and charred as if she'd been on fire. Her mast was down and there were holes in the hull and the wheelhouse windows, and ropes hung loosely over the side.

Cotton stared at her, his heart thudding suddenly in his throat. Shaw's voice, quiet and unafraid, made him jump.

'I think we'll go in there and have a look at her,' he said and, as Howard edged the throttles forward, *Claudia* began to move ahead again.

Even before they had entered the inlet, the sound of the engines running at low revs began to reverberate from the surrounding cliffs. Xiloparissia Bay was narrow – indeed the whole coast of Aeos just here was full of long tapering bays cut off from each other by high cliffs and half hidden by trees that grew down to the water's edge. The popple of the engines grew louder as the bay bounced the sound back and they were all busily staring at the shore when Cotton lifted his head. The engine note seemed to have changed, as if it were echoing off the cliff more noisily than before. It seemed to grow louder even as he listened, and suddenly he knew why.

'Aircraft!' he yelled, and dived for the 20 mm.

Coward was already on the starboard Lewis, swinging it quickly, while Patullo took the wheel to let Howard leap across the wheelhouse for the port gun.

The aircraft were Messerschmitts and they came over the cliffs at full speed, howling overhead and heading south. At first, it seemed as if they'd missed *Claudia*, but then, when they were about a mile out to sea, Cotton saw them swing in a wide arc and begin to come back. Remembering how much petrol they were carrying in drums on the deck, he found himself cataloguing and analysing his thoughts as he waited in grim fatalism. One shell into their deck cargo and there'd be such a bloody bang they'd all have wings.

'They've seen us!' Shaw yelled. 'Get a message off, operator, that we're being attacked!'

As Patullo opened the throttles, *Claudia*'s bow lifted and she seemed to leap across the water, rolling alarmingly on her beam ends as he dragged at the wheel. The wake trailed behind like an enormous paying-off pennant, white across the dark waters, then they had swung round and were hurtling out of Xiloparissia Bay. The Messerschmitts were heading directly towards them now, low over the water, and Cotton saw the snaking lines of tracer sliding over the masthead and heard bangs behind him.

It was hopeless running for the open sea. They would have been destroyed in no time, and Shaw decided to make for the shelter of the cliffs again. In one of the narrow bays, it would be almost impossible to hit them.

'Take her in there,' he yelled, pointing, and as Patullo swung the wheel, *Claudia* heeled over once more.

The Messerschmitts were coming round again now and Cotton felt the padded rests of the 20 mm shudder against his shoulders almost without being aware of pressing the trigger.

'Docherty!' he screamed.

Even as the gun stopped, the drum empty, he saw a piece fly off the leading Messerschmitt, then a puff of smoke, and he realized he'd hit it.

As the Messerschmitt swung away, losing height, to disappear over the cliffs, he became aware of Gully, the carpenter, his cap over one ear, scrambling out of sight beneath the platform that had been built for the 20 mm. The Lewises were going and Shaw, his head out of the wheelhouse hatch, was yelling at Patullo.

'Take her into Kharasso,' he was roaring. 'Take her in!'

'Docherty!' Cotton shouted furiously. 'Bring us another drum!'

But Docherty seemed to have disappeared and it was Bisset who appeared alongside him with the fresh ammunition. As he reached for it, Cotton saw a line of small explosions coming across the sea as the second Messerschimitt's cannon shells struck the surface. He was quite certain he was in the direct line of fire but they struck the boat forward of where he was standing. He was still struggling with the fresh drum when there was a crash behind him and, as he turned, he saw splinters fly from the wheelhouse roof. The radio direction finder jumped from the deckhead as if it had been ejected by a spring, and lifted up into the air in a clean arc to fall astern.

For a moment, the atmosphere seemed to be full of dust and flying fragments and he saw Shaw disappear through the hatch. The Messerschmitt's nose lifted and a fresh line of explosions jumped across the wheelhouse roof. Coward, who was aiming the starboard Lewis at the aeroplane, fell backwards. His head had gone and his body formed a curving arc through the air as it dropped into the sea alongside. Then Cotton saw it tumbling and rolling in the reddened foam of the wash as they swept past.

Claudia was heading into the bay at full speed and it was as the Messerschmitts disappeared and he lifted his head that Cotton realized the wheelhouse was full of gaping holes.

'Christ!' he said.

Gully was still crouching under the 20 mm, his face grey, yelling with fright. Docherty appeared at last through the engine-room door. He seemed to be staggering as if he were blind and was covered with blood, and it suddenly dawned on Cotton that the boat was out of control. It was pounding over the ripple of the sea in a series of small leaps and, with the wheelhouse roof reduced to splintered matchwood, it was more than likely that Shaw had been hit, and probably Patullo.

He couldn't see Howard at the port gun, and acting on an impulse, since there seemed to be no more Messerschmitts, he jumped from the 20 mm platform, crossed the well deck at a bound and was running across the engine-room deckhead without being aware how he got there.

Claudia was still heading into the bay in a wide curve that confirmed his belief that no one was in control. He had a brief impression of a steep cliff which seemed to run the whole length of this end of the island and had towered above Xiloparissia Bay, lifting high above them – even out of sight. Then they were heading for a small clump of jagged rocks that protruded from the sea, at a speed that took his breath away, and he saw trees on the shore to his right and a sharply shelving rocky beach just ahead. He almost fell into the wheelhouse, stumbling over something that brought him to his knees.

Scrambling to his feet, he wrenched at the wheel. The boat passed the rocks so close the bow wave covered them with a sheet of water, then as he dragged the throttles back and put the telegraphs to neutral, the engines died, and *Claudia*'s bow, high out of the water with her speed, dropped so that she halted like a charging wild animal brought to a stop by a heavy bullet and began to wallow as the following wake lifted her stern. As the bow wave slopped on to her deck, Cotton put her full astern, but he was already too late and the boat seemed to leap into the air as she touched the rocks fringing the shore. He heard the crashing and splintering of timber and the thunderous clangour of disturbed petrol drums; then things seemed to start jumping off the wheelhouse all round him. He was flung forward against the wheel, then to starboard. As the boat finally came to rest on her port side, the wheelhouse glass, broken by the shells from the aircraft and wrenched out of true, fell out of the windows on top of him, and a gout of water, which had shot up alongside, came down on the deck, drenching him as it slopped through the empty frames. The Packards were still screaming, the din coming through the open engine-room door like a wild animal in pain. Gasping, dazed, uncertain what had happened, he heard them die abruptly and realized that someone in addition to himself was alive enough to have cut them.

As everything became still, he dragged himself upright and, looking through the broken windscreen, saw that *Claudia* was lying motionless at an angle of forty-five degrees with her nose on the western end of the beach close to the trees. The tip of the mast with the torn ensign on it was among the lower branches and the wheelhouse seemed to be littered with broken glass and splintered wood.

Staring round him angrily, he turned to look for help and for the first time realized that the wheelhouse was full of blood. Shaw was lying head-down on the steps that lifted to the port door and hatch, and he remembered stumbling and realized he must have tripped over him. Patullo was tumbled in a heap just behind him where he'd been flung, and, as he turned, Cotton saw a pair of feet through the window, on a level with his eye and realized they must belong to Howard.

'Christ,' he breathed in awed tones, shocked by the fury of all the killing. 'Jesus Christ Almighty!'

PART TWO
Preparation

1

The shock that Cotton was feeling in Kharasso Bay was reflected on Lieutenant-Commander Kennard's face in Retimo.

'Am being attacked by Messerschmitts –'

The message stopped abruptly and Kennard knew only too well what it meant. They had been receiving similar messages in Suda Bay all day from ships around the Piraeus and the Greek mainland.

He screwed the paper up and tossed it down alongside the operator who retrieved it, smoothed it out and began to copy it into his log book. Watching them, Ponsonby lit a cigarette and passed the packet to Kennard without a word. Kennard stared at him, then frowned at his own unhappy thoughts.

'That,' Ponsonby said, 'seems to be that. We can say goodbye to our rifles and our money.'

Kennard looked at him bitterly. 'To say nothing of a good ship and nine good men.'

Ponsonby nodded, as though from an afterthought. 'Yes,' he said. 'Those too. I heard, by the way, that the Germans have reached Aeos. Perhaps we were too ambitious.'

Kennard scowled. 'Perhaps we were,' he agreed. 'I wonder if they'll manage to join up with the army. Perhaps it's not as bad as it sounds.'

In fact, it was worse.

The heat from *Claudia*'s engines was drifting through the boat, making the stench of blood seem stronger. With it was mixed hot oil, petrol and the smell of burned wood.

Cotton stood in the lopsided wheelhouse, bracing himself against the tilt of the boat, one hand on the telegraphs, his feet wide apart, his head hanging, almost like a calf outside a slaughterhouse. He was shocked, bewildered and horrified by what had happened and his stomach heaved at the smell of death and the sight of the mutilated bodies lying about him. As he recovered his wits, he saw Bisset lifting his head above the splintered wheelhouse from the well deck. He looked as scared and bewildered as Cotton.

'You all right?' Cotton asked in an uneven voice.

'Yes. You?'

'Yes. Anybody else down there?'

Gully's head appeared. The carpenter looked grey with fright. He had arrived on board pot-brave and had remained full of confidence during the trip to and from Iros because all had gone well. By sheer luck, up to that moment the war for Gully had been only the rub-dub of guns over the horizon, and the sudden shock of the disaster and the deaths of the men around him had changed his views in a second.

Then Docherty stumbled into view, his face covered with blood.

'You hurt?' Cotton asked.

Docherty shook his head, his eyes shocked. 'It was Duff,' he said. 'I was standing beside him.' He was just about to light a cigarette when Bisset put a hand on his arm.

'I should leave that,' he pointed out. 'There are a lot of holes and a smell of petrol. We might all go up if you strike a match.'

'Yeh.' Docherty took the cigarette from his mouth. 'Yeh.' He stopped. 'Holy Mary, Mother of God!' he said in an awed voice.

For a while, they all stood in silence. It was Docherty who had cut the engines, and round the stern Cotton could see the water, stirred up by the propellers before they'd stopped, turning into a brown clouded whirlpool that was just beginning to settle in dying whorls. He glanced along the narrow deck on the port side of the wheelhouse. All he could see was the bottom of Howard's feet. The boy was jammed against one of the stanchions that held the lifeline, and was hanging half over the side of the boat, one arm out, blood dripping steadily from the finger ends into the water.

The Messerschmitt had caught *Claudia* as Patullo had swung her to port and had raked her right across the beam. A shell from the first attack had struck the radio cabin cutting short Bisset's message and starting a small fire. Bisset had survived by a miracle in a shower of shell splinters and shards of black Bakelite. A second shell had hit the side of the forecastle, tearing a great hole in it, and a third had severed a petrol pipe. Fortunately, the drums of petrol in the well deck were untouched, though the smashing of the hull on to the rocks had flung them in a heap round the after door of the engine room. Two other shells had hit the boat. One in the wheelhouse had killed Patullo, Shaw and Coward outright and one in the engine room had killed Duff and wrecked the port engine. Howard was not dead but his left leg was torn open from thigh to knee by a splinter and there was a small hole in his stomach and a third wound in his left shoulder. Bisset, his face serious, bent over him.

'Is he going to die?' Cotton asked.

Bisset shrugged. From the way his fingers moved gently over the injured boy, he seemed to know what to do.

'Got any morphine?' he asked.

'We can have a look in the safe.'

'We'd better get the keys.'

Scrambling awkwardly on the tilted deck, they stretched Patullo out on the floor of the wheelhouse among the broken glass and splintered wood. His uniform was soaked with blood and sticky to the fingers, and as they probed inside his pockets his dead eyes stared fixedly at them all the time. Cotton couldn't take his gaze off them. It seemed inconceivable that all those brains, all that knowledge, had just simply disappeared. Wondering where it went to when a man died and suspecting that death was only darkness, whatever the sin bosuns said at Sunday divisions, to Cotton it seemed tragic that a man like Patullo, who had acquired his experience all over the world, together with all those languages and a great deal of humour, could have it all blotted out in a second by death.

Gully was watching them from the door, still grey-faced and shocked at the destruction. 'For God's sake,' he said in a shaky voice, 'put something over his bloody face!'

Docherty turned, unable to resist a sneer. 'Thought you were going to enjoy the war,' he said.

'I'm a civilian,' Gully said. 'I didn't come to get shot at.'

'What the hell do you expect the Germans to do?' Docherty yelled, his fear breaking out suddenly in violence. 'Kiss you, you daft bastard?'

Cotton scrambled to the captain's cabin and, tearing down one of the plush curtains, laid it over Patullo's head. The silence was what worried him most. The sound of the Messerschmitts' engines had long since died; and all he could hear now was the rush and gurgle of a little stream that fell among the rocks close by, the lap of the little waves against the side of the boat, and the drag of pebbles on the beach. When *Caérnarvon* had been bombed it had been just the opposite. There had been many more killed and injured but there had also been a great deal more noise – roaring steam, men running and the shouting of orders – and it had seemed somehow reassuring. The silence that surrounded *Claudia* seemed vaguely eerie. On *Caernarvon*, too, there had been someone to take control, to issue directions and co-ordinate the work of rescue and repair, and above all the presence of the captain, the Hon. Giles Troughton, calm, unflappable and knowledgeable because he'd been trained to know exactly what to do. Here there was no one – just Cotton, Joe Soap himself – and the disaster seemed more than ever complete as a result.

Unhappily, aware of the blood on their fingers, they searched Patullo's pockets, producing cigarettes, a gold pencil, a wallet and other belongings. Then Bisset held up a bunch of keys.

'These they?'

'People don't usually carry two bunches,' Cotton said. 'They must be.'

They went back to the captain's cabin. It was still luxuriously furnished with Panyioti's special dark-blue blankets and pillows such as never normally found their way into naval vessels. The safe was under the bunk and there were two jars of rum in it. Docherty grabbed one of them at once. 'Up spirits, stand fast the Holy Ghost,' he muttered.

Cotton snatched it from his mouth.

'For Christ's sake – !' Docherty's voice lifted in a whine.

'When we've attended to the kid,' Cotton said.

He wrenched the jar from Docherty's hand, leaving him hot-eyed, the red-brown liquid still dribbling down his chin. For a moment he looked as though he might snatch it back, but in the end he gave a little sigh and turned away.

They found the first-aid kit in the safe under a wad of Greek money. It included a syringe and morphine ampoules. Bisset filled the syringe clumsily and they climbed back on deck to where Howard was beginning to whimper as the shock died and the pain came.

'Give it to him, for God's sake,' Gully mumbled.

At first, Bisset found difficulty in inserting the needle but he managed it at last and they covered Howard with one of the lush blue blankets. Then they went down into the skipper's cabin again and Cotton slopped rum into the mugs that Docherty had found. Gully was looking sick and old.

As they drank the spirit, it reached down into their insides, warming them, making them feel better, clawing at their stomachs with hot, biting fingers. Then Cotton noticed the list he'd made for Shaw lying on the floor among the blood-scattered glass and torn charts. He picked it up and, remembering that from now on it would be his duty to keep the log, he used the pencil they'd taken from Patullo's pocket to put a stroke through the names of Shaw, Patullo, Duff and Coward. After Howard's name he wrote 'Wounded'.

'We'd better get 'em ashore,' he said. 'Take their identity discs and let's get on with it.'

They got a blanket under Patullo and, standing awkwardly on the lopsided deck, hoisted him out of the wheelhouse and up to the bow. Then, lowering a rope, Gully and Docherty climbed down to the beach and, with a blanket lashed round it, the body was lowered over the side to them. It was heavier than they'd expected and its limpness – like dough as it sagged in the sling – made Cotton feel sick. Docherty and Gully took the weight and carried the body up the sand towards the trees. Shaw and Duff followed and they laid the three corpses in a row under the branches. Climbing down to the beach, Cotton stared round him, oppressed by the steepness of the hill that rose from the rocks and the shadow it threw, and by the smell of death that mingled with the scent of foliage. His spirits were lowered further by the recurring thought that both the officers and the senior NCO had been killed and that he was now senior man. It was a daunting prospect, as heavy on his mind as the heat, the narrowness of the bay, and the crowding trees and rocks.

As they stood there, they heard the sound of aeroplane engines and they all darted for the rocks. The machine, a Messerschmitt, turned, low down as if it were looking for them. Then it disappeared beyond the cliff. A minute or two later it came back, flying the length of the narrow bay before disappearing once more over the cliffs.

They waited for a long time until they were certain it had gone, before climbing down to the beach again. Cotton stood a little apart from the others, still awed by the responsibility that had been thrust on him. Then he sighed and felt in his pockets for the identity discs and personal belongings they'd removed from the bodies.

'We'll bury 'em,' he said.

'Later,' Gully urged, his face grey. 'What happened to the other kid?'

Cotton indicated the bay. 'He's out there somewhere. About a mile back, I reckon. I saw him go over the side.'

'Hurt?'

'Dead.'

Climbing back on board, they stared at the unconscious Howard. His breathing was coming in snoring gasps now.

'What're we going to do about him?' Gully mumbled.

'We ought to get him into a bunk.'

Shaw's bunk in the captain's cabin was the only one to which they could move the injured boy without doing him more harm. They packed the angle of the cushioned seat with mattresses and manoeuvred him carefully into the wheelhouse and through the after door and laid him down.

'What do we do for him now?' Cotton asked.

'I don't know,' Bisset admitted, his face worried. 'I did a bit of first-aid before the war but that's all I know. His shoulder ought to be fixed and his leg stitched but, like the one in the gut, that's a job for an MO, not me.'

'Can we get a message back to base?' Cotton asked.

'Have you seen the sets,' Bisset looked white and shaken.

Cotton remembered the pigeons they'd taken aboard. 'How about the birds,' he said.

But the shell that had entered the forecastle had also done for the birds, which were now only a pulpy mess of flesh, blood, feathers and wickerwork cage.

'Think we could get the kid ashore?' Bisset asked. 'There'd be more room and we might find someone to help.'

'He'll die if we don't get him to a doctor.'

'How do we do that?'

Cotton frowned. 'Well, the Carley float seems to be all right.'

'You can't set off home on the Carley float,' Bisset said.

'Well, we can't just sit here hoping, can we? What about the engines?'

Docherty gave him a disgusted look. 'Port engine's nothing but a lot of old iron,' he said. 'And I reckon the prop's smashed.'

'What about the starboard engine?'

Docherty shrugged. ' 'S'all right,' he said. 'But there was a lot of vibration as it stopped. I think the prop hit something. It's probably bent.'

Bisset looked hard at Cotton. 'Why?' he asked. 'What had you in mind?'

Cotton was staring in front of him, holding in his hands the ensign which he'd taken from the masthead. He was mesmerized by an idea he'd had. It had arrived slowly, through a variety of processes, but now it had taken root.

'We've got a diving suit on board,' he said. 'And you're a diver, Docherty.'

'Not me!' Docherty answered as he answered everybody, his voice full of indignation and aggression, as if he were being accused of lying or cheating.

'Duff said you were.'

'Duff was talking through his earholes. I'd just started the course, that's all. I'm not going to do any diving.'

'Why not?'

'Because I'm scared. I'd probably drown myself.'

'Okay.' Cotton frowned. 'You'll have to show me and I'll do it.' He spoke calmly, making no complaint, just shifting position, but it had the effect of shaming Docherty.

'Well – ' he moved uneasily in his clothes ' – I could *probably* manage.'

Cotton stared at him, coming to life abruptly. 'The bloody boat's only in a few feet of water,' he said sharply. 'And there are plenty of us to see you wouldn't drown.'

'What's it for, anyway?'

'To go under the boat to see if the prop *is* bent.'

'Okay. I might do that. I might even do that without the bloody suit. Why?'

Cotton gestured. 'I was wondering,' he said,' if we couldn't repair her, drag her off and take her home.'

2

The report that landed on Major Baldamus' desk that evening was short and sharp and to the point. The Luftwaffe was none too pleased at having lost one of its machines and they seemed eager to lay the blame on him for having asked for it.

'It had to crash-land at Yanitsa,' Captain Ehrhardt explained. 'The pilot's all right but they're now short of one good Messerschmitt.'

'Fortunes of war,' Baldamus said. 'Were they annoyed?'

'A bit.'

Baldamus sniffed. Since Poland, Norway and France, the Luftwaffe had been fast growing too big for its boots, like its leader, that piffling parvenu, Goering. He shrugged. 'Can't see why they're getting so worked up,' he said. 'After all, I expect the advantage was all on their side. What was this damned boat armed with anyway? Quick-firing multi-barrelled pompoms?'

Ehrhardt grinned. 'One 20-millimetre cannon,' he said.

'And they're blaming *us*?' Baldamus smiled. 'I think the Luftwaffe must be scraping the barrel a bit. They lost too many of their best men over London and they're now having to make do with the leavings. Good God, three Messerschmitts against one boat armed with a 20 mm. What happened to the boat?'

'Ran aground, Herr Major.' Ehrhardt leaned over the map on Baldamus' desk and jabbed with a finger. 'Here. In Kharasso Bay.'

'Wrecked?'

'Messerschmitts say so. Complete write-off.'

'Survivors?'

'A recce flight soon after reported that everything was deserted.'

'Think they were picked up?'

'They've not been seen since.'

Baldamus smiled. 'I'll bet they *were* picked up,' he said. 'Did our friends in the Luftwaffe see any other boats?'

'They say not.'

'Doesn't mean there weren't any.' Baldamus frowned. 'I bet they didn't look. They don't seem very efficient, do they, getting themselves shot down by a little boat armed with a popgun? But you'd better send a party of men under a sergeant up to Kharasso Bay at first light to have a look for survivors and make them prisoners if they find any. I suppose we needn't worry about the boat itself just yet. It won't be moving, will it?'

If Cotton had his way, it would, though he was already meeting opposition.

'You're nuts,' Docherty said.

He was red in the face and panting as he clung to *Claudia*'s bent rudder, kicking with his feet in the water.

At first, Cotton didn't bother to dispute the observation. He probably was, he decided.

They were all beginning to recover a little now from the shock of the disaster and Cotton's mind was working, churning things over in his stolid fashion.

Patient as an ox, unopinionated as a spring lamb, he was nevertheless indomitable, virile, and astute; the nervy, brave Cockney of the London markets, who knew all the East End lingo of bulls-and-cows, whistles-and-flutes, rabbits-and-pork, and five-to-twos; supple, tough and able to bend with the wind so that he knew how to survive. He knew he'd probably get no thanks even if he succeeded, and he knew how little the people at home were interested in this forgotten corner of the war when they were occupied themselves with nightly air raids and the destruction of their homes. When it came to survival, most human beings were selfish.

All the same, the idea that had come to him had set his blood surging. He could probably even do some damage, he thought, given a chance. After all they existed to make war; so, okay, let them make it. The Royals who'd done their stuff in Egypt, the Sudan and China, and at Belle Isle, Jutland, Gallipoli and Zeebrugge hadn't stood around like barrack stanchions. England expected, after all. England expected a hell of a bloody lot sometimes, he thought. England expected a bloody sight too much even, but there was no getting away from it, and the idea of taking *Claudia* home seemed the most natural thought in the world to him. She belonged to the navy; he belonged to the navy. Obviously he must bend his efforts to seeing that naval property was returned to its rightful owners.

'The Marines captured Gibraltar,' he said slowly. 'Napoleon respected the Marines. It was three Marines that carried Nelson down to the cockpit after he'd been wounded at Trafalgar. At Navarino, in HMS *Genoa*, a Marine who'd had both arms shot off asked permission to go below. "I hope you'll allow, sir," he said, "that I've done my duty." '

They stared at him as if he were mad, but Cotton's mind was running on perfectly rational, straightforward lines. In the evacuation of Norway, when the Marines had been accused of keeping the navy waiting, they'd offered only a cold reply : 'It isn't the policy of the Royal Marines to leave its guns in enemy hands.' And that was how it was with Cotton now.

He knew he could surrender, but surrender simply was not consonant with good order and training, and he rejected the idea out of hand. He was acting on his own initiative with no one and nothing to tell him what to do but discipline, and he was in no doubt about where his duty lay.

He stared at *Claudia* lying on the rocks like a stranded whale. 'I'm not nuts,' he said at last.

'You must be,' Docherty shouted. 'Have you bloody seen her, man? She's a wreck! Half the island's sticking through her bottom !'

'It might be done.'

87

'How?' Bisset asked. 'How're you intending to repair a boat that's still in the water? She'd have to come up a slip for that.'

'Perhaps we can do it without a slip.'

'She's got holes in the side,' Docherty yelled. 'A big one in the bow. And one engine's nothing but a load of old iron!'

'What about the other?' Cotton asked. 'What's it like under there, Docherty?'

'One screw's smashed up completely, so there's nothing we can do about that. The other's got a kink in one of the blades.'

'How about the rudders?'

'One's sheered off. Other's bent.'

'Could we get the bent prop off and hammer it out and put it on the good engine?'

'No.'

Cotton glared, convinced Docherty was just being difficult. 'Why not?'

'Because the props turn in opposite directions to each other; to balance each other's torque. You can't put the port-'and prop on the starboard-'and shaft. It'd fit but it'd turn the wrong way.'

Cotton's heart sank. 'Couldn't you put it on back to front so it'd come right?'

'It's a prop, not a pair of bloody socks!'

Cotton was determined not to give up. Something, he felt sure, would turn up and he needed to know all about the workings of the propeller, the shaft and the rudder, things which so far he'd never considered his concern.

'How's it held on?' he asked.

'With a key, and then a castellated nut held in place by a split pin. The nut forces the prop on to the key so that it's held tight.'

'How do you get it off?'

'Tap the end of the shaft. That loosens it.'

'Suppose we could make it work—'

'We can't.'

'*Suppose*,' Cotton said doggedly. 'Could it be done under water?'

88

Docherty shrugged. 'It's been done,' he admitted grudgingly.

'Couldn't *we* do it? *If* we could make it work, I mean.'

Docherty stared at him as if he were mad. 'We *can't* make it work,' he said.

'*Suppose* we could?' Cotton felt like throttling him.

'Who's going to do it?' Docherty asked, going off at a tangent.

Cotton turned and looked at him. 'Couldn't you?'

Docherty's face went red. 'I'm not a fuckin' fish,' he said. 'Talk sense, you stupid Marine git.'

Cotton frowned. 'I *am* talking sense,' he said.

'Then, okay, tell me this: Even if we get the engines going, even if we repair the holes in her, how are we going to get the bloody boat back in the water?'

Cotton hadn't reached that point yet. He was a painstaking man who tackled problems painstakingly and he hadn't yet considered that difficulty. All the same, he remembered all that Patullo and the other two men in Retimo had told him when he'd first been dragooned into joining the expedition, and it seemed to him he ought to do something about it. He was known in the Marines' mess as stubborn, dim and regimental, but they were qualities that sometimes made a good Royal.

'There's supposed to be some other fellers on the island,' he said.

'What sort of fellers?'

'From the other boat – *Loukia*. Patullo told me. They sent a Blenheim over to do a recce and it reported seeing 'em on the beach by the wreck, waving. If they're still there, it's up to us to take 'em off, isn't it? Any case, we can't just sit here and wait for the Germans to come and take us prisoners, can we?'

That seemed to make Docherty think. 'No,' he said slowly. 'We can't.'

'Can't we *pinch* a boat or somefing?' Gully asked. 'All this about repairing this one's a lot of bloody balls. You might as well try to manure a forty-acre field with a fart. You've only to look at 'er. You've only to think twice. We ought to pinch one of them Greek boats?'

'How?' Bisset asked.

'Christ!' Gully grinned unexpectedly. 'How do you go about pinching anything? You walk up to it, put out your dirty little mitt, then grab it and run. Think we could make it back? It took us two days to get here.'

'Where are we, anyway?'

'This is the island of Aeos,' Cotton said. 'This is Kharasso Bay.'

For a long time, they stood on the beach staring at the stranded *Claudia*. Now that they were beneath her, on the sand, she seemed enormous.

'Only wants a few winkles and it'd be like Bridlington 'arbour,' Gully observed heavily.

'We *might* get the bent prop off and straighten it,' Bisset said.

'Then what?' Docherty asked.

Cotton's expression was murderous. 'I don't suppose it's ever occurred to you,' he said icily, 'that it might be useful on the *other* boat. They're sister ships. Same engines. Same props. Perhaps she's in better shape than this one.'

'She didn't look it to me.'

'We haven't examined her yet. And if she is, we might be able to get her going with bits from this boat.'

This obviously made Docherty think again but he didn't give up easily. He was a product of the back streets, wary, cautious and unyielding. Everything he'd had in life had been acquired by craft, wiliness or nerve, but he'd never done anything without thinking it out first.

'She looked a mess to me,' he said slowly.

'We're not going to go full belt.'

'Suppose she's got a bent rudder like this one? How're you going to manoeuvre?'

'We only want to go home,' Cotton said. '*Creep* home, if you like. So long as we don't stay here. Couldn't we rig a jury rudder or something? Gully could make one, and we could change the props and so on. We've got a diving suit.'

'Oh, Jesus!' Docherty said. He seemed to find Cotton trying.

'If you won't do it,' Cotton said savagely, 'I will.'

Docherty's voice rose. 'What about petrol?'

'Christ – ' In his frustration, Cotton was shouting, too, now ' – we've got a boat *full* of petrol! Shaw was going to fill up from these drums when we arrived, for the journey back. We've got about five hundred gallons. That's fifty miles or more – more still if we stretch it out.'

'What's fifty miles?'

'It's fifty miles away from here,' Cotton snapped. 'And that's halfway back to Suda.'

Docherty glared at him. If Cotton had been an officer, he'd have done as he was told without arguing because that was how he'd been trained. But Cotton was only a junior NCO and a Joey into the bargain, and that gave Docherty the right as a Stoker, RN, to state his view of the case.

'Ask a bloody mud-crusher how to do things,' he said, 'and he'll give you all the answers – the wrong ones. Okay, you daft Marine twit, so we've got the petrol. But you haven't seen the other boat yet.'

'We can soon organize that.'

'And, in any case, you're asking us to do something that would take a fully-equipped marine workshop and a boatbuilder's yard to do.'

'We can try, can't we? There must be villagers. Perhaps they'd help.'

'How do you know there are villagers? I've not seen any.'

'We saw houses as we were coming in. Patullo said it was called Ay Yithion.'

'Hi who?'

'It's a village.'

'It's a bloody funny name for a village.'

While they'd been talking, Gully had been wading round the fore part of the boat, studying the holes.

'Can it be repaired?' Cotton asked. 'We've got planks aboard.'

Gully shrugged. 'Not enough for this lot,' he said. 'Ribs is gone. And, Jesus, we're high and bloody dry!'

'We'll get the planks ashore, all the same,' Cotton decided.

'Why?'

'Why not?'

Bisset managed a twisted grin. 'Can't we wait?'

'What if the Germans come?' Cotton said.

'They might not.'

'We hit an aeroplane, didn't we?' Cotton pointed out patiently. 'I saw a bit fall off. When he got home, he must have reported what happened. If he didn't get home, then his pals would. That's why that second one came to have a dekko. It won't have taken him a minute to do a bit of the old dot-dash on the buzzer, will it? The Germans are going to start looking for us.'

'Perhaps there aren't any Germans here yet.' Gully like Docherty, seemed to be determined to be argumentative.

'Patullo said there were. It was on the radio. Anyway, it won't be long before there are, will it? We ought to hide.'

'Where?' Bisset asked.

Cotton stared about him. It was a good question but it seemed best to shelve it for the time being.

'Okay,' he said, ignoring Bisset. 'We'll get the dinghy and the rubber raft ashore and hide 'em. Then, if they do come, they'll think we've tried to row away.'

Bisset stared at Cotton. 'Well, that's not a bad idea,' he admitted.

'We've got plenty of grub,' Cotton went on. 'Apart from normal ship's stores, we took extra rations aboard.'

'It's worth a try.'

Docherty considered it for a while. In the end, even he couldn't find much wrong with the idea. 'What about them lot?' he asked, indicating the bodies lying in the shade of the trees at the side of the beach.

'We can leave them for a bit. Let's get the petrol drums ashore.'

Gully grinned nervously. 'He thinks he's bloody Nelson or something,' he said.

'We're in the bloody war to fight,' Cotton growled. 'What's wrong with trying to?'

'*Who?*' Gully flapped a hand in a deprecatory gesture. 'You, me and us two? You after a Victoria Cross or something?'

Cotton glared at him. Discipline was what counted, he thought. Morale. What the sergeant at Eastney Barracks had called *es pritty corpse*. 'Behaving like a sick headache don't help, does it?' he rumbled, and picking up one of the mooring ropes, he began to make a parbuckle.

Between them, they lowered the drums of petrol from the boat to the beach and Bisset and Gully rolled them up among the trees and covered them with foliage and stones. Cotton followed them, sweeping the marks from the sand with a dead branch he found among the rocks.

'What you think you are?' Gully asked. 'General Custer fighting the Indians?'

'Can't you think of anything bloody better to do?' Cotton snapped. 'Except find fault?'

Gully flexed his muscles. 'I'll have you know, mate, now that them lot – ' he gestured towards the silent shapes up the beach, then stopped. Cotton waited. For all his bounce, Gully wasn't a man of deep moral fibre.

'The bloody thing won't run! It's broke!' Gully's voice rose to a shriek and he seemed to lose his nerve for a moment in his despair. 'The engine's broke! The propeller's broke! The bloody bottom's broke! It's full of holes! Them three – ' he gestured again helplessly ' – *they're* full of holes!' He seemed to find Cotton wearying. 'Oh, Jesus,' he moaned.

Cotton remained quite unmoved by the outburst. 'We'd better get the dinghy and the raft and the Carley float ashore next,' he said. 'Then the blankets and anything else we can salvage.' He looked up. The thudding of the distant guns that they'd heard ever since they'd left Suda Bay was still with them. 'We'd better have the tinned food ashore too,' he went on. 'And then we'd better start rationing it out.'

'Proper Robinson Bloody Crusoe, aren't you?'

Cotton ignored the jibe and got them throwing down to the beach the tins of bully beef, peaches, sweetened milk and biscuit.

93

The planks and timbers they'd carried, Gully's big tool box, Docherty's smaller one, and the wooden box containing the diving gear followed.

'There are a lot of rocks and big stones up there,' Cotton said. 'We can stick 'em among 'em somewhere and pile things on top of 'em.'

'It'll take all day!'

'Okay,' Cotton said. 'We'll take all day.'

'What about the kid?' Bisset reminded him.

'Let's go and see him,' Cotton said wearily.

They climbed back on board. Somehow, now that they'd moved everything movable, *Claudia* looked a worse wreck than ever. The blood on the sloping, splintered deck was drying, black and ugly in the increasing heat of the morning. The flies had already found it and were buzzing loudly in the wheelhouse.

Howard was moaning, his head swinging from side to side in his agony, his skin grey and dead-looking.

'Oh, Christ,' Gully mumbled. 'Can't you do somefing for 'im?'

'What?' Cotton snapped.

'Well, Christ – !' the wounded boy moaned again and Gully's eyes rolled like a frightened foal's ' – Jesus, it gets up my wick!'

'It probably gets up his a bit, too,' Cotton growled. 'Shut your trap and be thankful it wasn't you.'

Bisset was bending over the boy now, his face strained.

'He wants a drink,' Gully said. 'That's what you give 'em when they're wounded.'

'Not with stomach wounds,' Bisset said. 'It'd kill him. I think I'm going to use some more of the morphia to try to sew up that wound in his thigh. He's losing blood and it might stop it.'

'Know how to do it?' Cotton asked.

'Not really.' Bisset gave a twisted smile. 'But I once saw my little brother's eyebrow sewn up by a doctor when he split it. It's just like sewing a tear in your uniform. There's some gut and needles.'

They gave Howard another shot of morphine and Bisset started to sew, with Cotton holding the lips of the wound together. They were both startled at the toughness of the flesh and Bisset was sweating as he worked. The wound looked better when he'd finished but was still by no means pretty. As they bandaged it up again, Bisset gave Cotton another smile.

'Might work,' he said. 'But he needs to be where he can be looked after.'

They spent a wretched night in the wrecked launch, with Howard moaning and crying out in his pain. Cotton was unable to sleep and after a while he went to the boy. To his surprise he found Bisset there, giving him another injection.

'It'll help,' he said. 'But it's almost all gone now. We shall have to get him to a doctor.'

When he'd assumed command, the agony of wounded men hadn't occurred to Cotton any more than the responsibility of getting treatment, and he frowned.

'Think he'll be all right till tomorrow?'

'I suppose so.' Bisset seemed dubious. 'I don't really know.'

As they helplessly watched the boy gasping, Gully appeared with Docherty.

'How is he?'

'Bad,' Bisset said and Cotton crossed himself. Seeing him, Docherty did the same.

Gully drew a deep breath. 'I wish I was back in Crete,' he said heavily.

As soon as it was daylight, Cotton made up his mind. Something had to be done about Howard. His torment was getting on top of them. Nobody could do anything for listening to his tortured breathing, which had seemed to echo round the whole boat all night.

As soon as they'd swallowed a cup of tea and a hard biscuit, they began to construct a stretcher made of two poles with blankets lashed across it. It was crude but it worked and they started to get the boy out of the cabin. His agony was unbearable and once he screamed as they manoeuvred him up the lopsided steps, in a way that echoed round the boat and shocked them all.

'How the Christ are we going to get him ashore?' Gully muttered.

But Cotton had thought of that and they lashed the boy to the stretcher and lowered it over the side to the sand where Gully and Docherty were waiting.

'Get him under the trees,' Cotton said. 'It's cooler there.'

His mind was stiff with the problems that filled it. There was just too much to think about and he began to realize just how much Captain Troughton, of *Caernarvon*, had supported on his shoulders. Captain Troughton had two decorations, a lot of gold braid and a considerably bigger salary than Corporal Cotton. Suddenly aware of what he had to carry around with him in a ship of 8000 tons and a complement of 500 men and conscious of his own small load, Cotton felt he was more than welcome to them.

They carried the boy up to the trees, where the other bodies were still lying.

'Oughtn't we to bury 'em?' Bisset asked.

'We'll get the rest of the stuff ashore first,' Cotton said. 'The boat and the rafts. Just in case the Germans come.'

They lowered the dinghy and hid it behind the beach in the rocks with the rest of what they'd salvaged. Howard's cheeks had fallen in when they went to the stretcher and Cotton peered anxiously at him. The party had been halved and somehow it bothered him that Howard was hurt. He had no wish to lose any more by death.

'Is he dead?' Gully asked.

'No,' Bisset said. 'In fact, he's breathing easier. If we could get him to a quack, he might pull round.'

'We'll try,' Cotton said. He drew a deep breath. 'We ought to go over to the other boat now,' he went on. 'To see what we can find. We can probably take him to the village while we're at it. We've got to look for the other boat some time. They might have seen us coming in and be waiting for us.'

As he spoke, he saw Gully staring over his shoulder, his eyes wide, his jaw dropped, and he whirled round, expecting to see that the Germans had arrived. Instead, standing in the shallow water by the rocks at the other end of the beach, he saw two men and a girl. They were all young and wearing civilian clothes, and the men were both armed.

3

For a long time the two groups stood motionless, staring at each other. Cotton's first thought was that the two men were survivors from *Loukia*, but then he saw they weren't British and they certainly weren't servicemen.

The warmth in the narrow bay suddenly seemed oppressive and the thud of the guns to the north seemed nearer. The newcomers appeared to have materialized from nowhere, and Cotton realized they must have climbed down to the beach from among the rocks. There were plenty of these, towering above him in strange mysterious shapes, the burden of stone like battered forts and castles, each joined by bastions and buttresses of gritty earth and clumps of genista, brambles and oleander. His eyes swung back from the tangle of stony sentinels to the civilians and it occurred to him then that if they could descend the hillside without being seen, they must know a footpath, and a footpath was what he, Docherty, Bisset and Gully needed just then.

'You'd better get talking,' Bisset pointed out softly. 'They look as if they aren't very keen on us.'

The strangers had begun to move forward now. The men had unslung their weapons – a tommy-gun, Cotton noticed at once, and a Lee-Enfield rifle – and they were moving along the beach, their feet in the shallow water, holding the weapons in front of them as if they suspected a trick. They stopped a few yards away. The man in front was thin and brilliant-eyed like a gypsy, with a heavy moustache and a feverish fanatic look. The other man was little more than a boy. The girl was roughly the same age as the younger man; not one of the plump lovelies Cotton had seen in Crete or on Iros, but a slimmer girl with natural grace and charm, her face like a waxen mask. She was bare-armed and bare-legged in a one-piece dark dress, her hair like a dark wave on her shoulders. She had charcoal-black eyes and an attractive mouth which looked as though at other times it might smile easily. Though she was not beautiful in the accepted sense, there was a serene quality about her that indicated she hadn't always been in the habit of accompanying armed men.

The older of the Greeks, the thin man with the feverish fanatic eyes, said something which Cotton didn't catch, and the girl spoke in English, her voice low, addressing Docherty who was standing to one side.

'This is your boat?'

Cotton answered in Greek and three pairs of black eyes switched from Docherty's face to his.

'Whose side are you on?' the thin-faced man demanded sharply, with a marked aggressive hostility.

'Whose side?'

'Are you for ELAS?'

'What's ELAS?'

'ELAS is the Greek Communist party,' the girl explained.

'I'm not Greek,' Cotton said stiffly, irritated as he always was if someone suggested he was anything but a pure-bred Englishman able to trace his ancestry back to Anglo-Saxon darkness. 'I can speak some Greek,' he added.

The man gestured at *Claudia*. 'What happened?' he asked.

'We were coming to the island to look for a boat.' Cotton pointed towards the cape. 'It's over there. In the next bay. We saw it. But we were seen by Messerschmitts and they shot us up.' He gestured behind him and the newcomers stared solemnly at the three silent shapes wrapped in blankets.

'They are dead?' the girl asked, her voice low and grieving.

'Yes.'

She looked at Howard. 'And that one also?'

'No,' Cotton said. 'But he's badly hurt. He needs a doctor. We were going to take him to the village.'

She said nothing, staring at the injured boy with a frown on her face, trying to work out what they could do. In the silence the man with the moustache spoke.

'Why were you looking for the other boat?' he asked.

'We thought we might find survivors.'

'There are no survivors.' The words came quickly, as though the speaker were anxious there should be no doubt about the matter.

Cotton frowned. 'None at all?'

'None. They're all dead.'

'All of them? I was told there *were* some. They were seen standing on the beach waving. A recce plane saw them.'

The Greek glanced at the boy alongside him, then he shrugged. 'There were seven alive,' he said. 'But the Germans came and killed them all. They arrived three days ago. The Western democracies have failed to stop them. The British will leave Greece soon and go back where they came from, and leave *us* to face the Germans.' He seemed to be a Communist and Cotton remembered the worried Mayor of Iros.

The Greek offered cigarettes. Cotton took one and was about to light it when he removed it from his lips and stared at it.

'These are English cigarettes,' he said.

The Greek shrugged. 'There were a lot left behind.'

'Left behind where?'

'Here.'

The girl glanced quickly at the Greek as if she didn't believe him, and Cotton frowned. 'I didn't know we'd been here,' he said. 'I thought we were the first.'

'Oh, no! A ship came in. They had no drachmas so they exchanged cigarettes for wine.'

The girl looked worried and interrupted quickly. 'What do you intend to do now?' she asked in her quiet, deep voice.

Cotton gestured at *Claudia*. 'We were wondering if we could repair one of the boats,' he said. 'This one or the other.'

'There is nothing here,' the Greek said quickly, almost too quickly, Cotton thought. 'This is a poor island and this end is the poorest part of it.'

'You'd better hide,' the girl put in. 'The Germans know there is a boat here.'

'How do you know they know?'

'We have ways of finding out. We have friends who have been taken on by them to clean their quarters in Kalani and at Yanitsa. And friends who own the cafés they use and listen to them talking.'

Cotton studied her grave face. 'What about you?' he asked. 'Who are you?'

'My name is Akoumianakis. Annoula Akoumianakis.' The girl gestured at the older Greek just behind her. 'This is Petrakis, Chrysostomos. He is my cousin. He comes from Crete. My uncle was a government official who was sent there from the mainland. I come from the Piraeus, which is the port for Athens.' She gestured at the other man. 'This is Cesarides, Gregorio. He is only a boy. There is another one up the hill, watching. His name is Xilouris, Giorgiou. *He* comes from Antipalia on the mainland.'

Cotton said nothing for a moment. In its trudging regimental way, his mind was working. Something told him that the feverish-eyed Greek was not to be trusted. 'And the guns?' he asked. 'Why are you carrying guns?'

The girl glanced at Petrakis. 'My cousin prefers the hills to the towns now that the Germans have come. I was in Ay Yithion just over the cape. It is a fishing village. He came for me and brought me along, too, because I speak a little English.' She gave a twisted smile and shrugged. 'But not much. My cousin lives up there.' She indicated the hills to the west. 'There are other men, too, and more will join.'

'How many?'

The girl glanced at Petrakis and he answered brusquely. 'My cousin says there are many,' she said. 'Very many. He has a lot of support.'

Cotton was aware of Bisset watching him, urging him to get on with it so they could continue with what they'd been doing, but he was deliberately slow.

'How far is it?' he asked. 'The other boat?'

'Three cigarettes,' the man said.

'Three cigarettes?'

The girl explained quickly. 'He is a Cretan and this is how they measure distance on Crete. The time it takes you to smoke a cigarette.' She smiled gravely. 'But I warn you, although Cretans can move fast in the hills, they are no judge of distance.'

'Is he starting a Resistance movement?'

'We aren't fighting for the Western democracies,' Petrakis interrupted. 'We're fighting for Greece. And that doesn't mean the king.'

The girl glanced round her at the cliffs. 'The Germans will come soon,' she said uneasily.

'Where are they?'

'The north side of the island. They're building a new airstrip at Yanitsa. It's flat there. There is nothing but windmills and they are already pulling them down. You ought to hide.'

'Where?' Cotton asked and she indicated the shrub-covered hills.

Petrakis gestured at *Claudia*. 'What about the guns?' he said sharply.

'What about them?'

'The Germans will take them when they come. We'll look after them for you.'

Cotton looked at him coldly. He had already decided he didn't like Petrakis very much and the thought of handing over Royal Navy guns to a stranger took his breath away.

'We'll look after them ourselves,' he said sharply.

The 303s were no problem because they were on temporary mountings and had only to be lifted off. The 20 mm was more difficult, but Cotton knew what to do and they carefully detached the barrel and recoil spring. They had just finished removing the gun when there was a whistle from the top of the hill and the two

Greeks turned at once and ran for cover, splashing in the shallows until they reached the slope. Leaping from boulder to boulder, they disappeared from sight.

'It's the Germans,' the girl said. 'That was Giorgiou Xilouris.'

Bisset looked towards the three stiffening shapes lying under the trees. 'What about that lot?' he asked.

'There's no time,' the girl said. 'Hurry!' She gestured at Howard. 'Quickly!'

'What about the guns?'

Cotton stared about him. It would take them too long to get the guns up the beach and hidden. 'Over the side,' he said. 'As far under the stern as we can get 'em. They'll not notice 'em there with a bit of luck and they're well greased. It was my job to see they were, and we can get 'em back before they come to any harm.'

They pushed the guns overboard, so that they dropped under the stern. Then they climbed from the launch's deck, taking the ammunition, the drums and the breech blocks with them. The girl was still waiting for them, fidgeting anxiously as she watched Cotton's painstaking preparations.

'Hurry,' she called.

Dropping to the beach, loaded with metal objects, they lifted the stretcher as she began to run along the edge of the sea. Then she turned and gestured. 'In the water,' she said. 'Or they'll follow the footprints.'

They splashed along in the shallows until they reached the rocks. Then, manhandling the stretcher, they followed her up the slope. Behind them there was no indication of where they'd gone, only the footprints round the bodies and the wrecked launch, and the marks on the sand where they'd struggled with the dinghy.

As they hurried after the girl, they heard the sound of vehicles beyond the hill and shortly afterwards saw soldiers climbing down at the other side of the bay. They wore square German helmets and they could hear their shouts.

Petrakis and Cesarides had disappeared and only the girl

remained. They all crouched among the rocks, praying that Howard, who had been roughly handled during the climb, would not cry out.

Watching between the clefts of stone, they saw the Germans, led by a sergeant, reach the beach. Baldamus' instructions that they leave Kalani at first light had been thwarted by the arrival of another two Junkers and the need for vehicles to unload them. The sergeant seemed irritated, as if the stuffy heat in the narrow bay was causing the thick clothes and equipment he was wearing to chafe his sweat-damp skin.

As they reached the sand, they crossed to the three blanketed shapes under the trees. For a while they stood in front of them, talking; then they scrambled aboard *Claudia* and began to move about her decks. As they stopped by the 20 mm and 303 mountings, one of them pointed out to sea.

'What's he saying?' Cotton whispered.

'They think we've bunked with the guns,' Bisset said. 'They think there were two boats and that we've been picked up.'

The sergeant gestured and one of the Germans ran for the cliff and began to toil upwards.

Bisset watched him. 'He's been sent to warn the Luftwaffe that there's another launch in the area with survivors.'

After a while, the Germans climbed down from the boat and the sergeant sent two more men up the cliff. They returned with spades and began to dig.

'Now what the hell are they up to?' Gully demanded.

'They're digging graves, you bloody fool,' Bisset said.

The Germans scraped three shallow holes at the head of the beach and laid the bundled shapes in them, then the sergeant, who'd been poking about in the trees, reappeared with three short stakes which he stuck in the sand above the graves. They saw him writing in a notebook, then he tore three sheets out and fastened them to the stakes, while the soldiers stood still for a moment by them. After a second or two the sergeant pointed at *Claudia*.

The men who'd first disappeared up the cliff had returned now and they began to swarm all over the boat. The luxurious blue blankets that Spiro Panyioti had provided for his comfort were tossed down. The sheets followed, together with other articles.

'They've got the rum,' Gully groaned.

The Germans were passing the rum keg around, swigging from it as it went from hand to hand. When they'd drunk, they poured the water from their bottles and, filling them with the rum, tossed the keg aside. By now they were laughing and joking among themselves.

A few tins of food that had been overlooked were also passed down and stacked on the beach, and the sergeant set up a carrying party which began to lift their finds up the cliff. As they went, one of them, an older man with a lined face and bowed legs, vanished among the bushes.

'What's he up to?' Bisset said.

'The bastard's hiding the other rum jar and one of the blankets,' Cotton said.

'What for?'

'What for?' Gully's words were almost a moan. 'So he can come back later and nick it for himself, I expect.'

Carrying the boat's equipment up the cliff required several trips and Gully was complaining all the time.

'All them lovely blankets,' he said. 'They'd have fetched a quid apiece in the bazaars in Alex.'

When they'd finished the Germans stood on the beach talking, the sergeant shouting to a man on *Claudia*'s bow.

'They are saying they will come back to pump out the petrol tanks,' the girl said.

'Can *you* understand them too?'

'Yes.'

He didn't ask her how or why, but just accepted the information. 'When are they coming?'

'Tomorrow.'

'Are they going to destroy her?'

'They haven't said so. They haven't destroyed the other boat.'

By the time the Germans disappeared it was evening and the sun had gone. When they heard the German lorries drawing away and were certain the coast was clear, they stood up, easing their muscles.

Cotton looked at Howard, comatose now in the shadows on the stretcher. 'We'd better get him to the village,' he said.

The girl shook her head. 'It's too late. And the path is bad. Can he live through the night?'

Bisset nodded and she gestured. 'Then keep him here. I'll get them to send a boat round. If you try to take him over the top tonight you'll kill him.' She gave Cotton a smile which transformed her sobersides little face. 'You are safe from the Germans now. This is the high part of the island, and they prefer to stay in the plain near Kalani. They know there are a few groups of patriots who have hidden in the hills. That's why they don't go near the other boat. My cousin says they took away the guns and set fire to it. He put the fire out. It had a good engine, I think, and there are less holes in it than in this one.'

'Will you come back tomorrow and show us how to get to it?' Cotton asked.

'If they'll let me.'

'Who?'

'Chrysostomos and the others. They haven't finished with it yet.'

'What are they doing to it?'

She smiled again. 'Mostly arguing. They are good democrats and believe nothing should be done without everybody having his say first. I expect they'll still be arguing when the Germans decide to come back and tow it off.'

'Can it be towed off?'

'Chrysostomos is thinking of towing it off.'

Cotton's heart thumped. 'Will it float?'

'With a few holes plugged up, it will, I think. The fishermen thought so too.'

Cotton looked at Gully; then he turned back to the girl. At that moment she seemed the most beautiful thing he'd ever seen. 'We'll wait for you here on the beach,' he said.

As she turned away and began to climb in the growing darkness, Gully rounded on Cotton. 'It's going to rain,' he complained. He pointed at the sky which was changing in the west to a deep violet-grey. 'We should have gone to the village. We're going to get wet.'

Cotton turned and glared at him, his face only inches away from the carpenter's. 'Okay,' he said. 'We'll get wet. But we're staying here.'

'Why?'

'Because it's my guess those bloody Greeks'll be back first thing tomorrow morning to get our guns.'

Gully's jaw dropped. 'What!'

'I'll bet my last bob the bastards were watching us from up there somewhere.' Cotton gestured towards the slope of the mountain and, as he did so, he noticed that the first spots of Gully's rain were falling. 'I expect they want 'em for their gang of bolshie patriots or something.'

'Well, why can't they 'ave 'em?'

'Because they belong to the navy,' Cotton said. 'And I want 'em myself. That lot couldn't do a thing with them. They don't know how.' He had all a trained soldier's contempt for amateurs. 'That's why when they come back tomorrow to fish 'em out, they'll find I've been there first.'

4

'You know what?' Gully said.

'What?' Cotton asked.

'I think you're bloody barmy.'

'That's what Docherty thought,' Cotton pointed out. 'I think he was wrong. I think you're wrong.'

He was quite unperturbed by Gully's opinion. Though Gully had been right about the weather, and it had not only rained, it had poured, and he had spent a wretched night under an overhang in the stream bed with Howard, hidden from the boat, damp, chilled and miserable, watching the trickle of water by his feet grow wider and faster until it lapped his shoes. But at least Howard had been dry and it had seemed safer there than on the boat where they might have been surprised and unable to get him away.

Docherty studied the lopsided launch. With her tilted deck and mast and the smashed wheelhouse, she looked a total wreck. 'Suppose the Germans come and set fire to her?' he said.

'And suppose they don't,' Gully added. 'What's the difference? She won't shift. So we've got guns and petrol but no bloody boat.'

'There's the other boat,' Cotton pointed out patiently. 'That girl said she was in better shape than this one.'

Gully grunted. 'I still think you're barmy,' he said.

Cotton shrugged. He'd been called a few names in his time. 'It takes all sorts to make a Marine,' he said, unperturbed. 'We once had a woman in the corps even. She was wounded six times at Pondicherry and finally kept a pub at Wapping.'

Gully stared at him as if he were mad but Bisset, guessing what it was that was driving Cotton, broke into an unexpected grin.

Gully shrugged. 'I still think you're barmy.'

Cotton didn't bother to answer. What was in his mind would never have made sense to a civilian. Though Gully didn't know it, he'd been prowling round even before first light, looking for a safe place to hide *Claudia*'s guns, the dinghy and the petrol.

'I mean – ' Gully was just beginning to get properly wound up ' – what can four of us do to a set of Germans?'

'I don't know yet,' Cotton said calmly. 'I expect I shall think of something.'

'I mean – getting us up at this bloody hour, with nothing to eat in our bellies, swimming around picking up guns and things!'

Stark naked and looking like a large skinned bulldog, Cotton sat in the dinghy between the two dripping Lewis guns, shivering. 'I'm doing the swimming,' he pointed out. 'Me and Docherty. You're just sitting in the boat pulling on the oars. I don't know what you're complaining about.'

'What are you going to do with the bloody guns anyway?'

'Shoot Germans, I expect,' Cotton said off-handedly. 'I haven't worked it out proper yet.'

They landed the Lewis guns and, while Cotton stripped them down, Bisset carefully wiped the parts and greased them well. When they'd assembled them, Gully and Bisset rowed the dinghy out again, towing Cotton in the water behind. Docherty had started working in the silent engine room.

'Did you ever swim the Channel by any chance?' Gully asked.

'No.' Cotton answered seriously. 'You need a lot of fat on you for that. Like you.'

While Gully and Bisset waited in the dinghy, Cotton took the end of the heaving line and dived down into the clear water among the rocks and the waving seaweed and the sea urchins under *Claudia*'s stern, and attached it to the barrel of the 20 mm. As he burst to the surface, gasping, Bisset and Gully began to heave.

The rest of the weapon followed and Bisset pulled for the shore, with Gully sitting in the stern and Cotton swimming alongside. Cleaning and pulling the gun through, they greased it like the Lewises; then, wrapping all three weapons round with shreds of clothing rescued from the forecastle, they stuffed them under the rocks in a hole Cotton had found, and covered them carefully. Cotton was in no doubt about what he was doing. His mind was clicking along precisely now, like a ship's chronometer, ticking off each item as it occurred to him.

When they'd hidden the guns, he cleared the beach of footprints with a branch torn off one of the overhanging trees. As he finished, he found he was standing near the graves the Germans had dug. The papers the German sergeant had stuck on the stakes all read the same thing : '*Ein unbekannter englishche Matrose,*' a small gesture of respect from one fighting man to another.

He glanced to the north. The faint thud of guns which had died away during the night had started again. The high hills seemed to muffle the sound but it was always there, insistent and menacing.

They were among the bushes in the stream bed, bending over Howard, when the girl returned. There were three men with her this time, the third one the same age as Petrakis, wearing black shabby clothes and tall boots and carrying with him the smell of an unwashed body. Cotton noticed that Petrakis was carrying a towel and the third man, whom he assumed was Xilouris, was leading a donkey laden with a folded rubber dinghy, encouraging it along with cricket-like noises made with the mouth. 'Psoo ! Psoo !'

'*Kalò ksiméroma,*' the girl said. 'Good morning.'

'Where's the boat you promised?' Cotton said immediately, his face full of suspicion.

She gestured towards the sea. 'The Germans came to the village,' she said. 'They are commandeering boats. It was difficult.'

'The kid'll die if he doesn't see a doctor.'

She knelt alongside Howard. He seemed to have recovered a little and managed to smile at her. 'Hello, Mum,' he said.

The girl lifted her face. 'Tomorrow,' she said. 'They will come

110

tomorrow. Please understand. They are willing to help. They will look after him in Ay Yithion.'

Cotton wasn't so sure and his mind was full of nagging doubts. 'What about the Germans if they find him?' he said.

'It's a chance we must take. We are Christians and there is a doctor. They would never turn him away.'

Cotton searched his conscience. He'd heard of Germans deporting or even shooting people who hid British prisoners of war. He wasn't sure that he had the right to ask. He stared at Howard. The boy's face was grey and he knew they certainly couldn't care for him themselves much longer. He nodded, still unwilling to push the responsibility on to someone else.

Petrakis interrupted. He had listened to the exchange with barely concealed irritation, as though a dreadfully hurt boy was no concern of his. He pointed towards the hill.

'She will take you to the other boat,' he said.

He seemed eager to be rid of them and Cotton frowned. 'Aren't you coming, too?' he asked.

'No.'

'The Germans'll be back soon,' Cotton said. 'To pump out the tanks. They'll be coming round by boat. We heard them say so.' He looked at Howard. He felt dreadfully hampered by the wounded boy and for the first time he realized how it was that senior officers could take the decision to leave their injured behind. It had always seemed a cold-blooded thing to do but at that moment he knew just what prompted it.

For a moment they were at a loss what to do with the boy. The three Greeks hadn't waited to see what decision they'd make and had already begun to head towards the beach. Cotton watched them, narrow-eyed and suspicious; then Bisset volunteered to stay behind with Howard while the rest of them went to inspect *Loukia*.

'He's all right here,' he said. 'He's out of the sun and well away from the boat, and he won't be seen if the Germans come.'

They seemed to have no choice and, leaving Bisset sitting under

111

the overhang where Cotton had spent the night, they set off after the girl.

The cliffside was full of heather and thistles – all occupied by outsize hornets – saxe-blue flax, magenta covered with butterflies, and pink and white roses. Here and there were deep ravines, their bottoms filled with the carmine of oleanders, and among the shrubs yellow-throated bee-eaters and hoopoes moved. Over it all, the polished quality of the Grecian light seemed to make everything crystal clear, while the sea behind them shimmered like a peacock's feathers.

The girl talked all the time they were climbing the cliff. She seemed in far better physical condition than Cotton and didn't even pant.

'This island is supposed to have been the home of Aeolus,' she said. 'He was the wind god. The one who brought all the breezes. He was supposed to have lived in a cave below the sea and stirred them all up and sent them out to cause storms.'

They were fairly high by this time, following a shallow ravine, and the sea looked a metallic blue, with leaden shades in the shadow of the cliff. The heat had not started yet, but it was still very warm scrambling up a muddy path that the previous night's rain had made a stream bed, with stones and lips of rock underfoot.

After a while the girl looked at Cotton and stopped as something occurred to her.

'You understand Greek very well,' she said.

'Yes.'

'Where did you learn it?'

'In London.'

'At school?'

'No. From a Greek family.'

She gave him a quick smile and for a second he realized just how attractive she could look when she wasn't wearing her grave, preocupied expression. But it faded quickly and she gave a little frown.

'Greeks are very inquisitive,' she said. 'You have only to arrive

112

in Greece and immediately someone questions you on your origins, family, work and why you have come. I think that's why Greeks are so hospitable. They really only want to know about you.'

Cotton didn't attempt to enlighten her about his background. 'What about you?' he asked. 'Where did you learn German?'

'At school. We learned English also. We have never forgotten that your Lord Byron died for Greece. But we also learned German because Germany isn't far away and we always had many German visitors. I worked in a hotel for a long time and I learned to speak it well.'

'And now?'

'I was visiting relatives on Spiridos for a holiday when the Germans invaded Yugoslavia. I set off home at once but when I reached here the ferries stopped because they had bombed the Piraeus. The harbour suffered terrible damage. The radio said the noise could be heard in Athens.'

'And your parents and family?'

Her face showed no emotion, as if it had all long since been expended and her tears had dried. 'We had a house close by the water,' she said. 'I managed to telephone my aunt and she told me they had all disappeared. She said there was nothing left. I think I will stay here.'

Cotton said nothing. He couldn't even try to imagine what she was feeling. How did you offer sympathy to someone whose country was collapsing about their ears?

She paused, her eyes troubled. 'I didn't like the thought of German soldiers on Greek soil,' she went on. 'My cousin was the same. He was in Kalani. He went there because there was more work than in Crete.'

She seemed to be talking for the sake of talking and, when Cotton didn't reply, she tried another tack.

'Greece is the birthplace of democracy,' she said. 'And Greeks are all fighters. Alexander the Great was a Greek, and so was Leonidas the Spartan, who held off the Persians at Thermopylae.' She gave a sad little smile. 'Unfortunately, our forebears lived in a golden age and we have little left now of our greatness. But perhaps our past is useful. Chrysostomos thinks so. He was always in trouble with the police for his political views and he never got himelf a job. I stay in Yithion and have started to do odd jobs for Dendras Varvara. He owns fishing boats and is very kind.'

Cotton glanced back. Petrakis and the other Greeks were launching the rubber dinghy. 'Is your cousin a Communist?' he asked.

'He's always been anti-Fascist. There's no harm in that.'

Cotton frowned. 'So long as he's fighting the Germans, not me,' he said. 'Are all Greeks Communists like your cousin?'

She laughed. 'You should see them at church listening to the blessed Eucharist! You can't believe in Christ and in Communism as well. The fishermen are very devout. They are so much at the mercy of the Lord as they go about their business. Why?'

'We need their help,' Cotton said. 'I'm going to get one of these boats off the beach and take her away. You could come too, if you wanted.' He was offering a bribe in the hope that it would encourage her to drum up assistance. 'Anybody else as well. Perhaps those people the Germans might imprison.'

They stopped on the ridge at the top of the cliffs. From there the sea looked as dead as a pane of frosted glass, but the wide green valley inland came into view, perfect, full of a thousand greens and with the sort of blue sky above it you saw nowhere except in the Mediterranean. As they set off down the other side they could see even to the north shore of the island, the blur of grey that was Kalani, and a scattering of houses to the west which was a village. As they descended further, they passed dog roses, poplars, ilex, and cacti, and a few wild figs. Then, as they turned, they saw a promontory and beyond it, just below them, another group of white houses.

'That's Yithion,' the girl said. 'The fishermen have all been to see what they can salvage from the boat. But there's nothing left now and Chrysostomos has claimed it.'

'Are they afraid of Chrysostomos?'

She shrugged. 'He has guns. You saw them.'

'What does he intend to do with it?'

'The same as you, I think. Repair it and escape from the Germans.'

'Then why won't he help us so we can all escape together?'

She gave a sad, disillusioned smile. 'Perhaps because you are not a Communist. He is very stubborn. Giorgiou Xilouris arrived from Antipalia some days ago. I think he is a Communist too, and they keep their help only for people who believe as they do. They're planning to take the boat away together.'

5

As Major Baldamus studied the intelligence reports that dropped on his desk, things began to become more clear. Ever since he'd arrived on Aeos he'd been wondering what his purpose there was, because he didn't imagine for a minute that the High Command was taking over the island for no special reason and they'd certainly not occupied the other islands in the immediate vicinity.

But then, as promised, General Ritsicz had fed reports to him from Belgrade and, as he read them, daylight began to dawn, because they all referred to Crete, further south, a bigger island than Aeos, occupied by the British. As he compared them with the reports on the way the airstrip at Yanitsa was being developed and expanded, the whole thing began to fit together.

The Junkers were arriving regularly now, bringing spare parts, fuel, men, typewriters, papers, weapons. In addition, there was the Messerschmitt flight to be maintained, to say nothing of all the men Baldamus had brought with him, a few others who had arrived since and a group of experts concerned with logistics, packing and routing. The Junkers came from the Italian airfields in Albania, flying out in a wide sweep and arriving from the west so as to avoid the British fighters. So far there had been no accidents and the build-up had gone well, with everything camouflaged so that no wandering RAF Blenheim from a Greek airfield would be likely to spot anything more than the normal vehicles which had always been on the airstrip and the two wrecked private

Desoutters and the wheel-less Rapide which were all that had remained of the strip's pre-war importance.

The British had shown no interest, but that of course was undoubtedly because they were preoccupied with what was happening in the plain of Salonika. They already had their hands full and, according to the reports from General Ritsicz, even on Crete, which had been under occupation for six months now, little had been done to defend the place, chiefly on the mistaken assumption that Britain's command of the sea would make it impossible for any invasion to be sustained.

'Prime Minister Churchill,' the reports stated, 'has urged that the island be turned into a fortress bristling with everything from tanks to road blocks and defended by armed natives as well as British and Commonwealth troops. He believes this to have been done.'

Baldamus turned to the sheet which gave the exact lay-out of what actually *had* been done. It didn't seem to be much. The suggested defences had not been constructed and none of the essential reconnaissance of terrain that the Wehrmacht was so good at had been undertaken. Nor, it seemed, was there any clear Intelligence understanding about German intentions, and it seemed quite obvious that the British commanders did not believe that any great build-up could be made by the Wehrmacht so soon after the final conquest of Greece itself. They also seemed to have no idea how they might confirm their beliefs, and there were only 3500 Greek troops on the island, with only one rifle between six men and three rounds of ammunition each.

'Existing airstrips have not been mined,' the report continued flatly, 'and proposals to build hidden airstrips in the hills have not been carried out. In spite of the plentiful supply of Italian prisoners of war who could be used for the work, landing stages have not been constructed on the south shore nor roads to link the south of the island to the north.'

And since – as Baldamus knew from his pre-war wanderings on Crete – the only decent road ran along the north coast where the main towns were situated, with that road and those towns within reach of German bombers from the Greek mainland and the British forced to land troops on the south side of the ridge of mountains which formed the spine of the island, it was going to be damned difficult for them. Supply ships from Egypt, which would have to circle the islands, would be in danger throughout the whole trip and the subsequent unloading.

'There are good reasons for them to hold on to the island, however,' the report went on. 'The triangle of naval bases it forms with Alexandria and Benghazi gives the Royal Navy a grip on the Eastern Mediterranean such as it has not previously enjoyed and it is firmly expected that the British will fight for the place. They will not dare to give it up; yet, because they will not be able to reinforce it, we have an opportunity here to wipe out a large portion of their Mediterranean forces and weaken them in North Africa to leave the route open to the East. All of this should be aided by the fact that there are hardly any tanks and a fatal lack of radio and telegraphic equipment.'

Baldamus drew a deep breath and read on. 'It is believed that any approach would be unopposed and that air cover has been – or will be – withdrawn. Weapons will be landed separately. The Royal Navy is watching to the north, but a sound plan has been devised and details have been worked out, which must at all costs be kept secret.'

Baldamus put the report down and sat back in his chair staring into infinity. His role and the role of Aeos were suddenly quite clear to him and he could expect the tempo to increase from now on. The only danger he could see was the possibility of a leakage of information and for that he had to be on his guard.

He pressed a bell and Captain Ehrhardt appeared.

'Ehrhardt,' he said. 'Have we given any thoughts to the coasts of this island?'

'We've got a grip on Kalani.'

'That's not what I said. Kalani isn't the coast, and there are at least two fishing villages in addition to Kalani.'

Ehrhardt looked puzzled and Baldamus tried to explain without telling him too much.

'You ever wondered why we're here, Ehrhardt?' he asked.

'To occupy the place?'

'But why? There must be a reason. Haven't you wondered what it is?' Clearly Ehrhardt, a normal, unthinking soldier who did what he was told, didn't question it any more than he sought the wider pattern of strategy, and Baldamus went on cheerfully. 'There *is* a reason,' he pointed out. 'And we're part of it. And since we *are* part of it, it's just possible that, unlike you, a few of the natives have been putting two and two together and making guesses. They're probably all the wrong guesses, but somebody might just hit on the right one, and, without telling you what I think is our role in the pattern of strategy, it does seem that if any of them escaped – and we must remember they have boats – they might be able to tell the British enough for their Intelligence to make a few inspired guesses. We have to protect our coastline, Ehrhardt.'

Ehrhardt waited. He was well used to Baldamus' long-winded lectures. He considered Baldamus a self-satisfied young man but the lectures did no one any harm and they kept Baldamus in a good temper.

'We'll need some sort of temporary marine craft, Ehrhardt.'

'We'll be lucky,' Ehrhardt said. 'Only the Italians and the British have armed boats in the Mediterranean.'

'There are such things as caiques,' Baldamus said. 'Kalani harbour's full of them. Can't we mount machine-guns on a couple of them and have them circle the island?'

Ehrhardt agreed unwillingly and Baldamus smiled. 'Better see to it then,' he said. 'They could be useful. Perhaps even easier and safer for us to get to the south of the island than wheeled vehicles. After all, some time soon, some idiot's bound to try taking a pot-shot at us with a fowling-piece. We'd be harder to hit if we went by sea.' He lit a cigar and puffed at it for a moment. 'That sergeant you sent down there might even have enjoyed such a trip. Did he find anything, by the way?'

'Only bodies and bits of equipment. He thinks the others escaped by sea.'

'Just as well.' Baldamus nodded, satisfied. 'We wouldn't want the British having men on the island who might find out what's going on, would we?'

As the party from *Claudia* began to scramble down the lower slopes of the hills to Xiloparissia Bay, a German aeroplane went over and they all crouched among the rocks and froze.

'Recce plane.' Docherty said. 'Probably flying south to see what's lying in Suda.'

As the German's engines faded, they became aware once more of the faint thud of guns to the north.

'Some poor bastard's copping it.'

They stood listening for a while, their eyes on the speck of the German machine disappearing southwards. Then Cotton turned and began to scramble across the last of the boulders to drop the few remaining feet to Xiloparissia beach. Immediately, he saw *Loukia* lying at the side of the narrow bay under the overhanging trees. She was blackened by fire and the branches that threw their shadows across her were charred. The splintered mast lay over the stern, its tip in the water, a tangle of wire stays and halyards. From where he stood, she looked a total wreck and his heart sank, but then, as he drew nearer, he saw that ropes had been attached to the shore

'Who put those there?' he asked, gesturing as the girl appeared alongside him with the others.

'Chrysostomos,' she said.

'She's high out of the water,' Docherty pointed out.

'She's bloody nearly afloat,' Cotton agreed. 'It looks as if they've pumped all the petrol out.'

When he questioned her, the girl agreed that her cousin and his friends had probably emptied the tanks.

'Where's the petrol?'

'Ashore somewhere. Hidden, I think. I suppose they'll sell it, because the fishermen would like it. I think she was almost empty when she ran ashore. Perhaps her crew were expecting to take on more at Antipalia.'

'How do you know she was going to Antipalia?'

'Chrysostomos told me.'

'How did *he* know? He couldn't have found out from the crew. The Germans murdered them all, he said.'

'Perhaps Giorgiou Xilouris told him. He was an engineer in the boatyard there.'

Cotton paused, waiting until Docherty and Gully had moved ahead. Apart from Patullo, and Shaw and perhaps Chief ERA Duff, he'd been the only man in *Claudia* who'd known about the money and guns *Loukia* had been carrying, and he'd only been told, he suspected, to encourage him to volunteer for the job of getting them back.

'Where did Chrysostomos get his tommy-gun?' he asked. 'I wouldn't have thought there were many of those about.'

She shrugged and he went on. 'Did he find anything on board?'

'Tinned food. I think they got a lot of that.'

Docherty had managed to scramble aboard *Loukia* now, climbing along the bow of a tree and dropping to the deck. He disappeared inside the engine room.

'What's it look like?' Cotton shouted up to him.

'Engines look all right,' Docherty said. 'Except some bugger's stripped a lot off 'em.'

'What, for instance?'

'Plugs, for a start.'

'Could they be made to work?'

'No.'

'What if we replaced the missing bits with the same bits from *Claudia*? They're sister ships.'

There was a pause then Docherty's head shot up above the well deck, his eyes wide. The simplicity of what Cotton had suggested had startled him. 'Yeh,' he said. 'By Christ, I think they could!'

'How about the propellers?'

Docherty climbed down to the beach and stripped off his clothes. Indifferent to the girl, he stood stark naked, his body white and knotted with muscle, studying the stern of the boat.

The girl was watching with interest but no sign of embarrassment. Docherty grinned. 'She's never seen one like mine before,' he said. 'Ask her if she'd like to hold it, Cotton.'

Cotton said nothing, faintly embarrassed that the girl might have understood, and Docherty waded out into the water and started to swim. Drawing a deep breath, he disappeared under the stern of the boat. He came up panting.

'One screw's okay. One's lost a blade.' He looked excited suddenly. 'We could hammer out that bent one on *Claudia* and put it in its place. It's the same side.'

'How about the rudders?'

'Twisted like a dog's hind leg. Both of 'em. You'd never use 'em.'

'That the lot?'

'How much more do you want?' Docherty frowned. 'You still ain't got a rudder, remember. You ain't got a single sound bloody rudder between both boats.'

'Why not drop 'em out and rig a jury rudder? We've got a chippy with us. Why can't he make one? Or why not straighten the bent rudder from *Claudia*? Build a fire. Get it hot and hammer it straight. Can it be done in the water? We've got a diving suit.'

Docherty frowned. 'It might.'

There was a long silence and Cotton's impatience broke out once more. 'We've got one bent screw which we ought to be able to straighten, one good screw and one bent rudder! Surely to Christ we can do *something*! We'll have two good engines. We can manoeuvre with *them* at a pinch.'

'It's a hundred and fifty miles to Crete.'

'In a straight line. With a sea that's mostly flat calm. We've only got to get her out of this bloody bay and point her south. After that, all we've got to do is keep her on course.'

His heart thumping excitedly, Cotton climbed to the deck of *Loukia*. The wheelhouse was blackened by smoke and flames but it seemed intact. He tried the wheel. It wouldn't move.

The compass, the chronometer, the binoculars and the charts had all disappeared, together with the Anglepoise lamp from the chart table. The chloro-sulphonic container for making smoke was still on deck, however, as though whoever it was who had stripped the boat had not understood what it was and left it there.

'The buggers got the rum,' Docherty said in a grieving voice.

The captain's cabin had been denuded of everything and the radio cabin contained only shards of ruined bakelite and the remains of a transmitter. There was no sign of the receiver beyond a few power leads. A fire had also started near the engine room but had been put out before it had done more than char the wood-work of the alleyway and buckle the doors. There was no sign of the equipment normally carried on deck – the scrambling net, the dinghy, the Carley float, the rubber raft and the boathooks. Even the mountings for the Lewises had been removed while the 20 mm seemed to have received a direct hit from a shell and was hanging half over the stern, the barrel split, the empty drum a torn rag of steel, the recoil spring and breech shattered.

'That's no good,' Docherty said.

'Mounting's not damaged,' Cotton pointed out flatly.

Gully was standing chest-deep in the water by this time, his hand on the hull, staring at the chine where it had been splintered by contact with the rocks.

'What's it look like?' Cotton asked.

Gully lifted his head and smiled. It lifted Cotton's heart because he knew it meant good news.

'A bloody sight better than *Claudia*,' he said. 'She's almost afloat and all the holes are above the water line.'

'Can they be repaired?'

'Nothink that can't be sorted out with a bit of good 'Onduras me'ogany. Aft, when she settles under way, the 'oles would be under water and they'll have to be fixed. But, lying like this, I could work on 'em. I'd 'ave to make a raft or somefing. But it could be done. There are some 'oles forrard, too, but none of the ribs is damaged.'

'Could it be done quickly? We'd have to be quick in case the Germans came, wouldn't we?'

Gully nodded. 'Yes, it can. There are a lot of small 'oles,

o' course – bullet holes, but they can be plugged. What about aft? I can't see underneath her. Is there much water in her?'

Cotton went through the boat systematically, lifting the floor boards and examining the bilges. There was no sign of weapons or money, he noticed. He climbed on deck.

'A bit forrard that must have got in as she came in here,' he said. 'Aft, there's not much at all, so she must be all right there.'

'That's all right, then.' Gully grinned. 'I could make some makeshift rivets and put canvas over the 'oles forrard, then put planks over 'em and screw 'em in place.'

'What about aft?'

'That'll 'ave to be mended proper. Take out the planks and put in new ones.'

'Can you do it?'

' 'Course I can, if I give me mind to it.'

Cotton frowned. 'Then give your bloody mind to it,' he said.

As they met on the foredeck, they were all grimy from climbing about the charred interior of the boat.

'What about the Germans?' Gully asked as they climbed down again to the beach. 'Won't they come?'

Cotton asked the girl but she shook her head. 'Chrysostomos heard them talking in the café in Kalani. They think she's a total wreck.'

They had to admit that she looked a wreck but, though to a landsman she presented the picture of irreparable damage, to a sailor it was clear that with a little effort she could be made to float again.

'We'd better get back to *Claudia*,' Cotton said. 'And shift everything we want off her before the Jerries come back to pump out the petrol.'

They stood on the beach, staring up at the battered boat, all of them suddenly more cheerful. Until that moment, their future had looked bleak. Now there seemed a modicum of hope.

'Let's get cracking,' Cotton said.

They turned and set off across the beach, walking in the sea as the girl had shown them, to avoid leaving footprints in the sand. But, halfway across, a man emerged from the rocks and dropped to the shingle. He wore khaki shorts and a shirt and carried a revolver.

They all stopped dead and Cotton wondered for a moment if they had at last met the true Resistance on the island. Then he realized that on the torn sleeve of his shirt, the newcomer wore three blue stripes and he was grinning at them.

'Sure glad to see you boys,' he said. 'I'm Kitcat. Fred Kitcat. Canuck Air Force.'

6

Kitcat was a small man, completely unlike the pictures of the traditional Canadian that Cotton had in his mind. He was blond, his skin burned and peeled by the sun, and his face was covered by a large moustache and several days' growth of gingerish beard.

'A goddam Messerschmitt got us near Kotlinos,' he said. 'We were flying a Blenheim and they say that if you jump from a Blenheim you hit the tail or get your head cut off by the aerial, so we rode her down. Only me and Travers got out. I got into the dinghy and pulled him in after me. He sure looked bad, and it seemed as if it was all up with me.' He gestured towards *Loukia*. 'Then this goddam boat appeared round the corner of the island. Jeeze, man, I've never been so pleased to see anything in all my life.'

Cotton's face showed his surprise. He'd always imagined Canadians to be strong, silent types eight feet tall, thick-set and granite-jawed. Certainly those he'd seen in Canadian ships bearing strange names like *Nonacha* and *Talkeetna* and *Athabaska* that he'd bumped across always seemed to be. It was something to do with the Rocky Mountains and all the forests they had, he believed.

He wasn't to know that Kitcat had been a shop assistant from a small town called Pickle Elbow in Ontario, who'd never lived an outdoor life and whose job would have made it pointless being either strong or silent, anyway.

Besides which, since he hadn't spoken to anyone for several days, his pleasure at seeing Cotton and his party quite overcame any Canadian reticence he might have had, and his words tumbled eagerly over themselves as he explained what had happened.

'They pulled us aboard,' he went on. 'But Travers died right off. They were going to Antipalia.' Kitcat's face changed and seemed to close down, as if a shutter had dropped across it. 'Some mission they were on, I guess. It was decided to take him on there and bury him. But then these goddam MAS boats appeared and that was that. This guy, Samways, who was in command, decided to run for this place. The Eyeties kept hitting us but we weren't doing so badly because it was only bullets. But then they got a shell on the cannon. That killed three of the crew and put holes in the stern. Then they put one in the forecastle and it hit the stove and set the kerosene on fire and started an explosion in a can of petrol by the engine room door. We were on fire as we ran in and the boat was full of smoke. The mast came down as we hit the shore.'

Kitcat paused and drew a deep breath. 'Samways put her on the beach so she wouldn't sink under us,' he went on. 'He thought we might salvage her, do a bit of juggling with the engines to get one going, and get out far enough to wait for the navy or something. But we hit a rock as we came in and I guess the props are done for.'

Cotton pointed at the hill. 'What were you doing up there?' he asked.

'Just sitting,' Kitcat said warily.

'Got a gun?'

Kitcat grinned and waved the revolver. 'Yeah. I've got a Bren too.'

'A Bren, for God's sake!' Cotton's heart leapt, and his brain started to click-click again. Three-oh-three, twenty pounds weight, rate of fire 450–550 rounds a minute. One of the best infantry weapons in service, its only fault that it was so accurate all the rounds hit the same spot. But, at least, what it hit it demolished. 'Where'd it come from?' he asked.

Again the shutter came down across Kitcat's face. 'We had one or two on board.'

'On a boat?' Docherty asked. 'What for?'

Kitcat ignored the question and Cotton didn't ask why, because he already knew the answer.

'It'll be useful,' he said. 'Got any ammo?'

'Six magazines and a spare barrel.'

Cotton smiled. 'Can you use it?'

'Rather use a Browning or a Vickers K.'

Cotton's smile widened. 'We've got two Lewises.' He glanced about him. Xiloparissia Bay was narrower than Kharasso Bay, with two large clumps of rocks in the entrance. How *Loukia*, in her damaged state, had run between them without hitting them he couldn't imagine. 'What happened to the crew?' he asked.

Kitcat frowned. 'The Germans shot 'em,' he growled.

'Couldn't you stop 'em? With the Bren?'

'I couldn't see 'em. The trees were in the way. I just heard the shooting. When I got down to the beach the whole goddam lot were dead.' Kitcat indicated a large blue-grey rock close to the water's edge. 'They were lying in front of that thing. They'd stripped 'em of their watches and wallets and everything. They'd even cut one of Samways' fingers off to get his ring. It was a good one. I'd noticed it.' His face twisted in a spasm of unhappiness, and as he turned and pointed, they saw that there was a line of graves at the other end of the beach.

'I buried 'em,' Kitcat said. 'I didn't do it so goddam good but I buried 'em. Then I thought the Germans might come back so I went on board for food. There was some left but they'd already stripped the blankets and things. After that I went up the slope there and lived for four days under some bushes. I came down when I saw you. You come to pick me up?'

As Cotton explained why they were there and what had happened to *Claudia*, Kitcat's face fell.

'Oh, Jesus,' he groaned. 'I'm right back where I was then, aren't I? In the shit. All the same,' he continued, 'I guess it's better being in the shit with friends than being in the shit on your own. If your boat's wrecked, what are you doing here?'

'We think we might repair this one,' Cotton pointed out.

Kitcat's eyes lit up but his enthusiasm died quickly. 'You must be joking,' he said.

'Samways thought you might, didn't he?'

'Well, yeah, I guess he did at that.' Kitcat shrugged. 'You can count on me anyway.' He indicated his stripes. 'Don't take no notice of these. They're only aircrew stripes. Until I became an air gunner I was just a goddam fitter.'

'Engine or airframe?' Docherty asked.

Kitcat stared at the stoker. 'Engine,' he said. 'I was going to re-muster as a flight engineer for one of the new four-engine jobs, as a matter of fact. Anything's better than a Blenheim.'

Nobody was listening to him and Docherty grinned at Cotton. 'We've got help,' he said. He swung back to the Canadian. 'Can you swim?'

Kitcat gazed at him, puzzled. 'Yeah,' he said. 'I'm a good swimmer.'

'Under water?'

'Yeah, sure.'

'That makes three of us,' Cotton said. 'Where's the Bren?'

Kitcat gestured. 'Up there.'

'Get it. Go with him, Docherty. I think we're in business again.'

When they returned to *Claudia*, however, Docherty let out a howl of fury.

'The Germans have been!' he yelled. 'They've pinched the bloody spares!'

Cotton ran to the wheelhouse. The blood had dried to black now but the place was full of flies and loud with the sound of their buzzing.

'It wasn't the Germans,' he growled. 'It was those bloody Greeks.' He gestured at the girl who was watching them with a worried face. 'Her cousin and his pals! They're going to use 'em to repair *Loukia*.' He turned to Gully. 'Get Bisset! Quick!'

By the time Bisset appeared, Docherty was quivering with disappointment and rage.

Cotton glared at Bisset. 'Where were you?' he demanded angrily. 'That bloody Petrakis has pinched everything!'

Bisset didn't lose his temper. 'I was up there,' he said, gesturing. 'Building a shelter for the kid and fetching him water.'

'Couldn't you have stopped the bastards?'

'If you go up there – ' Bisset refused to become angry – 'you'll notice you can't even see the boat. And if I *had* seen 'em, I could hardly have stopped 'em. You had the rifles.' He looked gravely at Cotton who flushed as he realized the injustice of his accusations. 'Finally,' he went on quietly, 'it seems to me that instead of arguing how we lost the things, we'd be better occupied bending our minds to the problem of getting 'em back, don't you think?'

Cotton came to life and whirled on the girl. 'Where are they?' he demanded. 'Where have they gone?'

She looked scared and backed away. 'I can't tell you.'

'You'd better.' Cotton lifted the tommy-gun and, cocking it, pointed it at her chest. 'Where are they?' he demanded.

'They're hiding.' She looked agonized and desperate at his change of manner. 'What have they done?'

'They've stolen everything we possessed,' Cotton said. 'They've been over the whole boat.' He stopped dead, thinking, then he whirled round. 'Bisset, you and Chippy go and check the stuff we took ashore! The food. The planks. The dinghy. *And* the guns. Don't forget the guns.'

Without a word, Bisset turned and climbed from the boat, followed by Gully. Cotton pushed the girl against the engine-room bulkhead and pointed the gun at her again.

Kitcat's jaw hung open. 'What's she done, for Christ's sake?' he asked.

'It's not what *she's* done,' Cotton snarled. 'It's what her bloody cousin's done! We were going to transfer everything from this boat to *Loukia* and repair it. The bastards have taken the lot.'

Docherty glared at the girl who stared back at him with huge dark eyes. 'You know what she wants, don't you?' he said.

'Shut up, Docherty,' Cotton said. Even now, in his fury, he was embarrassed by Docherty's suggestion.

'She wouldn't worry. Them wops go at it like ferrets.'

'Shut up!'

Docherty was about to continue but changed his mind and stopped. Cotton's face was dark with anger and for a moment Docherty thought he might even turn the tommy-gun on him.

Bisset reappeared. He looked as calm as if he'd just been to fetch the milk from the front step. 'Nothing's been touched,' he said. 'Petrol, wood, dinghy, guns. They're all there.'

'That's something then,' Cotton said. He gestured at the girl with the muzzle of the gun. 'Where's Petrakis?' he demanded.

She hesitated before replying. 'He's in the goatherds' shelter,' she said.

'What's that?'

She pointed to the hill. 'It's up there. It's a big cave with room for the animals in winter.'

'Do you know where it is?'

'Yes.'

'You'd better show me the way.'

Her face became anguished. 'I daren't.'

Cotton grew angry. 'Who is this cousin of yours, for God's sake? God Almighty? I want back everything he took off this boat. It belongs to the Royal Navy, and I want it.'

She gazed at him for a long time and he could see she was trembling; then she nodded.

He went on staring at her for a moment longer, his eyes angry, then he turned. 'Gully, you look after the kid. Docherty, get everything ashore we're likely to need. I'll go after that lot with Bisset. Christ knows when we'll be back but we'll be bringing what they took. You can bet your life on that.'

Docherty didn't argue and Cotton was about to climb down from the boat with Bisset and the girl when he stopped and thrust one of the rifles into Kitcat's hands. 'Can you use one of these things?' he asked.

131

'I'm better in a turret.'

'I expect you'll manage. Keep your eyes open.'

He thrust the second rifle at Bisset and gave the girl a push. Without speaking, she led them along the water's edge to the rocks and began to climb.

Halfway up she tried to explain. 'It was none of my doing,' she said.

'Never mind that,' Cotton said sharply. 'Just show us where he is.'

She didn't speak again, but kept on climbing. As he started to pant, Cotton wondered if she'd try to run. He knew he'd never be able to catch her if she did and he knew he couldn't shoot her. He hoped she'd not try to run.

The night's rain had left the path running with water and slippery. It was an old stream bed and climbing it was like going up a rickety staircase which was always in danger of collapsing. Constantly, their feet slid away from them as the surface crumbled, and Cotton was wearing only rubber-soled pumps so that the stones dug into the soles of his feet.

Near the top of the hill, the girl branched off from the stream bed between two boulders, and they saw they were in a second smaller stream bed that fed water to the other. They continued to climb across the purple-brown boulders, their shoes everlastingly slipping in the mud, and again the girl turned, this time by a huge rock overhung by cactus. In front of them, Cotton saw a pile of manure and realized that for sime time he'd been treading in the small hoofprints made by a donkey.

'How much farther?' he asked.

'A long way still.'

'If you try any tricks –'

She gave him a cold look. She seemed frightened no longer, only full of dislike for him. 'I shan't try to trick you,' she said.

They went on climbing until the bay below seemed only a cleft in the rocks, and they could no longer see the boat between the trees.

'Chrysostomos will have others with him,' the girl said. 'He has men up there and might not want to give you back the things he's taken.'

'He'd better,' Cotton growled. 'How many of them are there?'

'Chrysostomos says there are many.'

'Right.' Despite his ancestry. Cotton had the Englishman's contempt for dark-skinned foreigners. He'd often heard it said that an Englishman was equal to two Germans, three Frenchmen and any number of wops, and he believed it. It was nothing to do with race, only background and that sense of superiority the British had enjoyed for generations.

He turned to Bisset and indicated the rifle. 'Can you use that thing?' he asked.

'I'm a Regular like you,' Bisset said. 'Among other things in peacetime, they taught you to shoot and not to panic when disaster's hanging over you.'

Cotton looked quickly at him, wondering if the airman was suggesting he was getting hot under the collar too soon, but Bisset had the placid self-assurance of a butler bringing in the port and Cotton could only admit to himself that, if there were one thing that Bisset was not, it was excitable.

The girl's steps had slowed down now and she began to look uncertain, even unwilling. Cotton gave her a push. 'Don't stop,' he said.

She gave him a bitter glance and began to climb faster so that it took Cotton all his time to keep up with her. Eventually they reached a small plateau, backed by a low brown escarpment.

'There's a cave,' the girl said.

They moved forward more slowly, keeping close to the cliff and treading warily. At last, they saw the hole in the cliff face. There was no sign of life.

'That it?'

'Yes.'

'Do they live there?'

'Yes.'

'All the time?'

'Yes.'

The bareness, the starkness of the landscape, startled Cotton. 'How?' he asked.

'They've got fires. And blankets. They carry water up.'

The sheer graft of it troubled Cotton.

'Girls?'

'I don't know.'

'Have you lived here?'

'No.'

'But you've been here before?'

'I helped them carry bedding up when the Germans came.'

'Are you a Communist too?'

'I believe in God,' she said. She spoke simply and Cotton didn't doubt her word.

'Then why do you help them?'

'Because he is part of my family and Greeks are very close. I expect eventually, when things grow better, I shall live in the cave with them.'

'With all those men? Aren't you afraid?' Cotton noticed that, in his concern for the bleakness of the life she was choosing, he'd forgotten to be angry with her. She hadn't forgotten to be angry with him, though.

'Chrysostomos is my cousin,' she said coldly. 'He'll look after me. Besides, by then there'll be other girls. *Someone* must resist the Germans.'

'*We're* doing our best,' Cotton said.

She sniffed. 'But, at the moment, it's not very good, is it?' She spoke simply and, remembering Norway and Dunkirk and France and the men being evacuated at that moment from the Greek mainland, Cotton had to admit she was right.

He stopped. The cave lay just ahead, sheltered by creepers and saplings. He gestured to Bisset and they moved again, the girl behind them now. At the entrance to the cave, they halted again, then Cotton drew a deep breath. God alone knew how many men there were inside and how many of them were armed. He looked at Bisset.

'Right?' he said.

'Right!'

They entered the cave at a rush, the girl following them. Then they stopped dead. Inside were Chrysostomos Petrakis, the two other men, Xilouris and Cesarides – and the donkey, munching at a pile of dried grass.

Cotton stared round him. The cave represented living at its starkest, devoid of comfort beyond mattresses made of ferns and a fire on which a blackened pot simmered.

'Where's the gang?' Cotton demanded.

Petrakis and the others said nothing and Cotton jeered.

'This all there are?' he said, realizing at once that Petrakis was a man who fought with his mouth, persuading people he was a great leader when his band consisted only of himself, a donkey and two men who were little more than boys.

The three Greeks had straightened up. They had been bending over a pile of sacks and Cotton saw at once that they contained all the things they'd carried from the boat. Tools. Spark plugs. Spare parts.

'I've come for that,' Cotton said.

Petrakis smiled. 'It is only *klepsi-klepsi*,' he explained. 'A little stealing. All soldiers do it. It's even permitted if it isn't too much.'

'That lot belongs to His Majesty King George VI.'

'King George VI?' Petrakis' eyes glittered. 'Who is he? I don't bother with King George VI. Or King George of the Hellenes either. I am a Communist. I supose you know what a Communist is?'

'We have Communists in England.'

'*Pò-pò!*' Petrakis sneered. 'British Communists are British first and Communists afterwards. Greek Communists are different.'

'I've noticed.'

Petrakis' face was dark with anger as he gestured at the sacks. 'This is ours,' he said.

'It belongs to the Royal Navy,' Cotton said stubbornly. 'You stole it. I've come for it!'

'No!' Petrakis barked the word angrily. '*We* need it.'

'What for?'

Petrakis glanced at the other two Greeks. 'Because you are losing the war,' he snarled.

'We'll win in the end.' Cotton had never been in any doubt about that. He towered over the Greek, burly, strong and black-haired, the tommy-gun in his fists. 'Put it in the sacks,' he said. 'Then get the donkey loaded. We're taking it back with us.'

Petrakis looked at the girl. 'You brought them here,' he accused. As he stepped towards her, his hand lifted, Cotton moved in front of him and jammed the muzzle of the tommy-gun into his stomach. Petrakis' hand dropped and he stared at the girl with glittering eyes.

'You'll pay for this,' he said.

For a moment she stared at him, confused by her loyalties. Then she drew herself up. 'You do not believe in God!' she burst out. 'You have told me often! Your god is the Communist party!'

Cotton pushed her aside. 'Load the donkey,' he said.

Unwillingly, Petrakis and the other two stuffed their spoils back into the sacks and tied them across the back of the minute beast.

'Better search the place for weapons,' Cotton said to Bisset. 'I wouldn't want to be shot in the back.'

Bisset moved further into the cave. He returned with two rifles and a tommy-gun.

'That's a help. Any more?'

'I didn't see any. But there are plenty of places they could have hidden 'em. I didn't think now was the time for a prolonged investigation.'

The girl looked at her cousin and then at Cotton. 'I must come with you,' she pointed out. 'I cannot stay here now.'

'No.' It didn't seem unreasonable. 'Okay. You'd better go ahead and lead the donkey. You go with her, Bisset. I'll back you up. There's a manoeuvre for this. It's called leap-frogging. A hundred yards down the slope – at a nice easy range where you could hit what you aimed at – make yourself comfortable and shout. I'll pass through you. If they shove their heads out, let 'em have a shot to make 'em pull 'em back quick.'

As Bisset and the girl set off down the side of the hill with the donkey, following the winding path that curved like a discarded snake skin towards the sea, Cotton waited behind the rocks outside. Up against the escarpment in the sun, the heat seemed stuffy and oppressive. He could hear the mutter of guns to the north and somewhere out of sight the low hum of an aeroplane engine. He shifted restlessly, wanting to be away.

Petrakis was watching him from just inside the cave and he was aware of his stare of hatred like the blade of a knife. Then he heard Bisset's shout and, without looking back, he turned and began to march down the path.

7

'All right.' Major Baldamus looked up at Captain Ehrhardt. 'So these survivors were picked up and there *was* another boat, and the Luftwaffe missed it.'

Ehrhardt shrugged. 'According to my sergeant, Herr Major, there were no footprints leading from the beach – only into the sea – and he could only imagine, since the boat and the rubber dinghy were missing, together with the weapons – two light machine-guns and a 20-millimetre cannon by the look of the mountings – that this boat must have been accompanied by the third boat you mentioned, and that when the Luftwaffe had gone, they paddled out and were taken on board with what they could salvage. They're doubtless now back in Crete.'

Baldamus shrugged, nagged by doubt. There was a lot at stake and he felt it was unsafe to assume too much. 'But just suppose they *weren't* picked up?' he said.

Ehrhardt shrugged. 'There was no sign of them.'

'Even so, we'd be unwise to risk any more men down there yet. It's *just possible*, I suppose, that we could be wrong, in which case they're in those hills with two machine-guns and a cannon. Not exactly something to argue against. Fortunately, they can't harm us so we'll leave them alone. However, we'll have a watch kept – from the sea, as I suggested. What have you found us?'

Ehrhardt grinned. 'Two large caiques have been taken over, Herr Major. We found them in the harbour here. We're mounting machine-guns on one of them at this moment. I've sent the other down with drums to lay alongside the wreck in Kharasso Bay and pump out the petrol. It's better if it belongs to us than to the Greeks.'

'That was quick thinking, Ehrhardt.'

Ehrhardt grinned again. 'Well, the other one was stripped and pumped dry by the islanders,' he said. 'Just before we arrived. It occurred to me they might try to do the same with this one. When the sergeant went through it yesterday he removed everything that was left.'

'And doubtless at this moment he and his merry men are flogging half of it round the market place in Kalani.'

'It's soldier's pay.'

'Indeed. So long as we get *some* of it. Just for the look of the thing.' Baldamus lit a cigar and drew gently on it for a while. 'When your caique's finished pumping out, have her armed like the other. Their job will be to make sure none of the Greeks slip south to say what's happening in Yanitsa. They'll make a daily circuit of the island and keep their eyes well open.'

Baldamus drew on his cigar comfortably and glanced at the papers on his desk. The build-up at Yanitsa was still increasing; he was erecting tents all round the edge of the strip now, and clearing families from the houses in the village alongside to make billets. A bar had been taken over as a headquarters for the Luftwaffe captain who was running the place, petrol was being stacked in heavy jerricans inside the wire compound that was being put up. Marquees for workshops had been erected and a separate mess arranged for the flying crews of the Junkers of *Fliegerkorps IX* and the Messerschmitts and Dorniers of *Fliegerkorps VIII*.

The place was beginning to look important. If it grew any more important, Baldamus decided, it would need someone with the rank of colonel to run it. And that colonel, he intended, would be Renatus von Boenigk Baldamus. General Ritsicz had promised it.

'Make it clear that no one's to leave the island, Ehrhardt,' he said. 'It's absolutely essential that no one knows we're here. All fishing vessels are to report nightly and I've asked the Italian navy to supply us with a launch. It's due to arrive tomorrow. General Ritsicz's got the Wehrmacht to supply an officer and an NCO with sea experience, together with two or three sailors and engineers and someone to fire a gun. After all, the British might decide to do something mad here.'

As it happened, the British were already doing something mad. At least, some of the British were.

A sunset like watercolours on wet paper was just fading into darkness as Cotton and Bisset climbed down to Kharasso Bay. Over the noise of the stream they could hear the croak of frogs so that the silence sounded like the silence of a Hollywood thriller. Then a nightingale started singing among the bushes and somehow it relieved the tension.

Then, as they were walking down the hill, Cotton sensed that everything was not right. He touched Bisset's arm and stopped. As he listened, he heard the clatter of stones, then, through the foliage, he saw a man picking his way up the slope, moving as fast as he could go, his breath coming in sobbing pants. Under his arm in the last of the light they could see a blue blanket and a jar, and then in the undergrowth they saw a bicycle.

'It's that chap who hid the rum,' Bisset said. 'He's come back for it.'

Cotton's eyes glittered. 'And the way he's moving,' he said, 'he's seen somebody on the boat. Get over there. I'll wait here.'

The girl was watching them silently, her eyes wide, and Cotton pushed her into the bushes. His stomach heaving, he reversed his rifle and held it by the barrel.

She put her hand on his arm. 'What are you going to do, Cotton?' she whispered.

He brushed her aside. 'If we don't stop him,' he said, 'we're all prisoners and you're probably dead.'

He weighed the rifle in his hands, his throat working. The German was still climbing as fast as he could go, his breath coming in wheezy gasps. Then, as he rounded a curve in the path, he came face to face with Cotton. There was just time for an expression of terror to fill his eyes before the rifle came round to crash against his temple. The blanket went flying and Cotton heard the rum jar smash at his feet. As the German crumpled up, Cotton grabbed a stone and fell across him, pounding until the German managed to squirm free and started to run with little agonized bleating sounds in the back of his throat. He had gone no more than one or two steps when he crashed into Bisset and the two of them went down together. Scrambling up, Cotton jumped with his knees in the German's back and the three of them struggled in the half-light, Bisset's hands on the German's throat, Cotton bashing sickeningly with the stone until the German became still. When he stood up he saw there was blood on his hands and shirt. Bisset rose up with him, his jaw hanging open.

'I think I killed him,' Cotton said.

Bisset's eyes narrowed, then he shrugged. 'You or me.' He bent over the German. 'He's dead all right,' he agreed.

Cotton drew a deep breath. 'We'd better bury him,' he said.

He stared down at the dead man. His uniform was shabby, stained and rumpled, and there were greying whiskers among the blood and fragments of bone in the shattered face. He turned away from the single bloodshot eye that stared up at them.

The girl crept forward. Her eyes dilated, she stared at the body, a look of sick horror on her face.

'You have killed him,' she said.

Cotton nodded and wiped his big paws on his trousers. She gazed at him, pale and strained, then she turned away, her face buried in her hands.

Cotton drew a deep breath. 'Come on, Bisset,' he said. 'Let's get rid of him. I bet he's a deserter.'

They hid the bicycle. Then they scraped a shallow hole under an overhanging tree and, shoving the body into it, kicked earth and stones over it. Finally they rolled heavy rocks on top. It was like shoving guilt out of sight.

When they'd finished, without a word they picked up the

weapons they'd dropped and set off down the hill again. Eventually they saw the dim shape of the boat by the light of the stars but there was no sign of Docherty, Gully or Kitcat, and as they stopped on the beach, over the hill, muffled by the height, they could still hear the mutter of guns.

As they waited, there was a faint reedy pipe from the trees that sounded like an owl. Cotton waited and it came again. He whistled back and heard Docherty's voice. As they moved forward, they saw dark figures move forward along the beach. Docherty was grinning. What Cotton had to say wiped the smile off his face at once.

'A German? He didn't come down here!'

'He didn't have to,' Cotton growled. 'He'd hidden what he was after up the hill. Did the other Jerries come?'

Docherty nodded. 'They had a caique and they pumped the petrol out into drums. It took 'em bloody hours.'

There was a long silence. They were all a little afraid, and the death of the German deserter bothered Cotton. Kitcat was the first to throw off the feeling. It had taken some courage for him to live alone above Xiloparissia Bay for days, and, with all the others around him, he felt anything was bearable. He gestured towards the boat.

'We've rigged up the forecastle,' he said as they unloaded the donkey. 'We've stopped up the holes and shaded the ports and Docherty's fixed a light.'

As he lifted his hand to drive the donkey away, Cotton caught his arm. 'Moor her up,' he said. 'We might want her again. How's the kid?'

'No worse. Gully said he might even be better.'

It was then that Docherty noticed the girl standing nearby in the shadows. 'What's she doing here?' he demanded.

'She decided it was safer with us,' Cotton said.

Docherty grinned. 'Who're we to complain?' he said. 'Who's she sleeping with?'

They hoisted the sacks on board and Docherty began to check the contents with the engines. As he worked, Cotton drew

Kitcat on to the foredeck. The sky was studded with stars, and they seemed to glow instead of glittering as they did at home.

'Those guns *Loukia* was carrying?' he said.

Kitcat looked sideways at him. 'What about 'em?'

'There were a lot, weren't there?'

'Were there?'

Cotton scowled. 'You know damn well there were.'

Kitcat hedged. 'Well,' he said. 'One or two.'

'I think there were more.'

Kitcat looked up at him quickly. 'How do you know?'

'I was told. Before we left Crete. What sort were they?'

Kitcat studied him in the semi-darkness. 'I dunno,' he said. 'I heard 'em say they were old British issue.'

'Did you see what happened to 'em?'

'No. The Germans took 'em, I suppose. When they murdered Samways and the others. When I got back they were gone.'

'How many were there?'

'I dunno. They had 'em stacked in the captain's cabin, in the alleyway and under the floorboards. I saw 'em when we got Travers aboard and into a bunk. I should say there were four or five dozen rifles, some boxes of ammunition, a few grenades, and one or two Brens and tommy-guns.'

'They were carrying something else as well, weren't they? Money. And there was a lot of it, wasn't there?'

Kitcat frowned. He'd known about the money all right but he'd been told to hold his tongue and so far he had done. He decided that since Cotton seemed to be well in control there could be no harm in admitting something he already knew.

'Yes.' He nodded. 'There was. Samways got us to carry it up the cliff and hide it. As soon as we ran ashore. It was heavy, so there must have been a lot. We put it in a hole we scraped under a rock shaped like a toad and piled stones on it.'

'Could you find it again?'

'Easy.'

Cotton drew a deep breath. 'Then keep it to yourself. Nobody else knows about it.' He thought of Gully and Docherty. 'Perhaps it's as well,' he ended.

They made arrangements for the night and when the girl promised that a boat would be round in the morning from Ay Yithion, they decided to carry Howard down to the captain's cabin aboard *Claudia*. By the time they'd installed him, Bisset had managed to set up the paraffin stove and he and the girl were organizing a meal.

'If we 'ad some 'am,' Gully said gaily, his mouth splitting in a wide grin that showed his awful false teeth, 'we could 'ave some 'am an' eggs if we 'ad some eggs.'

There was tea but only two washed-out tins to drink it from because every mug that hadn't been broken in the initial disaster had been taken by the Germans. There was also bully beef, tinned peaches and biscuit, and though it was spartan enough they were all hungry and nobody argued, either about the food or the discomfort of the splintered forecastle. Docherty was in a cheerful mood and kept eyeing the girl with merry, lecherous, boot-button eyes, making suggestive remarks about her while she tried to avoid looking at him as he tormented her.

As she finally rose to go, pink-faced and clearly understanding, Cotton rose with her. On deck she turned to him. 'You must be careful,' she warned. 'Chrysostomos is a Cretan and Cretans are a savage people. They never forgive an injury, and you have made him look silly in front of Xilouris and Cesarides.'

Cotton remembered what Patullo had said about the Greek sense of honour. '*Philótimo,*' he said.

She hesitated. 'I'm sorry he took all those things, Cotton.' She gave him a little smile. 'But it is all over now, I think.'

Cotton stared upwards at the dark path through the trees. 'You'd be better staying here with us,' he urged. 'Suppose he's up there.'

She touched his hand in a curiously Greek gesture, as though to indicate all was well again between them and that she'd forgiven him for his brusqueness with her earlier.

'Tomorrow,' she agreed. 'Perhaps you're right and tomorrow

I will. But I must go back to Ay Yithion tonight, to bring the Varvaras round. I'll take care and I'm not afraid, and there is plenty of darkness.'

Then she was gone, melting quickly into the night, and Cotton heard her splashing along the fringe of the sea and the soft clatter of stones as she began to climb.

8

The signal was in code and began with the instruction that it was to be deciphered only by an officer of the rank of major or above. Baldamus' eyebrows lifted and he vanished into his office, closed the door and started to work. When he'd finished, he reappeared and called for Ehrhardt.

'What's the state of our transport, Ehrhardt?' he demanded.

'Not very good,' Ehrhardt said. 'Consists mostly of cars.'

'Lorries?'

'Five.'

'We need sixteen.'

Ehrhardt grinned. 'I doubt if there are sixteen lorries on the whole island,' he said.

'There'd better be.'

'What are they needed for?'

'You'll see when the time comes. Arrange for another eleven to be commandeered. I want them on the airfield by tomorrow evening.'

Ehrhardt scratched his head. 'Where the hell am I going to get another eleven serviceable lorries?'

'You'd better seek divine guidance.' Baldamus smiled. 'Because I've had instructions that they're to be ready by first darkness tomorrow night. See to it, Ehrhardt. Send your men round the villages. I think we ought to be able to produce them if we look hard enough. After all, this island was being developed as a holiday area for exhausted Greek millionaires, and Panyioti

146

owned that damned great museum of a place at Xinthos. I've had a look at it. It's full of furniture, so there must have been lorries to carry it there.' Baldamus' voice was gentle but Ehrhardt knew that by hook or by crook he would somehow produce the eleven extra vehicles.

'I wouldn't like to guarantee that they'll all be the same, Herr Major,' he pointed out. 'Some will be open. Some might even be pantechnicons.'

'I don't think anyone will argue,' Baldamus said. 'We have to move approximately two hundred and fifty men at great speed in the dark.'

'Why?'

'Never mind why. And since we've been talking about that residence of Panyioti's, we'll inspect it as billeting accommodation. Our two hundred and fifty men have to be housed.'

'We could use tents.'

'No tents.'

'There are huts on the airfield.'

'Not on the airfield.'

'A hotel in Kalani?'

'Not in Kalani, either.' Baldamus' voice grew a little firmer because he knew now what General Ritsicz had meant when he'd talked about the Panyioti residence. 'I think Panyioti's palace is handy both for the city and the airstrip. See to it, will you, Ehrhardt?'

It was Cotton who did the watch that night. Someone had to, because he didn't want the Germans to return and catch them asleep, and despite the climb he'd made with Bisset and the girl, he didn't feel tired and knew that the next few days were going to take a lot out of Docherty and the others. He had no skill with tools himself and it would be Docherty, helped by Kitcat, who would have to reassemble the engines; and Gully and Bisset – who claimed some skill as a carpenter – who would have to work on the hull. All Cotton could do would be tea boy, look-out and general dogsbody.

He could hear them all arguing through the open hatch of the forecastle, the old boring forecastle argument he'd heard hundreds of times in HM ships.

'She did,' Docherty said.

'She didn't,' Gully retorted.

'She bloody did, you know.'

'She bloody didn't.'

He wondered who they were talking about.

'Disarmed, disrobed and de-bloody-flowered in one hour flat,' Docherty insisted. 'I was always good at it. Left 'and behind her back so that when you pushed her down it was underneath. Her right in your left and what have you got – ?'

'Rape.' Bisset's voice sounded bored.

Docherty chuckled. 'Well, you've got one spare hand,' he said. 'And that's a distinct advantage. You'd be surprised how many times it worked. Anyway, half the time they're saying "no" when they mean "yes".'

'What happens when they mean "no"?'

'Well, that's bloody hard luck. Sometimes I used to ask 'em: "Do you rape easily?" I got a few clouts across the kisser, but I got a few rapes too.'

'Didn't you ever make a mistake?' Kitcat asked.

'Plenty of times. But I got a lot of birds as well.'

Cotton couldn't understand how they could be so indifferent with Howard probably dying, then he realized it was a sort of defence mechanism that allowed them to shut their minds to suffering and concentrate simply on being alive.

'It's them books,' Gully was saying. 'That *No Orchids* and that *Fig Leaves Forbidden* thing you got down there. They get you worked up. You go on the way you are, you'll end up like the last rose of summer.'

Cotton, who'd been brought up as a good church-goer with high moral beliefs, listened to them with disgust. Then, guiltily, he found himself thinking of a girl he'd been with the last time he'd been on leave in London. She'd had pale-blue veins in the porcelain whiteness of her breasts, he'd noticed, but her breath had smelled of whisky and there'd been a picture of a soldier in uniform on the mantelpiece.

Gully and Docherty were talking now about their war experiences, each trying to horrify the other.

'When they bombed Liverpool,' Gully said, 'you could scrape 'em off the walls.'

'All the time I was in the drink,' Docherty countered, 'this foot in the grey sock kept bobbing against my bloody 'ead.'

Bisset's voice came, weary and bored. 'This grisly ritual of shocking each other with horror stories takes some talent for lying, you know. And you two haven't got it.'

'Who's a liar?' Gully said.

'I dare bet *you* are. And so bloody boring you give a chap a headache.'

'You can chew my starboard nipple,' Docherty said cheerfully, then, as the voices died, Cotton heard Gully's battered concertina and his breathy voice singing in a low monotone.

'Roses round the door, kids upon the floor –'

Cotton sighed. For the first time in his service career, he began to see what command was all about. He'd often thought of ships' captains as privileged people spoiled by too much attention and too much spare time, but suddenly he realized why. They needed their time for thinking. Cotton had become the leader of the little group of men struggling for survival, not by order of the Admiralty or by reason of superior intellect or training, but simply because he'd been the only one with any ideas about self-preservation. The others had accepted his leadership without question and now he was realizing what a lonely position he'd created for himself. No wonder the navy revered Nelson like a saint. Slight, tough, strong-willed, yet emotional as an actress, he knew exactly what moved men to perform miracles. Cotton wished he did.

Eventually, the muttering below died away and while the others slept he went to the captain's cabin to check that Howard was all right. His breathing seemed to be quieter now, and Cotton began to think he might survive if they could only get him to where he could receive treatment. As he stared down at him, Howard opened his eyes. 'Wotcher, Royal,' he said.

'Go to sleep,' Cotton said. 'It'll be all right.'

Howard's head nodded weakly. 'Hurts a bit,' he said. 'What happened to Coward?'

'He's all right,' Cotton lied. 'Tomorrow we're going to try to get you to a quack.'

'Right.' Howard nodded and slid away again into a shallow sleep.

Cotton sighed, wishing he hadn't so much to think about. Climbing on deck, he drained the water tank into the empty rum jar the Germans had left and did anything else he could find to do. Then he completed the log, stating in simple terms – because he wasn't capable of more – exactly what had happened to *Loukia*'s crew, how he had decided to take over *Loukia* in place of *Claudia*, and everything that had happened between him and Petrakis.

It rained soon after midnight and for the rest of the night he sat in the shattered wheelhouse staring at the sky and nursing the tommy-gun as he listened to the bassooning of the frogs in the stream and the high creak of the cicadas. At the back of his mind there was a nagging worry. He wasn't quite sure what it was but it remained there all night. It was like something he was trying to grasp but couldn't quite find in the darkness.

He was still sitting in the wheelhouse when he heard the first aircraft of the new day to the north. It sounded louder than before, as if it were not far from the island, and he noticed the muttering of guns from the mainland had begun again.

It stopped raining as the first faint colours of the morning came in the east and, going below, he made tea for the others. Gully sipped it warily.

'Tastes like it's been made outa shellac,' he said.

He looked grubby and unwholesome and Cotton wondered why God had had it in for him so, to land him with a pair like Gully and Docherty.

Docherty yawned. 'I was just dreaming about my bird,' he said. 'I was making a bloody good job of it too.'

'I've forgotten what it's like to have a bird,' Gully observed. 'I won't know what to do next time.'

'It's like riding a bike,' Docherty pointed out cheerfully. 'It all comes back when you get on.' He paused, scratching his head, his eyes far away. 'My bird was the wife of a corporal of Marines.' He looked pointedly at Cotton, his face full of malicious glee. 'Dim bastard, like most Joeys. I met her in a pub. Had a big bed, she did.

'The corporal bought it for himself, only she was more often in it with me than him, see. Welsh, she was, and she had the nicest tits and legs you ever see. She was sitting on the bed starkers, all white and pink with green eyes, just taking off her stockings and looking at me like they do. You know – with her tongue going over lips – ' He gave a shudder and groaned. 'Oh, Jesus,' he said. 'Why did I have to wake up?'

The light was increasing as Cotton returned on deck, and the day was spreading from the sea in long pale fingers into the heavens like violet ink rising through the veins of a tulip. Then he realized that above the rumble of artillery to the north he could also hear the low thud of an engine.

Terrified that they'd been caught, he dived below and got the others moving. They were still struggling to get Howard out of the captain's cabin when a caique nosed round the headland. Standing on the bow was a small figure that was quite clearly Annoula Akoumianakis. Cotton climbed to the deck, Docherty just behind him, and as the others joined them another caique appeared. They were small vessels – one brilliant red, the other a blistering blue – sloop-rigged, low-waisted, with clipper bows and rounded sterns. There were fishing nets on the deck and they were both low in the water.

As they edged between the rocks and nosed slowly towards *Claudia*, he saw there were several men on board, apparently led by the captain of the electric-blue vessel. The girl was waving, proud of herself, and, as she gave Cotton a special smile, he found he was pleased to see her and glad she'd forgotten the dislike she'd felt for him the previous day.

'This is Dendras Varvara,' she said, indicating the captain of the blue caique, a stout, elderly man in a striped jersey. She pointed to a grave-faced, shock-haired young man on the other boat. 'This is Athanasios, his son. They have come to help. They will take your wounded man to Ay Yithion.'

Cotton grinned, delighted and relieved at this first sign of friendliness.

'Thank you, *Kapetáne*,' he said.

The old man spoke a harsh unfamiliar Greek that was hard to understand at first. 'She is a good child, this one,' he said, slapping the girl's behind. 'May she prosper.' He nodded towards the wrecked *Claudia*. 'That is a sad sight, my son.'

He offered a bottle of raki which they passed round. '*Eviva*,' Varvara said. 'One should always start the day with a drink.'

His son was watching the sea. He seemed nervous. 'We came early,' he said. 'Before the Germans are out.'

'What Germans?' Cotton asked.

'Two boats from Kalani have been armed,' the young man said. 'They are going to patrol the coast.'

'E-boats?'

'No.' The older Varvara shook his head. 'Just caiques. Fast caiques. You'll need to post a look-out.'

He turned to one of his crew, a boy no more than fourteen with ragged trousers and shirt, and pointed to the end of the promontory.

'He'll keep watch,' he said as the boy climbed ashore. 'They start their patrol today. If they come, we drop everything and head out to sea. We're fishing, if they ask. No one's said we mustn't – only that we have to report.'

They didn't waste any more time. The two boats, their diesel engines thumping and filling the air with fumes, edged nearer. Docherty unwillingly stripped off his clothes and, as he stood in a ragged pair of underpants, they began to festoon him with the diving equipment – the helmet and goggles, the counterlung and

152

absorbent canister and the gas cylinders. He gave them a nervous grin as he adjusted the canvas straps between his legs.

'I hope nothing goes wrong,' he said, 'or I'll be no bloody good to the birds.'

'Can you work it?' Cotton asked.

'I think so. Christ, I hope so! I don't fancy floating head downwards under water.'

They attached the lead weights to the harness and he thrust his feet into the heavy boots.

'I'll come down and help you,' Cotton offered.

'How you going to breathe?'

'I've got lungs.'

They had already attached a heaving line to one of the blades of the propeller and, as Bisset manoeuvred the dinghy against the stern of *Claudia*, Docherty hung a pair of pliers, a heavy spanner and a hammer round his neck with lengths of fishing line, and began to march into the water. When it was up to his chest, he hesitated so that Cotton began to wonder if he was going to be able to do it, then he waved and vanished abruptly beneath *Claudia*'s stern. When he emerged, the water streaming from his hair, he held a split pin in his fingers. He seemed excited suddenly. 'Hang on to that,' he said. 'We ain't got any spares. Now for the nut.'

Knowing there would be little he could do later when the real work started, Cotton borrowed a spanner from Varvara and, lungs bursting, head throbbing, watched Docherty working underwater at the nut until he had to surface.

'I think it's moving,' he said.

Eventually, his fingers cut, his shoulders scraped and bleeding, Docherty came up with the castellated nut in his hand. He handed it to Bisset and reached for a hammer.

'Now for the prop,' he said. 'I'll need a hand. We've not got to lose the key.'

Cotton was about to follow Docherty again when he felt a hand on his arm. Old Varvara was holding a length of rubber tubing.

'One end in the mouth,' he said. 'The other above water. With cotton waste in the nostrils you can breathe.'

Cotton smiled and, attaching one end of the pipe to a cork float from the caique, he put the other in his mouth and went down after Docherty. Between them, they began to attack the propeller. Gasping and spluttering, Cotton shot to the surface with it already moving. Docherty followed.

'One more go,' he said.

This time the propeller moved more quickly than they'd expected and Cotton saw it drop away through the shining water. The heaving line Docherty had attached to it jerked taut and, just before he burst to the surface, gasping, Cotton saw the propeller swinging gently on the end of it just above the sea bed.

Docherty appeared alongside him, grinning. 'I got the key,' he gasped. 'Haul her in.'

Bisset heaved the big bronze propeller into the dinghy, and they stared at it eagerly, indifferent in their excitement to the kink in one of the blades. Docherty's new enthusiasm was infectious, and he stared red-eyed at Cotton and Kitcat and grinned.

The younger Varvara was looking at his watch now and his father was staring out towards the sea. As they did so, the boy they'd posted on the headland whistled and pointed.

'The Germans!' the old man said.

Bundling everything into the dinghy, they pulled it ashore and carried it up the beach to the trees. The caiques were already under way and, as they passed the rocks in the entrance to the bay, the crews started throwing nets over the side. From the slope above the boat, Cotton watched carefully through the trees. Annoula was beside him, pressed close against him by Bisset who was crouching on the other side of her. Her body was soft and warm against Cotton and, as he turned to look at her, he saw her eyes flicker away, as if she'd been studying his face.

As they watched, they heard the thump of an engine and a moment later, the two big caiques appeared round the point. They were fast-looking boats, each with a small wheelhouse aft and a stern-mounted machine-gun. They stopped alongside the Varvaras' boats and they could hear the shouts across the water. Old Varvara offered a bottle, and they saw one of the Germans studying *Claudia* with a pair of binoculars. But they seemed satisfied that she was a complete wreck and eventually they chugged off again.

The blue caique came slowly into the harbour once more.

'They said they'd try and tow her off when it's all over,' Varvara said, as he casually tossed a line over *Claudia*'s stern cleat and cut the engine.

'When what's all over?'

'They didn't say. They seemed very security conscious. I expect they've got something unpleasant up their sleeves.' Varvara frowned. 'It goes badly on the mainland,' he went on. 'Yugoslavia surrendered yesterday and the German wireless said the British intend to leave Greece.'

The news, the first they'd heard since they'd arrived, was depressing to say the least. Evacuation was bad enough but an unsuccessful evacuation was worse.

'What about us?' Cotton asked.

Varvara laughed. 'They think you were picked up. They thought there must have been two launches.' He gestured. 'Now we will take your injured man. It is much better this way than carrying him up the cliffs.'

By the time they'd transferred Howard's stretcher to the blue caique, the boy who had acted as look-out had climbed down to the boat.

'We shall keep him aboard until evening,' Varvara said as Cotton took a last look at the wounded man. 'He's safe with us.'

'I can't tell you how grateful I am,' Cotton said and the old man held up his hand.

'You do not need to. It is balm to my soul to hear our beautiful language in the mouth of a foreigner. You speak it well. There are not many English who speak Greek.'

As he climbed back aboard the caique, he passed across canvas, nails, screws, oakum, grease and tallow. 'You will need these,' he said. He reached into the wheelhouse and produced a basket of fruit, rock bread, onions and dried fish. Candles, a lantern, a tin of paraffin and a rubber-covered torch followed, and finally he grinned and dug out a bottle which he tossed to Cotton.

'Raki,' he ended. 'Doubtless it will be of use.'

Putting the engine astern, he waved and chugged out of the bay to join his son before they both thumped off slowly round the headland.

Cotton stood watching them for a minute or two, unbelievably thankful to have got rid of the responsibility for Howard. The morning was already full of heat and the air seemed full of gold, with the sparkle of waves on rocks, and beyond that the blue-green haze of the sea. For a moment, his mind was full of thoughts. He turned to the girl.

'Get the donkey,' he said. 'We'll start moving over to Xiloparissia Bay straight away.'

9

As they climbed the ridge, struggling with the box of heavy diving equipment, they all carried rifles except Bisset and Kitcat, who carried the two tommy-guns they now possessed. The day had become sultry and heavy with a watery, lemon-coloured sun pushing through a thin layer of cloud. The mud had dried and in the gulleys it was stifling enough to make them sweat.

It was no surpise, as they crossed the ridge and began to descend into Xiloparissia Bay, to see figures on the deck of *Loukia*. The girl recognized the red shirt of the man by the wheelhouse at once.

'That's Chrysostomos,' she said.

They crossed the beach in the shallows as Annoula had shown them and stopped in front of the boat. Petrakis appeared from the wheelhouse.

'What do you want?' he demanded.

'We've come to take over.'

Petrakis scowled. 'It is *our* boat,' he pointed out.

'It belongs to the Royal Navy,' Cotton said. 'We're going to salvage it.'

The Greek gestured. 'The laws of salvage are well known; especially in Greece which is one of the great maritime nations of the world. It is *our* boat. We moored it to the trees.'

Cotton looked up at the Greek, unafraid and calm. 'Salvage doesn't apply to naval vessels in wartime. This is a naval vessel.' He wasn't sure he was right but it seemed like a good guess and he thought his bluff might work.

Xilouris and Cesarides appeared on deck. They were carrying

157

rifles once more and Cotton noticed that, as before, they were Lee Enfields.

'We are keeping this boat,' Xilouris said. 'The first man who tries to climb aboard will be shot.'

The three Greeks were standing on *Loukia*'s bows, staring down at the group on the beach, their backs to the trees. There was no question but that they held the whip-hand. They could hold off Cotton's party as long as they chose.

Petrakis appeared to be well aware of his advantage and was grinning. 'I think this time, Englishman, that you will have to concede defeat,' he said.

'I don't think so.' Cotton's voice was infuriatingly cheerful. 'Don't look round now, but just behind you there are two tommy-guns and they're both aimed at your backs.'

'Sure are!' The voice was Kitcat's and it came from the trees.

Petrakis' head turned slowly and Kitcat waved at him from the rocks among the foliage. The Greek's face reddened with anger but he climbed sullenly over the side of the boat, followed by the other two, and dropped to the beach. As they straightened up, Petrakis stared at Annoula and spat. The spittle landed on her shoulder and, her face tragic, she brushed it off without a word. Then, as he passed, he swung his arm and she went reeling away, her black hair lifting like a dark wave, to fall to her knees in a scattering of sand. Cotton's fist came up at once and Petrakis sprawled on his back alongside her. As Xilouris lifted his rifle, Docherty jammed the muzzle of his weapon under his nose.

'Leave it, you bastard!' he roared.

Cotton stooped over Petrakis and, picking up the Greek's weapon, flung it from him.

'Disarm 'em,' he said.

Xilouris and Cesarides handed over their weapons without arguing, and Cotton jabbed at Petrakis with his rifle. 'Get up,' he said and, as the Cretan climbed to his feet, Cotton jabbed him again in the ribs.

'From now on,' he said, 'there'll be a sentry here all the time. If you come back, you're likely to be shot.'

As the Cretan marched away across the sand, followed by the other two, Cotton glared after him angrily, his mind in a turmoil. It was a bit confusing having to look out for both Germans *and* Greeks, he decided. The bloody Greeks were supposed to be on our side, weren't they? This sort of situation didn't seem to be within the scope of a mere corporal of Marines.

The girl was watching him, tears in her eyes.

'You must forgive him,' she said. 'He's an unhappy man.'

'I'm not so happy myself.'

'He's uncertain what the future holds.'

Cotton turned and stared at her. 'So am I,' he barked. 'By God, I am!'

He dropped his burden on the sand and started unloading the donkey. Bisset was studying the shell-smashed mast and the stays and halyards draped about the deck.

'Never mind that lot,' Cotton said sharply. 'Leave it. It makes her look more of a wreck and it'll discourage Jerry from coming in and bothering with her. We'll get rid of it at the last minute, and we've plenty else to do for the time being.'

Bisset studied him for a second and Cotton thought he was going to be as awkward as Docherty. Then he smiled, nodded, and moved to help with the donkey.

Cotton sighed. 'Docherty,' he said, 'get cracking on the engine. We'll fix the prop later. The rest of us'll clear the beach so that if those German caiques arrive they'll see nothing.'

They carried everything they'd brought from Kharasso Bay under the trees and hid what they didn't need among the rocks. Cotton noticed that nobody argued with him. 'Gully can get stuck into the hull,' he said. 'The girl can keep a look-out for you.'

She gave him a scared look and as he saw Docherty's eyes flicker he changed his mind abruptly.

'Perhaps on second thoughts,' he said quickly. 'I'll take her with me.'

As the two of them set off back to Kharasso Bay with the donkey, they could hear Gully's hammer already at work on the hull and the clink of tools from the engine room. The sun was high by this time and the afternoon was hot. The tinned meat they'd eaten had been a greasy mess as they'd turned it out of the tins, and Cotton was rapidly coming to the conclusion that what they were trying to do was mad. Up to now he'd never had to think for himself, because there'd always been the ship's captain and the captain of Marines to do it for him, and it wasn't patriotic fervour which drove him now, simply an instinctive belief that he shouldn't stand idly by and let the Germans win the war.

The girl was walking in silence alongside him, tense and un-happy. Cotton had a big man's gentleness and with her quiet enigmatic face she was just one more of the things that worried him, something he was unable to understand in his frustration and anxiety.

On the ridge of the hill they paused. Cotton could hear the mutterings of the guns and wondered if the Germans had already bypassed the new British line and were heading down towards Athens. He'd once visited the Piraeus in *Caernarvon* just before the war. The locals had laid on a dance for the crew. The officers had gone to some swept-up affair but there'd also been beer and wine for the lesser mortals from the mess decks. The experience had left him with a warm affection for Greece – something quite apart from his ties of blood with the place – and it troubled him to think of jackbooted Germans stamping all over it, probably bullying his own aunt and cousins into the bargain. Then his mind was jerked back to the present with the sight of a small group of aeroplanes swinging in a wide arc over Cape Asigonia to the north. They began to drop lower and lower to land until eventually they disappeared from sight.

What was happening on the mainland was a nightmare and the lack of news troubled him. It was obvious that the conquest of Greece would be followed in good time by an assault on Crete, and if the invasion of Crete *were* in the wind, it was not surprising that the Germans were too preoccupied to bother about salvaging *Claudia*. There'd be plenty of time for that when they'd consoli-dated themselves across the sea approaches to the mainland.

There was no sign of life near *Claudia* and the three graves on the beach had sunk as the soil had settled under the rain that had fallen. They seemed smaller, somehow, and Cotton found it difficult to realize that one of them contained Patullo. He'd got to know Patullo so well, it was hard to believe he was dead.

They loaded the two Lewises on the donkey and added anything else they thought it would carry.

'It'll die of heart failure,' Cotton said.

Annoula smiled. It was only a small smile but it pleased him to see it return. 'Greek donkeys are very strong,' she said. 'And better that the donkey struggles than that the Germans find them.' She paused. 'They say in Yithion that they've collected all the big boats from Kalani.'

'Why?'

'Perhaps they're going to attack the British in Egypt.'

Not in caiques, Cotton thought. The navy was heavily beset and the army and the air force had more on than they could safely handle, but he thought they could still manage to stop an invasion by caiques.

'Suppose the Germans come to Yithion?' he said.

She shrugged and he went on, curiously troubled by what would happen to her. 'What will you do?' he asked. 'Have you no other friends on the island? People you could trust?'

'A few.'

'You could come with us to Crete. Every destroyer that evacuates troops seems to have its quota of girls. I expect they're taken care of by the British government or somebody. They're probably earmarked, anyway, by some soldier. Have *you* been earmarked?'

She gave him a sad little smile. 'No. Not me. Perhaps I am too plain. And I am not clever.' Her head came up proudly. 'I have once been to London, of course. It was a long way and very expensive so that I had to stay with relations.'

Cotton said nothing, feeling faintly guilty because he couldn't bring himself to tell her about his family.

She lifted huge dark eyes to him and managed a smile, and he thought at that moment she looked anything but plain.

'I'm already older than most girls when they marry,' she went on. 'Greek girls marry very young. Are you married, Cotton?'

'Not me,' Cotton said stoutly. He'd been resisting his mother's blandishments for years. 'When are you going to marry, son?' she was always asking him. 'Soon you'll be so old, the confetti will knock you down.'

'It's good to be married.' Annoula had been silent for a while and her words brought him back to the present.

'Yes,' Cotton said.

To the right bird, he thought. *He* wasn't going to end up like his Old Man. Cotton wanted to be accepted as an Englishman, and a blonde wife and fair-haired children seemed a good investment.

'Yes,' he said again. 'To the right person.'

10

Most of the damage to *Loukia* was aft and, apart from splinter holes, there was remarkably little forward. By evening, Gully had constructed a platform out of a door and a couple of big rocks they'd pushed into the water, and was already at work patching the bow with canvas, oakum, tallow and wood. Docherty had almost reassembled the port engine already and was pleased with himself.

'We need a drink to celebrate,' he suggested.

Cotton passed round the raki that old Varvara had given them and Gully pulled his concertina from the drab pile of rubbish he called clothing and started to play 'The Lambeth Walk'. Immediately, Docherty's feet started moving and he grabbed the girl and began to dance with her on the sand. Her face lit up and she responded at once, her eyes merry. Cotton watched them, aware how attractive she looked when she was happy, and even faintly jealous. In his mad fashion, Docherty had a way with him and Cotton could see how he managed to get the girls.

Then he pulled himself up sharp. What's this bloody regiment coming to, he thought, dancing when the Germans were only on the other side of the hill? It was as bad as that Roman geezer fiddling while Rome burned. On the other hand – Cotton paused, newly aware of the trials of command – all work and no play made Jack a bloody dull sailor and Docherty was the sort of man who needed lightness in his life. Cotton rubbed a big hand over his face. Jesus, he thought, no wonder ships' captains always seemed so bloody wise. They needed to be trick-cyclists, commanders, disciplinarians, teachers and bloody fathers to their crews all at the same time.

'Shorter cruises, longer boozes,' Docherty grinned. 'I used to be dead smashing at this. Rammer Docherty, the hearts and flowers kid of Tyneside. There's nothing like a smoochy last waltz to strip a girl's good intentions down to her ankles.'

He gave Annoula a salacious grin but she obviously hadn't properly understood him and Cotton decided it was time the larking stopped.

'That's enough,' he said sharply. 'We got work to do.'

'Ach' – Docherty flashed his mad grin at the girl – 'you've got more bull and flannel than a battleship. What's wrong with a bit of fun? A bint and a tiddly bit of music. It's just what we want.'

'It's enough,' Cotton said and Annoula gave him a frightened glance and backed away from Docherty.

'Marines,' Docherty observed, 'are about as much use as a blind bunting-tosser. You're as bad as that lot on the bridge with all the poached egg on their caps, Royal. Always spoiling a matelot's bit of fun.'

'We've got a lot to do,' Cotton said stiffly. 'We haven't time for stand-easies.'

Docherty scowled. 'What wouldn't I give for a pint of wallop, a plate of fish and chips and a turn round the Palais with a willing bird.' He grinned at Cotton. 'NCOs and petty officers come in three sizes – them with stripes but no authority, them with authority but no stripes, and them with neither. Join the navy and see the world. Join the Marines and scrub it.'

He went back to work, defiantly singing, 'Officers don't worry me – not much!'

As the sun began to sink Cotton set off to fetch the dinghy with one of the drums of petrol. Bisset and Kitcat went with him, and they took the donkey to bring back the propeller Docherty had detached.

It was already dark by the time they reached Kharasso Bay but there was a moon now and they were able, by the use of the torch, to uncover the drums and roll one of them down to the beach. Covering the others again with the rocks, they unearthed the dinghy and loaded it with the drum. There was still plenty of freeboard, so they pushed the rubber dinghy into it as well and fastened two or three planks across the stern. Then, waist-deep in the water, they launched the dinghy and Cotton started rowing.

It was hard work and by the time he reached the point, he was sweating heavily and his arms were aching. When he reached Xiloparissia Bay, the girl met him on the beach and together they dragged the boat up the sand.

'I was worried, Cotton,' she said.

'About me?' Cotton grinned. 'I've been dragging heavy weights around for years.' He was showing off a little for her, the same he-man act he'd performed a dozen and one times for the girls in Pompey, the big, straight backed, broad-shouldered Marine, muscular in body and mind, uncomplicated, proud of himself and the way he looked. *Philótimo,* he thought. Greek self-satisfaction. It was no different.

Docherty appeared through the darkness. He was whistling and, as he approached, he did a few dance steps, slipped his arm round the girl's waist, and whirled her round so that she laughed. Then, as he released her, he slipped his hand under her breast and squeezed it so that she gave a little scream and wriggled away from him. Cotton stared at them disapprovingly.

'We'd better get the stuff up the beach,' he said. 'The others'll be back soon with the propeller.'

Docherty was still smiling as they rolled the drum of petrol up the beach towards the rocks, chattering all the time – about the engines, about Alexandria and Suda Bay, about the war, about all the girls he'd had and hoped to have in the future. Silence was a thing Docherty could not endure and he was as irrepressible as a rubber ball, always ready to bounce back after a disaster, morally untrustworthy, uncomplicated but indifferent to conditions and hours of work; probably the sort who'd kept the navy afloat throughout its whole history.

'One day I'll be a dirty old man,' he was chirruping. 'And that's bad. But at the moment I'm a dirty *young* man, and that's fine.'

He glanced at Cotton's disapproving expression. 'You look like you swallowed a bun,' he said.

'You talk too bloody much, Docherty.' Cotton spoke heavily, feeling that, if he wished, Docherty had the ability to dance quick-silver-like round his more stolid mind.

They hid the drum of petrol among the trees and, as he turned away, Cotton saw that Docherty was with the girl again, talking to her, and she was laughing and pushing him away. He scowled.

'Let's get the planks ashore,' he snapped and Docherty patted the girl's behind and waltzed up to Cotton.

'Let them begin the beguine,' he was crooning. 'Bring back a night of tropical splendour. How about a dance, Royal?'

'Get stuffed.'

'How about a drop of raki then?'

Cotton gave him a look that would have spiked a gun. 'We got things to do,' he said. 'Get Gully.'

Docherty turned. 'Gully!' he yelled.

Cotton grabbed him by the arm. 'You want the whole bloody German army to hear you?' he snapped. 'You give me the bloody pip, Docherty! You do, straight up!'

Docherty grinned. 'I'm bleeding internally.'

Gully appeared to claim the planks and as Cotton turned away he heard him speak to Docherty.

'What's up with *'im*?' he demanded.

Cotton scowled. Though it took some doing to admit it to himself, he knew very well what the matter was. He was jealous that Docherty could make Annoula laugh whenever he wanted while he, Cotton, who could even speak her language, could only talk to her of the most mundane things, dead serious as they discussed her future or the hatred her cousin bore for them. Neither of them, he realized, were subjects which were likely to raise a song in her heart.

Cotton slept outside the wheelhouse for the rest of the night because Docherty was still in a lively mood and he was afraid he might find the bottle of raki he'd hidden in the bilges under the captain's cabin. The discomfort didn't improve his temper and when they started on the propellers the next morning, Docherty seemed to enjoy tormenting him. He had the girl in the well-deck, holding one of the lines by which he transmitted his instructions to those on deck, and he was constantly chaffing her, making her laugh and adding lewd comments to Cotton as they splashed around in the water out of earshot.

With the experience they'd gained from removing *Claudia*'s propeller, it was easier to remove *Loukia*'s. Getting *Claudia*'s undamaged one back in its place was more difficult.

'We'll need a staging of some sort for it,' Docherty pointed out. 'You can't tread water with fifty pounds of copper-bronze in your arms.'

It took Gully only half an hour to attach wooden blocks to a plank to hold the propeller upright. Then, standing on the stern with heaving lines tied to the ends of the plank, they manoeuvred it beneath the boat. The weight of the propeller prevented the plank from floating and, with directions from Docherty in the water in the diving gear, they began to pull on the ropes to lift it to the end of the shaft.

Docherty's head appeared. 'Only needs a shove now,' he grinned. 'As the actress said to the bishop when he jollied her into a shop doorway.'

Holding the key, he ducked beneath the water, emerging a minute later, with the goggles slipped and his eyeballs red. 'It's on,' he panted. 'Gi'e us the nut.'

They had the propeller in place and secured in surprisingly quick time, and Cotton allowed them all a swallow of raki.

'Will it work?' he asked.

'Anything I fix,' Docherty said, 'stays fixed. Ask any bird I've been with.'

Cotton scowled. Docherty seemed to be deliberately goading him. 'What about the bent blade on the other one?'

'I'll do it tomorrow. Get it off, shove it on a stone and tap out the kink. Ought to be just what the doctor ordered. So long as all the blades are the same, they'll be okay.'

'What about the rudder?'

'What about it?'

A dreadful thought had occurred to Cotton. 'When we let it go, won't the water come in through the hole and sink her?'

Docherty looked at him pityingly. 'Christ, trust a bloody Boot-neck to ask a stupid question like that. The stock of the rudder goes up through a tube inside the boat and the top of the tube's above water level.'

Cotton wasn't really sure what he meant and he stared at Docherty, faintly ashamed of his lack of technical knowledge. He decided to persevere.

'But will the water come in?' he asked.

'No, you stupid twit.'

Cotton nodded, satisfied. 'And will it get us home?'

'If we're careful.'

'Suppose we have to use full speed.'

Docherty shrugged. 'Well, the stern can only drop off,' he said.

The bent propeller took less time than they'd expected and by evening they had it on the other shaft. But the day for Cotton seemed full of tensions. The girl even appeared to enjoy Docherty's company and he went out of his way to make her smile, singing snatches of popular song to her whenever he saw her, clutching his chest with one hand like an opera singer and gesturing with the other so that she couldn't help laughing, doing tricky little dance steps round her as he passed her on the deck in a way Cotton with his big feet could never hope to. By dusk, Cotton was actually looking forward to rowing round the point for the next drum of petrol.

'Why not let someone else go?' Bisset suggested, but Cotton shook his head.

'I'm strongest,' he said, feeling that strong arms and a weak head were the only assets he possessed.

Once again Bisset and Kitcat were going with the donkey, to dismantle one of the mountings for the Lewises, and this time, unexpectedly, Annoula wanted to accompany them. But, with Docherty and Gully busy, she had to remain behind as look-out. She seemed unhappy about the arrangements and it puzzled Cotton because he couldn't imagine that, after the way Docherty had made her laugh all day, she wished to come simply to be near him.

Once again, it was dark when they reached Kharasso Bay but, with the moon and the experience of the previous night, loading the dinghy was much quicker this time and Cotton pushed off and started rowing. It seemed no nearer and no easier than it had the previous night, and he came to the conclusion that he was the mug for the whole party.

Then – unexpectedly, because when he had set off the sky had seemed full of stars – the rain came, slowly at first and then in a drenching downpour so that he began to fear the boat would be swamped and he'd have to swim for it, losing the drum of petrol and the dinghy as well.

Just as unexpectedly, however, it stopped, but as the hiss of the rain died, he heard another sound, a growling metallic sound that came quietly at first, threateningly, then growing in sound until it filled the heavens. Resting on his oars, he stared upwards, picking out eight aircraft which seemed to be approaching the island from the west in formation, their lights on so they could see each other.

He was still wondering who they were, half-hoping they were the RAF come to give the Germans at Yanitsa a taste of their own medicine, when the lights changed position as the aircraft swung clear and formed up in line astern. Then, one after the other, as they came lower, the engines were cut until they passed over the tops of the hills and disappeared from sight towards the north of the island.

169

The heavy rain that had soaked Baldamus and Captain Ehrhardt had stopped when they first heard the aircraft approaching.

'There they are!'

The lights in the sky drew closer and they could hear the engines approaching as the aircraft came down out of the darkness, slipping secretly into the landing strip at Yanitsa at an hour when all the Greek workers had left.

Only Major Baldamus, Captain Ehrhardt and a few men were there to see them arrive. There were eight aircraft, all of them big Junkers 52s and 53s, and as they touched down, swung round and came into line, one after the other, they headed slowly towards where the lorries were waiting in the darkness. As the first of the machines came to a stop, its motors still running, the door opened in the side and men began to pour out. They wore overalls and small pot-shaped helmets, different from the lipped helmet that hung behind the door in Baldamus' office. Without any instructions from Baldamus, they hurried towards the lorries, climbed aboard the first two and were immediately driven off. As the lorries vanished and the aeroplane swung round and headed for the end of the landing strip, the second aeroplane took its place. Once more it emptied of men, and as they were also driven off in the next two vehicles, the aeroplane moved away and the third machine appeared through the darkness.

The operation was repeated until all eight aeroplanes had emptied and all the lorries had gone. As the first aeroplane took off into the night, heading north into the darkness, the second pushed into its place, and the third moved up close behind. By the time the last aeroplane's passengers had been driven away, the fourth machine was already in the air. Within minutes, the remaining four aeroplanes had taken off and the operation was ended. The landing strip at Yanitsa was as empty as it had been before the machines had arrived.

Ehrhardt watched with his mouth open. Baldamus smiled.

'That, in my opinion,' he said, 'was a beautifully executed operation.'

Ehrhardt drew a deep breath. 'Does anybody else know about this?'

'Just you and I and a few others. See that it remains that way.'

'Where are they going?'

Baldamus smiled. 'I'll give you three guesses,' he said.

'They're Special Air Division troops.'

'I can see you're a *good* guesser, Ehrhardt.'

As Cotton pulled into Xiloparissia Bay he was soaked and there were several inches of water sloshing round his feet in the bottom of the boat. The rain hadn't helped to cool him off much and his arms felt like lead. There was no sign of a light aboard *Loukia* and he assumed that Docherty and Gully were still working. Then he realized he couldn't hear the chink of tools or the thump of Gully's mallet on a chisel and he supposed the rainstorm had driven them below deck. But no one came towards the boat as it grounded on the sand and he angrily decided that they hadn't bothered to keep the look-out and that the girl hadn't seen him.

Heaving the boat up the beach, he lifted out the anchor and trod it into the sand. As he straightened up, he heard a half-muffled cry from *Loukia* and he swung round at once and started running. At first he thought Petrakis had arrived but then he realized that the cry was feminine, despairing rather than panicky, and he knew at once what it meant.

Climbing on to the rocks, he began to scramble to the deck. As he did so, he heard the cry again. Lifting the forward hatch, he dropped through. Gully was snoring on one of the bunks, the bottle of raki, almost empty now, on the deck alongside him.

The cry came again and was as abruptly cut off. Snatching open the forecastle door, Cotton bounded through into the wheelhouse, his wet clothes leaving a damp smear on the blackened paint-work. The light came from the captain's cabin and he saw the girl's legs framed in the doorway, uncovered up beyond her thighs. As he jumped forward, he saw that Docherty was holding her down on the bunk, one of her arms underneath her, pinned by her own weight, and was gripping her other wrist with one hand. Her dress was open to the waist and Docherty was sprawled across her trying to force her to submit to him. For a fraction of a second, her terrified eyes saw Cotton over his shoulder; then Cotton had wrenched the stoker aside and punched him in the face. Docherty crashed into the door as the girl sat up, pulling at her clothes, and his hand reached out for a heavy wrench on the table. Cotton hit him again, with both hands, and then again. The wrench clattered to the deck and Cotton, uncertain what drove him on, smashed Docherty into the bulkhead until he yelled to him to stop.

'You bloody fool,' Cotton said in a low furious voice. 'You bloody Christ-damned fool! We've got no friends on this island that we know of and the only people who've helped us so far were those blokes with the fishing boats. She's our only contact with them. Do you think they're going to help if they learn she's been raped by a bloody fool stoker from the Royal Navy?'

Docherty's anger diminished to a sullen scowl as he wiped the blood from his mouth. 'Don't give me that,' he muttered. 'You're all flannel! She wanted it. She was asking for it.'

'You're a bloody liar!'

'She came down encouraging me.'

'I don't believe you! I've a good mind to blow your bloody head off, Docherty! You might have buggered up our chances of ever getting away. We depend on these geezers' goodwill –'

'We ain't seen so much so far!'

'But we've seen a bit and we need all we can get. If you lift a finger to her again, I *will* shoot you. Tomorrow night *you* can row round the bloody point and fetch the petrol. It might do you good. It might make you so bloody tired you'll not have the energy for that sort of thing.'

As Docherty climbed to his feet and vanished, Cotton stood in the doorway, staring after him, his chest heaving, his mind whirling with his problems. There seemed to be so much to think about and so much to remember.

He turned slowly. Annoula had risen to her feet and was fastening her dress.

'I'm sorry,' he said awkwardly. 'It won't ever happen again.'

She gave him an agonized look and the tears welled up into her eyes. His arms went out to her and pulled her to him, and she dissolved into incoherent sobbing against his wet shirt.

'It'll be all right,' he kept saying, overwhelmed by her smallness, the protective feeling he felt for her, and the odd satisfaction that, despite Docherty's crazy charm, she had fought him off when he'd expected her to submit. 'It'll be all right.'

After a while, she managed to become coherent. 'I did not ask him,' she said.

'I'm sure you didn't.'

'He made me laugh, that's all. It's a long time since I laughed.' She became faintly hysterical. 'It's my fault! I should have stayed in Yithion!'

He held her tighter, his comfortable soul curiously eased by her dependence on him. 'It isn't your fault,' he said. 'He's a fool. He always has been. It's my fault. I should have seen what he was up to. I never did have much brains.'

Her fingers tightened on his. 'You are a good man, Cotton,' she said.

He made her sit down. Then he went to the forecastle for the raki bottle. Seeing Gully still snoring on the bunk, he suddenly saw red. The carpenter was a typical seafaring man, boozy, stupid and unreliable ashore, never getting further than the first bar when his ship docked and he had money in his pocket. Consumed with rage, he grabbed his feet and swung them to the deck. Gully rolled off the bunk and crashed on to his face. His eyes wide, he sat up, staring at Cotton's bedraggled figure.

'What the 'ell – ?' he began and, as Cotton wrenched him to his feet, he moaned in anguish.

'Steady on, mate! I'm more keel than funnel at the moment!'

'You bloody fool,' Cotton said. 'You got drunk!'

'Only an eyeful! It started raining.'

'I hid the bottle!'

'Docherty found it. It didn't seem to do no harm.'

'You nearly finished the bloody bottle,' Cotton snarled. 'And Docherty knew you would. He tried to rape the girl.'

Gully seemed unconcerned. 'Confucius 'e say "No such thing as rape. Lady with skirt up run faster than man with trousers down.".'

Cotton grabbed him by the shirt and shook him furiously, so that Gully had to clap a hand over his mouth to stop his false teeth falling out.

'From now on there'll be no boozing aboard this boat,' Cotton snapped. 'I said I'd shoot Docherty if it happened again, and if *you* let it happen I'll shoot you too. Okay? We can get back to Crete without either of you if we have to.'

He left Gully gaping after him, still uncertain what had happened, and, snatching up the bottle, went back to the girl. Sloshing some of the dregs of raki into one of the cans they'd been using for drinking, he sat beside her on the bunk, one arm round her shoulders as she sipped it, gulping her sobs back.

They were still there when Bisset and Kitcat returned, both of them as wet as Cotton from the rain. Bisset's face was bewildered.

'What's up?' he asked. 'Gully's sitting in the forecastle with a fat head and Docherty's scowling at the floor in the engine room. We heard a lot of aircraft and we thought at first they'd shot the boat up.'

Cotton gestured angrily. 'Keep Docherty away from me,' he snarled, 'or I'll probably murder him.'

He told them what had happened and Bisset frowned. 'Fat lot of help we'll get if it gets to Yithion,' he commented.

The girl shook her head. 'I shall not tell anyone,' she said in English. 'Soon it will all be over and you'll be gone.'

His face concerned, Bisset gently took the tin from her and put the last of the raki into it. 'Here,' he said. 'Finish it. Then try to sleep. It'll seem different tomorrow.'

As they closed the cabin door, leaving her lying curled up on the bunk, her face to the bulkhead, Bisset's eyebrows rose.

'Did he – ?' He left the sentence unfinished and Cotton shook his head.

'No. I arrived just in time. The dinghy's still on the beach with the petrol in it. We'd better get it.'

Despair and hatred for Docherty darkened his face. He was well aware of his own lack of skill and it infuriated him that he was dependent on such fools as Gully and the stoker. The consciousness of his isolation swept over him again. Even Bisset, always calm, always helpful and encouraging, couldn't take from him the load he'd shouldered – probably a bit too bloody fast, he thought bitterly. But having shouldered it, he couldn't push it off on to any of the others. Not now.

Bisset was watching him as if he could read his thoughts.

'Cheer up,' he said. 'The news isn't all bad. We brought back *both* mountings. We'll fix 'em on the deck tomorrow. Then, if those bloody Greeks come back, it won't take a second to jam one of the Lewises in place. You could use it on Docherty at a pinch if you felt like it.'

11

The following morning, the Varvaras arrived in the blue caique. They brought news that Howard was much better and a load of oakum, tallow and three pots of paint. One of the pots contained black, one red and one the electric blue of Varvara's boat.

As the sun rose higher, they brought round the 20 mm cannon. Considering it safer to stay behind, Cotton sent Bisset and Kitcat, while he remained near Annoula. She seemed to have recovered and sat on the wheelhouse roof, watching the sky for aircraft, her face pale and set. Gully worked on the hull, frowning as if he had a headache. A bit of fun and games with a girl had never troubled his conscience before, and he knew that if it hadn't been Docherty it might well have been himself. Sailors were never noted for their high moral tone and he couldn't understand what Cotton was getting hot under the collar about.

His face pulpy, Docherty sullenly began to assemble the starboard engine. 'I reckon you've broken my nose,' he complained.

'You're bloody lucky,' Cotton said briskly. 'I might have broken your neck.'

'Just for a bloody wop 'ore!'

'Docherty,' Cotton said, 'she's no more a whore than you're a ponce. She's done a lot to help us. So drop it, Docherty. Drop it or I *will* break your neck.'

Docherty still seemed to want to argue but Cotton turned away and left him to it. During the morning, they removed everything from the deck and hid until the German caiques had passed the end of the bay. Cotton stared after them as they vanished. 'What do you reckon they're up to?' he asked Bisset.

'Looking for us, perhaps?'

'I wondered if they're doing a guard to stop anybody getting away from here to Crete. Patullo said they were expecting them to invade.' Cotton frowned. 'Still, everybody knows *that*. Even me. Let's get these rudders off.'

'Tomorrow,' Gully pleaded. 'My 'ead's like a setpot.'

Cotton reached out with a big hand and, grasping Gully's shirt, dragged him forward until their noses were inches apart. '*Now*,' he said.

For a moment, Gully glared feebly but he was neither big enough nor in a fit enough state of health to argue. Docherty hadn't waited for instructions and was already in the after hatch, throwing out rope and unlashing gear. As he removed the last bolt and whacked the end of the stock with a leather mallet, the starboard rudder began to slip downwards. As it dropped away, Cotton noticed with a certain amount of surprise that, contrary to what he'd expected and exactly as Docherty had predicted, the sea didn't rush in and fill the after compartment.

At the end of the afternoon, Cotton again told Docherty that he was going to have to row the next drum of petrol round.

'Why me?' Docherty said. 'I been at it all day and there's work to be done in the engine room.'

'Tell Kitcat what to do. *You're* so bloody strong, it might do you good to row round to Kharasso Bay and back.'

While Docherty set off for the headland in the dinghy, Bisset and Kitcat took the donkey over the hill to bring back what they could. Cotton watched them go, wondering if Docherty would simply go on rowing to Kalani and give himself up. The previous night's affair had brought a new problem – how to organize his manpower so that whenever the girl was aboard, there was some-body reliable at hand in case it happened again. With Docherty and Gully his only two skilled men and the rest of his team having to make the journeys to Kharasso Bay, it wasn't easy.

The night passed without incident, however. Rather to Cotton's surprise, Docherty returned with another drum of petrol and more planks, and the following day they removed the surviving rudder from *Claudia*. Bringing it over the hill on the donkey's back, Docherty built a fire in an attempt to straighten out the bend in the stock.

He wasn't entirely successful but they decided it would work. The top of the stock had been narrowed and squared to take a tiller for hand operation in emergency, and there was a hole through it for the big split pin that held the nut which secured the rudder arm when it was connected to the main steering. Threading a long wire from one of the mast stays through the hole, they passed the other end under the boat and up through the rudder tube into the after compartment where Cotton, with an ugly soldier's knot, bent on a heaving line to give them a grip for pulling. Then, with the same arrangement of plank, lines and rope they'd used for the propeller, Docherty manoeuvred the rudder into position beneath the boat and pushed from beneath as Bisset and Kitcat hauled on the heaving line. As the stock was dragged up through the tube, they secured it in position and Docherty eyed it with a satisfaction that was only marred by the crooked look his bruised nose and eyes gave his face.

'Right,' Cotton decided. 'Now we'll dismantle the pump from *Claudia* and shove it aboard to give us double suction. There's time to do it today.'

Docherty sighed. 'I wish I was a millionaire's bastard,' he said.

Three days later, Dendras Varvara's caique turned up again and they got him to bring round the last of the gear from Kharasso Bay, the heavy batteries from *Claudia*'s engine room and what was left of the drums of petrol. It was now the 18th, and since they had no idea what was happening to the north, it was essential to find out. Cotton had not forgotten the instructions that had been given to Patullo before they'd left Crete. In addition to rescuing *Loukia*'s survivors and her cargo of money and weapons – enough in all conscience, it seemed now – they had been ordered to find out what the Germans were up to. And in his heart of hearts, Cotton was also hoping that somehow he might get news that would counteract all the gloomy items he'd been hearing over the past few days. He drew Bisset and the Canadian to one side.

'I'm going to Kalani with the girl,' he said. 'We've got to find out what's happening. She says there's a bus from Ay Yithion and I can speak the lingo.'

Since he had to rely on Docherty to carry on working while he was away, he also felt obliged to tell him what he intended. He was relieved to see Docherty grin his old grin again.

'And this is a warning to the hearts and flowers kid to behave hisself, eh?' he said.

It surprised Cotton that he was so good-humoured about it. 'Yes,' he said stiffly.

Docherty did a few dance steps and looked up at Cotton. 'Y'know,' he said. 'I wasn't trying to rape her. It was just the old Docherty technique. Only this time it didn't work. If she'd screamed I'd have stopped.'

'She was probably too frightened to scream.' Cotton was handing out nothing in the way of forgiveness.

'Yeah – well – ' Docherty left what he was going to say unfinished ' – you needn't have clouted me like that. I thought my eyes was going to fall out and roll on the deck like ping-pong balls.'

'Touch her again and they will.'

'Okay, okay.' Docherty raised his hands in submission. 'Come to think of it, I'm not sure I like Greek bints anyway. Compared with what we've got on Tyneside, I wouldn't give you a fly button for the lot of them. She's all yours.'

Cotton's head jerked round. '*I*'m not interested in Greek bints either,' he said.

Docherty grinned. 'Then why,' he said, 'are you always goggling at her like last week's kippers?'

Between them they managed to equip Cotton in civilian clothes – a pair of flannel trousers from Docherty, a ghastly pink pullover with holes in the elbows from Gully, a checked shirt from Bisset. It was significant that only Cotton himself, a Regular to his

179

fingertips, had nothing civilian to contribute to his garb.

'We need some more petrol,' Docherty shouted down to him as he climbed ashore. 'We'll not get to Suda with what we've got.'

Cotton stared up at him. 'I'll buy some in Kalani,' he said sarcastically. 'There's bound to be a Woolworth's.'

They caught the bus where the road curved up from Ay Yithion. It was packed with people taking produce to the island capital. The rear portion was filled with fish boxes, while among the seats there were chickens in wicker cages, a trussed sheep, and baskets of fruit. The road wound through the marshes of the central plain where the island sank like the centre of a shallow plate, and they could see herons among the weeds and dozens of what looked like large versions of children's windmills. The ground around them was white with camomile, the flame of genista, rock roses and patches of red poppies.

To their right they could see Cape Asigonia projecting out to sea between a curve of the steep hills that ran round the south of the island. At the junction of the road to Skoinia, another batch of people crammed more baskets and another sheep into the back of the bus. As they passed the airstrip at Yanitsa, Cotton sat up. There was a large wire compound near the road where impounded civilian vehicles were carrying jerricans of petrol to stacks that had already been built.

'What do they want petrol for?' he muttered. 'Caiques run on diesel.'

There were half a dozen trimotored Junkers at the far end of the strip, three Messerschmitt 110s and what looked like a Junkers 88. There also seemed to be an enormous number of Germans, all wearing peaked caps and in their shirt sleeves, but no one stopped the bus and it was allowed to pass without incident. The end of the road from Kaessos produced more people. Then to the east of Kalani, as they passed a group of red-roofed buildings among the trees in the distance which Annoula identified as Panyioti's holiday home, they saw German soldiers at the end of a lane. They were tormenting a couple of girls carrying baskets of vegetables. They had surrounded them and kept touching the girls' breasts

180

and behinds and were pretending to lift their skirts, and the girls were giving little screams of terror that were drowned by the deeper laughter of the soldiers.

The Germans were all young and they all looked remarkably tough. They wore the ordinary short-jacketed grey-green uniform of the Wehrmacht but all distinguishing badges had been removed and they had an air about them that seemed to indicate they were not the same as the rest of the German soldiers on the island. They had a look of capability and self-sufficiency and didn't seem like men to be trifled with.

As the bus drew level with them, they left the girls and started to run towards it, shouting and waving their arms. The bus driver panicked, as though he feared there might be trouble if they managed to get aboard. His foot went down on the accelerator and the ancient vehicle began to labour, its engine roaring. The increased speed was slight but it was enough to put it beyond the reach of the running men, and one of them dragged a pistol from a holster and fired several shots into the air. A woman screamed and Annoula turned towards Cotton and hid her face against his chest.

Kalani was a small place, shabby for the most part, and the main road had been taken up for repairs so that the bus had to stop outside the centre of the town and they had to walk the rest of the way over a path made of planks and flat stones.

The weather was still unsettled, with a fluky wind threatening rain. The sea had risen and the waves were punching at the cliffs, and, as they approached the town centre, the rain finally came. The stones shone in the grey light as it pounded down. Everybody vanished from the streets into the shops and taverns, and the slanting alleys and the climbing steps among the tiers of white cube houses ran with water.

They found a café and ordered wine. Through the window they could see the jetty and the masts of the boats almost misted away by the rain. A giant acacia shaded the terrace but provided no shelter against the downpour that blew and spat and crackled against the windows. A dozen broad streams rushed down the steps and across the square, carrying pebbles and twigs and scraps of paper with them.

The café was jammed with people, talking or playing cards. The whitewashed walls were hung with prints of steamers and ferry-boats, and there was a gilt mirror and a picture of a girl in Edwardian dress alongside a photograph of the King of the Hellenes. Everybody seemed nervous and ill at ease, the wireless blaring out in a crackling drone that obscured the voices of the customers. The programme seemed to be one long news bulletin that appeared to consist only of a long list of military disasters. The centre of Belgrade had been destroyed by Nazi bombers which, unopposed and skimming the rooftops, had rained down their missiles on the stricken city for three days. Thousands of people had been killed. 'Yugoslavia must be crushed,' the Germans were declaring. Meanwhile the Greek army, which had successfully resisted the Italians for six months, was now on the brink of capitulation before the German might. For Britain, Greece had proved nothing but another Norway. Her expeditionary force of sixty thousand men had been overwhelmed by the sheer weight of metal and, with inadequate air cover, was disintegrating into a nightmare.

Cotton listened with a stony expression. He had come to find out what was happening and the news was shattering.

'It'll come right,' he kept saying to himself, but however hard he searched for a tiny gleam of encouragement, it eluded him. Of a good church-going family, he felt that somewhere there should be divine retribution against the forces of darkness that were oppressing the world, but nowhere – nowhere – could he see any sign of God's justice.

From where they sat, they looked over the harbour. But there seemed to be no unusual activity, no ships that could be used for an invasion of Crete or Malta or Egypt, nothing but a lot of caiques, small boats and one lost ferry. It puzzled Cotton, because he couldn't understand why the Germans had pushed so far ahead of their main army to capture Aeos if they weren't using it as a jumping-off spot.

As the rain stopped and the sun came out, they saw the two caiques they'd spotted off Kharasso Bay towing in another vessel with a charred black mark along its side. Its bows were pitted with bomb splinters and it was packed with khaki-clad men, British, Australian and New Zealand soldiers who had tried to escape from the mainland. Some of them were wounded and all of them were saturated.

Cotton watched them climb ashore, sullen and defeated under the laughter and jeers of the triumphant Germans standing on the jetty. His face wore the same set look it had worn as he had listened to the news, and he sat in grim silence, Annoula's tragic eyes on his face.

They hung about Kalani all day. But the trip seemed to have been pointless. Whatever the Germans were up to on Aeos, they were keeping very quiet about it. There weren't even any rumours and, apart from the sight of the British prisoners of war, the only untoward incident involved more of the tough-looking soldiers they had seen near Panyioti's house, who had tried to stop the bus they were on. Occasionally they had seen some of them about the town, swaggering along the narrow streets and pushing the islanders into the gutter. Only one boy, hot-blooded enough to be defiant, had disputed their passage, and he was slammed against a wall and left huddled at its foot, his face bleeding, feebly spitting out teeth. Cotton's great fist clenched but Annoula had dragged at his arm and pulled him away.

They ate bread and sausage in a bar as they waited for the bus back across the island, drinking a solitary thin beer between them. The German soldiers puzzled Cotton. They had learned there were about three hundred of them, billeted in Panyioti's place, and Cotton couldn't make out why an island the size of Aeos – which had already been subjugated – needed three hundred tough soldiers in addition to the Luftwaffe units, lines of supply troops and engineers.

The bus was late and, as they continued to wait, the soldiers from the captured caique were halted nearby, their eyes bitter and angry, while the German soldiers who guarded them chatted to German pioneers who came up to stare. Cotton's heart felt like ice. How much longer would it be before the whole of the civilized world was standing sullen and cowed in front of the triumphant Nazis?

One of the staring Germans, a blond, blue-eyed, ideal Nazi superman, pushed forward. He was staggeringly handsome and eager to show off his ability to speak English.

'I sink ze var goes bedly for you, eh?' he said to one of the soldiers. 'But perhaps you do not know how to fight a bettle, hein?'

The man he addressed, a short, sturdy New Zealander with a face like a terrier, looked up under the lock of greasy dark hair that fell from beneath his helmet.

'Fuck off, you Nazi bastard,' he said quite clearly.

The other Germans gave a shout of laughter and the one who had spoken swung his fist in fury. The soldier staggered away, his lip bleeding. As he straightened up, the German glared.

'Vat do you say?' he demanded.

'I say "Fuck off, you Nazi bastard",' the soldier repeated firmly.

The German was about to use his fist again when he was dragged away by his friends and a ripple of clapping ran through the café. The New Zealander heard it and gave a mock bow as he wiped the blood from his lip with the back of his hand.

Cotton's big hands gripped the table in front of him. His face was like granite, his heavy jaw set, his eyes glittering and angry, and it required a tremendous physical effort to sit still. Annoula saw his distress and put her hand on his, staring at him intensely with her huge black eyes, transmitting her own quiet spirit through the touch of her fingers, trying to express without speaking her sorrow and her sympathy.

Then the German guards threw away their cigarettes and began to push the soldiers into line again. As they tramped off, their heavy boots crunching against the surface of the road, Annoula leaned forward. 'It will not always be like this,' she said.

Cotton found it hard to see a time when it might be different. The Nazis were swarming all over France, Holland, Belgium, Denmark, Norway, Bulgaria, Rumania, Yugoslavia and now

Greece. How much bloody worse could it get, he thought in an agony of shame.

Her hand was still on his, clutching it with thin strong fingers. It seemed to calm him and, as his heart stopped thudding in his chest, he let out his breath in a long shuddering sigh. Defeat was a terrible thing to watch.

The bus was already almost full as it arrived for the return journey. It seemed a good idea to go on into Ay Yithion to see Howard and ask the Varvaras' help in the matter of extra petrol, and Cotton sat in silence the whole way, unaware that he was clutching Annoula's small paw in his great fist.

Howard lay on a shabby bed in a whitewashed room, staring at the ceiling, and though he looked bored he seemed better and recognized Cotton at once.

' 'Lo, Royal,' he whispered. 'Gi'e us a kiss.'

Cotton smiled and pushed a couple of packets of cigarettes into his hand.

'We goin' to get away, Royal?'

'Yes,' Cotton said with certainty. 'We've nearly got the boat fixed. When we have, we'll come and collect you.'

'You won't forget?'

'No. We'll not forget.'

'Good old Royal. Always one to remember.'

Cotton flushed. 'They're red hot on remembering in the Marines,' he said gruffly.

Out in the blinding sunshine again, Cotton felt faintly depressed at Howard's weakness. Annoula was watching his expression. During the day, she had constantly studied him, almost able to read his thoughts. Her own family had been easy-going, devious and careless. Cotton was quite the opposite – meticulous, detailed, rigid in his attitude to duty and painfully honest in his execution of it. Disaster had drawn them together in a flood of fearful uncertainties and she had been conscious for some time of a growing warmth between them.

'He'll be all right,' Cotton said to her, trying to reassure himself more than anything else, and she listened to him solemnly, worried by a sense of uncertainty and insecurity such as she'd never known before.

As they entered the café, looking for the Varvaras, the questioning gaze of twenty different people settled on Cotton; but then the Varvaras entered and, as they sat down alongside him, the suspicious eyes turned aside, satisfied.

'They thought you might be a German,' old Varvara explained. 'There have been strangers about. They're looking for partisans.'

'*Are* there really partisans?' Cotton asked, thinking of the wretched group round Petrakis in the goatherds' cave.

Varvara's eyes blazed. 'Greeks are fighters,' he said. 'Didn't we throw Mussolini out? There are men in the hills near Cape Asigonia.'

'Communists?'

Varvara looked shrewdly at Cotton. 'There are Communists and Fascists and farmers and probably a priest or two. They have no politics. They are simply Greeks.' He shrugged. 'Unfortunately, they have no guns and soon they'll need guns.'

His son indicated the radio. 'They say the Germans are after the Corinth Canal. If they get that, they'll cut off the Peloponnese peninsula from the rest of Greece. There'll be no Thermopylae this time. It would leave the passes over the Pindus Mountains unguarded.'

His father leaned forward. 'You have this from the Prime Minister – Koryzis himself?'

The young man slammed a hand down on the table. 'I read!' he snapped. 'I listen to the radio! I am not blinded by a pride left over from the Golden Age. It's the end of the British army. The Germans are already saying that they will start the final evacuation of the mainland any day now and that then their aeroplanes at Yanitsa will have a better killing than they did in France and Norway! After that there will be only local resistance – and without guns.'

Cotton had been listening gloomily, feeling hopeless and helpless. Then he remembered he was a Royal – not somebody out of the back row of the chorus at the Windmill Theatre. He was supposed to know what to do, because his training told him what it was. And even if he weren't *sure* what it was, he could still go on trying, couldn't he?

His head jerked up. 'I know where there are guns,' he said abruptly.

The Varvaras sat up. 'Where?'

'In the goatherds' cave on the slope overlooking Xiloparissia Bay.'

The girl's eyes lifted quickly to Cotton's face but he ignored her.

'You sure?'

'May my eyes fall out.' Cotton fell back on his mother's way of insisting. 'May my tongue dry up.'

Varvara looked at the girl then back at Cotton.

'Do you know the cave?' Cotton asked.

'Everybody knows it. We shelter there when we're searching for snails. They come out when it rains and everybody goes looking for them. Sometimes we get caught in a second storm.'

'There are guns there. They were being carried by the British boat in Xiloparissia Bay to Antipalia for any resistance movement that might be started when the Germans came. When the Germans searched her, they missed them. They were taken up there by Greeks.'

'Which Greeks?'

The girl lifted her head. 'My cousin Chrysostomos,' she said quietly.

The Varvaras exchanged glances. 'That man!' In the old fisherman's words there was a whole world of contempt. 'He's nothing but a gangster, good only for boasting round the Kalani bars. Who's with him?'

'Two others. One of them came from Antipalia. Perhaps he learned about the guns there.'

Varvara reached across the table and laid a hand on Cotton's arm. 'You have done the island a great favour, my son,' he said.

'I want one from you in return,' Cotton said frankly.

187

The old man sat back and glanced at his son. 'Which is?' he said slowly.

Cotton explained their need for any extra petrol they could get.

Varvara smiled. He seemed relieved it was no more. 'Leave it to me,' he said.

When Cotton started back the track was deep with mud, and rivulets of water were running off the mountains, but suddenly the clouds rolled back and the sun came out hotly, and steam began to rise from the rinsed earth. Somehow it gave him encouragement. At the top of the hill, looking down into Xiloparissia Bay, he stopped, listening to the hum of an aircraft. A flight of Junkers 87s – the dreaded Stuka dive-bombers – were flying along the coastline and he watched them swing inland to where the new airstrip was being built, knowing that they meant death to some poor bastard, and probably the end for some fine ship.

Feeling unbelievably alone, he set off down the hill in silence. At the bottom, Docherty met him. He seemed to have forgotten the beating he'd received. 'See anything?' he asked.

'Only a bunch of swaddies the caiques brought in. The poor bastards were marched away to be prisoners of war.'

Docherty said nothing because the idea of being a prisoner, of standing behind a barbed wire fence for the rest of the war, without girls and dancing and fornication, was a horror beyond his imagination. Then he forced a grin. 'One thing,' he said. 'I've finished the starboard engine. Tomorrow I'll finish the port engine. All we need now is some more petrol.'

Cotton was so surprised at Docherty's success he managed a smile through his depression. 'I've arranged it,' he said.

Docherty whistled and did a few fancy steps round him. 'Good old Royal,' he chirruped. 'You're enough to make a man grow two heads.'

Suddenly Cotton felt better, and part of a team once more.

12

Lieutenant Ehrhardt's face was worried. 'Our two hundred and fifty friends at Panyioti's place,' he said. 'Perhaps the islanders don't know who they are, Herr Major, but you know and I know, and, now it seems, so do the men at the airstrip.'

Baldamus' eyes grew cold. 'I hope they're not talking,' he said.

'Only among themselves. They're grumbling that they ought to be used to help. They claim there's a hell of a lot to do and they feel they should give a hand.'

Baldamus' nose wrinkled. 'It's nothing to do with them. If they want special treatment, they should join special units.'

Ehrhardt shrugged. 'It's not as simple as that,' he said. 'We're also getting complaints from the villagers at Xinthos. A girl was raped. Chickens have been stolen. Pigs have vanished. They know damn well who was responsible and they'll soon start asking themselves, who the hell *are* these damn people?'

Baldamus said nothing and Ehrhardt went on indignantly. 'They need to do something instead of simply sitting on their backsides wrecking Panyioti's place. According to my information, they've torn it apart. What they haven't stuffed into kitbags to take back to Germany, they're burning to make fires, or swapping with the villagers for food and booze.'

Baldamus stared at his fingernails. 'Try having a word with their commanding officer, Captain Haussmann,' he said. 'I'm told he's a reasonable chap.'

'Not that reasonable,' Ehrhardt said shortly. 'I can't get near him. I've tried. They're not allowing anyone within a mile of the

189

place. They've thrown up road blocks and they stop everyone who goes near. Needless to say, nobody tries.'

Baldamus began to frown again. He hadn't really expected trouble of this sort and it was clear that Ehrhardt's sympathies lay with the men at the airfield.

'They're not very popular, are they?' he said.

'Élite units never are. What they need is some hard work or some hard fighting.'

Baldamus pulled a face. 'I suspect they'll get plenty of both of those before long,' he observed mildly. 'Very well, I'll go and see Haussmann. Perhaps he'll listen to me. I'll tell him my instructions about keeping the place sweet, and ask him to keep his men under control. After all, they're not barbarians. They've got to measure up to the rules. If necessary, I'll see that one or two of them are picked up by the Provost Department and offer to court martial them. That ought to make them think.'

'Unless it brings the whole damn lot down on our necks,' Ehrhardt said. 'These special units are very much their own masters; especially since Holland and France. They've got it firmly in their heads that they've won the war and deserve special treatment.'

'Not from me,' Baldamus said. 'There's too much going on, on this island.'

There was indeed, even beyond the scope of Baldamus' command.

The following day, they decided there was nothing much more they could do and that night they were all so exhausted they slept like logs. Except for Cotton, who sat dry-mouthed and red-eyed on the deck on watch until Bisset appeared, languid as ever, just before dawn to take his place.

'I'll try to get a couple of hours,' Cotton said.

'Make it four.'

'Two'll do.'

Cotton woke as if to an alarm clock to get them all on their feet. Shoving the canister of chloro-sulphonic from *Claudia* alongside the other, they poured the contents of two of the drums of petrol into the tanks by means of a home-made funnel.

'If we use one engine at a time,' Cotton said, 'we can stretch out the juice.'

'Not to Crete,' Docherty pointed out.

'Doesn't matter. However far away we get from here, we're that much nearer safety. The number of RN ships there are in this neck of the woods at the moment is bound to help. We've only to get across their course for them to spot us.'

They examined the work they'd done on the hull and the engines minutely, and during the afternoon Annoula returned from Yithion with a basket of food and two bottles of wine. Her eyes were alight and she seemed pleased, as though their escape was a matter of great importance to her. She seemed even to have forgiven Docherty, who went out of his way to exert his crazy charm on her. With Cotton she was thoughtful and silent and he had a feeling that in her silence there was an accusation.

'I *had* to tell the Varvaras about the guns,' he explained. 'They weren't brought here for your cousin and his friends. Men died bringing them. Besides, I don't trust him and I'll feel safer now he's not got them.'

For a moment she remained silent. Then she lifted her head. 'Of course,' she said. 'It is safer that way.'

He felt relieved that she understood. She reminded him a little of his sister, Rhoda, the best one of the three, the one without the spiteful tongue. She had married a Greek waiter who worked with his father and had a horde of black-eyed children who screamed around the place, not in good King's English but in a jargon of two languages that had always irritated him.

'What will you do when we've gone?' he asked. 'Petrakis is a fanatic and he'll probably think you betrayed him.'

She gave a shrug. It had an element of hopelessness about it that wrenched at Cotton's stiff soldierly heart.

'I will get the Varvaras to take me to Mykos as soon as they can,' she said. 'I have friends there. They will look after me.'

'Good friends?'

'Not very. But they are kind.'

It seemed a wretched sort of future for her, especially after she'd jeopardized her life on Aeos by the help she'd given, and suddenly the idea of leaving without her seemed cold and harsh. 'Come with us,' Cotton said.

She shook her head. 'I belong here,' she said. 'I am not English. I am Greek. I would be lost among the English.'

Again Cotton almost told her of his own background, but he'd spent so much of his life dodging it that the words stuck in his throat, and he backed away from the warm feeling that had taken hold of him.

Among other things, she had brought the news that the Greek Epirus army had folded up and that the rest of the Greek forces were disintegrating and were expected to surrender any day. The Royal Air Force, hammered over Athens and the Piraeus in an attempt to protect the capital, had reached the end of its tether, while the British army was clinging to the last ditches of Thermopylae. The shadow of catastrophe, as great as that of Dunkirk, hung over them.

During the evening, as Gully started on the final repairs to the stern, Cotton slapped the paint the Varvaras had brought over the patches he'd put on the bow. When he'd finished, they all stood back and studied the effect.

'Looks like a bloody big dipper at 'Ull fairground,' Gully said. 'A burnt-out big dipper.'

Certainly *Loukia* presented an odd sight. Outwardly, with her scorched sides and smashed wheelhouse, she still looked a wreck, but by this time they were all growing enthusiastic because the next step would be to start the engines. Below, in the forecastle, the two Lewises and the 20 mm, stripped down, checked and freshly oiled by Kitcat, waited only for mounting. On Cotton's instructions, Gully unscrewed the splinters of the engine-room door.

'You'll get a bloody row through there,' he pointed out.

'We'll chance it,' Cotton said. 'And at least, I'll be able to keep an eye on Docherty.'

No one came near the bay and they continued to wonder why

the Germans showed no more interest. When he brought the ropes and blocks they were going to use to haul themselves off, old Varvara gave them some hint.

'There is something going on,' he said. 'We went round to Kalani with a load of lambs. They told us there are more caiques at the Piraeus and hundreds of Germans. They are clearly planning something.'

'What about the British?' Cotton asked.

'A few of them have got across into the Peloponnese. The Germans are trying to cut them off. If they get the bridges over the Corinth Canal, they will be marooned in Thessaly and Sterea Hellas, within reach of the bombers on the Salonika airfields. They are also on Rhodes, and that means their bombers will be right across the route of your ships from Egypt.'

'And here?' Cotton asked.

'They are still working on the airstrip. They've pulled down all the windmills and they are landing drums of fuel for the aircraft.'

'Stukas?'

Varvara shrugged. 'Some. But transport planes too.'

He left them a bottle of raki which Cotton hid ashore as soon as he'd gone.

The next day they installed the extra pump aft and Docherty primed the engines. There was a tremendous feeling of excitement and Docherty's face was tense, as though he knew what rested on his skill. They had put the anchor out to port so that they couldn't be pulled on to the shore by the creep of the engines, and Cotton stood on the stern, watching while Docherty finished his preparations in the engine room. He could hear him whistling between his teeth and occasionally addressing remarks to Kitcat alongside him. The starter motor whined but there was no response and Cotton's heart sank.

'Try a new flint,' Bisset said softly.

There was a long silence and they could hear Docherty muttering. Eventually his head appeared.

'Hold your hat on,' he said. 'This time.'

When the explosion of the starboard engine starting came, Cotton wasn't expecting it, and it made him jump. Docherty grinned briefly at him through the door of the engine room, then the port engine exploded into life too. Docherty's face appeared again, a beaming smile across it.

'Told you they'd work,' he said.

Cotton stared at the cliffs. 'Think the Germans could hear?'

'Only if they're listening.'

Cotton swung round to Bisset. 'Let's get the mast clear,' he said. 'It's time to spruce up a bit.'

With the exhausts poppling encouragingly astern, they unlashed the lines and unscrewed the shackles and turnbuckles that had supported the shattered mast and pushed it ashore among the trees.

'Unless we run into a gale,' Cotton said, 'we ought to be able to make it in easy stages: Serifos. Sifnos. Sikinos. Folegandros. Then a dash for Suda Bay.' His smile died. 'If the Germans haven't got there first,' he ended.

They rigged up ropes to the trees further out, and dropped a heavy anchor well astern from the dinghy, with the rope running to the stern post. Then they hauled in the chain to their own anchor which they'd dropped off the port quarter so they couldn't swing unexpectedly on to the rocks.

'We ought to make it,' Cotton said. 'She's floating pretty high astern without the 20-mill and the petrol.'

Annoula was smiling at them from alongside the wheelhouse.

'You have done it,' she said.

Cotton pulled a face. 'Not me. Them. I'm not clever.'

'You are cleverer than you think.'

He took her hand and pulled her into the wheelhouse. 'This is where you'll have to leave us,' he said. 'Unless you come with us.'

Her smile died and she shook her head.

'I'm a Greek,' she said.

'You needn't worry about that,' Cotton said. 'There are plenty of Greeks in London.' Then, before he realized what he'd done, he'd blurted out the very thing he'd tried all along to hide. 'I'm one.'

Her eyes lifted to his, wondering and doubtful.

'You are Greek?'

He felt like biting his tongue but he was a blunt man who believed in facing up to things and, having betrayed himself, he could see no point in trying to hide it any more. 'My mother was Greek, wasn't she?' he said. 'She came from the Piraeus. A long time ago. She came to London to work for relatives there and stayed when she met my father. His father was a Greek. He came from Athens, I think. I don't really know. I never met him and I've never been to Greece except with the navy.'

She still seemed very doubtful and he pressed on. 'How do you think I learned to speak Greek?' he said. 'Nobody in England learns Greek at school. Only French and German, and not so bloody much of that.'

He hadn't ever intended to tell her but it had slipped out as a means of helping her in her distress. She was clearly tempted but then she gave him another look, her eyes large. There were dark rings under them, as there were under the eyes of them all. They had all worked harder in the last few days than they'd ever worked in their lives before, and had slept a great deal less. Now that it was finished, though, he could see she was uncertain of her place in his world, afraid to leave her homeland and the familiar things of her own country. She shook her head again, firmly, and turned away.

'I will make tea,' she said quietly.

It was late afternoon and dusk was not far away when the Varvaras' caiques arrived. The old man seemed excited.

'I have told Nichomacos Delageorgis about the guns,' he said.

'Who's Nichomacos Delageorgis?'

'He owns land near Skoinia and when the Germans came he went into hiding in the hills near Cape Asigonia. He is much respected. If anyone can lead a resistance on this island, he can.'

'What about Petrakis?'

'Aie!' The old man's hand came down in a chopping motion.

'That one is only a talker, a back-street brawler who uses ELAS as an excuse for what he does. Delageorgis will deal with him.'

The younger Varvara was staring out to sea. He seemed nervous and anxious to start work. 'We haven't much time,' he said. 'We have to report back before dark, and they've set up a look-out post on Cape Kastamanitsa to stop anybody escaping to the south.'

Wire hawsers were attached to the caiques' sterns and the two boats started their engines. When the hawsers were taut, Docherty started *Loukia*'s engines. The thump and crash as they exploded into life seemed loud enough to be heard all over the island.

'Right,' Cotton said. 'Bisset, Gully, Kitcat – lay on the kedge rope.' The girl was alongside him and he nodded to the quarter rope. As she took hold of it and began to pull, he waved to the caiques. 'Give it all she's got, Docherty,' he yelled.

The water astern began to thrash and boil. The whine of the engines grew higher and a dirty froth floated forward as the screws churned up the sea bed. For a long time, Cotton thought they weren't going to do it. Then he felt a shiver run through *Loukia*, different from the shuddering the engines were causing, and he knew she was sliding into deeper water.

'Pull!' he yelled and, leaving the girl, he added his weight to that of Bisset, Gully and Kitcat. The water at the stern of the caiques surged. Then suddenly he realized the rope in his hand was no longer taut and he was hauling it in, and the boat had settled comfortably, her bows lower, like a duck taking to a pond, afloat and alive once more.

His wash-out signal stopped the caiques and, as they came alongside, he grinned at them and held up his thumb.

Bisset had taken a boathook and was probing down by the stern. 'We've got a good three feet below the rudder, I reckon,' he said. 'That's enough for safety. When do we leave?'

Cotton frowned. 'What about the petrol?' he said.

Varvara grinned. 'I know where there is some,' he said. 'My brother-in-law found it. I'll be round with it in the morning before daylight.'

That evening, after the Varvaras and the girl had gone, Cotton wrote up the log and they sat round the forecastle table to discuss their next move. They were all irritable now and worried with the fretfulness of exhaustion. They were dirty and oil-stained, their clothes marked by the blackened ash of the charred interior of the boat. Bisset's sleeve hung loose where it had caught on a bramble as they had crossed the ridge, and their legs and arms were all scarred and marked. Cotton's face was blue-black with bristle and the others all had varying degrees of beard, differing in colour from Docherty's Irish black through Bisset's yellow fuzz to Gully's mottled grey, as tatty-looking as the skin of an old terrier.

Cotton knew he had driven them too hard at times, but he'd also driven himself because he'd known all along that they hadn't any time to waste. On the night when Docherty had fixed the pump in place he'd ended working by the light of Varvara's candles.

The mutter of guns to the north sounded louder and the sky seemed full of aeroplane engines.

'Something's starting,' Docherty said.

'Probably the evacuation of the mainland.'

'Poor bloody navy!'

Cotton had made up a rough chart from the torn and blood-stained fragments he'd salvaged from *Claudia*'s wrecked wheel-house. It wasn't very satisfactory but it gave him some idea of the sea around Aeos and a rough direction to steer. His mind churning slowly, he had applied himself to it as he'd seen Patullo and Shaw and other officers do.

'We'll leave as soon from now as we can,' he announced.

'My engines'll get us home,' Docherty said.

Bisset gave him a look of contempt. 'They probably will,' he agreed. 'But it isn't your engines that are getting us back to Suda.'

Docherty's head jerked up. 'It isn't?'

'No.'

'What is it then?'

'Guts.'

Docherty looked bewildered. He hadn't noticed much in the

way of guts about. To Docherty, guts were something that went with fighting. In his bar-room brawl of a career, he had always mistaken strength for courage.

'Whose guts?' he asked. 'Mine?'

Bisset gave a shout of laughter. 'You, old son, are nothing but beer-cheapened hoddy-noddy! No, they belong to our good friend, Cotton. Just try to *stop* him taking you home. You might as well attempt to halt the Thames–Clyde express.'

Docherty stared at Cotton, then at Bisset, and though he would rather have died than admit it, he had a shrewd suspicion Bisset was right. 'You slay me,' he said.

There was a long silence and Cotton looked embarrassed. He pretended to fiddle with the lists he'd kept, cleared his throat, said 'Well – ,' then turned in desperation to Docherty in an attempt to restore his good humour.

'Are the batteries all right?' he asked. 'There'll be no mistake?'

'They'll start,' Docherty sniffed.

'Right.' Cotton looked round them, glad to be occupied again. 'When we leave, Gully'll have to handle the port Lewis, so you'd better show him how it works, Kitcat.'

Bisset watched him as he spread out the scraps of chart. 'Know anything about navigation?' he asked.

'Not a bloody thing! But if we head south we ought to make it.'

'What about the compass?'

'Ought to be swung. But *I* can't do it. I don't know how. But Crete's right across our path so we ought to hit it somewhere if we head towards the sun.'

'What about the extra petrol?'

'With what Varvara brings, we ought to get as far as Sifnos, perhaps even further. We might even make Iros and get some more out of that mayor.'

'A tommy-gun stuck up his nostril ought to encourage him,' Docherty grinned.

As they broke up, Cotton climbed ashore to look at the boat. Without her mast she had a sleek look about her, low and fast, and he decided it might even help them slip past any prowling Italian MAS boats that might be about.

She looked incomplete, however, and he climbed ashore with the axe and cut down a long pole from one of the trees. Trimming it carefully, he lashed it firmly to the stump of the broken mast.

'What's that for?' Kitcat asked.

'The ensign,' Cotton said. He studied the new mast from all angles; then he turned to the Canadian. 'Come on,' he said. 'We've got things to do.'

'Such as what?'

'You remember where you hid that money Samways was carrying?'

'Sure.'

'I think it's time to get it aboard.'

Concerned about whom he should leave on board, Cotton had decided Bisset was probably the most reliable. He was a funny bloke, but at least he had a cool head, a good temper, and a sense of humour; and Cotton had once heard it said that a man who could make you laugh was of more value when you were in trouble than a bore who could only shoot straight.

Bisset received the news without turning a hair. He gave Cotton an interested glance. 'Thought there was something I hadn't been told,' he admitted cheerfully.

Cotton looked quickly at him. 'Did it show?' he asked.

'At times, old son, I felt like hitting you over the head, because it was obvious to anyone possessed of an atom of intelligence that you were hugging some secret to your bosom.'

Cotton flushed. 'There was also money on board,' he growled. 'How much?'

'Twenty thousand quid.'

Bisset's eyebrows rose but he showed no other sign of interest. Perhaps, Cotton decided, it was because he came from a wealthy family and money didn't impress him much. He saw Docherty trying to catch what they were saying and, without thinking much more about it, he slapped a tommy-gun into his hands and told him what they were about to do.

'Money?' Docherty said. 'Where?'

'Up the cliff.'

'Whose money?'

'The government's. It was on *Loukia* when she ran aground.'

Docherty thought for a while. 'How much?' he asked.

'Twenty thousand quid.'

'How do you know?'

'Patullo told me. In Suda Bay.'

'Twenty thousand quid!' Docherty sounded awed. 'You're a close bastard, aren't you? That'd buy a few pints of old and mild. We could even nip away somewhere neutral like Turkey. With all the bints you want – black, white and khaki. Do we get to have a look at it?'

'The box's locked,' Kitcat said. 'Samways had the key but it disappeared with everything he possessed – his watch, his wallet – when he was killed.'

'Pity,' Docherty said. 'I'd have liked to have a look at twenty thousand nicker. I'll never get the chance again.'

PART THREE
Attack

1

The heat was on in Suda Bay. The whole place was working at a frantic speed.

Through the window of the hut near Retimo, soldiers could be seen digging gun pits round the harbour and pushing up barricades of sandbags. A lorry ground past, churning up the dust in a yellow cloud that coated the trees and turned the grass to a drab khaki. A staff car followed it, a general in the back, his face grim, staring ahead, busy with his thoughts.

'This place's beginning to look like Troy before the siege,' Ponsonby said. His grey suit shabbier now with dust marks on the elbows and knees, his collar stained and rumpled, he was staring from the doorway across the water.

Kennard said nothing. His mind was still on the boats and the men he'd lost at Aeos. The activity around him passed him by. The anxiety everyone felt, from the general down to the simplest gunner or ordinary seaman, was obvious. The Germans were coming but nobody knew which beach they were going to land on. Kennard tried to shove it out of his mind.

'You still worrying about those chaps we sent to Aeos?' Ponsonby asked.

'Of course I am. I don't like sending chaps out on a job and then abandoning 'em.' Kennard turned back to the list he was perusing. The names on it were all familiar to him. 'At Nauplia embarking troops – *Phoebe, Stuart, Hyacinth, Ulster Prince, Gleneard*. At Raftis embarking troops – *Calcutta, Perth, Glengyle*. On passage – *Grimsby, Vendetta, Waterhen, Themani, Zealand* –'

The list went on for another two pages and showed pretty well every available ship in the Mediterranean. What had started as a relieving expedition to snatch Greece from the hands of the Italians had turned into another Dunkirk. Already, it was clear there was to be no orderly embarkation but another scratch job in small boats from open shores.

As the ships came into Suda Bay, the weary, dusty men on board all told the same depressing story: shortages of aircraft, weapons, vehicles and petrol, with constant bombing and casualties, and behind it the threat of ultimate catastrophe. The unclouded sky and calm weather were a help and a hindrance at the same time. While they assisted in the evacuation, they also aided the Luftwaffe as they came over the mountains in the crystal-clear atmosphere that allowed the gaze to travel a hundred miles without interference from haze.

Among the indented rocky coasts with their doll's-house villages backed by the green of olive groves edging to deep blue waters clear for a hundred feet down, men were streaming south, searching for a safe place to embark. The situation was deteriorating hour by hour. With the Greek Epirus force laying down its weapons, the British army was clinging to its last ditch defences in a hopeless disarray of orders, counter-orders and lack of orders. Troops heading for the coast had no real idea where they were going and independent evacuations were starting everywhere in merchantmen, ferry-boats, caiques and yachts. Along the coast road, Dorniers, flying low over the sea, were shooting up the traffic so that the route was marked by burning vehicles.

Things had been left too late as usual, and the navy, trying to carry on with its mass of routine duties – succouring the army in North Africa, helping besieged Tobruk, escorting convoys through the eastern Mediterranean, victualling, fuelling, ammunitioning – needed time to marshal its resources. Kennard was well aware that the chances of being able to send help to Aeos were pathetically slim.

'I can't see what else we can do,' Ponsonby said.

Neither could Kennard, but he was still hopeful of trying. It was just possible that they might get somebody to take his ship to Aeos to have a look in case there was anyone on one of the beaches waving and hoping still to be picked up. Kennard had already broached the subject to the admiral and got a firm 'No' for his trouble, but there were more light forces due from Alexandria in the next few days and he might just prevail on some ship's captain. Kennard felt his responsibility keenly. He – and nobody else – had sent two boats into Aeos and he considered it his duty to make some effort to check whether the crews had survived. Two dozen men weren't many in the mass that were being lifted from the Greek mainland but he still felt he ought to try.

Major Renatus von Boenigk Baldamus had just finished an excellent dinner and was in no mood to exert himself much.

As he sat back the telephone rang. He picked it up, listened, then slammed it down again and looked up at Ehrhardt with a smile.

'The Italian naval launch's arrived, Ehrhardt,' he said. 'Armed to the teeth. I've become an admiral.' He fished among the papers on his desk and tossed a flimsy at Ehrhardt.

'Telephone message,' he said. 'Arrived this afternoon. Whoever it was, refused to identify themselves. It says there's aviation spirit in Ay Yithion.'

'Whose aviation spirit?' Ehrhardt asked.

'Have *we* lost any?'

'I gather some's been missed from the dump at Yanitsa. *Klepsiklepsi*, the Greeks call it.'

'Means scrounging,' Baldamus said. 'I think someone had better look into it.'

'Who?'

Baldamus moved a few papers about. 'Well, we've got an SS unit now to look after security, haven't we, and didn't we get a couple of the leather-coated fraternity from the Gestapo today?'

'That's right. Investigating pilfering of rations.'

Baldamus smiled. 'Well, let them investigate this too,' he said. 'It's right up their street. They'll probably tear the balls off some poor devil to find out where it is but I expect they'll end up with the petrol.' He turned up the sheet of paper he was looking for and glanced at it. 'Untersturmbannführer Fernbrugge. He's your man, Ehrhardt. Let him know, will you? I expect they'll want to lay on an operation to murder everybody on the island.'

Ehrhardt frowned. 'I don't like it,' he said. 'I don't have the conscience to accept the sort of things those bastards do.'

'It's something we all have to live with, Ehrhardt,' Baldamus said equably. 'When we've won the war, we'll all have to examine our consciences and find out if there isn't some way we can run Germany without these gentry.'

Cotton was the first awake. It was the sound of aircraft that brought him to life. They were transports and he wondered yet again what they were doing on Aeos.

Aware of being out of the mainstream of events and conscious of a feeling of not belonging, he watched the aeroplanes with a sick heart. Cotton was a man who needed other men about him and was at his best as part of a team. All his training had been devised to that end. It didn't alter the situation that he was still running the show, however. It was a hard fact to face but Cotton was a stubborn man, with the stubbornness of a bull in a bull-ring. The more he was goaded by adverse conditions, the harder he fought, and climbing into the dinghy, he rowed about the narrow bay in the growing light, dropping the lead line over at intervals and noting the readings on a piece of paper torn from the log. When *Loukia* had entered the bay, she had smashed her screws and rudders on a rock and he had no intention that she should do the same as she left.

They ate bully beef and biscuit for breakfast and were waiting on deck as the sun appeared. As its first glow came between tumultuous clouds, Cotton began to grow worried.

'Where's Varvara?' he said.

An hour later there was still no sign of the Greek caique and he felt he could wait no longer.

'I'm going into Yithion,' he announced. 'I want to know where that petrol is and arrange to pick up the kid.'

Taking one of the curtains from the captain's cabin, he rolled Patullo's revolver in it and pushed a few extra rounds into his trouser-pocket. The sky was dark with the possibility of rain as he set off up the slope. It was full of aircraft and he identified them as Junkers 87s and 88s, which could mean only one thing. The navy was copping it somewhere to the east.

Ay Yithion stood out sharply like a group of white stones. Even the gulls looked like spectres against the darkness of the sky, and the colour of the apple and peach orchards bordered by ilex, walnut and mulberry shone against the pink spurs of oleander. The place was quiet and there seemed to be an atmosphere of nervousness about it.

Annoula was almost the first person he saw. She was hurrying past the harbour, looking worried, and had more news of the German look-out post on Cape Kastamanitsa, set up to watch for Greeks trying to escape south.

Cotton frowned. A look-out with a radio meant that they'd be unable to escape until after dark. In daylight the Messerschmitts would be down on them in a matter of minutes.

'Where's Varvara?' he demanded.

Her eyes were scared. 'I don't know,' she said. 'Something's happening. They got a message from Kalani. But they're going to bring the petrol as soon as they can. I was just coming to tell you. They've heard that the Germans are coming and they've been hiding it.' She pointed beyond the harbour and Cotton saw the younger Varvara's boat moored there. 'Athanasios took his boat out,' she said. 'He thought it would be safer.'

The uncertainty that seemed to hang over Ay Yithion affected Cotton and he looked about him nervously. 'I'd better arrange to have the kid brought back to us,' he said. 'Then I've got to see Varvara. I'm scared something's going to go wrong because we've got to wait until dark before we can leave, and that's twelve hours away.'

As they headed into the village, they saw people lifting their heads and staring towards the north. At first Cotton thought it was aircraft they were listening to, then he realized it was the sound of lorry engines.

'The Germans!' The speaker was an old man who came hurrying down the flat steps of the main street. He looked terrified and was pointing over his shoulder. 'I saw them from my window.'

Immediately the place came to life and people began to hurry children indoors. The sponge fishermen, stuffing their work into sacks, vanished among the houses, and the old men mending nets for their sons packed up their twine and followed.

'Not the café,' Annoula said quickly. 'The church of Ayia Triadha.'

'I've got to get the kid.' Cotton turned but she snatched at his hand and pulled him with her. He had just wrenched his hand away again to go and find Howard when a man yelled and he was caught up in a flurry of running people. Annoula's fingers, thin but strong, grabbed his own again and this time, unwillingly, he allowed himself to be pulled into the church.

It was a tumbledown place full of washed-out colours and insipid pictures, and the smell of incense, herbs, beeswax, candles and candle-smoke. Faded and pale, the two main ikons of our Lord and our Lady had been prominently placed and Annoula crossed herself and kissed them devoutly. Then she bought and lit a candle and Cotton did the same, aware of the irony of Patullo's revolver clutched inside the curtain in his hand.

Other people seemed to have had the same idea and the church was full. The priest, a big man with a fringe of black beard who looked like a farmer, was invoking the saints as they kneeled, intoning the service with the aid of a cantor.

Outside, everything seemed to have become silent. Then they heard the grinding of the lorry engines.

'This is my Body . . . . This is my Blood. Thine of Thine Own we offer Thee . . . .'

The intoning voice droned on but, their ears tuned to what was going on outside, no one was listening. Lorry doors and tail-gates banged methodically and they heard the clump of nailed boots.

'By the Holy Spirit . . . .'

'Amen, Amen, Amen –'

The chant was cut across abruptly by a burst of machine-gun fire that jerked every head up as one. Frightened eyes stared towards the door.

The priest, who had been preparing to offer Communion, was standing as if petrified, holding the bread and the wine and the spoon he used. His face was expressionless but from the way his eyes were working Cotton could see he was thinking fast.

A man in front of Cotton rose to his feet and began to leave the church. As he did so, there was another long burst of machine-gun fire, then a scream, the harsh dry scream of a shocked woman, and a series of harsh shouts outside, and the man began to run. At once, other men rose and followed him, followed by the woman. The priest was still standing by the altar, motionless. As the church doors burst open and the congregation spilled outside, there were more shouts, then more shots and screams.

Finally the priest moved, beckoning the few remaining people in the church towards him. Annoula seemed to be petrified with terror and Cotton dragged her to her feet, and they ran down the aisle towards the front of the church just as the priest disappeared. Pushing through the door beyond the altar where he had vanished, they found themselves in a small room full of varnished brown wood and pink-washed walls, the register open on a desk, along-side it the pair of down-at-heel boots the priest wore about the village. A picture of the Virgin Mary, its peeling tinfoil frame held in place by a piece of sticking plaster, stared at them. The priest opened a door and pointed to a narrow alley beyond.

The few people who had been left in church crowded through after them and began to run, dispersing as they went. The shooting was coming more often now and the air was filled with despairing and agonized screaming and the shouts of men. The smell of smoke and the crackling of flames beyond the church grew stronger and, as they pushed past a line of nets and octopus drying in the sun, they caught a glimpse of German soldiers holding tommy-guns. They had dragged outside all the men who'd been in the café eating rolls and drinking their morning coffee and lined them up against the wall with their hands in the air. For a second they were fully occupied and Cotton snatched at Annoula's hand and dived into a whitewashed alleyway that rose in front of them, shallow step by shallow step along the hillside. Above them, Cotton noticed, the rain clouds had receded and the sky was full of long rinsed lines fading through apricot to yellow; then they were running along a lifting alleyway topped with wet bougainvillaea and dripping strands of honeysuckle and cacti against a stark white wall.

The shooting seemed to have intensified and kept coming in regular bursts now, and as they climbed they could see dark brown-yellow smoke lifting into the sky.

'What are they doing?' Annoula panted.

As they climbed, they heard a shout and the clump of feet behind them and had to dive into another alley running along the side of the hill. There was a yard full of dust and crowded with chickens, and they ran through them, sending them flying in a squawking cloud of feathers. Pushing Annoula over a low wall, Cotton climbed after her to fall on top of her on the other side.

They were on the outskirts of the village now, hidden from the road to Kalani, as it ran round the curve of the hill by a thick screen of aloes. Through the heavy spiked leaves he could see a blindfolded donkey, shaded by a walnut tree, plodding round a well, then he saw a German car moving slowly up the road with two civilians in it. There was a small scouting vehicle behind it and several men moving alongside. Grabbing Annoula round the waist, he pulled her down among the long stalks of dried grass.

'*Wo sind sie?*' The harsh voice was on the other side of the wall and, as the girl gasped with terror, he clapped a big square hand over her mouth and pulled her to him, enfolding her in his big arms to hold her still and quieten her terror. Her fingers clutched at his shirt and he could feel her shuddering in his grasp.

The voices sounded nearer now but, as he removed his hand from her mouth to unwrap the revolver, he realized the footsteps beyond the wall had moved away and the voices were growing fainter. For a long time, they remained silent, clutching each other in the shadows beneath the aloes, hidden from the road by the long grass.

'Why? Why, Cotton, why?' The girl's mouth was so close to his face he could feel her breath on his cheek. 'What are they doing? They're destroying the whole village.'

Her arms went round his body in terror and he felt her shaking violently. He pulled her closer, holding her against the wall, her face against his, one hand round her under her breast, so that he could feel the beating of her heart through her thin yellow shirt.

'Perhaps they found out that Varvara was helping us,' he whispered. 'Perhaps they learned about the petrol.'

'But how? How could they? Why should they do this to Yithion?'

The shooting seemed to have died away now, and all they could hear was the wailing of women. Then they saw the German car in the distance move away and the soldiers on the road move back to their own vehicle and climb into it. It moved down the hill nearer to the village and soon afterwards they saw it parked and four men moving forward carrying a stretcher made from a torn-off door. Even at that distance, Cotton could see that one of them was carrying a khaki blouse and he knew the figure on the stretcher was Howard.

'They've got the kid,' he said.

Her eyes probed the depths of his distress and, as he moved, almost as though he intended to dispute what was happening below them, she clung to him tighter, her fingers digging into the flesh of his arms. The lorry moved away and another half dozen vehicles, with soldiers sitting in them, upright like dummies, followed it. They seemed untouched, as though they had committed no crime, clean, wholesome-looking men, but they were sitting very still and not talking much.

They watched the lorries disappear over the brow of the hill but they still didn't move. The sun was hot now and the little hiding place against the wall was warm. Cotton, who had been peering at the road through the broad thick leaves of the aloes, turned. A pair of huge, frightened charcoal eyes were staring straight into his and for the first time he became aware of the warmth of Annoula's body against his, and the soft flesh of her breast under his fingers. Abruptly he snatched his hand away and stood up, moving the palm guiltily against his trousers as if to wipe away the feelings of warmth and life. Her eyes followed him. She looked desperately small and frail.

'I've got to get back,' he said. 'I've got to get to the boat.'

She seemed to come back to the present with a jerk. She pulled her skirt down where it had ridden up over her thighs and scrambled to her knees.

'We've got to get away,' Cotton said. It surprised him that he was able to make up his mind so easily, that he was able to abandon Howard without any agony of guilt. He supposed this was what ships' captains, generals and leaders had to do all the time but he'd never supposed it would ever happen to him or that he'd be able to face up to it so easily. But the elementary facts were clear. There was nothing they could do for Howard. He was a prisoner and it was beyond their strength and resources to free him. The only thing he could do now was make sure everyone else who depended on him was safe.

Annoula was staring towards the village and the smoke, her face desolate and wretched. 'I must find Varvara,' she said.

'For Christ's sake, take care!' For the first time, Cotton was thinking of her safety and she gave him a look that was frightened and uncertain.

He lifted his head cautiously and stared over the wall. There was no sign of life but he could see a thick column of smoke lifting above the houses near the harbour.

'Have they gone?'

'I think so.'

He pushed her over the stones and they moved cautiously down the alley towards the harbour, Cotton holding her hand in his. She made no move to withdraw it. Then they saw the body of a man lying in a doorway, blood splashing the white walls, and a sobbing woman crouched near it, clutched by two screaming children.

'Why do you leave us?' she was wailing as she pressed at her temples in her grief. 'Why must they do this to you?'

Sickened and shocked, they turned out of the alley and into the narrow, descending set of shallow steps that was the main street. Across one of the steps, a donkey sprawled dead with its load, its owner spread-eagled alongside it, his sightless eyes staring at the sky.

They began now to meet more people and see more bodies. The priest was intoning a vigil.

Down by the harbour the village was well ablaze and the air was full of flying sparks and crackling timber and the nauseating smell of death. Men and children were running with buckets from the sea, but there weren't many men and most of the women seemed dazed. There were two or three dozen bodies sprawled outside the café and Cotton stared at them with narrowed eyes. The Germans had clearly shot everybody they'd found inside.

'Don't go down there,' he warned.

As Annoula shook her head, he pulled her into a doorway. He needed to get back to the familiar sound of English voices and the feeling of being part of the navy.

'We'll be leaving at dusk,' he said. 'I wouldn't like to leave without seeing you again.'

She stared at him with an agonized expression so that he pressed on in a stumbling mutter, his eyes refusing to meet hers. 'To say goodbye.' He tried to explain. 'You know what I mean. That sort of thing. You've all put up with a lot for us.'

She waited until his eyes finally met hers. 'I go to church and believe in God.' She sounded like Cotton's mother on Sundays, arguing with his father who preferred to stay in bed. 'I'm not my

213

cousin Chrysostomos. I will do anything to help anybody stand up to these anti-Christs.'

Her black eyes blazed then she reached up on tiptoe to kiss his cheek.

'Go with God, Cotton!'

He answered her automatically, then, holding his hand for a second longer, she turned away through the pall of smoke.

2

In his headquarters in Kalani, Major Baldamus was growing
worried. He had suddenly seen the possibility that he might after
all miss that rise in rank to colonel that he'd been coveting so
much since his arrival on Aeos. He was due for another promotion
soon and it suited him best to have it here on Aeos. The Greek
campaign was virtually over. The British were in hopeless disarray,
lacking orders and heading south with no idea of where they were
going, and he'd heard rumours that another campaign was being
planned for the East. Russia, it was said, and since Major
Baldamus didn't quite see himself trying consequences with
moujiks, he was suddenly uneasy. What Untersturmbannführer
Fernbrugge had told him had made him so.

'He found his petrol,' he said angrily to Ehrhardt. 'Only two
drums, mind you, and he had to shoot two dozen people to get
even that.'

Ehrhardt scowled. 'Seems a lot of suffering for two drums of
petrol,' he growled.

'I don't suppose it was really for two drums of petrol,' Baldamus
said, his face grim. 'It was for the honour of the greater German
Reich. There's one other thing. He thinks there are British
survivors from those two boats we destroyed at the south end of
the island.'

'Where?'

'They've been seen in Ay Yithion. He radioed in. They found
a wounded British soldier from that boat the Messerschmitts shot
up. They didn't escape, after all, it seems. Fernbrugge, of course,

215

made sure that everyone in Ay Yithion learned the lesson that they mustn't harbour escapees.'

Ehrhardt looked as uneasy as Baldamus. 'Where's Fernbrugge now?' he asked.

'On his way to Kharasso Bay. I suggested he should go, but he was going anyway.' Baldamus sighed. 'I doubt, in fact, if I could have have stopped him under the circumstances.'

While Untersturmbannführer Fernbrugge was heading across the island from Ay Yithion to Kharasso Bay, Corporal Michael Anthony Cotton was climbing up the ridge that overlooked the sea.

His mind was seething with unhappiness because he'd just realized that among the other things a ship's captain had to suffer was the weight of guilt. The destruction of Ay Yithion was undoubtedly caused by the discovery of Howard and the petrol that Varvara had obtained for him, and now he had to learn to live with his conscience. In saving one life he'd caused the loss of twenty-odd others. He'd heard of this dilemma – the risk of many lives to save one. In fact, in *Caernarvon* when a man had fallen overboard, Captain Troughton had refused to turn the ship back for him because of the nearness of German bombers. There had been hidden catcalls from aft and a great deal of bad feeling, but when the ship was caught at the extreme length of the bombers' range and they'd escaped untouched after only a brief attack before the planes had had to turn for home, the ill feeling had died away and they'd realized the captain had been right. Perhaps what none of them realized, however, was what Cotton was realizing now: how much courage it had required to make that decision. Because he had generations of navy behind him, Captain Troughton had probably made it without too much searching of his conscience, but it wasn't that easy for Cotton.

As he climbed, his thoughts pressed in on him. A hundred and one questions bothered him and he even began to wonder if they ought not to have left the night before and taken a chance on being short of petrol.

When he reached the top of the ridge, the Junkers 87s and 88s were taking off all the time from the north side of the island and circling beyond Cape Kastamanitsa to turn on course towards the mainland. The thud of guns was loud now, and he guessed the Luftwaffe had found the navy as it escorted the troop transports. The strip at Yanitsa was right across their route south.

As he stopped above Kharasso Bay, the first thing he saw was a German staff car on the dusty road above the beach. Dropping flat among the scrub, he saw four Germans climbing down to the wrecked *Claudia* and he lay in a niche between the rocks, watching.

Two of the Germans were civilians and he recognized them as the men he'd seen in the car at Ay Yithion. The other two wore the black-collared tunic of the SS.

As they reached the beach, they marched across the sand in their arrogant strut, the hateful stride of men who knew they were conquering the world. Then one of them pointed and they started to run so that Cotton guessed they'd seen the planks that Gully had removed from the hull to repair *Loukia*. For a while, they stood on the beach, staring at the wrecked boat, talking and gesturing, then one of them climbed on board and disappeared below.

After a while he re-emerged in the well through the engine-room door, climbed on to the deck and walked to the bows, where he stood shouting down to the others below him. Cotton couldn't understand what he was saying but he guessed they'd jumped to no uncertain conclusions.

Eventually, they began to climb up the path back to the car and Cotton saw them drive off to the north of the island. As he hurried back towards *Loukia*, he saw the two German caiques making their circular tour of the coast; then, later, rounding the point as they disappeared, the brilliant red boat of the younger Varvara. Stumbling and slipping, his face wealed and scratched by twigs and brambles, he hurried down the slope just as Varvara's caique appeared.

217

He explained what had happened and, as they argued what to do, all faintly depressed by what had happened to Howard, the red caique nosed into the bay. As it moored up alongside *Loukia*, young Varvara emerged from the wheelhouse.

'I have two drums for you,' he said. 'My father had them hidden. We had four but when we'd loaded two, they telephoned from Kalani that the Germans were coming. We thought it was best to wait, so I took my boat out. I saw them arrive. They – '

His voice broke and he stopped.

'I saw what happened,' Cotton said. 'I was there.'

'They must have known,' Varvara choked. 'Someone must have told them. They took away the English boy.'

'I saw that too. There's nothing we can do about it.'

But it hurt, nevertheless, to be reminded of the promise he'd made to Howard only a day or two before that they wouldn't leave without him.

'They found the other petrol under my father's nets,' Varvara went on. 'They shot him and the doctor and the mayor and his secretary, and then everybody in the café.'

There was a moment's silence. There was nothing they could say to Varvara, who seemed less emotionally affected by this time than angry. His weeping had already finished and he was itching for revenge, and even his grief had not caused him to swerve from his promise of help.

'As soon as they'd gone,' he said, 'I went ashore to see my father. My brothers have taken the body. They said the Germans had been tipped off. They knew exactly where to look. They're going to search this part of the island now.'

'They've been,' Cotton said. 'I watched them in Kharasso Bay. They're heading now towards Kalani but they'll be coming back. I expect they've gone for reinforcements.'

Varvara frowned. 'There'll be more reprisals,' he said. 'They'll shoot more people. They'll wipe out my family.'

'I'm sorry,' Cotton said. 'I'm sorry we brought it on you.'

Varvara managed a taut smile. 'I don't blame you, *Kapetáne*,' he said. 'You have your orders. And the sympathy of all Greece.

But I think I shall go home now and collect my people and leave when it's dark. Perhaps you will stand by my boat until we're clear of the island.'

Docherty, who had been watching them uneasily as they talked, had picked up the drift of the conversation. 'If the buggers are coming here,' he said, 'we ought to bloody well hop it ourselves.'

'Or stop 'em,' Cotton said.

Docherty's eyes lifted to his face. 'You barmy?' he yelled. 'We can't stop the whole German army!'

Cotton's face was bleak. 'It won't be the whole German army,' he said. 'They won't send more than a couple of lorry-loads of men to sort *us* lot out, I bet. Perhaps we could stop *them*.'

'What with?'

'We've got guns. We've got the Bren, haven't we?' Cotton looked at Kitcat. 'How're you with a Lewis?'

Kitcat gave a nervous grin. Since starting to fly he'd been shot at more times than he liked to remember, taking off often in a cold sweat of anticipation and returning exhausted by holding his breath at the narrow escapes he'd had. He had a feeling that he'd already pushed his luck as far as he ought, but Cotton was a persuasive man, less from his command of words than from the inner conviction about duty that seemed to be behind everything he did.

He swallowed. 'Deadshot Dick,' he said.

'Let's have a go then,' Cotton went on. 'We've got to do something because we can't leave till dark. That bloody look-out on Cape Kastamanitsa would spot us straight away. A spot of the old dot-dash on a morse key and there'd be an aeroplane out one-time to investigate.'

'We can't hold a couple of lorry-loads off.'

'We can try. We'll not get away any other way.'

Cotton turned to Varvara and explained what he wanted to do. The Greek seemed more than willing, his eyes burning with hatred.

'The road from Kalani winds up the hill on the other side,' he said. 'Then it drops down to the bay here. There's a sharp bend near the top and cars have to go round it dead slow in low gear. you could wait there for them.'

One of his crew, a squarely-built man with fierce dark eyes, spoke quietly to him in Greek and he turned again to Cotton. 'Argine Papaboukas here says he'll be your guide. They shot his father and he's spoiling for a fight.'

As Varvara's caique headed out of the bay, Cotton, Kitcat, Bisset and the Greek gathered among the trees alongside *Loukia*. Solemnly, Cotton had entered the Greek's name in the log. Events, names, times and dates were meant to be in logs.

'You're in charge,' he told Docherty.

Docherty grinned. 'Trust me, do you?' he asked.

'You're in the navy. It's up to you if we don't get back.'

Docherty grinned again and Cotton went on. 'Don't panic, though. Even if you hear firing. We might just be winning. Wait to see what happens. You've plenty of time, so watch out for the rocks. Keep an eye on the slope and if you see the Germans coming, get cracking. They'd never be able to stop you.'

Docherty gave him a mock salute. 'England expects that this day every man will do his duty. I've heard that bloody lot ever since I joined.'

'Perhaps some it rubbed off,' Cotton said hopefully.

As they began to climb the hill, he began to wonder how far he was right to extend his trust to Docherty. He was immoral and irresponsible but he was a sailor as well as a stoker, and there was no one else who could handle both the engines and the boat. It *had* to be Docherty who stayed behind, and he had to chance that sufficient naval tradition had stuck to him to make him behave well if the need arose.

The sun was high now and it was growing hot as they laboured under the weight of a rifle, the Lewis, the Bren, one of the tommy-guns, a rope and what they'd considered to be a reasonable amount of ammunition. They were sweating when they reached the top of the slope.

The Greek led them down the road to Kalani and showed them the corner Varvara had mentioned. It was steep with a hairpin turn and there was no doubt that anything negotiating it would come almost to a stop.

They rigged up the Lewis to cover it, fixing it with stakes and ropes so that it couldn't run wild as it fired. Papaboukas, who claimed to be a good shot with a rifle, was left with Kitcat while Bisset and Cotton moved fifty yards further down the slope. 'I just hope Varvara's right,' Cotton said, 'and that they don't come in large lumps.'

They found a place where they could see well and, setting up the Bren, covered it with scrub. Then Bisset squatted down to watch the road to Kalani. As Cotton walked back to where Kitcat and the Greek waited, he decided that things were happening almost too fast and he was unable to keep up with them, because they had to hold the Germans off until dark and it was only just into the afternoon.

Kitcat was fussing round the Lewis.

'Think it'll hold?'

Kitcat grinned. 'I wouldn't like to tackle a Messerschmitt with it,' he said. 'But I reckon it ought to get off enough rounds to wipe out a lorry-load of Jerries before we lose control.'

'It might be more than one lorry-load,' Cotton pointed out.

'Okay.' Kitcat shrugged. '*Two* lorry-loads. We might well get 'em both. These things fire four hundred and fifty rounds a minute – if they don't jam.' He gave a nervous grin. 'They're noted for jamming,' he ended.

3

Untersturmbannführer Karl-Johannes Fernbrugge rested both his fists on Major Baldamus' desk and leaned forward. His manner was threatening.

'If there is one British survivor down that end of the island,' he said, 'then there are more than likely others too.'

Baldamus looked up. Fernbrugge's face was pockmarked by acne. It was thin and pale and reminded Baldamus of one of the ferrets he'd used as a boy. 'So?' he asked.

'So they were probably being looked after by the people of that fishing village, Ay Yithion.'

Baldamus sniffed. 'I gather you've already taken care of *them*,' he said coldly.

Fernbrugge gave a small smile. 'They won't hide any more survivors,' he said. 'I doubt if they'll be able to hide themselves now. There is one other thing.'

'Please go on,' Baldamus said coldly.

'You have a man called Festner on your muster roll.'

Baldamus shrugged. 'We *had*. He disappeared. The good Festner was not exactly a patriotic German. In fact, I understand his father was Austrian and his mother Hungarian. He didn't feel the same way about things as everybody else.'

Fernbrugge wasn't amused. 'As far as I'm concerned,' he snapped, 'your Festner could be a Polish warthog crossed with an Azerbaijan ferret. All I know is that he's probably dead.'

'Dead?' Baldamus' good humour vanished at once.

'When your half-witted sergeant inspected the boat, *Claudia*,

222

a few days ago, it seems your good Festner, who has a reputation as a scrounger, laid a little on one side for himself and a friend of his, one Pioneer Gunther. When Festner went back to find it he never returned.'

'Deserted, perhaps?'

'More likely murdered by your British survivors.' Fernbrugge slapped the desk. 'I want reinforcements! I've worked it out there might be around half a dozen of them in Xiloparissia Bay and I gather they have weapons – automatic weapons.'

Baldamus' eyebrows lifted. He had long realized such a possibility existed, but it was still news to him and, though he didn't show his concern, it wasn't particularly good news.

'It's my belief,' Fernbrugge went on, 'that they've been repairing the wreck in Xiloparissia Bay and you know what that can mean, don't you?'

'Tell me.'

Fernbrugge scowled at Baldamus' sarcasm. 'They're intending to escape. With news of what's going on here. We were sent to back up your security people who appear to have been remarkably slack, and this seems to me a case that ought to be investigated.'

'It does indeed.' Baldamus' face didn't change but his heart thumped annoyingly that somehow his command had slipped up.

'Why wasn't the matter investigated before, Major?'

'It was.'

'Then why wasn't it brought to a satisfactory conclusion?'

Baldamus stared at Fernbrugge, disliking him and everything he stood for. In men like Fernbrugge, he felt, there was only a thin veneer of civilization and the job they did very nearly wiped that away. Even so, there was a small feeling of doubt at the back of his mind and he was playing for time because he was well aware that when Ehrhardt's sergeant had jumped to the conclusion that the British survivors had escaped, the idea had probably been put into his head by Baldamus' own suggestion that there'd been a third boat. The eye saw what it wished to see and, because there'd been no sign of the British, they'd all assumed that they'd been taken away.

223

He forced himself to be calm. 'You'd better ask the Luftwaffe,' he said. 'They did the recce.'

Fernbrugge was eyeing him. He didn't like Baldamus any more than Baldamus liked him.

'I *intend* to ask the Luftwaffe,' he said. 'For the moment, however, I need men.'

'I have a few engineers.'

'I need *soldiers*,' Fernbrugge said contemptuously. 'Those people I took to Ay Yithion were useless. I sent them back.'

Baldamus didn't blink. 'Perhaps they don't enjoy murder.'

Fernbrugge was used to insults from the regular army and Baldamus' dislike ran off him like water off a duck's back.

'They have no guts,' he said. 'I want something better this time. If those survivors in Xiloparissia Bay have automatic weapons, I want men who know how to deal with them – not clerks and bridge-builders.'

Baldamus began to move the papers on his desk as an idea occurred to him. He had tried incorporating the troops at Xinthos – the so-called Special Service Battalion – into his own command, if only for discipline, and had even called on Captain Haussmann, their commander. There was a built-in self-reliance among them, however, which existed from the top to the very bottom and Haussmann had made no bones about it. His troops weren't going to answer to anyone but himself and he didn't intend to permit anybody to push them around.

Baldamus had had to leave unsatisfied, but there had been other means and a quick exchange of signals with Sofia had provided them. 'Subject troops,' General Ritsicz had pointed out, 'will conform in every way – repeat every way – with orders issued by your headquarters. Co-operation of the islanders is first essential and good behaviour of troops is of prime importance. Subject troops will be given duties but, bearing in mind the need for secrecy, will not be used except in security tasks and then only sparely.'

Baldamus smiled up at Fernbrugge. 'You'd better ask the captain in command of the special service unit at Xinthos,' he said. 'He's the man with the soldiers. Mine are *all* bridge-builders, clerks, pen-pushers and bottle-washers.'

Fernbrugge glared. 'That'll take time.'

'You wanted soldiers. They *are* soldiers. Splendid soldiers.'

As Fernbrugge turned away and the door slammed behind him, Baldamus stared after him, irritated and not a little worried. This was a damn fine kettle of fish for a peace-loving fighting man to find himself in, he thought cynically. If the British survivors they thought had escaped were still at the south end of the island and had repaired one of their boats sufficiently to take it away, it might prove highly embarrassing for him – especially if they *did* take it away! One of the instructions he'd been given by General Ritsicz had been that nothing should leak from the island about what was going on, and there was no knowing how much they'd seen or how much they'd guessed. It seemed a good idea to stir himself.

As he rang a bell, Ehrhardt appeared.

'Ehrhardt,' he said. 'Get someone to send my car round. I'm going to sea.'

Ehrhardt gaped and Baldamus smiled. 'We have a fleet,' he pointed out. 'Two caiques and an ex-Italian launch. And I'm the admiral in command. After all, we mustn't let the Gestapo take the credit for *everything,* and we seem to have put up a bit of a black about these British survivors.'

'I thought it was out of our hands,' Ehrhardt said.

'Not quite. I'm going to station my flagship south of the island, with me aboard her. *You'd* better stay around here. Our gallant friend Fernbrugge is bound to radio in.'

'Won't he contact Haussmann first?'

Baldamus considered. It had given him a great deal of satisfaction to present General Ritsicz's signal to Captain Haussmann, who had glared at it fiercely so that Baldamus had realized there would very soon be signals flying north from him in an attempt to rescind the order. He was probably already in touch with General Student, who was in command of all special air service units, and was doubtless prepared to go as high as Field Marshal List and –

if necessary – even to the Führer himself. That would take time, however, and by the time the dispute had penetrated into the inner sanctums, Haussmann's men might well be gone from Xinthos, and the situation – and Major Baldamus' reputation – might well be saved.

'I suspect Haussmann will be receiving Fernbrugge at any moment,' he said. 'When he found our order covered his group he told me, if his people had to be used for anything, then for God's sake at least let them be used for something worthwhile, because he was as bored as they were and was prepared to go with them.'

'And – ?' Ehrhardt was still puzzled.

Baldamus gestured and smiled again. 'And if our British are as clever as they seem to be, they're not going to surrender all that easily to the SS. They might even try to dodge them by going to sea. And if they do, the chances are that they'll run right into *my* hands.'

At the top of the slope, Cotton was peering across the plain, biting his nails. His mother had been in the habit of putting mustard on his fingers when he'd bitten his nails as a boy but he decided that this was a time when he might legitimately enjoy his bad habits.

'I hope to Christ there aren't more than *two* lorry-loads,' he said to Bisset. 'We'll wait for Kitcat to start and we'll handle the rear end.'

Bisset nodded, not taking his eyes off the plain. 'Right.'

As they waited, the sun began to sink and Cotton realized with gratitude that it was well into the afternoon now. Every minute they waited without anybody approaching was to their advantage. Then he began to wonder again whether he could trust Docherty and why Annoula had failed to turn up.

It was almost five o'clock when Bisset touched his arm and pointed. In the distance below them they could see a cloud of dust approaching.

'Here they come!'

226

Running up the road, Cotton waved to Kitcat. 'They're here!'

'How many?'

'Can't tell yet. I'll let you know.'

'Right!' Kitcat's small face was taut and his big moustache bristled with anticipation.

Cotton ran back towards Bisset and threw himself down. 'How many?' he asked.

'Can't say yet. Not a column, anyway. That's one thing, thank God, because I expect there'll still be *too* many. After all, there are only four of us. Six boy scouts would be almost too many.'

Bisset was frowning and Cotton looked at him. 'I'm scared,' he admitted. 'Are you scared?'

'Of course I'm scared. *You* scare me.' Bisset shifted his position and his eyes narrowed. 'Four vehicles,' he announced in a flat voice. 'There seem to be four men in the car in front and eight in each of the other three. Twenty-eight altogether.'

Cotton's heart sank. Twenty-eight! It was almost a regiment! He was tempted to call the whole thing off and take *Loukia* to sea and chance being caught by the aeroplanes off Cape Kastamanitsa. His whole soul cried out to him to bolt while the going was good, but the trained soldier in him told him it was up to him to do something positive.

He swallowed, deciding that this time he'd dropped himself in for something he couldn't get out of all that easily. Glancing at Bisset to find what he was thinking, he saw the wireless operator's face was blank and expressionless as he crouched among the rocks, holding the tommy-gun.

Jesus, Cotton thought, one tommy-gun, one Bren, one Lewis — not on a stand — and one rifle, against twenty-eight assorted weapons, some of them inevitably machine-guns! Then, suddenly, unexpectedly, he became aware of men among the rocks lower down and even a few near him, crouching over rifles. He saw a tommy-gun, a Bren, for God's sake, even Lewis-guns, mounted on home-made stands. He turned swiftly, alarmed and wondering where they'd come from, who they were and what the hell was happening, and as he did so one of the men dropped down

227

alongside him. Thickset with strong features and hot black eyes like Petrakis, he wore a jersey and an old felt hat, with smart riding breeches and long boots, and he was festooned with belts of ammunition.

'Delageorgis, Nichomacos,' he said. 'You are Cotton?'

'Yes, I am.'

'We are from Cape Asigonia. We went into Ay Yithion to kill the Germans but they'd all left and Varvara told us you were here.' Delageorgis gestured down the slope. 'You intend to destroy them?'

The German vehicles had started to climb the slope now and Cotton nodded. Delageorgis smiled.

'We will help you. We collected the weapons from the goatherds' cave. We owe you a little and we can now return it.'

Cotton couldn't believe his luck. He'd been doing a bit of quiet praying as he'd watched the Germans and it seemed that someone had answered his pleas. He remembered how his mother had always complained about his faltering attendance at church in the past and he resolved that if he got out of this lot he'd try to do better.

Then another thought occurred to him and he nodded at the machine-guns. 'Can you use them?' he asked.

Delageorgis' eyes flashed and he gestured with the flat of his hand. '*Pó-pó,*' he said. 'Not very well yet, perhaps, but we shall manage and there are plenty of us. We have an ex-soldier among us who showed us what to do. Many of these men work for me and I have a small debt to wipe out. My brother was in Ay Yithion.' He nodded at the approaching cars. 'I have told my people to fire when you do. Will that be all right?'

Cotton's relief exploded from him in a great sigh. 'That will certainly be all right,' he said.

As he explained what he intended, Delageorgis sent off a messenger to the other men gathered among the rocks, and Cotton could see him pointing.

The German vehicles were climbing towards them now. The first one was a staff car and contained the men he'd seen on the road outside Ay Yithion and later inspecting *Claudia*. The two civilians sat in the rear seat and one of the men in front wore a leather coat and the second a black uniform cap, so that he realized they were all security men. He'd never seen an SS man at close quarters before and, having heard of their ruthlessness and cruelty, he felt a little awed. But they looked ordinary enough men, not monsters. One of them even wore spectacles, and the second looked plump and overfed as if he wouldn't move very fast.

Then his eyes fell on the second vehicle. It was small, open and light, with small wheels, and was commanded by a full captain. The men who crammed into it all nursed automatic weapons and wore grey-green overalls and small round helmets that he'd never seen before. Suddenly it dawned on him who they were, why they drove such a small vehicle, and just why the men he'd seen near Xinthos had worn no badges on their tunics.

'Paratroopers!' he said in an explosive gasp. 'They're paratroopers, Biss!'

4

The realization of what they faced came as a shock. The men in the open vehicle were the men who had contributed to the defeat of Norway, Holland and France – highly trained, ruthless specialists drilled in every form of assault.

Bisset answered Cotton calmly, quietly, almost in a drawl. 'We have a few allies now,' he pointed out. 'What's more, they don't know we're here, which is a happy thought because thrice blessed is he who gets his blow in fust.' His sleepy smile widened. 'And, brother, what a blow,' he went on. 'I can see three Lewises now, two Brens, one tommy-gun and God knows how many rifles. That's firepower, old boy.'

Thinking of the captured soldiers he'd seen in Kalani, Cotton gripped the butt of the Bren more tightly. There were a few things he owed the Germans. There was the blitz on London. His parents had been lucky and still had their home but there wasn't much else left of the street where they lived. There were also the men who'd been killed when *Caernarvon* had been bombed, and all the men who'd died in Greece and at Dunkirk and in Norway. And now there was Ay Yithion. Hitherto, in spite of everything, the war had remained an impersonal affair of missiles launched by men out of sight or virtually out of sight, so that he'd experienced little feeling against them, but the butchery at Ay Yithion that morning had changed everything. Shifting his position, settling himself, savouring his hatred, Cotton felt a little better and drew a deep calming breath. 'You ever done this before, Biss?' he asked.

'I came out of France at Dunkirk,' Bisset said. 'I'm quite used to loud bangs.'

The four vehicles were climbing now up to the steeper part of the road.

'I'll take the second vehicle,' Cotton breathed. 'Kitcat'll stop the first. It's up to you and the Greeks to get the others.' He swallowed. 'We can't let anyone escape,' he said to Delageorgis.

The Greek smiled. 'Nobody *will* escape,' he said.

Cotton drew another deep breath. It seemed to come with difficulty as if his chest was tight. His stomach felt empty, as it used to before a football match or a sports day at school, and his heart was thumping enough to deafen him. Above the grind of the engines, a bird was singing. The song seemed to fill the air, liquid and quavering, almost as if it were sounding a warning.

Glancing over his shoulder, Cotton could see Kitcat fifty yards away. He was crouched behind the Lewis which he'd smeared with dust so that its bright metal wouldn't catch the sun and warn the approaching Germans. Doubtless in his forays from Malta and in the desert, he'd learned the trick of keeping anything that might pick up the brilliance of the Mediterranean sun well dulled, because everybody knew how the first invasion of Egypt in 1940 had been spotted and stopped because the sun had caught the windscreens of the Italian lorries turning down the escarpment at Sollum.

'Hundred yards,' Bisset said.

The four vehicles were keeping close to each other and none of the men in them seemed to be expecting danger. The SS men were slouched in their seats, clearly not anticipating meeting anything until they began the climb down to the beach at Xiloparissia Bay. The paratroopers, however, sat up, alert and clutching their weapons, and they looked as though they expected to be able to deal with anything that came along. But, Cotton noticed, they were jammed tight together, which would make quick movement difficult and provide a good target into the bargain. The captain in the second vehicle was armed to the teeth like the others but, unlike them, he hadn't bothered to don a paratrooper's smock, as if he expected his job to be quickly over.

Cotton glanced at Delageorgis, hoping and praying his men were as dangerous with the weapons as they looked. Then the grind of the engines grew louder and, as the German vehicles slowed for the steep slope and the tight bend, he heard the crunch of stones under the tyres. His head down behind the rocks, he caught a glimpse of the high-peaked cap of the SS man in the car in front passing slowly by; a moment later the round grey-green pot-shaped helmets of the paratroopers appeared in his line of vision. He was just wondering 'Why paratroopers?' when Bisset touched his arm.

'Now,' he breathed.

The leading vehicles had almost come to a halt as they negotiated the hairpin. It was only for a second as they changed into low gear, and Cotton thought Kitcat had missed his opportunity, because the SS men's car began to draw away again. Then the Lewis fired, in a long burst like the tearing of cloth.

The car containing the SS men came to a dead stop at once and slewed sideways, jamming the road, steam coming from the radiator. The windscreen disintegrated and Untersturmbann-führer Fernbrugge's hat flew into the air as, with his companion in the front seat, he dissolved into bloody rags of flesh. At a distance of thirty feet, Kitcat couldn't miss.

The doors had flown open and one of the men in the rear seat fell out, his head on the ground, his feet still in the car. The other was caught by the Lewis as he ran. A short tearing burst lifted him clean off the ground and flung him several yards away, rolling him over and over in bloody jerks that left red stains on the dusty road.

The open-topped paratroopers' vehicles had also come to a standstill and they could see the man at the wheel of the rear-most one struggling to put it into reverse. As he did so, Cotton fired. The driver was flung sideways over the door, and the car ran backwards in a short curve until one wheel dropped into the drainage ditch at the side of the road that carried the mountain rains away.

In the second vehicle Captain Haussmann had been thinking what a pleasant change it was to be away from the gloom and silence of the great house at Xinthos. Panyioti had provided comfort beyond all his dreams but, since he'd arrived, it had seemed like a prison and it had been harder than he'd imagined to keep his men inside. He'd jumped at the chance to join Fernbrugge in a fire-fighting party and had brought with him all his most intractable troublemakers to let them blow off a little steam. As the firing started he had reacted quickly to the ambush and jumped to the road, shouting and pointing out the direction of the firing; but the Bren was knocking whole chunks off his vehicle and the men struggling to jump clear fell about him like jointless dolls, the blood bursting from their arms and faces and bodies as the Bren's five hundred rounds a minute tore into them. They were so close they didn't have a chance, and Cotton let them have the whole magazine.

Haussmann had just realized that for the first time in the war he was facing defeat when three of the Bren gun's bullets hit him in the face, punching in his nose and eyes and dropping him dead into the dust. The tommy-gun, with its less accurate fire, had not done such deadly work on the other vehicles but the Greeks were blazing away now with everything they possessed, and the rocks echoed to the roar of musketry. His nostrils filled with the smell of cordite as he jammed another magazine into place, Cotton heard the chink and crack of bullets whipping overhead and realized that the Greeks in their enthusiasm were in danger of shooting each other and him.

One of the paratroopers in the third vehicle had dived out of the blind side, acting on an instinct drilled into him by training. Another man trying to follow was slower and, as he ducked from the waggon, Bisset swung the tommy-gun and the paratrooper sprawled in the dust and lay still. The man beside the driver seemed to panic and stood up, staring round, spraying the air with his weapon, but he was looking in the wrong direction and Bisset's burst lifted him clean out of the vehicle and dropped him flat on his back in the road.

By this time the Germans seemed to be all dead or dying except for a few who had dived under their vehicles. But the Greeks were spraying the ground round them and several of them were forced to make a break and started to run down the slope. Immediately, every Greek in the vicinity opened fire on them and Cotton's throat tightened as they were flung like autumn leaves across the road, the bursts of machine-gun fire tearing into their bodies and nudging them down the slope so that they left a bloody trail in the dust.

As the shooting died, only three Germans out of the whole twenty-eight, were still on their feet and they flung their hands in the air and started yelling for mercy. As Delageorgis rose and moved towards them, holding a tommy-gun, the Germans' arms became straighter. They seemed to be only boys and they watched the Greek with wide terrified eyes and hanging jaws. Using the tommy-gun, he herded them into a close bunch; then, without any show of emotion, pulled the trigger. The heavy bullets lifted them from their feet and dropped them into the drainage ditch. One of them was still moving and Delageorgis stood over him and pulled the trigger again.

Lowering the weapon, the Greek turned and looked at Cotton. 'Nobody escaped,' he said in a flat voice.

For a long time there was silence. Even the birds seemed to have stopped singing. The dust was still hanging in the air by the four vehicles and there was the smell of new blood and cordite. Then Bisset rose cautiously, holding the tommy-gun in front of him, and stepped out from the rocks, a fixed nervous grin on his face. Cotton followed, then Kitcat. They were all slack-jawed and sick-looking, shocked by the butchery.

Kitcat swallowed and Cotton saw his adam's apple work.

'Jesus,' he said softly, indicating the Greeks. 'I thought the buggers were going to kill *us* as well.'

Three of Delageorgis' men had been wounded by flying bullets – more than likely their own – one of them seriously. His jaw was hanging down in a bloody mash, but his friends seemed to show little sympathy and simply bound it up with a handkerchief round the top of his head.

'I expect he will die,' Delageorgis said bluntly. 'It will be impossible, of course, to take him to a doctor.'

He seemed unmoved by the slaughter and they cautiously approached the dead Germans, turning them over with their feet to see if any were still alive. One of them further down the slope moved and began to whimper – *'Mutter, Mutter,'* he moaned. *'Hilfe! Hilfe!'* – and one of the Greeks, holding his rifle in one hand, placed the muzzle against the German's ear and pulled the trigger. Cotton saw Bisset wince.

'God help them,' he breathed, 'when the tide turns the other way.'

The bodies were sprawled all over the road and the dusty surface was puddled with their blood. Several of them lay head-down in the drainage ditch and one sprawled with his back against a rock, his eyes wide open, his jaw sagging, an expression of startled horror on his face.

Bisset's throat worked. 'For Christ's sake,' he said. 'Let's get away from here!'

'Hang on!' Cotton knew his duty. 'Let's see if there are any documents. Pay-books and that sort of thing. They might tell the Intelligence wallahs something. One of 'em was an officer.'

Bisset pulled a face. '*You* can search him,' he said. 'I'm not going to.'

Gagging on his own bile, Cotton bent over the Germans and went through their pockets. Their pay-books were torn and bloodstained but he put them carefully into a scarf he took from the throat of one of them. The Greeks seemed unworried by the blood and were excitedly going through the jackets of the dead men, handing any papers they found to Cotton but pushing watches and money into their own pockets and posturing with the tommy-guns and grenades wrenched from the hands of the dead para-troopers. Occasionally a rifle cracked as they found someone still breathing.

Cotton looked at the papers he'd taken from Haussmann's body. 'You can read German, can't you, Biss?' he asked.

Bisset took the papers and looked at them. He seemed troubled by the blood on them.

'*Kriegsschauplatz*,' he said, reading aloud. 'That means "Scene of operations". "*Fallschirmtruppen* :" Paratroopers. "*Begleiten* :" Accompany. And isn't this the German for Crete? Must be, because it goes on about *Suda Bai* – Suda Bay – and the *Englische Königliche Kriegsmarine*. That's "English Royal Navy". Then it mentions Maleme, Heraklion and Retimo –'

He lifted his head and Cotton saw that his frown had deepened.

'What's the matter?' he said.

'These places are aerodromes,' Bisset said, then he went on in an awed voice. 'I think we've stumbled on orders for the invasion of Crete.'

'Well, that's something,' Cotton said. 'The navy'll be pleased to have 'em.'

'It won't make much difference to the navy,' Bisset said in a tight voice. 'Because they don't concern the navy all that much. They're not going by sea. They're going to do it with parachutists and gliders.'

5

For a moment there was silence.

'You sure?' Cotton asked.

Bisset nodded. 'There's a bit here that seems to have been copied from orders. It says Hitler doesn't intend to launch an operation against Crete, but it's been crossed out and it says "Generaloberst Lohr, Luftflotte 4, considers Crete can be captured solely by airborne and parachute troops." Then it says, "The Führer directs that an operation to occupy the island of Crete, Operation Merkur, is to be prepared, with the object of using Crete as an air base against Britain in the eastern Mediterranean." That seems plain enough to me.'

Bisset stared again at the papers, frowning, his nose wrinkling at the blood on them. '*Schlachtordnung*,' he said. 'Order of battle. I can also see "Maleme" and "Sphakio".'

He pulled a face as he wiped the blood from his fingers on his trousers and studied a notebook Cotton gave him, which had also come from the pockets of the dead officer. 'I don't know who the hell this bloke Haussmann is,' he said, 'but it talks about twenty thousand troops and five hundred troop-carriers and gliders from *Fliegerkorps IX*.' Bisset's face was pale. 'We haven't got that many men altogether in Crete, have we?' He read again. 'They've mustered 'em at Argos, Eleusis, Molai and Myli in Greece, and in one or two islands, including this one. *Fliegerkorps VIII*'s job is to deal with the navy.'

'You're sure about all that?' Cotton asked.

'It's pretty simple stuff.'

'I mean those big words. "Order of battle". That sort of thing.'

'I was in France,' Bisset said. 'We were running like rabbits from these buggers. We got to know a lot of big words then, and one I'll never forget was *Fallschirmtruppen* – para-troopers.'

'I think you must be right,' Cotton said. 'It would explain all that fuss at Yanitsa. And if that's the case, then we've got to get away tonight. Somebody ought to be told.' He looked at his watch. It showed five-fifteen.

'What about this lot?' Bisset said. 'When they don't return or radio in they'll come looking for 'em. And if they find 'em, they'll soon know what's happened, and that'll be the end of us. They'll have the Luftwaffe down on us like a ton of bricks.'

'Suppose they *don't* find 'em?' Cotton said. 'Suppose we hide everything? It took 'em three hours or more to get from looking at *Claudia* to Kalani and then back here again. Those geezers in Kalani don't know what's happened to 'em, do they? They didn't get a radio message off so they won't worry for another hour or two. More if we're lucky. And if they come and find nothing, that'll delay 'em a bit longer, won't it? In that case, they might not arrive here until after six or seven o'clock or even later. By that time, we could chance it. It grows dark quickly here and it'd be night an hour or so later.'

'So?'

'So we shove 'em among the rocks where they can't be seen and hide the vehicles.'

'How? By the look of 'em they won't go very far.'

Cotton studied the vehicles. The Lewis had smashed the engine of the SS men's car, burst the two front tyres and shattered the windscreen. The Bren, more deadly at a closer range, had smashed the second vehicle completely and the bodies of its occupants lolled from it like red-stained grey bags.

He crossed to the other vehicles. The engine of the third had stopped but it was still switched on. He tried the starter and the engine kicked, then stopped again immediately as it tried to drag itself from the ditch and failed. The last vehicle's engine had been caught in the crossfire from the Greeks, and its distributor was only shattered vulcanite.

He turned and stared towards the plain. 'It's downhill from here,' he said. 'And we've got plenty of time. Let's drive two of 'em down the hill and shove 'em in a ditch where they can be seen.'

'And?'

'Anybody coming from Kalani will spot 'em and investigate. They'll not find the crews but they'll see the bullet holes and they'll wonder what happened. They'll search down there, not up here.'

Bisset nodded his agreement and they lifted the bodies from the road and carried them among the rocks, sagging and sodden with blood. Then they turned the car with the smashed distributor and faced it down the road and heaved the other vehicle from the ditch.

'Can you drive, Biss?' Cotton asked.

Bisset grinned. 'Grand Prix,' he said.

'Get in and follow me. We'll take the rope. You'll probably have to tow me.'

He bent to pick up a few scattered items of equipment that the Germans had thrown off in their attempt to escape and began to toss them into the back of Bisset's vehicle with two or three of the pot-shaped helmets, a bullet-smashed gun and Haussmann's cap.

'What's that lot for?' Kitcat asked.

'To give 'em something to search for. While we're down there, you get everything ready for us to get away smartly when we come back. But keep an eye on us and if anybody comes and we're in trouble, leave the lot and run. Take the papers and make sure they're handed over to the right people.'

Just so long, he thought, as Docherty, hearing the firing, hadn't taken fright or fancied the money, or both, and bolted already.

They pushed the SS car into the ditch. Then, tossing the rope and a few more items of German equipment in with Bisset, they set off down the hill, Cotton leading. The hill descended steeply to the plain and rolled straight on as far as they could see before ascending gently to the other side of the island. Staring across the valley to the rise, Cotton thanked God that Aeos was one of the bigger islands and that the rest of the Germans were a long way away.

As they descended lower, three aircraft approached from the west and passed over them, before dropping in a slow, descending curve towards Kalani, finally losing height and disappearing behind a small hill as they came in to land. They reached the bottom of the hill in a cloud of dust, a good two miles from where they'd left Kitcat. A cart track ran at right angles from the road and in the distance they could see a ruined white farmhouse. Its windmill was broken and it was clearly deserted, a monument to the islanders' increasing habit of moving to the mainland. There wasn't a soul in sight.

Cotton allowed the impetus of the run down the hill to carry him on to the cart track. Its uneven surface soon slowed him so he stopped and climbed out. Bisset arrived alongside almost at once.

Cotton pointed. 'On the hill there,' he said. 'Alongside the house. It'll stand out against the white wall. It's a nice way from the road and high enough to be seen by anybody coming from Kalani. There are also a few walls and ditches to make them wonder if there isn't an ambush and the farm's full of guns.'

Bisset grinned as he took the rope. 'You ought to have been a paratrooper yourself,' he said. 'You've got a good eye for country.'

'I'm a Marine,' Cotton said simply. 'They're red-hot on country in the Marines.'

Towing the bloodstained car, they left it alongside the wall of the broken-down farm where it stood out clearly against the white. Then they scattered the items of equipment, the steel helmets and the smashed gun where they could be seen after a little easy searching. Finally Cotton tossed Haussmann's cap down at the foot of a wall alongside the cart track.

'That'll make 'em think a bit,' he said. 'It'll give us a few more minutes. Perhaps longer.'

Tossing the rope back into Bisset's vehicle, they drove back along the track and up the hill to where Kitcat waited with the Greeks.

Delageorgis greeted them. 'That was a good beginning to the war on Aeos,' he observed.

Cotton wasn't so sure. The Germans weren't known for taking the butchery of their men lying down and there'd be reprisals as there had been at Ay Yithion. If they could shoot men merely for the possession of petrol, they'd certainly not accept the wiping out of a twenty-eight-man patrol of paratroopers without hitting back.

'You are leaving now?' Delageorgis asked.

Cotton nodded and Delageorgis pointed in the direction of Cape Kastamanitsa.

'Remember there is a look-out post on the headland,' he said. 'They'll see you. They've put up two guns and a searchlight. They don't intend anyone to escape south.'

Cotton nodded. They weren't out of the wood yet, just in a different stretch of trees. Delageorgis seemed to understand how his thoughts ran.

'We'll attend to the Germans on the headland,' he said. 'They'll not be expecting anything. There are only twenty of them under a lieutenant and there are twenty-four of us. And we now have plenty of German grenades and automatic weapons.'

Up to a little while before, Cotton wouldn't have expected twenty-four untrained Greeks to be a match for twenty well-armed and organized Germans, but after the butchery on the bend he wasn't so sure. At least they knew the country and they were possessed of a burning desire to kill.

'As soon as it's dark,' Delageorgis promised. 'I'll leave three men here to warn you in case any more come.'

He gathered his party together, ragged men in shabby black coats and baggy trousers, jerseys, woollen caps and turbans. Some of them were old and leather-skinned, one or two mere excited boys.

As the Greeks moved off, they dumped the guns in the wagon

241

and Bisset drove over the ridge of the hill and down the other side towards where *Loukia* lay. At the end of the track they pushed the vehicle into a small ravine overlooking the sea and tossed branches and foliage over it until it was hidden.

'That ought to make 'em think a bit too,' Cotton said.

Scrambling down the slope, he was pleased to see *Loukia* still there under the trees. At least Docherty hadn't panicked and bolted.

'I heard the firing,' he said as they appeared. 'I thought the bastards had got you. What happened?'

'*We* got *them* instead,' Bisset said. 'Twenty-eight of 'em.'

'You're kidding!'

'We had a bit of help. A few Greek partisans turned up.'

'What about their pals from Kalani? Won't they come?'

'It'll take a bit to find 'em. We hid 'em.'

'I'm bloody glad you're back,' Docherty said feelingly. 'I'm no ship's captain and that's a fact.'

He was clearly in a highly nervous state and certainly didn't possess the fibre to make decisions. It made Cotton, still nauseated by the slaughter at the top of the hill, feel a little better.

Young Varvara returned soon afterwards. To Cotton's surprise, he came without the caique and leading a straggling file of people over the crown of the hill from Ay Yithion. There were five men, three women and three small children, and they were carrying haversacks, suitcases, wine bottles and what looked like petrol cans, together with a single fowling-piece that looked as if it dated from the last Turkish invasion.

'My brothers,' Varvara said. 'Two of my crew. Also their wives and families. We wish to come with you.' He indicated the petrol cans. 'We have brought you some more petrol. Not much, but as much as we could carry. It was very heavy.'

'We have brought our own food and wine,' he went on. 'There is no longer any point in our staying. The radio says that the British have started evacuating their troops and that Greece is expected to capitulate tomorrow. The Germans are across the Corinth Canal and already hold many of the islands to the north. It is the end for us. Yesterday they bombed a hospital ship in the middle of Piraeus harbour. It was packed with wounded and women and children, and almost everybody perished. They say the caiques the Germans have collected are for the invasion of Crete.'

Cotton frowned. The blows seemed to be growing heavier with every day.

'Will they capture Crete?' Varvara asked.

Cotton had a suspicion that they would and that eventually they'd all be jam-packed into the Egyptian corner of the Mediterranean waiting with their backs to the Suez Canal for another Battle of Britain to be fought in Africa. All the same, he decided, with a little foreknowledge they could make it a hell of a lot more difficult.

'Perhaps not,' he said. 'If we get there first.'

'We shall join the navy,' Varvara said. 'We have decided this. The radio said that Greek naval vessels are already assisting the British and that they will head for Alexandria to lay alongside your ships. They will be glad of us, I think.'

'Why didn't you use the caique?' Cotton asked. 'You'd be less crowded.'

Varvara gave him a troubled smile. 'The Germans have posted a notice in the village that there must be no movement of boats and there's a sentry on the harbour wall. We had to leave in ones and twos.' He made a despairing gesture. 'There's also a naval launch which has arrived from Kalani to make sure the order's carried out. It's lying off Cape Kastamanitsa with two caiques. We saw them as we came over the hill. They're full of troops. They came from Kalani.'

'What for?'

'For the invasion of Crete. What else? They're going to Isfos further south. They're grouping there. They're leaving tomorrow morning.'

'This launch you saw.' Cotton gestured. 'What's it like?'

'It looks fast.'

'Fast as this?'

'Perhaps. It also has a big gun on the stern.'

Cotton frowned and gestured at Bisset. 'Biss, get up the hill. Take the binoculars and stay where you can see the road. Come back if you see the Germans coming. If they do, we'll have to shove off and chance it. Come down before dark.'

In his heart he knew his decision to wait until dark was also influenced by the hope that Annoula would return. There'd been no sign of her since she'd disappeared in Ay Yithion and he'd been hoping all afternoon that she'd decide to throw in her lot with young Varvara and join them.

His eyes turned towards the slope. There was no sign of life beyond the donkey, which they'd set free, grazing quietly halfway up the hill; nothing but the purple-brown slopes burned by the sun.

He found Varvara alongside him. 'Did you see Annoula?' he asked.

Varvara shook his head. 'Perhaps she will come, *Kapetáne*.'

As Cotton moved towards the foredeck, restless, watching the ropes, checking that everything was ready for departure, Kitcat placed the Lewises on their stands, and the pans of ammunition over the breeches. The 20 mm was on the stern mounting, a drum in position, the remaining drums on the deck below ready to be handed up. Inside the engine room he could hear the clink of Docherty's tools and Docherty himself whistling with a surprising cheerfulness that lifted shrilly over the deep thudding of guns to the north.

Kitcat was explaining the working of one of the Lewises to Gully who was staring at it, bewildered.

'Fed by a circular magazine,' Kitcat was saying. 'This one. It's fixed horizontally over the breech mechanism and holds forty-seven rounds.'

He indicated which was the breech and Gully frowned. Cotton knew how he felt. When he'd first made the acquaintance of a machine-gun it had been nothing but a meaningless conglomeration of oddly shaped bits of shiny steel.

'Perhaps you'd better just pull the goddam trigger,' Kitcat said in disgust, 'and hope for the best.'

He removed the magazine and stood alongside Cotton, listening. The air seemed full of the sound of guns and the lower note of aircraft. It seemed to Cotton to make them more cut off. For days he'd been existing entirely on drilled-in discipline and the morale they'd shoved into him at Eastney, but it was beginning to wear a bit thin now. A man could live cut off from his friends only for so long, and they seemed to have been in the wilderness for ever.

Kitcat was watching him and he felt he had to say something. 'Somebody's copping it,' he offered.

'Navy.'

Cotton nodded, his head cocked, listening. 'If they're trying to lift the pongos off the mainland they'll be getting it thick and heavy, because the Jerries have airfields within easy distance of the coast now. Think they might just know in Crete what we know?'

Kitcat sighed. 'It's always been my experience,' he said, 'that they don't know a goddam thing about what's coming till it drops on 'em.'

A stone clattered ashore and he swung round.

'Somebody coming.'

Thinking it might be Bisset returning, Cotton called to Docherty to stand by, and Gully moved to the forward mooring rope.

But it wasn't Bisset. Three figures were emerging from the scrub. It wasn't possible to see who they were as they entered the fringe of trees but they saw the flash of coloured shirts and, as they came out of the trees, Cotton saw they were Chrysostomos Petrakis, and his two companions, Xilouris and Cesarides, wearing blankets in rolls round their chests.

They stopped among the dusty rocks alongside the boat. 'I am glad you have repaired it,' Petrakis said.

Cotton scowled at him. 'How did you know we'd repaired it?'

'We have been watching.'

'What difference does it make to you?'

Petrakis smiled. 'We are sorry we have caused trouble, but whatever our ideals and whatever yours, we are both fighting the same enemy.'

'It took you long enough to find out.'

'Perhaps.' Petrakis smiled again. 'But it's all over here now and we wish to go with you.'

6

'We may come aboard?'

Petrakis smiled and gestured towards *Loukia*'s foredeck. Cotton scowled. He disliked Petrakis and didn't trust him, but he had to suppose that anybody who proposed joining in the fight against the Nazis would be welcomed in Egypt. The fact that he didn't like him had nothing to do with it. If he'd looked through the army, navy and air force muster rolls, he'd doubtless have found plenty of men he wouldn't like.

'I thought you were going to stay here and fight,' he said.

Petrakis smiled and shrugged.

'And what about that army you said you had?'

Petrakis gestured at Xilouris and Cesarides.

'These two? Just these two?'

Petrakis shrugged again. 'We may come aboard?'

Cotton turned to Kitcat. 'I suppose they'd better,' he said grudgingly. 'Put 'em forrard and see they stay there. They're not to come on deck.'

'We're not proposing to steal your boat,' Petrakis said coldly.

'I'm not going to give you a chance,' Cotton snorted. 'The women and kids are to stay below too,' he went on. 'And Kitcat' – Cotton lowered his voice – 'stick around that forrard hatch. Just keep an eye on those bastards. I wouldn't put it past 'em to stir up trouble of some sort even now.'

Kitcat nodded and ushered Petrakis and the other two below. As they vanished, Cotton moved round the boat.

'Think she'll stand up to it?' he asked Gully.

247

The carpenter was bending over the port Lewis, frowning. With the chance of success round the corner, he had recovered his aggressiveness. His new courage took the form of confidence and he straightened up and grinned. 'If I do a job, son,' he said, 'it stays done. She'll get you there if the engines keep turning.'

'What about the holes?'

'You'll not get enough water through 'em to worry you. And they won't leak much in less than 'alf a gale.'

In the engine room Docherty was bent over the starboard engine. 'How's it going?'

Docherty looked up. 'They'll be all right,' he said.

The day seemed to drag through the last hours of the afternoon; the sun turned from piercing gold to bronze, and the shadows of the trees reached across the deck until they showed in the water at the far side. For the hundredth time Cotton looked at his watch, then at the two clumps of rock in the entrance to the bay, fixing in his mind exactly where they lay so that they could safely negotiate them in the dark. Finally he looked towards the hilltop for some sign of Bisset.

Nothing was moving and for something to do, he cleaned himself up, shaving for the first time in days, polishing his cap badge, trying to rub the spots off his trousers. He was a Royal Marine and it was his duty to look like one. He'd heard of the Marine colonel who'd acted as beachmaster at La Panne during the evacuation of Dunkirk; contriving to put on his best uniform to go aboard ship, he had made himself so smart the women doling out rations in the train to London had refused to supply him because they wouldn't believe he'd just come across the Channel. Cotton understood what lay behind the gesture and thoroughly approved.

Gully appeared. 'What are you polishing up for?' he said.

Cotton couldn't explain; he couldn't have explained why the colonel at Dunkirk had put on his best uniform either, even though he understood. 'They're red-hot on polishing in the Marines,' he said shortly.

Still nothing happened and he doggedly began to hum the

Marines' march, a little number called 'Sarie Marais' they'd picked up from the Boers in the South African War. Then he stopped dead as the Greek women started to sing, too; softly, perhaps to lull their children to sleep, a slight tuneless melody with a strange touch of the east, all half-notes that never quite arrived where they appeared to be going. Cotton guessed it was probably an inheritance from the days when Greece was a vassal of the Ottoman Empire.

'How's it going?' he asked Docherty.

Docherty looked up at him. Like Gully, despite himself he had been impressed by Cotton's single-mindedness. They only needed luck now to make their escape and, though he could never have told him so, he knew as well as Bisset that it was entirely due to Cotton's doggedness.

'You've already asked me that,' he pointed out. 'About five times.'

Cotton managed a smile. 'Bit on edge,' he explained. 'Bisset ought to be back soon.'

The Greek women's song stopped and they started another, and this time it was more lively, and he could hear the voices of the men also joining in.

'That lot sound cheerful,' Cotton said.

'More cheerful than I feel,' Docherty said. 'I feel like ten men. Nine dead and one with his foot in the grave. I'll be glad when we're away from here.' He indicated one of the boat's Mae West life-jackets hanging near the engine-room doorway. 'Blown up ready,' he said. 'Only bit of air support we'll get this trip.' He paused. 'I don't suppose we could nip off a bit early, could we?'

Cotton shook his head. 'With that armed launch off the cape, we haven't a chance before dark.'

A little later, they heard the thumping sound from the north again. It seemed to shudder the air and sent shivers down their spines.

'Luftwaffe after our ships,' Docherty said. 'I expect it's Dunkirk all over again.'

There was a long silence, as though the heat weighed heavily on them all. From the shore they could hear the high rasping of crickets. The sea looked like pale silk but seemed as solid and unmoving as metal.

'We'll single up,' Cotton suggested, itching to be off.

'Not till we've started the engines,' Docherty warned. 'She'll surge a bit. Leave 'em.'

Cotton nodded, seeing the sense. '*Will* they start?' he asked.

'Whatcha mean?'

'The batteries. Will they do it?'

'Once,' Docherty said bluntly. 'That's all. They're low and if they don't do it first time, that's it. We're here for the duration.'

The silence continued. The Greeks in the forecastle had fallen silent and Cotton wondered if they were asleep. He slipped into the wheelhouse. The women and children seemed to be dozing in the stuffy heat but through the door he could see Petrakis sitting bolt upright, smoking, and Cotton noticed that the cigarette packet he held in his hand was the familiar duty-free navy issue.

He went back on deck, staring round him, waiting for dusk, praying it would hurry. He glanced up at the hill for Bisset, but the skyline was empty. Then he looked at the hilltop in the direction of Ay Yithion, hoping against hope he'd see Annoula. But again there was nothing except the bare brown-purple soil and the scrub and the clumps of cactus.

He wondered where she'd gone to. She'd been seeking Varvara but Varvara had missed her, and still she hadn't come. He wondered if the Germans had found her and questioned her and, seeing her again in his mind's eye as he'd seen her when Docherty had flung himself down on top of her, with her dress open at the throat and the white flesh of her shoulders and breast, the thought of the Germans touching her, perhaps beating her, using cigarettes on her skin to torture her, made his stomach heave.

How long his bitter thoughts occupied him, he didn't know, but when he jerked to the present again he realized the sun had set and the high hills behind them were flinging shadows. There couldn't be more than half an hour left before darkness arrived. Bisset should be on his way down at any moment.

His eyes flickered towards the direction of Ay Yithion again. There was still no sign of Annoula, and his fist thumped softly on the top of the battered wheelhouse in his frustrated anger.

He glanced towards the sea. It still looked surprisingly bright, covered now by a metallic sheen so that the deep delphinium blue had become paler, almost the colour of lead. There wasn't a ripple on it and he knew that if they moved before dark they'd stick out like a sore thumb on its smooth surface.

'Another half-hour,' Docherty said, chewing at a matchstick. He looked worried and nervous.

'Perhaps less.' Cotton's eyes moved again to the hill-tops looking for the girl and Bisset. He'd given up hope now that Annoula would ever return, and he realized suddenly that he'd missed her since she'd gone that morning. They'd never spoken much to each other but there'd always been a quiet sort of understanding between them and a lot that had gone unsaid.

'Bisset!' Kitcat, sitting in the wheelhouse, spoke suddenly and Cotton heard a faint shout above them. After a while, he saw Bisset scrambling down the slope, carrying the tommy-gun, the binoculars swinging in front of him. He looked in a hurry.

'Stand by, Docherty,' Cotton said. 'Gully, take the stern! Kitcat, foredeck! We might have to leave in a hurry.'

The carpenter hurried down the narrow deck to the well, and Kitcat, dumping his tommy-gun by the winch, waited by the bow ropes.

Bisset was closer now, and they could see him pointing. He came scrambling through the trees, sliding down the last slope on his backside. As his feet thumped on deck, he looked round for Cotton.

'Jerries are on their way,' he panted.

'Where are they?'

'I've been watching them. They arrived some time ago.' He grinned. 'They found the equipment and the cap first and they've been mounting a full-scale attack on the farm. It was worth watching. They weren't paratroopers this time but they did all the usual crawling along ditches and behind walls. When they found nothing, they stood around talking for a long time, then started searching. When they saw that SS car we dumped they did it all over again. I think they're heading this way now. They'll not be here yet, though. They can't get their lorries to the top of the hill here so they'll have to walk and they've a fair way to come.'

'How long?' Cotton asked.

Bisset glanced up the slope where the last of the light was touching the scrub with paler shades. 'Half an hour from now,' he said, 'they'll pop up over that ridge.'

7

Major Baldamus' launch lay in position off Cape Kastamanitsa. The light was going but it was warm and the land scents were coming from Aeos, bringing the smell of dust mingled with flowers and pine trees. The southern aspect of the island looked like a flat wall from which the colours were going and the shadows were taking over as the land grew misty in the twilight. Nothing moved and there were no lights. A narrow spiral of smoke lifted slowly into the air from the direction of Ay Yithion, a reminder to Baldamus of Untersturmbannführer Fernbrugge's activities that morning.

The radio in the cabin below began to cheep and a moment later one of the Wehrmacht soldiers who were crewing the launch appeared alongside Baldamus with a message. It was from Ehrhardt and it had a faintly exultant note that did Baldamus' heart good. 'No word from Fernbrugge,' it said. 'Suspect he's got himself into trouble. Have sent out a party to rescue him.'

Baldamus glanced at the time of origin of the message and saw with surprise that it was more than four hours since Fernbrugge had set out to pick up soldiers and head south.

He clicked his fingers and the signaller gave him a message pad. Baldamus wrote quickly, ordering Ehrhardt to find out if Fernbrugge had managed to collect his soldiers from Haussmann's special battalion. If he had and had lost himself for four hours, then he *was* in trouble, whatever had happened. Baldamus could imagine nothing on Aeos to account for a four-hour silence, and Haussmann wasn't the man to lie down even before the SS.

253

As the signaller disappeared and the cheeping of his radio started again, Baldamus sat in the wheelhouse staring at the land. He lit a cigarette and someone handed him a mug of coffee which he drank in his slow fastidious way.

The young engineer-lieutenant who was in command of the launch appeared and Baldamus indicated the headland. 'Is this the best place for us?' he asked.

The lieutenant peered towards the land. 'If anything leaves the island we'll be right across its path,' he replied.

'Wouldn't it be worth poking our nose into the bay to see if they're still there?'

The lieutenant shook his head. 'It would be dark before we got there.'

'Haven't you a searchlight?'

'Perhaps they've got one too, and I wouldn't want to be caught where we couldn't manoeuvre. I gather they've got a 20-millimetre cannon.'

'Couldn't they slip past in the dark?'

The lieutenant shrugged. 'I'm not Kriegsmarine,' he said. 'I'm just an engineer-lieutenant who used to own a boat of his own at Rostock. I've not been trained to fight sea battles. Mind' – he grinned – 'with the gun we've got, I think we could stop anything that came near us.' He pointed towards the two caiques laying off his starboard quarter, fifty yards away and twenty yards apart, one slightly astern of the other. Like the launch, they were at anchor, bows to the breeze coming off the land.

'We're covering quite a bit of sea,' he pointed out. 'At the first sound of an engine, we can fix our searchlights on the entrance to the bay. We have the advantage. We're facing the way they'll come and, with the wind as it is, we'll hear their engines start.'

As they spoke, the radio cheeped again and a moment later the signaller appeared with the reply to Baldamus' message. It made him smile.

'Fernbrugge accompanied by twenty-four special service men. No signal yet but one of Fernbrugge's vehicles since seen alongside deserted farmhouse on south side of Kalani plain. No sign of crew or of Fernbrugge. Special service vehicle shot up. Suspect trouble he found bad – repeat bad – trouble. Investigating unit now moving on Xiloparissia Bay.'

Baldamus screwed up the paper. It seemed that Untersturmbannführer Fernbrugge had made rather a mess of things and probably got himself killed into the bargain, and he couldn't find it in himself to be very sorry.

He studied the two caiques on their starboard quarter. In the last of the light he could see the men crowding the deck and smoking, and the last faint gleam of light on the barrels of the machine-guns mounted on stands on the sterns.

'So long as they don't get in each other's way and shoot each other or us,' he observed cheerfully, 'we should be able to assemble quite a lot of firepower. It turns out to be rather fortunate for us that they've assembled here.'

And particularly fortunate for Major Renatus von Boenigke Baldamus, he decided. His plans for the future – especially with Untersturmbannführer Fernbrugge safely out of the way with his unpleasant friends and his suspicions of Baldamus' inefficiency – might still come to excellent fruition.

He stared towards the land and the dark patch that marked the entrance to Xiloparissia Bay. 'They'll appear after dark,' he said. 'I think Ehrhardt's people will be flushing them out like rabbits from a burrow any time now.'

While Major Baldamus was studying the land with a satisfied eye, Corporal Cotton was studying the sea, staring from the shelter of Xiloparissia Bay with a great deal of concern.

He glanced at his watch, then back at the sea. It had darkened suddenly and there was a hint of mist so that he felt they might creep out quietly and lay under the shadow of Cape Kastamanitsa.

'We'll go in a quarter of an hour,' he said to Bisset who was leaning against the wheelhouse, staring at the entrance to the bay. 'Did you notice the German launch?'

'As I came over the top,' Bisset said. 'She's off the point with the two caiques. Think she'll see us as we come out? We couldn't risk that.'

'She'll have the light behind her.' Cotton had spotted something that had escaped the notice of Major Baldamus and the engineer-lieutenant on the German launch. They'd stationed the launch so far offshore it was beyond the shadow of the land, while under the loom of the cliffs it was already growing dark. Taking advantage of the light was the oldest naval trick in the world and Cotton had listened to enough naval lore to be well aware of it. The Germans had had the advantage of it at both Coronel and Jutland, firing at British ships with the evening glow behind them while they themselves were protected by a darker horizon and the loom of low cloud. Cotton had the shadow of the cliffs.

'We'll be all right,' he said confidently.

'What about the engines? Won't they hear 'em start up? They make a row like the last trump.'

Cotton had been studying the belt of mist forming close to the shore, willing it to thicken so that it would hide them, and it was a moment or two before he became aware of Bisset's question. Starting up was something that had been worrying him too, but the thudding of the gunfire had grown louder now, as though the British ships engaged in the evacuation to the north were being heavily pursued to sea by the Luftwaffe, and he hoped it might drown the noise of the engines.

He stared up at the ridge of hills again. There was no sign of Annoula, and his heart sank and his stomach felt empty as he turned towards the wheelhouse.

'Tell the Greeks we're leaving, Kitcat,' he said. 'And tell them women to pray with all their Greek Orthodox faith that we'll make it. Then stand by the forrard rope.'

As Kitcat disappeared into the wheelhouse, Cotton stared round him, assessing the light. The brightness had gone from the sea now. If they could only get out of the bay without being seen, they might easily lay under the shadow of the cliffs until total darkness. He gave a final glance towards the ridge of the hill. There was no sign of anyone and he sighed.

The heavy rumble of guns came again, and he heard the loose glass in the wheelhouse give a vibrating rattle that seemed particularly loud. Then, over the rumbling, he realized he could hear aeroplane engines growing closer and, in the distance, the vanished sun glinting on the underside of their wings as they circled, he saw a flight of five machines. They were the same big three-engined Junkers they'd seen before, and they were turning in a wide arc out to sea to come over the hills to land on the strip at Yanitsa, dropping lower all the time as they lined up into the wind.

'Stand by!' he yelled.

The five transports came lower. The noise of the engines grew louder and Cotton peered upwards through the trees, wondering if *Loukia* could be seen. The aeroplanes were low in the sky as he hurried back to the wheelhouse.

'Start up,' he said.

Docherty disappeared and Cotton held his breath. For a long time nothing happened and he heard Docherty swearing.

'Oh, Lord,' he prayed, 'let 'em start!'

The aeroplanes were almost directly overhead as the starboard engine exploded into life. Normally it could have been heard in Ay Yithion but, with the roaring of fifteen engines above them, it sounded as if the big Packards had become mute. The second engine came to life a moment or two later and Cotton felt *Loukia* surge against the springs. The aeroplanes had passed overhead now and moved out of sight beyond the hills. Almost immediately it seemed as if the sound was cut off by a knife. The boat's engines had settled down now to a low poppling sound that was muffled by the intervening cliffs and the thudding of the guns.

'You've got ten minutes,' Bisset warned, looking at his watch. 'I shouldn't leave it any longer.'

'Stand by!'

'Hold it!' Kitcat's voice came thinly through the low rumble

257

of the exhausts. 'Somebody's coming! Down the hill there! It's the dame!'

Cotton's heart leapt and his head turned. Barely discernible against the purple shadow of the hillside, he could see her yellow shirt. She was waving and her mouth was opening and shutting, but he couldn't hear her voice because of the engines.

Docherty's head appeared. 'Okay,' he said. 'I'm ready.'

'Wait! We've got another passenger.'

'If we wait much longer, they'll be *German* passengers.'

The girl had reached the beach now and was crossing it in a stumbling run. As she began to climb among the rocks and into the trees, even in the growing darkness Cotton could see that the yellow shirt was torn from her shoulder and that there was a livid bruise down the side of her face. Her knees and hands were dirty and as she stumbled between the rocks he jumped ashore to swing her to the deck. She fell limply against him as he lifted her aboard, and he saw that her lips were swollen and there was blood along her hairline.

'What happened?' he said. 'Was it the Germans?'

'No!' Her voice was an incoherent gasp. 'It was Chrysostomos! He sold a watch in the village to buy wine. He said it was his and the owner of the bar gave it to me and said that, as Chrysostomos was escaping, perhaps he would need it and should have it back.'

She pulled a man's wrist watch from the pocket of her skirt and showed it to Cotton in a muddy palm. 'It has English words on the back,' she said. 'Chrysostomos couldn't read them and neither could the priest. But *I* could.'

Cotton struck a match. '*To Lt-Cdr Samways*,' he read. '*From MTB 19*.'

Immediately a great many things that were already in line clicked into place: Petrakis' interest in *Claudia*. The weapons he'd always been able to replace when he'd lost them. The fact that they were British, and that he smoked British cigarettes. The fact that the Germans had apparently murdered Samways and his men but had failed to remove *Claudia*'s cargo; that they'd behaved with reasonable reverence to the bodies on the beach at

Kharasso but had killed the men at Xiloparissia. It stuck out in clear blinding light. Petrakis had known all along about the bullion *Loukia* was carrying because Xilouris came from Antipalia and had probably even been part of the organization that was due to receive it, and they'd murdered Samways and his men in the expectation of finding it. They'd failed only because Samways had taken the precaution of hiding it before he was surprised.

Annoula was still sobbing incoherently. 'It was Chrysostomos who told the Germans the Varvaras had the petrol,' she was saying. 'It was the petrol they'd pumped from the boat. It was because Varvara told about the guns in the cave. He wanted his revenge on them – and on you. It was Chrysostomos, Chrysostomos!'

She spat the name out as though she couldn't stand the taste of it on her tongue. 'He's evil,' she sobbed. 'He was always evil. I couldn't believe that he could be *so* evil.'

They were all staring at her crouching against Cotton's chest. Gully stood on the stern about to haul in the spring, and Docherty had his head out of the engine room, indignant like the rest. Bisset was further aft near the well deck and Kitcat was by the winch holding the bow rope, wet and heavy from being in the water.

'Cotton!'

Bisset's quiet voice brought their heads up and, as he turned, Cotton saw that Petrakis had appeared in the dusk from the wheelhouse and that he had a revolver in his hand. Xilouris pushed through behind him with Cesarides. They also held revolvers which had clearly been hidden beneath the blankets they'd worn.

Petrakis pointed his weapon at Cotton and said something in Greek. Annoula clung more tightly to him.

'He won't put you ashore,' Cotton said.

'He doesn't want to! He wants me to move! He wants to shoot you!'

Petrakis spoke again but the girl only clung tighter.

'Shoot me,' she screamed. 'Shoot me! Leave him alone!'

Cesarides jumped forward and, as he grabbed her arm to swing her violently aside, Petrakis lifted the revolver and Cotton found himself staring down the muzzle. The hole in the end looked as big as the six-inch guns on *Caernarvon*.

The Greek's fingers tightened on the trigger and Cotton had decided he'd no more than seconds left to live when Kitcat's arm swung suddenly and the bow rope he was holding, soaked with water and heavy as lead, hit the Cretan across the face. As he yelled in pain, Cotton leapt forward. The girl, just scrambling to her feet, went flying again as Cotton kicked out and sent the revolver spinning through the air. As Petrakis reeled away, Cotton saw he had a knife in his fist but Kitcat, sweeping up the tommy-gun he'd laid down, lifted it to his waist and pulled the trigger. The burst hit Petrakis in the chest and lifted him clean off the deck to drop him with a splash into the sea alongside the boat. Xilouris, yelling with fright, was cut down by a second burst and slithered across the deck to fall half-through the broken window of the wheelhouse. The boy, Cesarides, flung his hands in the air at once and dropped to his knees, yelling for mercy, but Varvara's crewman, Papaboukas, stepped up behind him and, grabbing his hair to wrench his head back, slit his throat with a single stroke of his knife. The wheezy gurgle and splutter as his cries died sent a shiver down their backs. Coldly, Papaboukas wiped the knife on the body and pushed it away from him into the water.

Annoula, her face buried in her hands, was huddled on the deck. Cotton drew a deep breath. Then, dragging Xilouris' body clear, he pushed at it with his foot so that it rolled over the side to splash into the bay after the other two.

'Jesus Christ,' Bisset said quietly. 'We've seen some bloody butchery today.'

'We've also buggered up the whole operation,' Cotton said in a flat voice. 'Because those bloody Germans waiting on that launch outside must have heard the shooting.'

8

They had.

The engineer-lieutenant had been standing by the door of the wheelhouse staring towards the entrance to Xiloparissia Bay, and his head jerked up as he heard the sound of the tommy-gun.

Baldamus was alongside him in a second. He had been sitting in the captain's cabin listening to Goebbels' radio trumpeting the triumph in Greece. The crackle of fire from ashore had wrenched him savagely from a sense of euphoric satisfaction and he had leapt for the deck, leaving the door swinging on its hinges, its ringed handle clinking as it slammed against the stop.

'What's that?' he demanded.

'Machine-gun.'

'Where?'

The engineer-lieutenant pointed towards Xiloparissia Bay.

'Ehrhardt's men must have arrived.' Baldamus smiled in the growing darkness. 'He's either stopped them or he's driving them out to sea. We'd better keep a sharp look-out.'

As the lieutenant went inside the lighted wheelhouse, Baldamus glanced at the clock. Everything seemed to have hung together very neatly. Where Fernbrugge and his precious black-coated friends had failed, the operation initiated by himself had succeeded. He followed the lieutenant inside the wheelhouse and, lighting a cigarette, sat down to wait.

Inside Xiloparissia Bay, *Loukia*'s engines were still rumbling and they were all staring at Cotton as he lifted the girl to her feet. She clung to him, sobbing.

'They saw me leaving Ay Yithion,' she choked. 'They took me into the bushes and beat me. They – they – Xilouris – ' She gave a whimpering moan, her fingers digging into Cotton's arm, kneading the flesh in her distress. 'And he let them! He let them! Chrysostomos let them! He watched and he was – he was laughing.'

She gave a great gulping hiccuping sob. 'I knew while they were doing it, what he'd done. I remembered when he first went to look for the boat that he said to Cesarides, "We couldn't find it." I thought then he meant the boat but he meant money. They wanted it. They told me today. It's hidden on the hillside somewhere.'

'We've got it aboard,' Cotton reassured her. 'They must have seen us and they were intending to take over the boat somehow.'

She continued to cling to him, choking on her sobs and holding his hand against her cheek, as trusting as a child as he tried inadequately to comfort her.

'It'll be all right,' he said. 'It'll be all right.'

'Cotton – '

It was Bisset's voice and, as Cotton turned, he nodded silently towards the sea. It was practically dark now and Cotton realized at once that if they didn't leave now they might never find their way out of the bay.

Young Varvara's wife and the two other women had appeared on deck, wondering what had happened, and Cotton gestured to them to take Annoula below. They prised her from him and helped her through the wheelhouse, still sobbing, their voices soft and concerned, their eyes big and dark and sad.

'Okay,' Cotton said. 'Let's go.'

They moved to their places, Kitcat on the bow, Gully by the stern, Docherty in the engine room.

As the ropes splashed into the water, the boat went ahead gently against the forward spring so that the stern came out.

'Let go spring!'

As Kitcat let the spring slip free, Cotton put the telegraphs to astern and the boat began to edge gently away from the shadows of the trees in a tight circle to the centre of the bay, Cotton's eyes always on the shallow water over the submerged rock he'd found. As the boat slowed, he thrust the telegraphs from neutral to ahead.

Varvara, one of his brothers, and Papaboukas had reappeared in the wheelhouse and stood waiting quietly behind Cotton. There was a blue-grey haze beyond the black opening to the bay, hiding the lift of waves and rocks at the entrance. The slaty depths glistened with a strange sort of incandescence. Shoving the throttles to slow ahead, Cotton felt the propellers bite and, standing in the charred wheelhouse, he stared into the shadows. The stars were not bright yet and there was no moon, so that the mouth of the bay and the rim of the surf were barely discernible.

The entrance was narrow and he peered through the broken window for half-submerged rocks.

'There!' Kitcat pointed and Cotton edged the bows to star-board. A second rock appeared, like a pale shadow in the black-ness. Then they were edging through the entrance to the bay into the long deep swell and the low-lying mist that flattened the scent of the sea and the smell of wild thyme from ashore.

'What about the German launch?' Kitcat said.

'I'm hoping they don't know we're out.' Cotton cut the revolu-tions until the boat was merely wallowing on the swell. 'They probably haven't heard us.'

Kitcat stared over the side at the slow-moving water. 'Then why don't we get cracking?' he said.

Cotton's eyes glittered. 'I'm going to wipe the bastards out,' he growled.

Kitcat's head jerked up. 'There are three of 'em,' he pointed out. 'Two packed with soldiers, all armed.'

'P'r'aps they'll get in each other's way,' Cotton said calmly. 'The Marines was always good at cutting-out expeditions. Nelson knew that.' He glanced at Kitcat. 'How good would you be with the 20-mill?'

263

'I can hit what I'm aiming at, so long as I'm close enough.'

Cotton nodded grimly. 'We'll be close enough,' he said. 'Let's have Bisset and Gully on the Lewises. I'll use the Bren.'

'What about the goddam boat? You expecting it to steer itself?'

'Varvara's here, isn't he? He's got a boat of his own, so surely he can steer if I tell him what to do. I'll be right outside the door there, won't I? Papaboukas can act as loader for the 20-mill and the other Varvara for the rest of us.'

Kitcat stared at Cotton for a second then he slapped him on the shoulder and vanished to the stern with Papaboukas and Varvara's brother. Cotton turned to Varvara. 'Do you know what to do?' he asked.

Varvara studied the throttles. 'Yes.'

Cotton pointed to the duplicated controls. 'Telegraphs. Throttles. You work them together.' He placed a broad hand over the closely set levers, then moved it to the throttles and let it rest on the brass knobs. Understand?'

'Yes.'

Cotton pointed to starboard. 'I shall be there,' he said. 'I'll tell you what to do. All you have to do is as I tell you. Try it. Nice and easy.'

Varvara stood behind the wheel and eased the telegraph handles to ahead. The boat began to idle slowly through the water, the engines poppling.

'Try the throttles.'

As Varvara moved the throttles, the speed picked up and immediately Cotton gestured to him to pull the handles back. 'That's enough!'

Varvara did as he was told, frowning heavily with concentration.

'How she'll behave I don't know,' Cotton said. 'We haven't been able to have a trial run and the rudder's stiff. It's up to you.'

Varvara looked dubious, then he smiled. 'I have handled fast boats,' he said. 'I have worked in the Piraeus during the summer season with the tourists.'

Docherty appeared, irrepressible as ever. 'What's going on?' he demanded.

Cotton told him what he had in mind and his eyes widened. 'With this bloody wreck?' he said. Then he shrugged and did a little dance step. 'We put the bloody thing together to get us home, not sink the German navy.'

'That's what we exist for, isn't it?' Cotton said. 'Sinking the German navy.'

Docherty shrugged and Cotton pressed him. 'Well, come on,' he demanded. 'Will she do it?'

Docherty gave a sudden mad grin, his black boot-button eyes merry. 'I reckon she might. I expect the rudder'll drop off and the vibration aft'll shake my teeth out, so for Christ's sake don't keep her at high revs longer than you can help.'

Cotton glanced up at the makeshift mast he'd rigged, with the rag of the white ensign at the top just beginning to flutter a little as the wind off the land caught it. It wasn't much cop as a battle ensign but it would have to do.

'How long can we keep her at high revs?' he asked.

Docherty gave his mad grin again.

'Two-three minutes.'

'That's enough. Then we make smoke and shove off behind it.'

'Leaving 'em coughin' their bloody socks off.' Docherty was still grinning. 'Where'd you learn your battle tactics, Cotton? Off of Admiral Cunningham hisself?'

Gully's head reached round the door. 'What's up?' he demanded.

'We're going to war,' Docherty said.

Cotton nodded. They were indeed going to war. 'I think we owe these bloody Jerries a bit for what we've had to put up with,' he said.

Gully looked nervous, his new courage evaporating rapidly again. 'Don't forget I'm a civilian,' he bleated.

'Out to enjoy the war, you said,' Docherty pointed out with mad glee. 'You shut your bloody trap, Gully. If Cotton's gone barmy, then okay, for once I'll back him up.'

Cotton could have kissed him. Docherty was trouble, every kind of trouble, lazy, awkward, difficult, boozy and over-sexed, ready to drop everything for a dance or the chance to get a girl on her back, but somehow, somewhere, what made the navy had rubbed off on him. Cotton slapped his shoulder and followed him aft as he went to the engine room, to explain what he intended to Kitcat.

Kitcat was standing by the 20 mm. It was cocked and ready and trained as far round as he could get it.

'Will it go any further?'

'I'd fall off the stern.'

'If they're lying into wind,' Cotton said, 'then their bows are towards us. I'm going to cross their T.'

'What's that, for Christ's sake?'

Cotton stared at him, wishing he had a crew of sailors or Marines instead of the ham-handed shore-bashers he'd been given. He explained carefully.

'They've all got their weapons on their sterns,' he said. 'The caiques machine-guns, the launch something a bloody sight bigger. But if we cross their bows, they won't be able to fire at us along their own decks, will they, while you'll still be able to fire over to starboard at them. Right?'

He indicated with his hands what he intended and Kitcat nodded.

'I'm going to approach slowly,' Cotton went on. 'I shall get as close as I can with the engines idling. We've got to take our time, anyway, because we can't chance too much manoeuvring with that bent rudder. But there's a bit of gunfire and bombing and a few aeroplanes about, so they might just not hear us.'

'I hope to Christ you know what you're doing.'

Cotton ignored the jibe. 'Get the launch first,' he said. 'Go for the waterline so she won't be able to follow us. The petrol tanks should be aft of the wheelhouse. Bisset and I'll try to get any gunners who appear.'

'Right.'

Cotton looked down at Papaboukas standing with Varvara's

brother close to the 20 mm platform. Neither of them looked very happy.

'You afraid?' Cotton asked.

Papaboukas moved his shoulders in a gesture that meant nothing and everything at the same time. 'My wife is forward,' he said.

'I meant about the gun.' Cotton indicated the long barrel of the 20 mm just above his head and Papaboukas' shoulders moved again.

As the boat idled, wallowing in the water under the cliffs, the engines still poppling quietly, Cotton went forward to explain to Bisset what he wanted.

'I don't suppose Gully'll be much good,' he said. 'But he can keep down any opposition on his side. Leave the caiques until last.'

'Suppose they're waiting for us?' Bisset asked.

Cotton pointed to the cliffs. 'I'm hoping that those bloody Greeks up there will start something on Cape Kastamanitsa any minute now,' he said. 'It might just attract their attention.'

Bisset managed a twisted smile. 'I hope you're right,' he said. 'Personally, I reckon we've taken enough chances for one day and we're pushing our luck a bit.'

Cotton shrugged. 'Keep an eye on Gully,' he advised. 'Make sure he doesn't shoot you. He might if he gets excited.'

With a marline-spike, he jabbed two holes in the plywood of the wheelhouse deckhead and jammed the legs of the Bren's bipod into them. Young Varvara had grasped quickly what was in his mind, and he gave him a nervous smile.

'Stand by,' Cotton said, jamming a magazine into place and pulling the cocking handle. 'Dead slow ahead.'

They edged forward slowly, moving away from the cliffs until they were heading out to sea. By now it was possible to see the loom of Kastamanitsa point.

'Starboard.'

The bow came round as they crept south, close against the dark shadow of the land where they couldn't be seen. Cotton glanced aft at the wake. It showed faintly phosphorescent against the black sea but there was very little of it. The throb of the engines seemed loud enough to alert every German on the island. Then Varvara touched his arm and pointed. Just ahead he could see the big German launch he'd heard about. It was about a quarter of a mile away and was roughly the same size as *Loukia*. What looked like a four-pounder was mounted on the stern. If they managed to get a shot in with that, he thought, it would be the end of *Loukia*, and for a moment he wondered if he were doing right.

He knew how much things could go wrong and he knew what could happen if they did.

'*Any person . . . who, through negligence or other default, shall strand, lose or hazard, or suffer to be lost, stranded or hazarded, any of His Majesty's ships or aircraft, shall be dismissed from His Majesty's Service with disgrace, or suffer such other punishment as is hereinafter mentioned . . . .*' It was an instruction designed chiefly for ships' captains and officers, but Cotton had a pretty good idea it could apply to Marine corporals just as well, and here he was, not only about to strand, lose or hazard one of His Majesty's ships, but probably going to kill everybody on board into the bargain.

He swallowed. 'Port,' he ordered. 'Do it gently. Bring her round. We don't want any violent manoeuvring. Then I want a straight course across their bows. Okay?'

Varvara nodded. 'Okay.'

'Right. Dead slow. Neutral.'

Loukia came to a stop, wallowing in the water, the sound of the engines muffled by the mist. The sky beyond the loom of the cliff was flickering with flashes that appeared to come from the mainland where the fighting was dragging on as the navy tried to evacuate the army. The heavens echoed with the sound of aircraft and Cotton guessed their approach hadn't yet been heard. There were faint lights on the German vessels and here again Cotton thought he might have gained a slight advantage. He'd been at the Battle of Matapan and had been shouted at for introducing a light at the wrong moment to spoil *Caernarvon*'s bridge officers' night vision. The lesson had gone home, and ever since it had grown dark he had been careful to allow no lights on *Loukia*; he could see faint lights on the German vessels and he hoped that the Germans wouldn't see as well as he did.

He pointed out the boats to Bisset, then moved aft to Kitcat and pointed.

'I've seen 'em,' Kitcat assured him.

'Right, then. This is it.'

Returning to the Bren, he called out softly to Varvara. 'Dead slow. Ahead both. Keep her steady.'

The boat began to creep forward again. Cotton's heart was thumping in his chest and his breath seemed to gag in his throat. He thought of the women and children below and of Annoula, still shocked by what had happened to her. Any shots that came from the Germans would hit *Loukia*'s bows first. He forced himself not to think of it.

The Germans didn't seem to be expecting them and by now they were within three hundred yards. Varvara glanced at Cotton. The big launch was on its own about fifty yards from the two caiques which lay to starboard, one slightly astern of the other. They were all bow-on to them and he guessed they all had their anchors down, which gave him another slight advantage.

'Across their bows,' he directed and *Loukia* edged slowly round.

They crept closer until they were no more than a hundred and fifty yards from the German vessels. Then suddenly, above the engines, they heard the faint crackle of firing from the direction of Cape Kastamanitsa. Cotton grinned.

'It's the Greeks!' he said. 'Stand by!'

The firing on Cape Kastamanitsa came just as a radio message from Captain Ehrhardt was received aboard the launch. Ehrhardt had arrived in Xiloparissia Bay just too late, to find *Loukia* gone, and had immediately scrambled back up the slope to the lorry to scrawl the message for the radio operator sitting by the set in the back.

'*Boat gone,*' he wrote. '*Heading towards you. Will check Kharasso Bay.*'

The radio on Baldamus' launch cheeped and the wireless operator scrawled the words down and headed for the deck. Just as he emerged, the crackling of firing on the headland started, followed by a flash and a flare of flame that looked like a lorry set on fire by a grenade.

The look-out on the launch's bows swung round at the sound of shots and stood gaping sternwards over the wheelhouse towards the point. At his shouts, Baldamus and the engineer-lieutenant had appeared, followed by the rest of the crew pouring up from below. The wheelhouse door gaped open, throwing a yellow light on the waves as they stood staring towards Cape Kastamanitsa.

Pushing through the crowding men, the radio operator handed Baldamus the sheet of paper he was carrying. Baldamus glanced at it but it was too dark to read on deck and the firing on Cape Kastamanitsa was holding his attention. As he stared, there was another explosion, acid-white this time, that suggested ammunition had blown up, and he stared, puzzled, across the slowly lifting water to the loom of the cliff.

'What the devil's happening there?' he demanded aloud.

'Looks like someone's having a go at the look-out post,' the engineer-lieutenant said.

Baldamus frowned, wondering how much it was connected with the shooting they'd just heard from Xiloparissia Bay. Perhaps, he decided, Ehrhardt's men had driven the British away from their boat and they were now fighting some sort of running battle towards the point.

Stuffing the message into his pocket unread, he went into the wheelhouse, blinking in the light, to pick up a pair of binoculars. Outside again, he put them to his eyes but, apart from the glow of flames, he could see very little against the dark loom of the land.

He was faintly irritated because he'd hoped that the climax of the day's proceedings would lie with him not Ehrhardt, but at least Ehrhardt was acting on his instructions and any credit that was going would remain with him. He'd make very sure it would.

'It looks as though Ehrhardt's doing his stuff,' he said. 'I think we've probably got them.'

But he hadn't. Not quite.

Staring at the flare of light on the point, Cotton guessed that Delageorgis had got at the German ammunition and he wondered briefly in passing how many of the Greeks had gone up with it.

It was no time to dwell on possible casualties, however. Delageorgis had known what he'd taken on and what he was doing, and at least he was there with his men, not sitting in some headquarters in safety, moving flags and pins that merely meant other men dying.

Cotton's eyes flickered towards the three boats ahead of him. A light had appeared on the launch, bright and square as if a door had been opened. Then another light appeared on one of the caiques and against them they could see men standing on deck staring towards the cape.

'Now,' Cotton said. 'Full ahead! Straight across their bows.'

Varvara's hands moved and the engines exploded into full power. The bow rose as the stern sank; the big wave aft lifted and Cotton saw the wake widen and lengthen. They were within fifty yards of the Germans now, *Loukia* bucking like a frantic animal. Water leapt over the wheelhouse in slashing spouts that found their way through the broken windows, and what doors remained banged and clattered as she shuddered.

More lights appeared on the armed launch and against them it was possible to see the Germans on the deck beginning to turn as they heard *Loukia*'s engines. As they started running, Kitcat opened fire. The thumping of the 20 mm seemed to shake *Loukia* to the keel. The muzzle flash lit up Bisset's face as he bent behind the Lewis and pulled the trigger.

With speed came surging primitive courage. The forty-knot slipstream blasted Cotton's cheeks and the engines trumpeted beneath his feet. The boat was clear of the water for a third of her length now as the speed built up and she started planing, and astern the wake swept away with the whiteness of a mountain torrent. His senses and his brain responded to the storm of wind in a tremendous keenness to smash the Germans.

The wildly glittering peak of water and the vast cascades on either side of the bow, the sledgehammer jolts to the spine as the boat bucketed through the sea, and the exhaust smoke feathering astern in a furious elemental cacophony of noise, seemed glorious to Cotton. The odds were dead against him succeeding, he knew, but the excitement gripped him and he knew suddenly why it was the Light Brigade had managed to charge down their Russian valley without faltering. They'd probably been carried forward by elation rather than duty and had probably even enjoyed it in part as he was enjoying it now.

He'd held his fire, waiting to use the Bren to the best advantage. He could see Kitcat's shots going over the German launch, little slots of light vanishing into the darkness in a flat arc.

'Lower, lower!' he yelled, the words forced out of him by his excitement, and he saw the slots of light change course and begin to flash against the German launch. The windows of the wheel-house disintegrated and he saw one of the stays that held the mast snap so that it heeled to starboard, while great chunks of wood flew from the upperworks.

There was a group of men round the gun on the stern now but Cotton's first burst from the Bren sent them all diving for cover. Then he saw the 20 mm shells bursting all along the German's waterline, lifting splashes high above the deck.

The sudden appearance of *Loukia* just off the launch's port bow came as a complete surprise to Baldamus. He was standing by the door to the cabin alongside the engineer-lieutenant, Ehrhardt's message still unread in his pocket, staring towards Cape Kastamanitsa where there was a new outbreak of firing. He frowned, puzzled, and was just about to push below to read the message when he heard the first bellow of *Loukia*'s engines. Unlike Cotton, neither he nor the engineer-lieutenant had any experience of attacks at sea in the dark and it had not occurred to either of them to protect their night vision. Neither had they allowed for the sound of gunfire and aeroplanes drowning the sound of *Loukia*'s engines and they had quite failed to realize how well the loom of the land and the mist on the water could hide her shape. There had been no sign of a bow wave or a wake until now and the distraction on Cape Kastamanitsa had momentarily drawn their attention away from the point which held most chance of danger.

As Baldamus swung round, he saw a white curving wave and the faint bulk of a boat behind it, cutting across the bows of the launch at high speed; above it apparently unattached, the fluttering square of the white ensign.

'Fire!' he screamed. 'Fire!'

But it was impossible to bring the gun to bear because the wheel-house, with Baldamus and the engineer-lieutenant standing alongside it, were all in the way and the crew could only wait until the enemy had moved further to their starboard side.

'Fire!' Baldamus screamed again but it was almost as if the wrong people had heard because little slots of light began to float over his head. They seemed at first to come straight at him, then they appeared to change course and whip beyond the launch. The windows of the wheelhouse disintegrated, showering him with glass and he heard a twang as one of the stays that held the mast parted.

By this time the boat seemed to be falling apart all round him and huge splinters of wood were flying from the deck. The men at the gun on the stern were still waiting for their sights to bear when a burst of machine-gun fire flung them all to the deck and, to his horror, Baldamus realized that cannon shells were thumping into the side of the launch. He heard screams from the engine room and knew that men were being injured there. Then, as the crew of the stern gun tried once more to reach their weapon, he heard the high tearing sound of a high-speed weapon and they were literally lifted off their feet and flung over the side.

The British boat was passing close by the launch's bows now

and shells were probing her side between the wheelhouse and the stern where the petrol tanks were situated. A vast shaft of flame leapt up with explosive force, tearing at the deck to lift planks and metalwork and blast men's bodies, and as the heat burned his face and he felt himself blown over the side, his flesh scorched and charred, it occurred to Baldamus in a blinding flash of reality that seared through ambition, hope and guesswork, that all those fine plans of his had finally come to an end.

As *Loukia* drew clear of the German launch, Bisset was yelling with excitement. A last attempt to reach the gun on the stern had been stopped in its tracks and they were now crossing the bows of the caiques with no more than twenty-odd yards between them.

Men on the deck of the caiques were firing with rifles and sub-machine-guns now. There seemed to be dozens of them, packed in like sardines with more appearing from below. Cotton swung the Bren and pressed the trigger, knowing he couldn't miss and that they couldn't hide or dodge or run. It was hard to see for the muzzle flash but, as they roared past, he saw men falling in windrows, like corn before a scythe, and more of them jumping into the water.

Gully was screaming with excitement – 'I got 'im! I got 'im!' – and out of the corner of his eye Cotton saw him crouched behind the port Lewis. He had pressed the trigger and was letting the whole panful of ammunition go in one long roar across the top of the wheelhouse, the stream of bullets coming nearer and nearer to Bisset's head. Fortunately the ammunition ran out just in time and, as he started pounding the gun, Cotton heard him cursing.

'The fucken thing's stopped,' he yelled in disappointed fury. 'The fucken thing's stopped!'

'It's empty,' Bisset yelled back at him as he slammed another magazine on his own Lewis. And a bloody good thing too, Cotton thought.

Kitcat's cannon was doing deadly work and the big German launch seemed to be literally melting away as they roared past. The 20 mm swung as they surged ahead and Kitcat was shooting over the stern now. Then suddenly, unexpectedly, there was a tremendous flash and a flare of flame as the launch's petrol tanks ignited. In the glare they could see planks flying through the air and men hurled into the sparkling water.

For a second Kitcat stopped firing. Then he switched to the caiques, doing dreadful slaughter among the crowded Germans, the shells flashing and bursting among them, so that their screaming could be heard above the roar of the engines. The outside caique, its anchor up at last, was swinging away to safety, while the inside one lay wallowing on the sea, its crew still too shocked to make a move.

They were fifty yards ahead now, with Kitcat firing short bursts over the stern. In the glare of the flames, they saw the caique's wheelhouse start to burn and men jumping overboard. A man wearing an officer's cap tried to set up a machine-gun on a mount but one of Kitcat's shells hit him and he seemed to explode into tatters of bloody flesh. Then they saw the flames reach up in a great flare and everybody on deck started leaping into the water as Kitcat turned his deadly weapon on to the second caique.

A solitary brave figure fought to use a machine-gun by the wheelhouse and, as it started, Cotton seemed to be staring straight into the muzzle flash. Slots of light vanished on either side of him. Then *Loukia*'s remaining windows fell in and he heard Varvara yell in the darkness just as something exploded in his head and he was flung against the wheelhouse, half-blinded, his big fists still trying to clutch the Bren.

'Smoke,' he yelled and through the haze of blood he saw Bisset run aft and, in his excitement, pull the cocks of both canisters.

As the smoke poured out, forced away by the compressed air, it filled the well and trailed astern to cling to the surface of the water, and Cotton reckoned he'd never seen so much bloody smoke in his life. It seemed to fill the whole world, and Bisset and Kitcat and the two Greeks emerged from the well coughing and spluttering, their eyes streaming.

As *Loukia* lurched off course and was wrenched back again, Cotton staggered. For a moment, as he clung to the Bren, he was staring down into the dark rushing sea alongside him, the drenching sound of hurrying water filling his ears. Kitcat's gun had stopped now and in an explosive sigh Cotton let out the breath he seemed to have been holding ever since they'd left Xiloparissia Bay.

It was Bisset who grabbed him as he swayed. Then the boat hit a wave, and as it lurched both he and Cotton crashed down the wheelhouse steps to the deck, to sprawl just behind Varvara among the shards of glass and splinters of woodwork.

9

Loukia arrived off Suda Bay two days later in the first opalescent light of dawn at just about the same time as Captain Ehrhardt was fishing what was left of Major Baldamus from the sea off Cape Kastamanitsa and just as an air raid was developing from the direction of Rhodes.

There were two ships, packed with soldiers in a khaki mass along their decks, and the German aircraft hardly noticed *Loukia*. The aircraft were Junkers 87s but their attacks were indecisive and desultory, the machines skimming over the hills to do more of a low-level glide than a dive, so that their bombing was inaccurate. One bomb closely missed one of the transports, however, and they saw her heel over and steady, then come to a stop with steam coming from her engine-room ventilators.

They had managed to pick up extra petrol at Sifnos and Sikinos and, by using one engine at a time to conserve it, had crept southwards all day and all night. At first light on the second morning, unnoticed by the aircraft that swarmed overhead, they had slipped past as Stukas attacked a convoy on the horizon. They could see the columns of water rising alongside the struggling ships and hear the thud of explosions. God alone knew what the men on board were going through and had gone through already to get so far. But by this time the army was pouring out of Greek ports, and the only glimmer of brightness to penetrate the gloom was the hope of rescue by the navy.

There had been one or two nightmare moments when they'd seen flights of Junkers 87s going over, often with 88s higher up, but *Loukia* had remained an insignificant spot on the surface of the sea and nobody had bothered to investigate them until a British destroyer, already laden with troops, had moved across their path and stopped to ask them who they were.

It had even offered to take their passengers aboard but Cotton – and not only Cotton but the others, even Docherty – having made their own way so far, were in favour of completing the journey under their own steam and they'd rejected the offer. The naval officer on the deck above them had indicated the bandage on Cotton's head.

'How many wounded?'

Cotton gestured. 'Two,' he said. 'Only slightly.'

It hadn't seemed slight at the time, however, he'd thought, as he'd come round on the wheelhouse floor with Annoula crouched over him, her hair across his face like a dark wing as she wept.

'He's not dead,' Varvara had snorted, holding his own injured shoulder, and she snapped into efficiency, tearing at her skirt and bullying the other women to give up clothing to make bandages.

Cotton was just laboriously finishing his report when they caught the first glimpse of Crete and a convoy of ships packed with soldiers.

'We've arrived!' As they swung into Suda Bay, Bisset put his head into the smashed radio cabin where Cotton was working.

'Right.' Cotton put down his pencil and picked up the battered log, written up in his neat square hand. It was all there, right from the beginning, not very fulsome and lacking in resounding phrases, but there nevertheless.

'Casualties,' it ended. 'Dead: Lt Shaw, Lt Patullo, CERA Duff and Pte Coward RASC. Wounded and prisoner of war: Pte Howard, RASC. Wounded: Self (slightly) and one refugee, Athanasios Varvara (cut by flying glass).'

He signed it, and closing the log book, went on deck. The sight of Crete lifted his heart, though from the German papers in his pocket he knew the respite was only temporary. Vessels of all kinds were gathering there, caiques, motor boats and small local craft from harbours and coastal villages all round the island, their reluctant owners urged to help the hard-pressed British army. In

278

the bay, destroyers packed with men were still alongside oilers, unable to disembark the soldiers on to the ships that were to take them to Egypt because the berths alongside those ships were already occupied.

As they approached, a frigate came rushing towards them and men's heads appeared as they leaned over to gape at the strange multi-coloured launch, bald-headed without its mast.

'What ship are you?'

'*Loukia*. From a mission to Aeos. With Greek refugees and survivors from *Claudia*.'

'There's a wooden jetty at the far side of the harbour. You can get in there.'

The morning seemed to be dragging out, the sun apparently nailed to the sky, and everyone was on edge in case another flight of 87s, more determined than the last lot, arrived. But none came and they moored by the wooden jetty alongside a destroyer.

All round the bay gun positions were being erected, and the men on the destroyer said there were more going up at Heraklion and Canea and everywhere the Germans might get a troopship or landing craft in. The destroyer was due to leave for Greece at any moment to pick up more troops and bring them back to man the growing defences, and the crew were all busy, clearing away the rubbish left by the last lot, the scraps of letters, the fag ends, the pieces of bread and stale bully, and the lost items of equipment and steel helmets.

'It's bloody hopeless,' they said. 'Some of the bloody senior officers have given up hope and, while there's some regiments parading as if they were outside Buckingham Palace, as you go alongside there's others so disorganized they'll never get fetched off.'

The Jerries had got *Diamond* and *Wryneck*, and were expected to get a few more before they'd finished, while a Junkers 53 had landed on Milos and demanded that it surrender or they'd take off again and bomb it. Milos had surrendered.

They were splicing slings for stretchers, and lashing drums together to make rafts, because already it was clear that the men in Greece would have to find their way out from the beaches on anything that would float. Benches were being roped off for operations and the cooks were baking double helpings of bread. The sailors seemed fatalistic and indifferent, not bothering to clean up because they took the view that it wasn't much use if the pongos were going to come and muck it all up again.

Loukia had hardly got her ropes across when a car appeared, heading for the jetty in a cloud of dust. Its horn going, it edged along the planking until it stopped by the destroyer. The man who climbed from it was Lieutenant-Commander Kennard. He crossed the destroyer's deck in a series of bounds and dropped into *Loukia*'s well. Cotton threw him up a salute that was fit for the quarterdeck of *Caernarvon*.

'What in God's name happened?' Kennard asked. 'We thought we'd lost you.' He turned and stared round at the charred wood-work, the coloured patches and the damaged wheelhouse. 'This isn't *Claudia*,' he said. 'It's *Loukia*. Where's *Claudia*?'

'You might well ask,' Bisset said, a ragged, bearded Bisset suck-ing at a fag one of the sailors had tossed down from the destroyer.

'Where's Lieutenant Patullo?'

'Dead, sir,' Cotton said. 'With Lieutenant Shaw.'

'And Commander Samways?'

'Also dead, sir. Murdered by Greek bandits. We killed the Greeks.'

Kennard stared. 'Did you, by God?' he said. He indicated the bandage round Cotton's head. 'How about you? You hurt?'

Cotton stiffened. 'Nothing to speak of, sir. We also lost CERA Duff and Private Coward, and Private Howard wounded and a prisoner.'

He began to explain, anxious to get it off his chest and receive the reassurance that there was nothing else he could have done. Kennard gestured. 'You'd better tell me about it,' he said. 'Let's go into the captain's cabin.'

'Sorry, sir.' Cotton stopped him dead as he turned away. 'Three kids sleeping in it. It'll have to be here.'

Standing on the foredeck, he handed over the log and outlined what had happened, in a flat voice, unemotionally, leaving nothing out and adding no frills. When he'd finished, Kennard blinked.

'And the money?'

'Below, sir. The kids are lying on it.'

'And this boat?'

'It's a bit of *Claudia* and a bit of *Loukia*.' Cotton's mouth twitched. 'I reckon she ought to be called *Cloukia*.'

Kennard gestured. 'Did you do it all without a slipway?'

'There wasn't a slipway, sir.'

Kennard nodded. 'You did well, Cotton.'

'We were lucky, sir.'

'I'll take the money with me. What about the refugees?'

'They helped us, sir. It didn't seem safe to leave 'em behind. We brought their families with them. Three are women. I think the men would like to join the Greek navy, sir. If there is one.'

'That's something we've still to find out. We'll pass 'em south. It probably won't be very healthy here before long. We're getting out of Greece, Cotton. Did you know?'

'We heard about it, sir.'

'It's not going to be easy. We've got the Glen ships but we can't get 'em into the Piraeus. Bloody place blew up. They hit three ammunition ships – *Clan Fraser, City of Roubaix* and *Goalpara*. They took *Clan Cumming* with 'em. It was bloody hopeless from the start. There weren't enough airfields in the forward areas and a complete lack of aerodrome defence weapons, blast pens and even transport. We never got off the ground. We'd no sooner settled in than we started getting out again. Our recce planes tell us there are a hell of a lot of caiques in the Piraeus, and I expect they'll eventually be heading here or to Canea or the beaches.'

Cotton blinked. 'That's another point, sir,' he said. 'I think it would be wrong to expect a seaborne invasion.'

Kennard's head jerked round. 'What the devil do you know about it?'

Cotton produced Captain Haussmann's notebook and papers

and the torn and bloodstained pay-books and letters they'd taken off the men they'd killed.

'Where did you get these?' Kennard asked.

'Took 'em off some Germans, sir. Four of 'em were SS men or Gestapo or something. The notebook belonged to an officer. Bisset – that is, Leading Aircraftman Bisset – speaks German, as you know, sir, and he said they seemed to suggest an airborne invasion of Crete.'

'Airborne?'

'That's what he said, sir. The airfields at Maleme, Heraklion and Retimo. I think he was right too, because we got these papers off a lot of paratroopers.'

Kennard stared at the papers and then at Cotton. 'How, for God's sake?'

'We killed 'em sir.'

'The paratroopers?'

'Yes, sir. All of 'em.'

'Did you, by God?'

'We had a bit of help from some Greeks, sir. They were using the guns off *Loukia*.'

'Were they indeed? Well, at least we've started something that looks like resistance.'

'Yes, sir. We also sank one German caique – probably two – both full of troops – as well as a German armed launch.' Cotton couldn't resist a last prideful comment. 'She had what looked like a four-pounder on the stern.'

Kennard stared. 'Good God, Cotton,' he said, 'don't sound so bloody modest! You seem to have taken on the whole German garrison of Aeos – and beaten 'em too!'

Cotton didn't think it very odd. After all, that was what the Marines were for, and since Kennard had come up at his briefing with a quote from Kipling's poem about Joeys – one that Cotton had known almost since the day he'd put on his first pair of ammunition boots – he thought that, now that the thing was over and done with, he might toss it back at him.

'*An' 'e sweats like a Jolly*,' he quoted humourlessly. '*'Er*

282

Majesty's Jolly — soldier and sailor too! For there isn't a job on the top o' the earth the beggar don't know, nor do.'

Kennard's eyebrows had shot up and his mouth widened in a grin. 'There's a bloody sight more to you than meets the eye, Cotton,' he observed.

'Yes, sir,' Cotton agreed placidly. 'They're red-hot on that sort of thing in the Marines.'

'We might even get you a gong for this.'

Cotton coughed. 'I'm not much bothered about a gong, sir,' he said. 'There is one thing, though.'

'Go on.'

'I sort of promised these Greeks we'd look after their families. I'd be glad if you'd fix it with the padre, sir.'

Kennard looked up under the peak of his cap. 'Where do they want to go?' he asked.

'I don't rightly know, yet, sir. Except for one. She wants to go to England. That is, *I* want her to go to England.'

'You do?' Kennard gave him an old-fashioned look. 'It's not all that easy. Has she got somewhere to go?'

'Yes, sir.'

'Where?'

'My ma would take care of her.'

'Some relation?'

'Yes, sir. My ma was Greek. You'll remember there was some mention of it at the briefing. It wasn't something I liked shouting about the ship, sir. People get to thinking you're a Maltese or a Cypriot and *they*'re always stewards or canteen managers. That's how I came to speak Greek, you'll remember. It turned out very useful, sir.'

'I'm sure it did. And this woman?'

'Girl, sir. She's not all that old?'

'What relationship is she?'

'Cousin, sir,' Cotton said stoutly, staring the commander unflinchingly in the eye.

'Is she now? It was a fortunate coincidence you found her, wasn't it?'

'Yes, sir,' Cotton said. 'Very fortunate. But, then, I might have guessed. You know what these Mediterranean lot are like. Breed like rabbits.'

'I hope *you* don't, Cotton,' Kennard said. 'I don't think I'd like to meet a regiment of Cottons. Very well, I'll have a word with the padre. Under the circumstances, it's the least we can do. In the meantime I'd better get over to headquarters because I've heard there are only fifty ack-ack guns on the island and thirty-odd obsolescent fighters. You'll all be questioned by Intelligence, of course, and be expected to pass on everything to the admiral. To the army commander in charge here, too, for that matter. It looks like being Freyberg. Will that bother you?'

'No, sir.'

Kennard looked at Cotton's solid bulk and unemotional face. 'No,' he said slowly. 'I shouldn't think it would.'

As Kennard departed, Varvara and his family appeared on deck. Annoula was with them. She seemed strained and exhausted and she looked at Cotton with a worried expression. He marched straight up to her and, taking her arm, drew her aside.

'It'll be all right,' he announced. 'You'll be able to go to Egypt. They'll look after you.'

She looked at him sadly. 'I have nobody in Egypt.'

'You have me.'

She gave him an unhappy look. 'No.'

'Why not?'

'Egypt isn't your country.'

'It is at the moment. Alexandria's our base. Or it will be when they chuck us out of here.'

'But after that?'

It seemed to present no problem to Cotton. 'You can go to England. They send wives and kids home via the Cape.'

'I have nowhere to go in England.'

'I can give you an address. *My* address.' He wondered what his mother would say when she turned up. Probably fall on her neck and burst into tears of joy.

She shook her head. 'Not now. Not after – not after what they did to me.'

Cotton frowned. 'What bloody difference does that make?' he snorted.

'Nobody would want me after that.'

'I'd have you.'

Cotton frowned as he spoke. He'd done it now, he decided. Here he was, in spite of everything he'd ever thought, bloody well opting for the one thing he'd always fought shy of – a Greek wife, Greek relations and Greek kids yelling in a foreign lingo and having their teeth knocked out by the other kids in the street because they were wops. Perhaps it'd be easier not to take his discharge in a hurry after the war. After all, there were Maltese wives in the navy and nobody minded them, and it would give everybody time to settle down a bit. And perhaps the kids would be lucky enough to turn out as big as he was.

Annoula was looking up at him, her eyes filling with tears. To her Cotton represented security such as she'd forgotten existed. 'You are a good man, Cotton,' she said.

'No, I'm not,' he said bluntly. 'My parents were Greek and, because it was sometimes uncomfortable having Greek parents in London, I ran away and joined the Marines. I even pretended I wasn't Greek and never wrote to them much. I expect I'll have to change if you're there.'

'Perhaps they won't want me.'

'I think they will. I think my ma will fall over herself to get you in the house. I'll write and tell 'em you're coming.'

She stared up at him, moisture sparkling on her lashes, and her face split in a smile that was trusting, happy, relieved and joyful all at the same time. Cotton's stolid heart thumped as he realized how beautiful she could be when she tried. Then her face became grave again, meek almost, and dutiful.

'Very well, Cotton,' she said.

Jesus, he thought – and oddly enough for the first time it didn't shock him – she sounds like Ma.

Epilogue

On 28 April 1941, only a few days after *Loukia*'s return, confirmation of Corporal Cotton's opinion came when Winston Churchill signalled to General Wavell in North Africa to suggest that an airborne attack on Crete should be expected.

'It seems clear from our information,' he said, 'that a heavy airborne attack by German troops and bombers will soon be made on Crete. . . . It ought to be a fine opportunity for killing the parachute troops.'

Churchill's view was not an unreasonable one but unfortunately the garrison was far from sufficiently equipped to meet the attack, which came on 20 May. The first parachutists and the first airborne troops in gliders were killed almost to a man, but more arrived and their final capture of Maleme airfield was the turning point of the struggle. A German attempt to follow up with caiques from Milos, however, met with disaster. Four British cruisers – one of them *Caernarvon* – and four destroyers got among them, as *Loukia* had off Cape Kastamanitsa, and sank almost every one by gunfire or ramming, including the Italian destroyer which was escorting them. A second convoy was attacked on the same day and the Germans made no further attempt.

Because the attack on Crete had been expected, it cost the Germans one-third of their airborne invaders – 12,000 to 17,000 men – together with 170 troop-carrying aircraft. Never again did they risk their air division troops in so hazardous an operation. Their commanders had grown older and more cautious overnight because the cost of victory had proved too high, and in the end

Hitler turned his parachute regiments into infantry. Although the British were thrown out of Crete, they had blunted one of Hitler's most effective weapons, and it has always been believed that Crete delayed Hitler's attack on Russia so long he was just too late to capture Moscow before the Russian winter set in. The following year the German decline began.

As for Cotton and Annoula Akoumianakis, *their* story perhaps supplied the happy ending that was not immediately obvious in Crete. After an exhausting journey through a variety of refugee camps in the Middle East and South Africa, Annoula finally reached London the following year, when, as Cotton had suspected, she was swept delightedly into the Cotonou home. Being Greek, she was literally held captive by Cotton's mother until Cotton himself, wearing three stripes and a DSM for what he'd done on Aeos, returned from the Middle East to enjoy survivor's leave after *Caernarvon* had been sunk by a German torpedo.

He remained in England as an instructor until the time came for the British to return to the Greek islands in 1944. Rather to his surprise he was commissioned because of his ability to speak Greek. He even managed to pick up an MC – ironically enough for leading the attack on Kalani when Aeos was reoccupied. A little startled by his unexpected success, he remained in the Marines until 1955, when – still considered to be a bit regimental – he retired as a captain. For a year or two he did various jobs. Then, in 1960 when the tourist boom got going, Bisset, whose languages had landed him a job with one of the larger British travel firms, got in touch with him and he found himself appointed as Greek representative with a base in Athens. So that, in the end, accepting his Greek origins with far less trouble than he had ever expected, he got the best of both worlds.